BOOK TWO OF
THE APOTHEOSIS TRILOGY

EARTH'S SOWING

JAMES BISHOP

Published by Fantastic Journeys Publishing,
Boise, Idaho
PUBLISHING HISTORY
First Edition: James Bishop September 2014

The Apotheosis Trilogy is a work of fiction, and was written with the intention to entertain. Like any work of fiction, the ideas contained in this novel are not meant to be taken literally, or as a direct representation of the author's own spiritual beliefs. It is a story. Nothing more, and nothing less.

EARTH'S SOWING

Copyright 2014 by James Bishop

Cover art by Giuseppe Saitta and Lorraine Barreras
Cover layout by John Farmer
Interior formatting by John Farmer
Edited by Brady Sparks

ISBN:978-1-941276-91-4

To John

The three things I care about most in this world come from you. Thank you for everything. We'll meet again, someday.

Table of Contents

PROLOGUE

I am he that liveth, and was dead; and, behold, I am alive for
evermore, Amen; and have the keys of hell and of death.
- Revelation 1:18

The demons had been pushing them hard that month. Captain
Daniels had done a damned fine job keeping morale up, but that
wouldn't last forever. The men were smoking more, and as often
as not, when Markov looked at his brothers he saw the worry lines
etched deeper into the furrows of their brows. Thank God they at
least still had plenty of cigarettes. He looked outside of San Luis'
walls.

The jungle had been cleared to a full length of a stadium
green. He supposed once it would have been called a football field,
though no games had been played in a couple of centuries. At this
rate none ever would again. Books and film of the game still
survived, in the archives at the Sanctuary, though only the priests
had time to look at old world information at length. Soldiers, like
Markov, were too busy defending the walls. There wasn't enough
electricity to go around either. Entertainment was not a priority.

The Fort, which Markov now conceded was going to be called
a Sanctuary, was huge and ringed a giant area of fertile ground
which had been taken over by the army and fortified in the early
days of the invasion. There were some accounts of those first days
that survived, but not many. In the old days, he had been told by

priests, there was a way to share information instantly across the entire planet using satellites and computers. Computers still existed, but they couldn't do anything like they could before the Fall.

Markov gazed intently out over the twenty meter high walls, lighting another cigarette as he did. Without them, morale would fall to shit, and quickly. Everyone was committed to defending the fort... the *Sanctuary*... but a lifetime of this was hard enough even with nicotine and alcohol. Without them, he imagined that twenty meter fall would look damned inviting to a lot of soldiers.

He said a quick prayer of thanks to God for sugar, distillation, and tobacco. As long as they could grow sugar and potatoes, rum and vodka would follow. God bless the priests and the archives, too. Markov chuckled. At least some of them could run a still.

The Continental Divide ran all the way down what used to be North America, through the mountain range where the Sanctuary had been built, and further down into South America. No one knew if any people still lived down there, but if they did they were probably high in the mountains like Markov's soldier brothers and sisters. More than half a million survivors lived in the valley, and half of those served in the Temple military. There was a popular movement to start calling the soldiers Templar, though Markov didn't have much of an opinion on the matter. Templar or soldier. Both were just words.

"Markov. Care for a drink?" Luis called to him from the stairs leading down into the wall.

"Don't mind if I do, Saint *Lou-ee*."

"Fuck you Markov, I told you not to call me that. It's not my fault this place was named for some French king a thousand years ago. And it's *Lou-ees* not *Lou-ee*. Asshole."

Markov laughed, and offered Luis a smoke. It was good natured; Luis was his best friend here. "Careful soldier, don't let the Captain hear you say one of the old countries. New directive from the priests, or didn't you hear?"

"Fuck the priests, fuck the cardinals, and fuck the Patriarch. What, if I don't say the word *Mexican* that makes me not *Mexican?* Fucking stupid. So does your Russian ass want a drink or not?"

He smiled at his friend, and he grabbed an old metal coffee tin and nodded. "I don't disagree; just don't let Daniels hear you. Good guy, but he toes the line."

"Don't I know it? Did you hear Walters got the lash for wearing a cross? Crazy."

Markov nodded, but inwardly he cringed. Walters was a fine soldier, but she was stupid about shit like that. Rules were rules. No distinct religions. No old-world nations. No distinct ethnic, cultural, or social ties outside of officially sanctioned Temple ones. Walters getting ten lashes was a tough break, but Markov saw why Daniels had ordered it. It was simple enough to not wear a crucifix.

"I think the Temple is way too uptight about this shit, Markov. Demons are everywhere. Do they seriously think the Christians, Muslims, and Jews are going to stop fighting the Legion long enough to throw down? This isn't the old days, as they are so quick to remind us."

"No, Luis, I don't think that's it. The Patriarch is just doing everything he can to unify what's left of us. Besides, this isn't a San Luis thing. Remember the contingent from Fort Rio?"

"You mean the Rio Sanctuary?"

"What the fuck ever. Yeah, from Rio... those guys said all the other forts... fuck... *Sanctuaries* were doing this stuff too."

"I know, Markov, just seems heavy handed. The demons spill enough of our blood without us needing to do it for them... and for stupid reasons."

He nodded at Luis, though again inwardly he disagreed. He smiled and clinked cups with his friend. "You're a good man, Lou-ees."

"Same to you. Things could be worse here you know, man."

"Hell, it can always be worse..."

Smoke started rising from the tree line. He quickly put his cup down and picked up his rifle. Guns were slowly being replaced by primitive weapons like bows and crossbows as stockpiles of ammunition were depleted, but wall sentries still were outfitted with rifles if at all possible. The rifle was a standard 7.62, good at ranges even three times longer than the tree line, but for now he just needed the scope. As he feared, the smoke was caused by a Legion signal fire. They were about to be attacked.

"Luis, ring the bell." He continued to gaze through the scope and heard not just one, but at least ten bells signal the attack. The sentries had done their job. Luis called out farewell to him and raced down the stairs. He wasn't a sentry like Markov, Luis was an engineer and worked in the foundry making siege equipment and munitions. His place was there, probably loading black powder for the defense of the walls.

Markov prayed for the Eyes of the Eagle and for the Hands of a Statue. The priests had told him for years that it didn't matter what visualizations he used for his Invocations, but he always felt better when he was specific in his prayers. It no longer felt new or exhilarating to feel the enhancements flow into him from the Divine, though he shuddered to think how it was for the first soldiers to fight the Legion without them when the demons first burst forth from Hell.

With his aim steadied and his vision enhanced, he scanned the tree-line for targets. He did not have long to wait, and he was momentarily surprised when he heard half a dozen other rifles fire off rounds ahead of him. He was usually the first. He must be distracted. Frowning, he Invoked another Prayer, this time for the Focus of the Snake.

A giant, flaming bi-pedal ape burst through the trees and sprinted across the grass. He exhaled and found the demon's head aligned in his crosshairs. He squeezed the trigger and was already tracking another target when the thing's head exploded. Gunshots echoed across the valley as Markov and his brothers brought down more of the outriders. Ammunition was not scarce yet, but he half felt attacks like this existed for no other reason than to deplete their stores. The Legion was infinite. Bullets were not, no matter how much they tried to replace what they used.

Long minutes passed. Markov hoped to hear a signal horn from the demons calling for a retreat, but no luck. If it was a small exploratory force, and they saw that San Luis was well defended, perhaps it would be over quickly. He tracked the tree line for any movement, and more minutes passed as he felt his Invocations start to slowly lose their effect.

Maybe it was over, he thought, as a sight which terrified him to his soul shattered his hope. No outsiders came this time as the entire jungle came alive as far as he could see to either side. His rifle was not the only one which remained silent as an unbroken line of Legionnaires marched forth onto the valley floor. Shields, pikes, swords, and archers moved unwaveringly towards the walls, and in horror Markov realized that the bells were ringing all along the ramparts. This was not just the strongest portion of the Legion army attacking his station... it was this bad all around them. The Legion had come to break the Sanctuary. From what Markov could see, they had enough to do so, easily.

He shook the fatalism from his head with difficulty. He shrugged, and made his peace. It had been luck more than anything which had allowed them to survive for this long. The demons could have killed them much earlier if they had so chosen, but probably had better targets elsewhere. San Luis, the Sanctuary on the Divide, was isolated and little threat to the endless hordes. Why spare the time and energy for them unless the war was in hand elsewhere?

He breathed easily and calmly as he accepted what was happening. Half a million souls would join their Father in Heaven soon... but not too soon. The battle would be lengthy, and epic, and worthy of song. Unfortunately, no one would live to sing about it.

Markov grinned as he found a Legion officer on an infernal steed giving orders to his infantry. He fired and smiled wider as the flame-wreathed demon died. It wasn't a bad day at all.

For two months the Templar- the name was firmly embedded now- had held the walls from the largest force of Legion anyone, including Patriarch Quintus Salvius Meles, had ever seen. The old man had seen much in his life, and though the Fall had happened more than a hundred years before he was born, he remembered much of what the clergy had told him from that time.

When the Patriarch was but a child, and the old-world nations, religions, and armies still existed... though weakened mightily... he would listen to the old men talk about how things used to be. He remembered a conversation which must have happened more than eighty years ago, with a man who was probably eighty himself at the time, about the years soon after The Fall. The man spoke of incredible weapons used by humanity against the Legion, of tremendous balls of fire that blotted out the sun and laid waste to entire battalions of demonic troops. He spoke of great and terrible machines of sea, earth, and sky that massacred demons in such numbers that it was believed the war would be won with ease.

Thinking back on that conversation, it was not the wonder in the eyes of the old man which the Patriarch, now an old man himself, remembered. It was the sadness that even with all the formidable weaponry the old world had produced, the Legion was still winning. That sadness had settled into his heart that day and never left. Even now, with the end close, all he had left in him was regret that things had come to pass in the way that they did.

Gazing out from the Temple at the heart of the San Luis Sanctuary, all he could see was Legion campfires dotting the landscape. How many troops had come? One million? Two? It didn't matter. They brought enough. The food stores were nearly depleted. Ammunition and ordinance were gone, and so were the raw materials needed to make more. They could grow more food, mine more minerals, and start over if they got the chance, but the siege was almost over. The Legion was undaunted and the walls would be breached before long.

Surrender, perhaps mercifully, wasn't even an option. The demons never asked. Very little of their enemy was known, even after all the years of war, other than they slaughtered all opposition unwaveringly. There were no survivors after the Legion came through an area. It would be thus here.

Sighing, the Patriarch read the report in his hands from Captain Daniels once more. A request for a commendation for a young sentry on the walls named Markov. The man had killed fifty Legion officers. Truly, a remarkable achievement. Cursing, he wished they had more bullets. The man might kill fifty more.

"Page, tell Captain Daniels to grant the commendation. Also tell him to relieve Markov of duty for the night. Inform him that Markov is to be rewarded with a cask of rum from my reserve stock, and have him share it with whomever he wishes." The page nodded and ran off. The Patriarch wiped away exhaustion and frustration from his eyes. He should have told the page to inform the officers that there were no more provisions to dole out. He should have told the page to tell the men that it was over, and that by tomorrow they would be throwing rocks at the Legion. He should have told him all of it, but he couldn't bring himself to. It was over. Let them have one more night of not knowing so.

"I don't understand, Captain. I've done well enough to be relieved of duty?" Markov was tired, but defiant. Daniels looked terrible but there was a stubborn set to his eyes.

"Look, I know you want to fight. This is for morale though. You've done an incredible job, now take your booze and get the hell out of here. Take some friends, and get the hell off my wall. Be back in the morning. I want the *Templar* to see good work rewarded."

"Sir…"

"Dismissed, Markov. If I have to throw you in the brig by God I will. Take the night off. Go get laid. Get the fuck out of here."

Inwardly he fumed, but he knew Daniels wouldn't budge. He saluted and left his post. He hadn't made it twenty paces when he heard running, heavy footsteps behind him.

"You forgot your booze, jackass." Luis carried two full wineskins.

Markov wanted to yell at him, but had to laugh at the expression of pure joy on his friends face. "Stop sulking, I agree with Daniels."

"My place is here, Luis."

"No, your place *was* here, and is here again in the morning. Now your place is in town, with your trusty and faithful friend, and a goddamn cask of rum. I'd bring the whole thing if I could, but it's fucking heavy."

He sighed again, but what could he do other than not drink and not relax out of protest?

"Lucinda's?" He would not have thought Luis' face could grin any wider, but he was wrong.

"Lucinda's. I'm going to get Walters to go, too."

Markov awoke before dawn. His head was pounding, but he'd been worse. He extricated himself from the bed, doing his best not to disturb the girl sleeping there. Damned if he could remember her name, but he could remember she had been kind and quick to laugh.

He dressed and drained a pitcher of water by the nightstand like he was dying of thirst. He knew better than to look for Luis. Luis would still be sleeping it off, as he was not an early riser like Markov, even discounting the rum. They had only been at it a few hours, but he and Luis had each drained their wineskins, and drained their refills, and that was before Walters showed up and spent the next several hours drinking Luis stupid. By God that woman could drink. Luis had the wisdom to order a couple of porters to deliver the cask to Lucinda's, and for at least one night the common room was lively and joyous.

That it was a brothel didn't bother Markov. The Temple was fine with houses of ill repute, and so was he. Rubbing his eyes, he couldn't remember if the girl was earned or paid for, though with the amount of booze he and Luis had thrown around, maybe a little of both.

Dawn was beginning to break as he eased out of the room, and then out of Lucinda's after grabbing and devouring a hunk of bread and some cold sausage. He stopped at a cistern to drink his fill, and also filled his wineskin. If he was going to be of any use on the walls he needed to rehydrate. He hoped Daniels would be sleeping, but with his luck he'd be awake and not let Markov back at his post until the sun was completely up. To kill some time, he decided to head up to the ramparts at a different area of the wall. He was off-duty, and Daniels hadn't told him to stay away from the *entire* wall.

Yawning and stretching, he jogged for most of the trip, hoping to sweat out most of the rum and replace it with water. He felt almost human by the time he reached the wall, and nodded in greeting to the men and women standing guard. No one carried rifles, he noticed. It wouldn't be long then. The Legion would have little fear of arrows and stones. It would come to hand to hand combat, and the Templar were no match.

He went for a long walk along the ramparts, and it was without surprise when the Legion attacked. He made his peace, and returned to his post.

The fighting was bloody, and brutal. Templar fought with whatever they could. Some used bayonets from their rifles, some used knives, and some used more archaic weapons like swords and axes. Of late, those were getting increasingly popular, especially with the younger soldiers.

Markov was incredible with a rifle, but only good with a blade. He had an old antique American knife, a functional fixed blade that weighed less than a pound and had seven inches of edge. He had never had to use one at San Luis, but had gutted a couple of lesser demons while making a pilgrimage when he was a teenager.

As more and more Legion reached the walls with their ladders the fighting grew frantic. The sounds of thousands of Templar Invoking Strength, Grace, and Fortitude would have normally been a tumult of noise, but it was drowned out by the inhuman screams of the demon siege breaching the walls of the Sanctuary. There were a few isolated blasts of explosives throughout the morning but they had died out long before Markov rejoined his unit with Daniels.

There was no need for orders. Everyone was engaged in fighting on the walls. Markov ducked a claw swipe from a fanged horror reaching over its siege ladder and stabbed it quickly in the neck with a reverse grip. Blood splashed hot from the artery and the thing gurgled in agony as it grabbed its neck. A young Templar, a boy of no more than sixteen it looked like, saw the opportunity and helped Markov shove the siege ladder back. They both shared a grin as the ladder toppled back, taking a dozen demons with it.

Markov blinked as the boy's smile turned to horror as he looked to the sky. Markov followed his gaze and cursed. Three great winged forms had taken flight and now rushed the ramparts. Of course there would be Ba'al here, but three of them attacking? The Templar must have tried the patience of the Demon Lords. Fire and death would follow.

Markov left the boy there and ran to the nearest tower. Running up the stairs four at a time he broke into the daylight above to track the flight patterns of the Ba'al, and stood transfixed by the futility of their plight. He saw two more beginning to strafe the walls on the far side of the valley. Five Ba'al? By God what sort of force were they facing? Never had five Ba'al been reported in a single battle since the Day of Judgment. Two were a rarity, but *five*? This was a force meant to obliterate them. Screams all around him signaled the beginning of the end. He saw one of the Ba'al drop to closer than twenty paces away down the wall, and the thing looked almost bored as it batted away arrow shots and slowly landed on the ramparts.

A single, terrible and glorious laugh came from its mouth. "Mortals." The Ba'al then drew a blade which must have been half again as long as Markov was tall and clove the nearest Templar like wheat. Many Templar braved the thing, and all were cut down. No one near would survive that black blade.

"Signal the mercy killing! It's over, prepare for euthanasia!" Daniels' voice cut over the din from down below, and Markov collapsed to his knees, breaking line of sight on the slaughter below. He knew it was coming, but his mind hadn't accepted it yet. Daniels was right, though. Better a quick, clean and merciful end than how the Legion usually killed survivors. The stories alone were enough to justify the act.

He narrowed his eyes and stood. Anger darkened his vision, and he walked to the stairs. He would die today, but his blade would first taste the flesh of a Ba'al. He walked slowly, calmly accepting that his actions meant nothing and his own death was imminent. Within a quarter hour the potions would be distributed to the non-combatants and they would sleep forever. He Invoked every prayer he could remember as he walked purposefully down the tower steps. Never had his body and mind been so possessed with Divine Power. He left the entry to the tower and saw the Ba'al laying waste to all those who opposed him.

Markov saw that the Ba'al was turned away from him, having just taken the heads off two Templar with one blow. Markov ran towards the towering, winged figure and slashed with his knife with all of his Invoked Strength. He felt the knife bite flesh just a moment before he felt his ribs crack with the blow the Ba'al struck him with.

Reeling, and out of wind, Markov struggled to roll over to look at the Ba'al, who was staring down at the foot long gash along his infernal side. He turned towards Markov, who, knowing death approached mustered up his most insolent smile and taunted the Demon Lord. "Got you, fucker."

"Indeed, mortal. You drew the blood of Ba'al Abigor today, son of Adam. Does it give you comfort?"

The Ba'al knelt down to lock his darkly perverse angelic gaze to Markov's pained and dying one. He thought about trying to slash at the demon again, but he knew it was futile. The Ba'al was watching him. He'd rather die with dignity. "Not as much as you'd think."

The two of them stared at each other for a long moment before the Ba'al snorted. "Adam's Seed. Favored children. Pathetic." The Ba'al raised his blade, and Markov closed his eyes for the end, and whispered a final Invocation for Peace as his life neared its end.

In his mind, the quiet Prayer for Peace erupted into Fire and Wrath. Time slowed. A prayer he hadn't said aloud since he was a boy blossomed in his mind, the Invocation of the Sword. It was a useless prayer, esoteric and non-specific, used only for iterating and meditation. He saw it etched across his eyelids in an instant, and a fire so hot he could scarce comprehend it ignited him from within. He opened his eyes and saw the Ba'al in front of him frozen in time, and a golden nimbus of light burst forth from Markov's body... no... from his *soul* it seemed.

He should have been in agony, but instead he felt as if the torrent of the searing light was healing and empowering him. It flowed through his body and soul like a cascade of raw energy. He stood, and glanced down at his simple blade. He could scarce see the darker shadow of the weapon, enveloped as it was in a golden light so pure it hurt his eyes to look at it. Red sigils of a language he could not decipher danced and flickered over the nimbus faster than his eyes could discern. He looked up at Ba'al Abigor, stepped to the Demon Lord, and severed his sword hand as if cutting warm butter. He looked at the stump, and noticed that blood was only slowly pooling in anticipation of spurting out of the wound. Markov blinked several times, and sighed in deep contentment, then gasped as he felt the torrent of energy within him surge for a moment then stutter. Inexplicably, he felt that he must hurry, that this sensation would not last. He stabbed the Ba'al in the stomach, once cleanly, and then left the thing to die slowly. There were demons everywhere. The walls of San Luis were overrun. He needed to hurry.

The Patriarch stood in astonished silence from the top of the keep at San Luis' heart. His steward had provided him with a share of the sleep tonic, though he had no intention of using it. He knew what the Legion would do to him, but he owed it to his people to look their enemy in the eye if they were all to die. In truth, he had expected it to be over already, but the golden figure on the walls had stopped everyone in San Luis cold. The order to begin the mercy killings had been abandoned in mass as the Angel of Vengeance had slaughtered the Legion invaders faster than could be believed. Even now, the Patriarch was stunned as the figure simply appeared along the next section of the walls and demons fell apart, sliced into ribbons.

Why now, after all this time? God had abandoned them and left them to fend for themselves as the Legion came. There was no Messiah, there was no Rapture, and there was only war. Why allow the demons to slowly obliterate mankind over the last two centuries only to send help now? He shook his head to clear his thoughts. He looked through his spyglass and was simply amazed at the figure. It was a living avatar of golden fire, armed with a blade forged in Heaven itself. The Legion had panicked and broken as they fell by the hundreds over the span of heartbeats. As the Patriarch counted his breaths, the screams of the butchered demons echoed across San Luis. The Legion hadn't even descended from the walls. The city would be almost completely untouched. Templar had died by the thousands, tens of thousands, but their sacrifice most certainly was not in vain. San Luis would be depleted of almost all of its old-world supplies, but what of it?

Their crops were undamaged, their water was unsullied, and the population would be nearly intact. Beyond that, the entire invading force was in the process of being annihilated. He blinked again, and the walls were clear. He watched as the golden figure vanished on the far side of the Sanctuary walls, and flashes of light coming from the tree line indicated that not only were the walls clear and the city was safe, but that the Avatar was killing the demons far afield as well. He stood and watched for the better part of the afternoon, until at last the golden flashes had stopped. The city was deathly quiet, though down below he couldn't see a single casualty. It was the quiet of awe, and of deliverance.

He glanced down at the philter of sleep, and without concern dumped its contents onto the stone. The people of the Sanctuary at the Divide would have no need of such things.

Markov went about his grisly work quickly and efficiently. He found that the Legion weren't completely frozen in time, but to his eyes, they still moved as if stuck in tree sap. He was aware that his Invocations from earlier were still present, though they hardly seemed relevant compared to the power he possessed from the Invocation of the Sword. He incanted the verse softly to himself as he butchered the demons. Though he still felt as though the power within him was dwindling, he made short work of the invaders.

He jogged along the battlements, severing heads and piercing chests with ease, his blade giving him far greater reach than the simple knife within the halo of power should have. He should have tired, but he felt not even an increase of heart or breathing rate. Markov simply moved through the Legion, reaping the demons as if he was death incarnate. Time was hard to judge, but he had cleared the walls after only one complete circumnavigation of the city. The equivalent to running nearly a hundred miles, he was sure several hours had passed even at his inhuman speed. That first time he circled the Sanctuary, he killed nearly the entire Legion. After returning to the tower where he had first encountered Ba'al Abigor, though, he was surprised to see a few remaining infernal warriors still intact. He was also amused to see the Ba'al, hobbled in pain, sitting in agony with his hand pressed against his abdomen with a few Templar ringing him with pikes.

He paused long enough to stab Abigor again, this time in one of his eyes, before completing another circuit of San Luis. The Walls cleared; he noticed with sadness that very few Templar remained alive on the walls, though he also saw with pride that not a single Legionnaire had made it to the city itself. Civilians looked up at him with slow-moving eyes filled with awe as he passed. The city would not fall, and the people would live. Markov smiled, and felt another large interruption in the flowing energy within him. He was running out of the power source. Looking down outside the walls, he nodded and hopped down, landing lightly on his feet, unscathed from the huge drop.

He continued to butcher the Legion as he moved, slaughtering with ease every imaginable fanged horror as he went. He moved as fast as he could, and as day turned to dusk he grew tired. He began to move slowly, and as twilight grew closer the very few demons he still saw moved nearly as fast as Markov did. He still killed them easily, but it was not as it was earlier in the day. Night fell, and his pace slowed to close to what he could do normally, though few demons remained. A mighty yawn cracked his jaws as he stumbled through the trees into a clearing, feeling more tired than he could ever remember. He looked in surprise as he saw the scarce remnants of the invasion force fleeing through a burning portal easily three times Markov's height.

So that was how they came to attack San Luis unaware. An actual portal to Hell opened on the Sanctuary's doorstep. He laughed, and then had to brace himself against a tree as he nearly fell over. God he was tired. He could sleep forever. He lurched towards the remnants, weakly dispatching a couple of Legionnaire who made to stop him. His blade still moved through the demons like paper, but it glowed faintly like bronze, not the brilliant gold it once was.

He reached the burning portal, and was surprised that it didn't feel hot. The fire crackled and hissed so loudly that Markov was sure he should be burned to cinders even approaching it, but he felt not even slightly uncomfortable, even at arm's length. He yawned again, and had to blink hard to keep his eyes open. The demons were gone. Either dead or fled back to Hell from whence they came. Markov smiled, and closed his eyes. Sleep, he needed to sleep. It would be warm next to the portal, and if the Legion came back he would wake and stop them. Markov fell to his knees before Hell's Maw. He dozed off as the power flowing through him slowly died down to embers. His last thought as his eyes closed and he fell forward was that he had done well.

⛨ ☪ ⛨ ⚕ ⛰

"What do you mean it was a Templar?" The Patriarch was still in shock, though exuberant that excepting the death of so many Templar, the Sanctuary had been wholly and completely saved.

"You said Angel; I'm telling you it was a man. I know him, his name was Markov… he was my friend."

Luis, the engineer standing before him, reeked of stale alcohol and blood, but he couldn't bring himself to be upset. Incredible things had happened that day; he would not berate the man. "Why do you think that?"

The man was quiet for a moment, and then addressed the Patriarch with fervent eyes. "I saw him change. I had slept late… not derelict mind you, we were granted leave… but I had slept later then Markov. I went to find him with Captain Daniels but by then it was too late. I arrived just as Daniels was giving the mercy kill order, and there was a Ba'al there… killing everyone." Luis swallowed hard, but his eyes were nearly fanatical.

"Here, have a drink, son. Take your time." He offered a glass of wine, and watched with amusement as Luis drained it in a single gulp.

"The Ba'al... he was killing everyone, and I got to the battlement just as Markov slashed at him. Everyone was dead, and Markov was going to die too... I wanted to call out, but I couldn't. I just watched... as the sword came down."

"It's ok, Luis, no one is questioning your courage. Morale was broken, the enemy had won, and I myself gave the order to euthanize the city. We all know what happens to survivors when the Legion takes them."

"Markov... changed. I heard him Invoking the Sword... of all things, and one second he was on the ground, and the next he burst into golden flames and the slaughter had started. I blinked and he was gone, the Ba'al was doubled over bleeding out his guts like a stuck pig, and the Legion was ripped apart like leaves."

"I saw, but how do you know the golden figure was Markov? Couldn't the Angel have consumed him by accident?"

"Father, I don't want to argue, I'm just telling you what I saw. The figure *was* my friend. He... changed, and I know it was him because I saw his shape in that moment before the light hurt my eyes to gaze upon it. It was him, I know it. Markov did this... he saved us."

The Patriarch was quiet for a time, then smiled at Luis and dismissed him. He thought long about it, and in the end decided to believe the engineer. In the short term, the important thing was that the Sanctuary had been saved. True, they would have to replenish the Templar sentries with those too old or young, but in time that too would be fine. What was far more important was whether the man was right. Oh he assuredly believed what he was saying, but Luis could still be wrong. If he was, and it was an Angel sent by God to save them, well so be it, but why now after so long? More likely it actually was Markov.

If it was Markov, then a man had done those things to the Legion. A soldier, a Templar, a human being had wrought more destruction than could scarce be comprehended, and he did it without any old-world technology. He did it with prayer, devotion, and a righteous heart. If it was Markov... then it could be someone else, too. Invoked the Sword, Luis said. Interesting.

Looking out from the top of the Keep, he inhaled deeply in the wind and allowed thoughts of hope to hold his mind. If a man could do such a thing once, he could do it again. Or another could, if Markov had died or couldn't be found. Regardless, the tide had turned. Whatever Markov had done, it would be duplicated. The man had become Divine, and in becoming Divine had smote their enemies. He hoped to find the man alive, but even if he didn't, his gift would not be wasted. The Patriarch would spread word of what happened that day at San Luis. Markov's Gift would be given to every Sanctuary still standing. The Legion would learn to fear mankind. The war was far, far from over.

chapter one

His first-begot we know, and sore have felt,
When his fierce thunder drove us to the deep;
Who this is we must learn, for man he seems
In all his lineaments, though in his face
The glimpses of his Fathers glory shine.
- John Milton: Paradise Regain'd Book One

Priolt had lived his whole life in the High Sheol. His father had been a half-mortal mongrel that was unable to distinguish himself in the Legion, one of the poor souls born here in servitude. He served for decades in the campaign on Earth while Priolt, his siblings, and their mother worked in the eatery her family had owned since before the ash-Shay'tan invaded the realm of the mortals.

Holding the broken sign in his hands, he ran his thumbs over the wooden emblem. Although his eyes had been burned to near-uselessness a century ago, he still knew the emblem by heart. A simple, thick-cut Hart-Steak with a slab of butter and heat marks. The Restaurant was famous for its food and ale, and Priolt had always felt pride that it was his work with the fats and scarn-onions which made officers and Ba'al alike frequent the place.

His father, useless as he was, had managed to do nothing in his career to advance within the Legion and so when word arrived that he had been killed by Templar, Priolt could only laugh. A bad soldier was nothing compared to a good cook, and Priolt was one of the best. As a child, it had fallen to either Priolt or Kijk to learn the secrets of the scarn-onions, and Priolt had begged for the chance even as his brother wept and said he didn't want to lose his eyes. Weakness had always run in Kijk.

So as a child, he smiled through the pain as he peeled the bulbs and learned to work them. At first his eyesight recovered after a night of sleep, though after a few weeks his vision was always blurry and strained. By the House of Lucifer it was worth it though, as their establishment prospered more than any other public eatery in all the Empire, in any Province. Salt and Sear was booked a year in advance, and they received patronage by at least one Ba'al nightly, sometimes two. There was always one table in reserve for the Shay'tan, though of course if they needed room for anyone important it was understood that a Ba'al could displace any normal patron.

It wasn't just the scarn-onions, though they were a big part. Their fumes were caustic, and if eaten raw could bore a hole right through someone's stomach. Cooked properly, though, and the flavors were simply unmatched. Sweet, smoky, and complex. Priolt had made a small sacrifice in his mind. They also served only the finest ales and wines, only those produced by Houses in good standing with the ash-Shay'tan.

They served exotic meats primarily, as well as rare truffles and herb extracts. He still remembered serving Ba'al Moloch braised blood boar with truffle-oil from his own estate. Priolt had heard from the kitchen the lavish praise Moloch had heaped on Kijk for only providing the finest food in Hell. That was a fine night, as Moloch had overpaid for his meal by a hundred golden crowns and had even blessed their sister, Hylea, with a tryst. She hadn't emerged the next day damaged, or weeping, so Priolt had always believed that Moloch was genuinely pleased with the meal.

Sighing, he ran his thumbs over the sign and painful tears crept out of his ruined ducts. The onions had been worth it, but he was thankful he was not prone to emotion. Crying was excruciating. Today though, he couldn't help it. He couldn't see more than a few feet away, and badly at that, though his ears told him all he needed. His mother and siblings weren't the only casualties. The screams of the dying had stopped, thankfully, but the lamentations of the survivors were terrible. He had never experienced anything like the explosion which leveled Salt and Sear and if he had not been in the cold room trimming cured venison from a drying haunch he would be dead too. The metal walls had protected him, though he would just as well have died.

He had lost everything, and though he knew in his heart it was his skill with food which had made their life worth living, he also had to admit that his family, being not blind, was what enabled him to work at all. Maybe his father wasn't so worthless after all.

He sat, lost in his misery, for a time. It was the clatter of horseshoes on stone and the scent of priceless oils which broke him out of his trance. A Ba'alat, and one with money, was staring down at him.

Priolt wearily climbed to his feet, and bowed. "Pardon, m'lady. I am unable to accept any patronage at this time. I am truly sorry." He didn't fear retribution. Why take her anger out on an old blind cook? He was not responsible for what happened.

"Understandable, though regrettable. I've looked forward to meals here for centuries, long before your time, Priolt. Though I must say, once you took the mantle of kitchen master the food became unrivaled."

His eyes leaked more painful emotion. "Thank you for the kindness, m'lady. It may be some time before I can have the privilege of cooking for you again."

The Ba'alat was silent for a long moment before answering him. "Longer than you may realize. Do you know what has truly happened here?"

He again held no fear in answering. He had already lost everything except his life, and without Salt and Sear, that was worthless as well. It would gain this Ba'alat nothing to kill him. "I have heard that the Throne is all that remains inside the palace. The Cataclysm destroyed everything else inside the inner walls as well. Before the explosion, my brother told me Hellfire wyrms flew against the Shay'tan. After I crawled out from the rubble, I heard in the street that the dead walk outside Sheol, and that any who get close die of a horrible plague. I also heard that the House of Lucifer is no more, and that a mortal slew our immortal ruler."

She was again silent for a time before answering Priolt. "What will you do now?"

He pursed his lips in thought before he responded. No sense in avoiding the truth. "Likely I will die m'lady. I have no family to care for me, and my skill is worthless without a place to practice it. I could scrounge or beg for a time, though I care not to. I was a great man, and I should like to die as one. Perhaps my soul will flow to one who can make use of it."

"You ask for the kindness of my blade, then?"

"Aye, if you would grant it. A clean death at the hand of a Ba'alat is a greater death than I could hope for."

He stood, silently, and was relieved when he heard the whisper of her sword clear its scabbard. It would be a good death.

"Kneel."

He did so, and smiled. "Thank you, m'lady."

He felt the cold touch of the steel on the top of his head, and an intense, searing burn pierced his skull and shot down his brain and into his spine. He gasped, and lifted his head to look at the Ba'alat with sightless eyes.

"Rise, Priolt Ve'kal, Master of Kitchens to the House of Ve'kal. I shall have need of your services in my employ. Do you have any belongings that you need to gather?"

In shock, Priolt spluttered. "No... no, m'lady."

She turned away and spoke behind her. "Ha'jur, have him saddle with the column. We will set up at the Throne. Perhaps some of the tunnels beneath the palace are intact, and our new Master of Kitchens might find some provisions."

He heard the man called Ha'jur signal for a rider, and he found himself saddled behind a Legionnaire en route to the palace. He found his circumstances to be bizarre, though he could smell the devastation all around him. Even his nearly useless vision could tell that the structures were nearly all destroyed.

Master of Kitchens to a Ba'alat? The very one that had marched on Sheol to depose the Shay'tan? Remarkable. Perhaps Master of Kitchens to the ash-Shay'tan! She must have succeeded then, if she meant to take the Throne as her own. Even without the palace, the Throne would be the center of the succession. Any aspirants thinking to displace Ve'kal would have to do so within

27

the center of Sheol, assuming they could even field an army strong enough to break through whatever forces protected the city. If she couldn't hold it… well he was hoping for death only minutes ago. Certainly he could do no worse.

chapter two

But his flesh upon him shall have pain, and his soul within him shall mourn.
- Job 14:22

"Are you sure, Han? You don't wish to stay within the walls?" Piotyr spoke without any regret or pleasure, he simply wanted Han to do what he felt was best.

The giant of a man had not taken off his black plate armor yet, and still carried Moloch's spear, Eirygaile, like it was a part of him. Internally, Han chuckled. With the soul of Lokyrg imbued within it, it actually was a piece of him. He kept his greatsword strapped to his back as well, the one he had forged before he had met up with Han here in Hell, made of that same strange metal his armor was.

"Yes, my friend. Joshua and his plague-walkers can't stay within the walls, and we agree on this. We will retire to the hills above the city for a short while. It will keep most of the mortals who haven't yet been exposed safe, and the two of us may be able to create a vaccine."

Piotyr smiled and offered his hand. "Then I wish you both all the luck in the world. If you need something how will you reach us?"

He shook hands and answered his friend. "Kasim will be back and forth between our camp and Sheol Shay'tan. He can move quickly, and is unaffected by the plague. He travels with Joshua now to settle in up there on the bluffs. The real question is... are you sure you want to stay here?"

Piotyr was uncharacteristically quiet, almost sad, before answering. "Han, I know Jacob was a friend to us all. But in all things save blood he was truly my brother. I don't give a damn about that Ba'alat he was with, but until I know for certain what happened I shall hold vigil. Merethius might have saved us all. I will stay where he fell."

"As it should be, then. Jacob would never say so, but I know in his heart he held you in higher esteem than any Templar. It saddens me that he had to Invoke the Sword, Piotyr. I wish it had not been so."

"As do I, old friend. As do I." The silence between them said it all. Much had been lost.

"What of your family, Piotyr Lamja? Will they stay with you or take to hunting?"

"Both. Asya, Aruc, and Ulis are all going to stay here for now. They will patrol the countryside and report when the other Ba'al move on us." At their names, the two juvenile dragons lifted their heads from where they rested on the battlements and gazed lazily towards the two Templar. Their mother was out surveying the area.

"Then Godspeed, Piotyr. We'll be close by, ready to bring ruin and death if you need us."

"You as well, Han Fei-tze. If you call, my brood will answer."

Han smiled and walked out of the courtyard. He wanted to get to helping Joshua as soon as he could. Kasim would already be there. They may have won the battle, perhaps even the war ultimately, but for now, there was work to be done.

Piotyr worked at clearing corpses and looked up in surprise as a retinue of demonic nobility came into the courtyard. It was the woman Jacob had arrived with. Ve'kal. He snorted and went back to his efforts. Aruc and Ulis helped as well. The combined hellfire from the Templar and two dragons made short work of the bodies.

Pity that the bodies of Jacob and the Shay'tan both had been destroyed in the cataclysm. Piotyr would have liked to make a monument right where his friend slew the Devil.

"Hail, mortal. What are you doing here?" The woman had pulled up short of him by a few paces, and looked down as if she were his master. Piotyr would not tolerate such things.

"Call me *mortal* again, and we shall have discord, demon. My friend accepted your company, but I am under no such compulsion. I am here because I choose to be. That is enough for you."

The column behind Ve'kal stiffened. Piotyr smiled and casually slung his spear on his shoulders. *What, they think they equal us, father? Goad them again.*

No, Lokyrg. No need. If they seek our blood they will draw.

"I had hoped for a friend in you, friend of Jacob. I see that was a foolish notion. Do you mean to fight for the Throne your friend died to liberate?"

Piotyr snorted again. "Of course not. This is the Throne of the Devil. It's fit for a demon, not for me. I may not be a man any more, but I am no Ba'al. When I'm done here I'll be away. This is no place for me or my kin."

Ve'kal was silent a moment before answering. "You could stay. I know you don't have the same loyalty to my house that Jacob did, but as I cared for him I would count you as an ally, Piotyr Lamja."

What she means is when the other houses come to stake their claim she would like to have us there to fight for her. She thinks us stupid, father.

Indeed, son.

"Ba'alat Ve'kal, of House Ve'kal. Good luck in fighting over this damned thing. The life and soul of my best friend and brother bought it for you. I hope it suits you." He turned his back and went about clearing more of the debris and bodies.

This would be a slaughter, father. Must we stay our hand?

Lokyrg, she stood with us in battle. If she attacks, we will slay her. If she does not, I will allow her past allegiance with Jacob to stand. I will not strike first.

Quiet brooding emanated from Lokyrg but the spear stayed silent. Eirygaile was a wicked weapon when he ripped it from

Ba'al Moloch's dead hands, but with his son's soul imbued into it Piotyr could feel it hunger for flesh more often than not. Han had done well, and as a father Piotyr was very pleased. Though Lokyrg would not take wing ever again, his soul would live eternal. Not a perfect trade, nor one he would make on purpose, but it was far preferable to the oblivion awaiting his child had the Shay'tan simply killed him.

He noticed that Ve'kal and her entourage had dismounted and begun setting up camp. He for a moment started to chuckle, but then stopped. What else would she do? If she meant to take the thing it meant occupying the area, even if it was a smoking ruin. He sighed. He missed Jacob. The sacrifice was noble, just, and necessary. That didn't make it sting any less.

He finished clearing the area and looked around. Other than the Ba'alat's company, the Throne was deserted. She was giving him space, either from anger or fear. Piotyr didn't care which and was grateful for either. He blinked a few tears from his eyes as he did what he came to do, channeling hellfire and etching the stone in front of the Throne. He really wished he had Jacob's body to entomb.

Here fell Jacob Merethius, the greatest man who ever lived. Hell could not defeat him, and in his passing he slew the Shay'tan in single combat. He died to save all of mortal kind, but he is not alone. If ever a Shay'tan again rises to wage war upon us, Merethius will be avenged tenfold. Hell trembled before Jacob. It will weep if his sacrifice is forgotten.

Piotyr looked at the epitaph. Blinking more tears away, he lamented that he was weak with words. It seemed melodramatic to him, but he believed in what he wrote. He gathered up Lokyrg, appreciating that his son allowed him to grieve in silence. He met Ve'kal's eye as he left the courtyard. She looked away to the epitaph quickly, but Piotyr had no idea what she was thinking. He didn't really care. It was over for him, at least for now. He longed to be with his mate and other children, and away from the High Sheol. If he was fortunate he'd never have need to return.

chapter three

The seers say truly that he is wise who acts without lust or scheming.
- Renunciation through Knowledge: Bhagavad-Gita

"No, you fool. I told you the Throne is not vacant, not that I was stopping you from claiming it." Ve'kal had no patience for the game any longer. It had been over a week and Ba'al Geir was just the most recent.

"How is it that you expect us to take your word on the matter? The Shay'tan is dead, and you think it likely for us to believe that you simply chose not to claim the Throne?"

"I don't care if you believe me or not. If you think the Throne arcing with energy and forcibly blasting me away from it... if you think that is an act by me then you are more the idiot than I realized. I tell you, I did not claim it."

Geir glared at Ve'kal and flexed his hands, the cracking of his joints hinting at the violence the Ba'al would love to commit on the woman before him. Tall, and powerful, Geir would be no easy foe, though Ve'kal was confident in her own swordplay. Truthfully she didn't want to goad the man, but she was weary and angered by the constant questioning of her account of what had happened.

"Peace, Geir. I speak the truth; I am not the one who holds the Throne. I don't know what happened."

The large Ba'al snorted. "I am of a mind to be sure. No offense." He turned and waved over his eldest son, a deformed monstrosity, barely recognizable as kin. Ve'kal had heard tales of the hideous Obistal, but words did not do the boy justice. His face looked like it had been washed with acid.

"Obistal, fetch me a mortal from outside the palace grounds, as young and innocent as you can find. Bring it here so that we may slay it and then we shall see where the soul flows. If it flows to you, Ve'kal, it will be war."

"Father." The boy nodded and made to leave, though he didn't get the chance.

"A word, Ba'al Geir." The man stepping out of the shadows was unfamiliar to Ve'kal, though she thought she might have seen him before around the palace grounds.

Obistal stopped and turned to look at the man, unarmored and unarmed, who was staring at him. "Me? I am not Ba'al. My father is the Lord of House Geir."

"Impudent dog! How dare you address my heir as Ba'al? Ten days ago he was still in Thrall to the Shay'tan... there is no chance you could mistake him as Ba'al!" The air chilled in front of Ve'kal as the elder Geir drew his blade and stepped towards the man. "I must take offense, then."

The mortal had never taken his eyes from the maimed young man before him. Geir was perhaps four paces away and advancing, and the man still never turned away from the son. Obistal for his part looked confused and uncertain.

"As I said, a word, Ba'al Geir?"

From behind the human, hissing came from the lips of the Ba'al as he lunged out with his blade. Ve'kal had no sympathy, the human was a fool.

She blinked in surprise as Geir stumbled during his attack. She thought he was about to run the man through, but as he thrust, the mortal turned towards him and the sound of a gust of wind accompanied a grunt from the Ba'al.

Onlookers gasped, and Ve'kal stood in amazement. Geir turned towards the Throne for a moment, shock apparent in his eyes as blood poured out from a gash in his stomach. He fell to his knees in a rapidly growing pool of his own blood, eyes rolling back in his head.

The courtyard was deathly quiet; the only sounds were the weak gurgling of the dying lord. No one appeared to be concerned about the death, only in watching it happen.

The mortal hadn't moved since turning towards Geir, but still stood watching Obistal. "Do you need a moment, Ba'al Geir?"

The scarred boy looked at the mortal, eyes slightly wide in shock. "You killed him."

"I did."

"Are you going to kill me?"

The man was quiet for a long moment before answering. "Your face. Was it your father who did that to you?"

"Yes, at my mother's request. When it was time for me to be placed in Thrall, she said she couldn't bear for such a beautiful child to waste away in possession. They splashed hellfire on my face so that I would no longer be beautiful. I was told that it made it easier for her to accept."

Ve'kal knew Ba'alat Geir. The words from Obistal did not surprise her. Looking down at the former Ba'al laying still in the crimson pool, she felt sorry for the boy. She would never have done anything like that to Nezmyr.

"You speak of such atrocity without emotion. Does it not trouble you?" The mortal sounded sad.

"What matter if it did? It was a long time ago, and I was placed in Thrall shortly after. I only awoke recently. What Ba'al Geir said was true."

"I will not kill you, Ba'al Geir." The man paused to see if the title had sunk in. Obistal said nothing. "I will not kill you for what you were about to do. In exchange for your life, think upon the future. To murder someone simply for sport or to satisfy curiosity will no longer be tolerated. My friend gave up everything to kill the Shay'tan, and I will not allow it to be in vain."

Ve'kal's eyes narrowed as she listened to the man. It must be Kasim. Jacob had told her of the assassin, but she hadn't seen the man in person until now. She knew of the other Templar from Jacob's account, but Piotyr was the only one she had met personally. She had thought Jacob boasted of Kasim's skill. She now knew better. She wondered why the man was here.

"I will shed no tears for my father, but why kill him only to spare me? Do you not fear vengeance from my family?"

The man smiled, but to Ve'kal it seemed genuinely sad and not arrogant at all.

"No, I do not fear vengeance from your House. I spared you because you acted out of fear and blind obedience to a wicked master. I am not so foolish to think altruism and morality could grow here yet, but I am willing to plant seeds where I can. In your soul, you are still innocent. I've seen it before in the Thralls. Being placed into possession as a child protects you from becoming like the Ba'al. You can be taught."

"Taught what?"

He smiled again, this time it looked to be with warmth. "How to be human." He then bowed his head at the boy... at the new Ba'al Geir. "Justice will be swift and merciless in Hell. Horror and despair brought us to your Empire, but in staying here I will bring hope. Be better than your father, Ba'al. Peace be upon you."

The boy looked down at his father's corpse, and then up at the mortal... at Kasim. Ve'kal couldn't have guessed what was going through the boy's mind.

Kasim walked over to the Throne and nodded his head in greeting. "A word, Ba'alat Ve'kal?"

chapter four

Be angry, and you confuse your mind; confuse your mind, you forget the lesson of experience; forget experience, you lose discrimination; lose discrimination, and you miss life's only purpose.
- The Yoga of Knowledge: Bhagavad-Gita

"Kasim of the Sword. I am pleased to meet your acquaintance finally."

"No titles. Just Kasim, if you please. I am here to tell you of our plans, and of our expectations."

Ve'kal stilled herself. She had thousands of years behind her of thinking of mortals as weak, inferior, and mostly irrelevant outside of the use of their souls. While she rarely was outwardly cruel for no reason to mortals, treating them with respect was an alien concept. They were chattel.

"Kasim, my intent is not to offend, but even though you are powerful, and a friend to my slain consort, you are new here. Mortals do not give commands to Ba'al or Ba'alat."

The man smiled at her, though it seemed to Ve'kal more out of bemusement than warmth. "You assume that because I do not emit fire from my flesh that I am less of a being than Piotyr?"

She frowned. She had begun to think of Piotyr as an equal, at least in martial terms, but Kasim couldn't have known that. It was a thought she had barely begun to acknowledge herself. Could he read her thoughts? Such a thing worried her.

"I mean no offense, Kasim, but surely you must see the difference between the two of you, not to mention his dragons."

The bemusement turned to genuine mirth. "Aye, Piotyr is mighty; you shall hear no argument from me. Know this though, I *will* tell you of our plans and expectations. If you choose to consider them issued from a simple mortal, that is your choice, but I assure you it would be unwise not to heed my words."

She thought to argue, but something about the man seemed to direct her gaze to the former Ba'al Geir. The Demon Lord had been a formidable warrior, and this *simple mortal* had gutted him in the blink of an eye... over a command issued to his son to kill another mortal. Prudence won out. She had underestimated Jacob, too, at first.

"Very well, Kasim. What would you ask of me?"

"Not just of you, but of all of your kind. Starting today, you are named acting Shay'tan. The four of us have convened and decided. You shall rule Hell for the indeterminate future."

She blinked, and swallowed before answering. It would be of no benefit to her to lose her patience. Nor did she care to explain the intricacies of the Throne or the succession to this ignorant man.

"While I appreciate the gesture, *Kasim*, that won't work. The other Ba'al will never accept a pretender, especially one vested by the seed of Adam." She expected him to bluster and apologize for being so foolish.

"Second. You will command all mortals be freed across the Empire, and all remaining Thralls be released immediately, upon pain of death. Most should be free already, but make an edict mandating it. There will be no slavery of any kind in Hell. All souls stored in the bowels of Sheol will be kept, for now, until Han and Joshua have had a chance to decide what to do with them, but no more will be gathered by the Ba'al... and that includes House Ve'kal. It ends now."

Wearily, she sighed and rubbed her eyes. "Shall I ask Heaven to send us fine food and flowers as well?"

Not even a hint of anger in his eyes answered her sarcasm. "Hah! Splendid notion. Feel free, though I suspect you have less of a chance of that request being granted than the many we asked for over the long years of our apocalypse."

"Ok, I'll speak plainly since you don't appear to grasp the situation. I simple cannot..."

He calmly raised a hand to forestall her. She should have been enraged, but the gesture seemed both respectful and conciliatory, though she didn't know how.

"Ve'kal. I have told you of our expectations. Now hear our plans. Bear in mind that this is told to you after *much* deliberation among us, and this plan of action is not proposed, it is absolute. It will bear out, and you shall do your part. By your leave?"

How could the man be so damnably polite? He had just butchered a Ba'al in cold blood, and from some accounts of the fall of Sheol he had stood in mortal combat with the former Shay'tan. The man must have ice in his veins. "Yes, Kasim, let's hear it."

"Very good. Starting tomorrow the first of the Destroyer's supporters will begin to arrive in the valley of Sheol. They have come to see the succession play out, some of them perhaps to curry favor with the new Shay'tan, some to perhaps make the claim themselves. Either way, you will greet them here, in the courtyard, at Jacob's memorial. They will pay homage to you, or they will die."

Her eyes widened. "You mean to kill any who oppose me?"

"For a time. As I said you will be *acting* Shay'tan. We Fallen Templar will be directing you. Those who accept you, and through you, us... will be allowed to bend the knee and take a place alongside the changes coming."

"That will be almost none of them."

"No, I expect not at first. But still, the offer will be made. Those who accept your rule may remain, and help rebuild."

"That will work briefly, but after word gets out I expect those who would choose neither to accept me nor perish will gather their power elsewhere to strike. Your plan is flawed."

"Indulge me. Yes, what you predict will happen. When it does, Joshua will take his walkers and destroy any organized opposition. Those that flee, Piotyr and his brood will take on the wing. Those that lurk near and sow discontent and treason to your rule, I shall ferret and eliminate. However, if any come close to being able to actually threaten The High Sheol with a real gathering of force? Han has enough power here to obliterate a thousand Legionnaires with a single thought. Do not question me on this, Ve'kal. If you think Piotyr a man of power you would quake to understand a fraction of what Han can do."

She was listening now, and frighteningly, she believed him.

"Within six months, resistance to your rule will be scattered and broken. Within a year, it will be gone."

"So you will help me consolidate my false claim to the Throne, direct my actions, and what do I get out of it?" Almost, she believed him. Ba'al Apollyon made his plans more complicated, though.

"Not an altruist then?" His eyes sparkled when he chided her. How could he be so calm? "Fair enough. In exchange, once our plans are complete in Hell, we shall leave you to rule it in fact. By then, challenge to your rule should be a forgotten thing, and you can do what you will."

"Why go to this trouble if you intend to leave me to it? What is to stop me from undoing all that you change?"

"In truth, nothing, though it would be unwise to assume that mortals would never again come here. I think the rules of this particular contest have changed."

"Fine, then what *are* your plans for Hell? Again, why go to all this trouble?"

"For now, I am not inclined to divulge everything, but suffice it to say that our short term goal is to liberate the mortals in Hell, free all Thralls, and change this place of misery into something better. In the process, Ba'al Apollyon will be forced to deal with us. That will give our brothers time to rebuild, regroup, and start over."

Her eyes widened. The last thing she wanted was for Abaddon the Destroyer to come back with any cause to be displeased with her. "Do not think to stand against him as you did these trifling, lesser Ba'al. Apollyon is every bit the equal of the Shay'tan. If he marches here with the Legion he wages war with on Earth..."

His eyes changed in a flash. The amusement was gone, replaced by what could only be regret, or perhaps sorrow. Ve'kal was at a loss, so she just sat silent for a moment.

"No one alive knows better than I not to underestimate him. I did so once. I shall not repeat my mistake."

The silence between them grew heavy. It was she who finally broke it. "I agree to your terms. I shall do as you wish. What else would you have me do to prepare for the bloodshed to come?"

The man called Kasim shook his head, clearing the regret from his eyes. "Nothing, Lady Ve'kal. Prepare your petitioners whatever hospitality you can in this broken place. Treat them as your supplicants. Perhaps more of them then we suspect will find the role suits them, and the bloodshed will be minimal."

She nodded her head, though in her heart she did not believe it would be that way. "Perhaps."

Chapter Five

The Sanctuaries are falling. Not quickly, but inevitably. Death is patient, and more than willing to wait for us.
- Patriarch Quintus Salvius Meles

The sky above shone down in a light red, soothing midday sun. He blinked, and felt the stirrings of one waking from a long nap underneath the clouds and the wind of a pleasant afternoon.

It was warm, not hot, and soft where he lay. The sounds of trees blowing in the breeze soothed his ears as well as the babbling brook flowing gently but swiftly near the sandy bank he was on. He sat up, and looked down at his tattered clothing. He had wondered what would happen when he died, here. It was strangely somewhat as he expected.

He had tasted the pain and suffering of this place, and now that he was dead, it was a pleasant surprise that he was not enduring torment.

He stood up, brushed sand off his legs, and looked at his surroundings. Idyllic, was all he could think of. Mountains surrounded him, and he was in a very small valley that he could walk across in probably a quarter-hour. The water smelled clean and reflected the sunlight peacefully. Altogether, it seemed about as nice a place as he could ever remember visiting.

He inhaled deeply, and smiled. Death was not so bad. There were far worse things than this which could have awaited him.

Still, it was the mountains, and the warmth would fade with the sun. He needed shelter, and it was a task that he took to with relish.

Driftwood abounded, and ample grasses grew in the sandy soil along the banks of the water. He bundled what sticks he could carry and made a simple den large enough for him to sit up in. It took him a couple of hours, as he worked at a casual pace. If he needed to enlarge the burrow tomorrow he would, perhaps even make a smoke hole and a fire pit. For now, though, he relaxed in his new home, and watched the sun set. No, Death was not so bad at all.

It was clear to him that there was someone else living in his valley. He had been there a long time, and he knew it well. He had awoken that morning and all was as it should be. He left his cabin, taking his fur cloak and hat off the wall as he went. As he always did, he walked the boundaries of his purgatory. Lacking the need for food, it was really his only daily requirement... his only compulsion in this place.

He didn't call it Hell, he knew better, but after being here for so long it was hard to view it as anything other than a prison. He had tried to leave, when he first arrived, but the hunger grew in him so fierce and fast as he approached the valley's edge that he had to turn back. Over the years, he had tried off and on to again escape the valley, but always failed to overcome the incredible gnawing in his stomach. Only when he tried to leave, though. Otherwise, hunger was foreign to him.

After so long being trapped, he had memorized every stone, tree, and bush. So it was that he knew exactly when it was that another being had arrived in his home. He felt it like an itch. He did not view it as an attack, or an invasion, but it was a curiosity, and there were scarce few of those to be had. He didn't investigate at first. He allowed his new guest the chance to acclimate his or herself, and he returned to his cabin. He looked over his rustic home, and for a moment allowed memories to wash over his mind. They were all he had. He went to sleep that night thinking about things long forgotten, and smiled as he dozed off. In the morning he would seek out his guest, but for now was content just to remember that there was anything outside of the valley.

chapter six

Knowing others is intelligence; knowing yourself is true
wisdom. Mastering others is strength; mastering yourself is true
power. If you realize that you have enough, you are truly rich.
- Lao Tzu: Tao Te Ching

Ve'kal had been right. The first petitioners from the Crusade on Earth, from House Rhy'gajna, had laughed in her face. Then they had spat upon Jacob's memorial and drew blades. Brown cloaked wraiths had appeared from the dust and the stone and House Rhy'gajna had died within heartbeats.

She blinked, and the wraiths were already departing. Kasim was true to his word. "Priolt, please offer the refreshments meant for House Rhy'gajna to the next supplicants. Have this cleaned up as well."

Her master of kitchens had been a fortunate and wonderful find here. He was giving legitimacy to her claim by virtue of his skill with spice and salt.

She awaited the next group, and this time it was House Toly'm, who she knew was old, but not powerful. Ba'al Toly'm was not an imposing warrior, but instead gave the impression of books, ledgers, and boredom. She did not expect him to draw upon her.

"Ba'al Toly'm, do you come in supplication to Shay'tan Ve'kal?" The title burned her tongue. Not because she didn't deserve it, but because it wasn't actually hers. The Throne wasn't vacant. Maybe these fools didn't know it, but she did. The lie tugged at her pride.

"Yes, mistress. House Toly'm will gladly serve your Throne in whatever capacity you require. Do you have any requests to make?"

His tone caught her off guard. Surely that was not... his eyes were turned towards her, leering. He was proposing a union. Disgusting. Inwardly she fumed, and decided then and there to destroy him. Jacob was not even a fortnight dead and already she was being propositioned by suitors.

"Yes, your ancient and noble house will serve me best by being an example of loyalty and honor. You will be my official emissary to House Apollyon. My stewards will prepare statements of greetings for you."

The color draining from his face as he left did little to diffuse the soiled feeling she had from the lecherous old goat. How could he think to equal Merethius? Had he not seen the man?

Sighing, she realized that almost no one had. Her lands were remote, and Jacob had arrived from the far corners of it. The only denizens of Hell who had spent any real time with him had been in her estate or accompanying them on their march to Sheol. The battle had been quick, and brutal, and Jacob had died long before many Ba'al would have had even a remote chance to know of him.

Not that it would have mattered, she supposed. The Ba'al would have treated him as a mortal, and either challenged him or tried to subvert him. She was saddened by the loss of the man. Mortal though he may have been at heart, he was still unequaled by any she had met over her millennia of life. She had known he would die in the fight, but she still missed him. She missed his touch... and the look on Nezmyr's face when Jacob smiled at the boy. She truly wished things could have been different. Unkind, for the other mortals to have lived when her Jacob had died.

Gazing out across the plaza, she allowed her eyes to linger on the memorial the mortal Piotyr had wrought. Water, weak, foolish water came unbidden to her eyes. Would that things could have been different.

"Is it done, Han?"

"No, not done, though it is being done as we speak. Not much longer, I think."

Joshua, feeling wretched as always, took small comfort in the words of his friend. "How many examples do the fools need?" Kasim and his disciples could keep this up forever. In his mind, Joshua had no fear that any Ba'al could challenge the plans he and Han had created, unless The Destroyer broke siege and marched on Sheol.

"They are a prideful and arrogant bunch, it is true. I don't think their minds can adequately process that mortals have come and shaken their society to its core. Perhaps they lack the gift we humans have in questioning our circumstances."

"Perhaps, Han. Though I wish they could at least accept the overwhelming truths in front of them. They bring arms and armor where we bring death itself. Hellfire, disease, and whatever it is that you command Han... they cannot hope to stand against us."

The older man smiled at his younger, if sickly looking friend. "I told you, I command all the suffering endured in Hell since time began. Regardless, just as water is wet, these beings will challenge Ve'kal. It is in their nature, and we are but mortals to them."

A snort came from the corner of the pavilion tent. The First had sat silently during their exchange, though now it was clear to Joshua that his new closest friend had something to say on the matter.

"The dead walk and dragons fly under your banner. No one but a fool could call your forces mortal. The Ba'al are not needed, only their soldiers. Unleash your walkers, cleric. Let there be an end to discord."

It was Han who answered, though his Templar brother said almost exactly what he himself thought as well.

"True we do not need their sword-arms, but I would wager that their Legion will fight harder and better if there is true loyalty at play. I would not hesitate to destroy any Ba'al deemed necessary, and in truth that is what Kasim is doing down there with his bloody work. However, if there are any Ba'al which could be brought to our side with actual conviction? So much the better. We can wait a fortnight without damaging our cause."

"You think the Destroyer will wait a fortnight as well? Cleric, tell your friend he is a fool."

Joshua smiled and looked at the old philosopher, who was smiling as well. He was glad that the First had chosen Han to call a fool, instead of Piotyr. Han was as humble a man as Joshua had ever known, and had a self-deprecating humor hard to find in the Temple. Piotyr would have drawn steel. Han merely chuckled.

"Han, are you a fool?" He laughed as he said it, but phlegm rattled in his chest and ruined his humor.

Han's grin turned to concern. "Not all the time. I also think that a fortnight might do us well. Joshua, we must look to your disease. You deserve better than this, and there must be something we can do."

A coughing fit took him, and he struggled to find breath as he waved his friend down. "I'm open to suggestions, Han. I don't prefer this."

Another snort from the First turned both the Templar to the attention of the Zombie-King. "Your sickness made you powerful, cleric. Never forget that." With that the undead man, now unrecognizable from other humans, walked out of the tent to go do whatever it was that he did when on his own.

"Do you think he has a point? Will you lose your ability to create the walkers if you are healed?"

"Yes. I do think that, and I'll gladly accept the trade. Han, I can't live like this. I'll ask Piotyr to burn my flesh to ash if I can't find a cure. Suicide is preferable to this intolerable existence."

"Careful. If you asked, he would do it."

"Of course he would, he's a friend. He might think us poor soldiers, but he respects us in his own way. Besides, if he didn't, I'm sure Asya would."

The name caused Han to shudder briefly. The dragon still unnerved him, even after he had saved Piotyr's son. Joshua hadn't asked him why he feared them so.

"True enough. Enough talk of suicide, though. How can we cure you?"

Joshua reached over for a draught of tonic. Wine made him feel much worse when he imbibed, but a cask of liquor found in the outer city of Sheol had done well by him once fortified with citrus and honey. It wasn't based on prayer, but rather was a simple remedy rooted in nature. "The illness is demonic in nature, of that I am sure. It will not be cured by the will of a man, even men such as us."

"So you think to find a healer amongst the Ba'al?" Han didn't appear to be surprised, though he likely wondered at the logistics of finding a competent healer who could or would help Joshua willingly.

"There will be more of a chance among the mortals living here in Hell. The Ba'al will have their methods, though I would first trust to a descendant of Adam... though it would have to be one who survived my plague."

Han grabbed himself a drink as well, simple table wine from an inn. "Ah, that. I think our vaccine will be successful. Your blood should give inoculation if the recipient can be kept in quarantine and properly cared for while it works."

Joshua smiled sadly, and nodded his head. "I agree. It should give inoculation, though I fear many will die from exposure before immunity is granted. The thing is virulent."

"They would die anyway, Joshua. At least this way there is a chance. We also aren't forcing anyone to take it. The vaccine will be voluntary. Those who want to simply flee, can."

Joshua steeled himself and nodded to Han. This was Hell. Nothing was easy or mild. "Agreed, and I will be setting up the infirmary tents tomorrow. For weal or woe, we must try to save all we can."

Han smiled and raised a glass. Joshua followed suit and waited for his friend to speak.

"For weal or woe."

chapter seven

The sorrows of death compassed me, and the pains of hell gat hold upon me: I found trouble and sorrow.
- Psalm 116:3

My love, this does not seem important, or necessary. Why are we doing this?

Asya had been, by Piotyr's reckoning, incredibly patient and understanding while he wrapped up the mess left after Jacob had died. She had let him do what he needed to, and hadn't asked him for anything while he grieved. He owed her far more than just his love, though she had that from him for the rest of his days. He also owed her honesty and information.

My heart and soul, we are looking for any organized resistance to the rule of Jacob's former mate. Though he is dead, the Lady Ve'kal asks in his name to unify the forces of Hell under our cause. If any oppose that, Kasim will cut them down if they are in the city. It falls to us to do so if they are in the wilds. Piotyr had finally mastered the art of communicating with his mate and his brood telepathically. It felt so much more natural than speaking. Asya had been surprised that their children had matured enough to do so as quickly as they had.

Why though? What benefit is it to us for Hell to unify under this Ba'alat? Fractured and isolated, our prey is weak. Why strengthen them?

As usual she was insightful, though all of her thoughts were filtered through a lens of predation. His mate cared nothing for war or politics; she only wanted to hunt, both for food and for sport. This was not the first argument they had like this since the battle of Sheol, but she may never understand. The concept was alien to her.

Asya, you have lived here your whole life, and know of no other place. The Ba'al have hunted the dragons near to extinction, as have they hunted humanity. I am too late to save the slain wyrms, but we can still push the Legion out of my home. To stand against the Destroyer, we have decided to do all we can to increase the power of our forces.

Why do you want to go home? Are you not happy with us here?

Never have I been happier. My desire to liberate Earth is not out of longing to return there, it is out of a desire to vanquish my enemies. Humanity deserves better than annihilation, and I am of a mind to aid them.

Confusion came over his empathic link with his mate, but no anger or bitterness. She would follow his lead, and for that he was grateful. *Besides, my love, though it is not the case with you, I find myself to be a greater hunter when I am focused on a specific objective. As a warrior, I will greatly benefit from this campaign of unification. The feeding will be plentiful for our children, as well.*

They were silent for a time as they flew towards where the targets were. Piotyr knew from Kasim's information that Ba'al Mirish and his retinue from the portal had killed Ve'kal's messenger inviting him to offer fealty at the Throne. Mirish was a powerful Ba'al with several thousand Legionnaires with him, all battle-hardened veterans from the War on Earth.

Asya as always took the lead, with their son Aruc and daughter Ulis following near a quarter mile behind. Lokyrg as usual kept silent while the family hunted on the wing.

It was past twilight when they spotted the entrenched fortification. Ba'al Mirish clearly expected an attack from Ve'kal's Legion, as the encampment had a triple ring of sharpened pike walls encircling the command tent. Cook fires, guard posts, archer's nests, and picket lines greeted Piotyr's eyes as the wyrms circled far above. He Invoked a Prayer of Farsight to get better detail on the camp.

The guards were disciplined, and reacted quickly to the sight of the dragons. He mused in his head and was briefly surprised when Asya answered his thoughts. He still forgot about the link they shared.

Yes, Piotyr, there will be those among these soldiers that hunted my kind in centuries past. Ba'al Mirish is an old name, and a feared one. He will be no easy prey.

Piotyr peered intently down at the fortifications. *Stronger than Moloch?* Lokyrg pulsed in his hands, vibrating with a palpable desire for bloodshed at the name.

No, not stronger, though close. He is known for his prowess with a bow, rather than a spear. If Moloch is like to you, then Mirish would be as Kasim.

Piotyr smiled with pride. A month ago Asya would not have even thought to use a nuance of his speech. The comparison meant she was trying to learn his language. It pleased him.

Well, he won't be familiar with our tactics. His arrows won't find our flesh today, my love.

I know that, Piotyr, I am merely sharing what I know. Shall we do this as we usually do? She banked and waited for Aruc and Ulis to close and for Piotyr to give the signal.

Aye. Attack.

Asya plummeted like a stone towards the earth. As she fell, Piotyr Invoked Grace and Prescience. His role was to support the dragons, and direct them. His skill at arms would be secondary.

The Legionnaires truly were disciplined. The rain of arrows was loosed at precisely the right moment to cause maximum damage to the cavalry charge. Piotyr allowed his hellfire to coalesce around his body and burst outward in an expanding sphere of protection. The projectiles turned to ash in a deluge of small immolations. As the fire caught, he kept up the cascade of flames as more and more missiles were launched from the archers.

Asya pulled up for her strafing run and Piotyr could hear the screams of the Legion as first the larger wyrm's breath washed over the encampment and then the sides followed suit from Aruc and Ulis. Fire and death came in a torrent to Ba'al Mirish's forces.

There were a few isolated Legion who survived the initial salvo, but their morale was broken and they fled in terror. By the time the first pass was over, the fortifications were cinders and the only rival to the screams of the dead and dying was the crackling of timber.

They made a second pass, and Asya pulled up suddenly. Piotyr had to shift his grip to keep his balance, surprised at the sudden change in their attack pattern.

He was about to put the words of uncertainly to his lips, but then he saw what had caused his mate to stop short. The command tent was not burning, was not even singed. His Farsight enhanced eyes could see clearly the figure standing in front, looking up at them in cold, calculating focus. Piotyr also saw the three-span longbow drawn back just an instant before it loosed.

Agony struck the Templar as stark as the shock. A jagged length of freezing metal protruded from his shoulder near to the length of his forearm, having punched clean through his armor. He grunted in pain, and made to grab the shaft to remove it from his flesh. His hand closed around the arrow and went numb from the cold, all his strength draining from his closed fist. Steam rose from the wound like a venting geyser. What devilry was this?

Asya, fall back out of his range! The thought contained barely restrained panic, answered in kind by Asya as she was also struck by one of the freezing quarrels. A dragon her size had little to fear from a lone arrow wound, but the thickness and heat of her carapace should have been more than enough to keep her safe from the Ba'al firing from below.

Through his pain, and turning his head to watch Ba'al Mirish as Asya retreated, he could see clearly the smooth draw and release as the Demon Lord fired quickly at the now retreating brood.

Father? Why do we flee a lone Ba'al without his Legion?

Aruc was right to question. Other than the battle at Sheol, Piotyr and his family had never tasted defeat. They had been pressed at times to exertion, but had never been forced to withdraw. Piotyr inwardly fumed at his arrogance. To assume victory was the quickest way to defeat. He had become overconfident and foolhardy. This was Hell, and he had nearly forgotten it.

Asya had finished her turn and was now fleeing the fortified encampment, and Piotyr noticed with concern that the Ba'al had taken flight and was pursuing them. Huge black-tipped copper tinted wings beat in time to the painful pulsing of Piotyr's throbbing wound. By God he was cold. The numbness was creeping slowly down his torso and into his belly. No blood flowed down his chest that he could feel. He began to feel drowsy. He thought he should be more concerned, but couldn't bring himself to call out as he slipped off Asya and plummeted to the ground.

Father!

My love!

Cold... so cold.

By my blood, washed away on the sword of the Shay'tan, wake up father!

He faded in and out of consciousness as the dragons roared in rage and pain around him. The earth churned as blasts of hellfire warmed his numb body briefly. Piotyr struggled mightily to remain awake; noticing as he glanced down that his entire torso was turning green-black with frostbite. Strange, that it didn't hurt.

The arrow was still embedded in his shoulder. He was so weak he could barely keep his eyes open, let alone stand. The roars of the dragons around him... his family, let him know that they were in pain. Piotyr gasped for breath and Invoked Strength. Power trickled into his body. Not the torrent he expected when in the midst of war, but instead just barely enough to allow him to sit up.

He wheezed with the effort, but was able to stay upright and managed to get to his knees. Ulis and Aruc were engaged with Ba'al Mirish. They were trying to flank him, but by God the Fallen was fast. He wasn't hovering exclusively, but was landing frequently and using his wings to great effect in bursts of speed keeping him out from between the larger dragons. Numerous arrows protruded from their hides, and Piotyr grit his teeth in hatred. Between the three skirmishing foes and Piotyr, Asya stood protecting Piotyr with her wings out and directing hellfire breath over the Ba'al. What should have immolated Mirish instead dissipated around him in waves of great steam.

Piotyr wondered briefly about the Ba'al's immunity, but instead focused on the arrow. If he could just get it out of him...

He tried grabbing it again, but found he had no strength in his hand. It was useless to try to pull it out. Curse his stupid pride that day. It was selfish, lazy, and now his family was paying for his pride.

Father, use me.

Piotyr looked to where Lokyrg called him from. Only a pace away, the spear had fallen in some rocks. He sadly shook his head. He couldn't even grab an arrow, wielding a spear was impossible. He was going to die.

Use me, father!

He hadn't the energy to argue... then it dawned on him what Lokyrg was suggesting. It might work. Grinding his jaw with the effort, he crawled to the rocks where his spear rested. The spear was heavier than most greatswords, and if he could just brace it properly...

He was barely able to wedge the butt of the spear into a gap in the rocks, its point solidly resting perhaps two feet in the air at a sharp angle. Pushing down on it, he was pleased that it hardly gave. He rolled up against it, angling his shoulder to meet the edge. He felt the pressure, but his shoulder was completely numb. For that, he was grateful.

Hurry, Ulis is about to fall!

He heaved himself into the point as hard as he could, shifting his weight so the spear would have the benefit of gravity to help the thrust, necessary to help the spear force past his pauldron. He found that his shoulder was *not* completely numb.

Piotyr screamed as the arrow met Eirygaile and he almost blacked out again as he pushed as hard as he could down against the spear. Agony pierced his skull and he had to fight to stay conscious. He had to keep going. If he stopped they were all dead. Spittle flew from his mouth as he heaved himself further down the spear. The blade was flat, but the shaft wasn't. Nearly three inches in diameter, he might die anyway from blood loss if he couldn't get the freezing barb all the way out of his body. He heaved again, and this time the pain was almost blissful as Eirygaile shoved the vile ice arrow out of his body. He could sense his son's soul sigh in relief as the spear he was bound to completely pierced his father's torso.

Blood started to pool around the wound, slowed by the acidic residue on the spear. Piotyr blinked and watched as Ba'al Mirish put another several arrows into the flesh of his children, laughing at them and their roars of pain as he dashed up and away out of reach faster than the drakes could pursue.

He grit his teeth as the cold leeched out of his wound and he felt his strength return. Hellfire leaked out of his eyes and mouth as he growled in hatred at what the Ba'al had done to his mate and children. Asya. Gather the drakes and heal them.

My love! I can't leave you or he will slay you!

Never in his life had he hated anything as much as he hated Mirish in that moment. *ASYA NOW!*

Piotyr roared as his body erupted with Hellfire and he felt his wound close with the consuming flames that burned the grasses and rock around him into ashen dust. He saw the drakes, his beautiful children, look to him in pain from the dozens of arrows piercing their flesh and a veil of red descended over his eyes. He stood from his knees, grabbing Lokryg as he did. He felt the longing of his son to let blood flow, through Eirygaile.

Ba'al Mirish turned from the drakes to meet Piotyr's eyes and Piotyr saw a glint of humor in the demon's eyes. He would not suffer such mockery. He Invoked Speed and rushed at the Ba'al with the fury of a hurricane. As he passed Asya his aura washed over her in a cascade of healing flames. The Ba'al turned to fire the ice arrows towards him and Piotyr spun Lokryg faster than a willow branch. Arrow after arrow fell to the ground harmlessly, parried with precision as he closed to the Ba'al. The coward kept falling back, firing shot after shot at the Templar, but in his rage, with holy grace pouring through him... Piotyr swatted them aside like gnats.

The mirth in Mirish's eyes faded into concentration, and as Piotyr finally closed within a spear length the Ba'al dropped his bow and drew two short blades which dripped arctic frost from their blue-black metal.

Finally. A foe with flesh for me to taste.

Piotyr howled as he thrust the spear over and over at Mirish, spinning and twisting it to meet the whirling slices of the Ba'al. Time and time again he neared the flesh of the Ba'al but was unable to finish him. He grew angry at his own incompetence, but realized that Mirish wasn't trying to actively kill him. The Demon Lord was parrying without any attempt to counterattack. Why?

The answer came from his son. *Father, the cold... beware the cold. He means to sap your strength again.*

He frowned, and stepped back from his assault for a moment. Eirygaile was frigid, and he could feel the cold slowly penetrate his aura of hellfire into his hands. Cursing, he knew the tactic would work in time. Could he end this quickly?

He didn't think so. Not with Mirish only trying to deflect his weapon. Ba'al Moloch had wanted to kill him, and that fight had been over in moments. Piotyr had little experience fighting an opponent with no desire to fight back. This encounter favored the Ba'al.

Asya, Ulis, Aruc. Slowly spread out and encircle him. Aruc stay to the ground, Ulis take wing and hover behind him a body length into the air. Asya. Wait until they are in position and then fly down from above to flush him to one of us.

Thoughts of affirmation came, and Piotyr flexed his hands on the spear. The cold would eventually numb him, but not for a while yet.

He feinted a couple of attacks towards Mirish, but did not press over-hard as his offspring, at least partially healed he hoped from Asya's breath... took up their positions. He grinned with anticipation. This would now favor the Lamja family.

Mirish gazed up as Ulis flew over their melee and frowned in consternation. He looked at Piotyr briefly and then beyond him at Asya.

"Well fought, human." The Ba'al spoke in a lyrical, pure voice, tinged with malice and frustration. "We shall meet again."

Piotyr's eyebrows climbed high on his head, and he blinked as Ba'al Mirish fled underneath his daughter. Asya was not even close to being in position. The Ba'al had surmised what Piotyr had intended.

Asya made to fly in pursuit, and Aruc and Ulis did too.

No. Let him go. He caught us unprepared. It will not happen again.

Growls of frustration and disagreement came into his thoughts, and he agreed with them, but he knew he was right.

We will meet again. For now, help me gather his arrows. This is a weapon I fear, and I would know more of it. We must take these to Han.

His children and wife were silent, but he could sense how they seethed. Piotyr did as well, but he would not risk another encounter with Mirish at that time, unprepared as they were.

Agreement came from a most unlikely source.

Bound though I may be to this steel, father, I agree. I do not wish to feel the bite of that ice again.

Lokyrg was not alone in that.

chapter eight

Knowing it birthless, knowing it deathless, knowing it endless,
forever unchanging, dream not you do the deed of the killer, dream
not the power is yours to command it.
- The Yoga of Knowledge: Bhagavad-Gita

Kasim walked the ruin of inner Sheol in quiet introspection. The cataclysm had left almost nothing standing close to the Throne, but surprisingly many buildings in the outer city were intact. Many more could even be repaired. The reconstruction had begun, but over the last week little more than the removal of debris had occurred. It was a start.

His words to Ve'kal had not given him much hope in her conviction to improve the quality of life for mortals in Hell, though she was sincere in accepting aid from him and his brothers in securing the Throne. She could not hold it on her own, but between the four of them, the Templar could do it for her.

The campaign had been largely successful, with the supplicants arriving either bending knee to Ve'kal or dying at the hands of Kasim and his disciples. The undead threat had been enough to prevent any military action against the city. There were still isolated pockets of resistance out in the provinces, but Piotyr had been incredibly successful wiping those out. Things were progressing well, and soon all of Hell would be united... either under Ve'kal or fleeing to The Destroyer. Many more Ba'al than

Kasim had anticipated had joined with Ve'kal. Their plan would work.

Dhermina smiled at him and held his hand as they walked. Her face lit his heart with warmth and for a time he forgot violence as he walked with his love. If the other acolytes walking behind them took notice, he was unconcerned. They would all come to find their own love, in time. For now, it was his.

"Soul of my soul, Dhermina, what say you to...?" Kasim broke off as hissing sharply came from the street they were walking on. The smell of chemicals assailed his nostrils for but a moment as he turned in confusion to look back up the street towards his followers from Sagarmatha, his most trusted friends and companions.

He could see nothing, but the smell intensified as horror overtook him. Time slowed to a crawl as he saw a cloaked figure step out of an alley and fire a rounded arrow into the street. "RUN!" Was all he had time to say as he grabbed Dhermina and shoved her as hard as he could further down the road and ran to follow. It was too late. Fire erupted above the cobblestones and danced up their flesh. Kasim blinked as the flames washed over the monks from Sagarmatha and their teacher. As one, the screams reached his ears even as he willed his legs to keep running. The hellfire seared his nerves even as he called the wind to sheathe his skin to protect him.

The area of the attack was small, and Kasim was nearly at the edge when the fire erupted. His shove had saved Dhermina, and the wind had saved him, though the flesh of his legs was scorched and smoked in searing agony. The fire burned in a near perfect square where his disciples had walked. He collapsed to his knees, the pain throbbing below his thighs nothing compared to the pit of despair he felt in his stomach as he looked at the fires.

Ozra, Kishien, and Jio had stopped twitching; their flesh blackened and flaking from the residual wind Kasim's elemental cloak gave off. Tal and Qor instead writhed in agony, screaming as they bat futilely against the flames melting their skin.

"No! My God, no!" Dhermina wept, lurching to her feet from where Kasim had thrown her. Grief warred with pain in his heart.

"Dhermina... fetch Joshua. NOW!"

She coughed and looked at him, wide eyes from shock and misery, but the command in his voice moved her to action. She left at a dead sprint while Kasim stood in mute horror as his friends and students burned. He had grown to love the other monks, and as Tal and Qor grew silent, his heart grew laden and the pain in his legs paled to the despair in his soul.

The smoke in the air stunk of burned flesh, and glancing down he knew that without Joshua he would never walk again. The wind had saved him; his unique gift from the demon soul imbued into him by the Patriarch had allowed him to live. Hellfire was too strong to merely be undone by wind, though. Without the healer, Kasim would be a cripple.

"Is this what you want, Son of Adam?" Kasim looked up to see the cloaked archer walking through the flames unscathed. "You come to our domain, and think yourself master of it. Look and behold the cost of your arrogance."

Kasim didn't have the strength for hatred, then. He looked up at the man while the figure smiled and drew back another arrow in his bow. The flames danced upon his vestments, but did not burn them. Kasim wondered at that, as he looked into the eyes of his killer.

"May I have the name of my slayer? My pride has killed us. Might I humbly ask who has done the deed?"

The assassin's smile vanished. "We have no names, horseman." He shot Kasim through the heart.

Kasim smiled, then, though it was the hardest thing he could remember doing in his life. The irony was not lost on him.

The intrusion of the newcomer into his valley had changed from a curiosity into an amusement. He had lived there for so long he had forgotten what it was like in the beginning, and it all came back to him now watching the stranger.

The stranger was not a novice woodsman, though not as accomplished as he, the valley dweller was. The dweller could kill a hare with a sling without fail from across the clearing, but never felt hunger unless he tried to leave. Sometimes he lingered near the boundary just to feel that hunger. When the gnawing in his belly came, he would hunt, and eat, and remember things long forgotten.

He watched with wry amusement the stranger cooking his meal over his fire. Two perfect looking rabbits turned expertly on a spit while the man watched them marinate in their own juices. Any man would be drooling in anticipation of the meal after spending a day hiking around the valley. He almost laughed as the man kept turning the hares, poking them to see if they were done, and finally just took them off the fire and looked at them. No hunger would find him here in the center of the valley.

Frowning, he wondered how long it had been since he last neared the boundary to hunt and eat. Weeks? Surely. Months? Perhaps. It did smell fine, but he was reluctant to call out to the stranger. The dweller was enjoying the novelty of change, and was hesitant to chance interruption. What if the stranger was hostile, or worse, annoying? No, he would wait for now, and watch. He would learn more about this man before he came to him. Perhaps it was deceitful, but another day or so would not hurt anything. Smiling wryly, the dweller realized that he had nothing but time.

Ve'kal could see the ruin of everything cascading down around her. The dragon woman, Asya, and Piotyr were fighting in the courtyard, with Asya in her human form shouting at the man. Kasim lay dying on a cot next to Merethius' marker. The attack had not claimed him, but she had seen the work of the Watchers before. Kasim would die screaming.

"Han, were we so arrogant that we thought ourselves safe here?" The healer had tended to Kasim, and his burns looked to be better, but the poison would turn his veins to stone within days.

"Not now, Joshua. Let Piotyr have his moment and we will address it then."

Fools. Ve'kal knew enough of these men to know they were woefully unprepared for the true horrors of Hell. Piotyr and the dragons had brought back samples of the arrows Ba'al Mirish had used to nearly kill all of them. To their credit, they had completely obliterated Mirish's Legion, and consequently his chance at challenging for the Throne. However grateful Ve'kal was to have another challenger, a strong one at that, removed did not negate how one Ba'al had almost severed one of her support pillars in a single afternoon.

She glanced over at the table where the arrows lay. Heart of Cocytus was rare, but not unknown. It was much easier to handle than hellfire, and not nearly as deadly. The table radiated cold, but it was safe to touch the ice, if only for a moment. What was more of concern was that Mirish had so much of the stuff. At least four quivers of arrows, his blades, and his armor would be worth a fortune, and House Mirish was simply not that wealthy.

It was possible that it was an heirloom set, and Ba'al Mirish *had* been a wyrm hunter of great renown, but coinciding with the attack on Kasim and his disciples? Ve'kal sensed the hand of Ba'al Apollyon. The Destroyer was the only being other than the Shay'tan powerful enough to easily make a trek to Cocytus. She had not heard of The Destroyer breaking camp outside of Haven's walls, and she would have if that was the case. More likely he sent Mirish to collect his own stock from his estate, thinking both to send Mirish to take care of a threat and also that it would be easy to replenish his supply later.

"No Asya... please don't go." The quarrel had spilled out into the courtyard.

"You know where to find us when you are finished with this madness. I told you I would follow you, and I did, but I will not send our children to their deaths for *politics*. This ends for us. Lokyrg has chosen to stay with you, and even that pains me. Farewell, my love. Should you decide to leave the demons to their own fate, I would long to see you again."

The large Templar watched as the three dragons took flight. Ve'kal said nothing, but could see from his face that he was not the man he was only yesterday. Her support crumbled around her.

"Piotyr, I know this is not a good time, but we must speak of Kasim." Han, the smaller and least intimidating of the Templar had a way with words. Was he as mighty as Kasim had boasted?

"What?" His shoulders slumped. "Oh, yes. I understand he is sick? Can you not heal him, Joshua?"

"I healed the wounds as best I could, but hellfire has taken his legs and he has been poisoned by something I am unfamiliar with. His strength wanes, and will die soon."

"I am sorry to hear that." No fire at all in the man. Ve'kal cursed inwardly. He was broken.

Han hissed and walked over to Piotyr, and shockingly struck the giant man hard in the face. "There is no time for this, Piotyr!" The image would have been comical, had not Han's eyes burned with wrath. Piotyr must have outweighed him nearly three to one, but it was the warrior who shrank before the philosopher.

"Your family nearly died and Kasim's followers... no... *his family* did die, and all because we failed to remember why we are here. You will *not* give in to self-pity. We need you, and we need you now!"

The healer, Joshua, his eyes had climbed into his stinking, rotten forehead. Han continued to glower, to his credit not giving an inch of ground. Piotyr merely looked at the ground for a moment, and spat out a small amount of blood before looking at the smaller Templar. There was no fire in his eyes, but Ve'kal could see no despair either.

"What would you have me do?"

Kasim faded in and out of consciousness. The times when he was aware... then he could see Dhermina through blurry eyes, and could feel her clutching his hands tightly. He could sense the loss of the others from Sagarmatha like a wound in his soul, and the pain pulsing through his body was worse. Kasim could sense the toxins and the minerals in the poison coursing through his veins and turning them hard and brittle. The passage of time was hard for him to follow, but he knew he was not long for the world of the living.

He remembered smiling as the arrow pierced his chest, and did so again as best he could through the pain. It was not a good death, but it was a death nonetheless. He did not know how much success he could claim here in Hell, but he could claim that they had slain the Shay'tan, he had known his true love, and soon he would join Jacob in oblivion. There were worse fates. He squeezed Dhermina's hand as he faded out of awareness again.

Before him stood five doors.

chapter nine

Out of whose womb came the ice? and the hoary frost of heaven, who hath gendered it?
- Job 38:29

"You say this substance is known to other Ba'al? This... Heart of Cocytus?" Han spoke conversationally, as if all was right in their world.

"Yes, it is at the center of a great pit of ice and despair. It has been spoken of before, by poets of your world." Ve'kal was familiar with the work, though much of it was wrong.

"The concept of Nine Hells is an old one, and a false one at that. Hell is infinite, just as Heaven is. How does one get to the center of an infinite plane of existence?" Han sounded sure of himself.

"The same way our portals opened up to your world. It is not a matter of distance; it is a matter of placement. At least I believe that to be the case. I have never been, nor has anyone I know of. All I know is that the ice exists, and has been brought out before. There is some in the armory under the palace ruins, if you doubt me." Ve'kal hoped they were not angry she had not mentioned it before. In truth she had not found it relevant.

"I do not doubt your belief. What I need to know is how to get there."

"You are mad. The cold would sap your strength and leave you dead within minutes."

The Templar glowered at her, and for a moment she felt her life being weighed in his gaze. Surely he would not...

"I *was* mad, Ba'alat Ve'kal. Do not call me such again. I seek to save Kasim, and if Cocytus flows into a frozen lake then so too will the other waters of Hell."

"Kasim cannot be saved, Han Fei-tze. He dies the slow death of one touched by Watcher's Venom."

"Tell me again what cannot be done and we shall have discord, *Ba'alat!*" The shout rang across the courtyard. Piotyr looked back and forth from Ve'kal to Han, and Joshua stared intently at the stones below him.

"Fine, I won't stand in the way of your doom. I will send for the Seneschal, and he will assist you on your *journey.*" *I will kill this man.*

"Thank you, but I won't be going. Someone needs to stay here to protect the city. Piotyr, how do you feel about traveling with the undead?"

Everything was on the brink of ruin, but Han wasn't ready to give up yet. One thing at a time, Kasim had to be saved.

"Why me, and why send Joshua's walkers? Hell what am I talking about, how would we even get to this place?" Piotyr appeared to be focused. Good, Han needed him alert.

"I am sending you... sorry. I am asking you to go because of how the substance hindered you and your family. It is a weakness for you, and someone knew it. It would be to our benefit for you to overcome that weakness, and the best way to do that is to confront it directly. Go to this pit of ice and despair, find the Heart of Cocytus, and learn how to master it." Han waited for Piotyr to nod before continuing.

"As to the walkers? I only wish to send one. Joshua, would you object to the First traveling with Piotyr?"

"You might ask him yourself. He is his own man. Is it my preference? No, I enjoy spending time with him, but as I said he is his own man. He can go wherever he pleases. Why send him at all though? Piotyr can fetch the ice without the First. What else do you have in mind?" Joshua coughed and hacked as he finished.

"To help Kasim, and also you. We are recently to Sheol, and beyond that have seen little of Hell. I came quickly to the dungeons of Ba'al Moloch, and quickly after to the battle with the Shay'tan. This I know, however. Hell *is* infinite, and it contains many mysteries older than we could imagine. If those weapons and armor are made from ice found in Cocytus then we will find the other unholy rivers flowing through our destination as well. I need the Waters of Lethe, Acheron, Cocytus, Phlegethon, and Styx. With those I believe I can heal Kasim... and you, Joshua."

Joshua looked hard at his friend, and his chest rattled and rasped as he spoke. "Don't get me wrong, Han, but what manner of divination led you to think you can heal either of us with those waters?"

"I have... *communed*." Han didn't know else to put it. "This place is evil, but it has great knowledge. The temptation is there to use that knowledge for terrible things, but I am strong enough to resist that seduction. For now, the knowledge is enough. Hell tells me what I need to know, and I know that these waters can heal your malady and stop the poison in Kasim's veins. I just need to get some from the sources."

Joshua was silent a moment before answering. "Then I shall do my best to persuade the First to go. Will the two of you get along alright, Piotyr?"

Piotyr snorted. At least some of his humor was resilient. "I imagine there could be no greater company for me at the moment." *Asya is right, old friend. This is not her war, it is ours.*

"Then we have preparations to make."

The Seneschal was silent as he led the three Templar and the Zombie Lord into the catacombs beneath Sheol. He had survived as long as he had by learning not to speak. He knew that these three mortals were not the equal of his former master, but they had stood against him, and lived to tell of it. He would not risk their wrath.

In truth he didn't miss the Shay'tan in the slightest. Obviously he was meant to die, but the Seneschal did lament not having the chance to serve his slayer. This Jacob Merethius by rights had earned the palace, its treasures, and the service of its dwellers. Oh well, Ve'kal was not an unkind mistress. She was, however, unfit. The Seneschal only wanted to serve the greatest.

He had collected the maps as Ve'kal had ordered, and had escorted the mortals and the unnatural plague walker underneath the ruins of the plaza and down through the cellars. The cataclysm had destroyed the palace, but the warrens underneath were mostly intact. Food, drink, valuables in storage, vaults with wealth and mundane items both, even lodging for palace servants were connected by passageways going for miles and miles beneath the Throne.

It was quiet down in the tunnels. The Seneschal had spent centuries serving the House of Lucifer and never had the absence of suffering been so stark. The dungeons were one level below, but had been designed so that the torture rooms had excellent sound projection. The Shay'tan had liked to hear the screams near constantly, whether taking a meal or a bath or entertaining in his chambers. The Seneschal never understood that. The screams didn't bother him, but they did make it hard to concentrate. A meal should be taken in silence, he always thought. Or better yet with an interesting treatise. He had been no stranger to violence in his years of service, but there was a time and a place for such things.

The fact that Ve'kal had ordered the dungeons cleared of mortal prisoners originally had made his jaw drop. Fortunately she was wise enough to ask the mortal called Han Fei-tze to join her on a tour, and she was also wise enough to first release those mortals who had done nothing to earn their fate other than be chosen to please the Shay'tan in some manner. Han didn't seem surprised when she brought him down to the darkest depths of the palace, and showed him those that *deserved* to be there. He was shown the absolute worst offenders in the Shay'tan's domain, and Ve'kal had asked the Seneschal to politely explain their crimes and if he, Han, wanted them released as well. The Seneschal chuckled to remember the exchange.

"This one stole and consumed sixteen mortal children alive before he was caught. He believed it would grant him longer life. He has been here ten years, so I suppose in a way he was right."

"This one snuck into the homes of Ba'al and raped their Thralls in the night. Should he be released?"

"This one killed his family with poison; he hated them so, and ground them into sausage to feed customers in his restaurant. Hundreds got sick and died. From the contaminated meat. Perhaps a pardon is in order?"

Of course his purpose was not to offend. The Seneschal knew better than to anger his betters, and he was no Ba'al. It used to bother him that he had no title and no land, but there was prestige in his service. That service required knowing when to be silent, and always how not to offend. None were better at those skills than he. Still, Han Fei-tze must have felt at least some humiliation in the circumstances. Those were just the mortal prisoners he was using as examples. Fell creatures of unspeakable horror were imprisoned in the depths, from wraiths and other soul eating undead to those that preyed on flesh and blood. It was unknown to all but himself, the Shay'tan, and the chief gaoler that there was even a masque broodmother kept down here. That was a secret he hadn't even shared with Ve'kal. Some things were best kept buried under dust and secrecy.

Still, those that remained in the dungeons were quiet, now. They had been broken long ago, and existed now for no real purpose. The Shay'tan kept them for amusement, but Ve'kal did not share that love of sport. Of course, she was no *real* Shay'tan. She hadn't bested the last one in combat, and rumor had it she couldn't complete the ascension as required. She held the Throne, but it was not hers and no one had seen her grace it herself. A true King of Hell would not have been so squeamish with his toys. Han had requested that they remain incarcerated, though why he would want them to continue to be fed was beyond the Seneschal. If they weren't to be abused, might as well discard them.

He walked quickly past the wing where the horrors were kept. He looked back to see how quickly the others followed and was displeased to see Han give a lingering look that direction. *Clever, that one. He knows something of what lives here.* To the benefit of the journey, Han said nothing and they continued on. The dungeons led lower into the catacombs. Few Ba'al wished to be buried outside of their estates, though on rare occasion it happened. Most of the sarcophagi were from the Fall. Those that followed the Morning Star and lost their lives during the War in Heaven were enshrined here in honor. The Seneschal always felt reverence when accompanying the Shay'tan here. Mortals should not be here.

He gazed with rapturous eyes on a large crypt they passed as they entered the catacombs.

Here lies Uthazel, brother and friend to Lucifer. Slain in single combat by Uriel. May he be avenged at the end of all things.

He sighed as they continued. So many entombed, so much death. *Slain by Michael, slain by Gabriel, slain by Uriel...* the names were not all the same, but most of them were. The War in Heaven was before his time. It was before the time of the last Shay'tan as well. The Ba'al who were there did not speak of it, but accounts were common in the Librarium. The surviving Fallen were bitter at their loss, and wont to describe it in detail. The names of the Seraphim were cursed more than any others, save Adam himself.

He watched Piotyr and Han as they walked in silence. Would this place mean anything to them? So many Fallen, Angels too for that matter, had died over the seed of Adam. Did these descendants even care?

The one called Piotyr snorted, and the Seneschal had to bite his tongue. Impudent creatures. He hoped the river would drown them. Thinking on the zombie with them, he wondered if the undead even *could* drown.

Hard to call this thing they called The First an undead. He looked healthier than any creature the Seneschal had ever seen, save the Heirs of Lucifer. He had flawless features and his eyes seemed to burn with an inner fire. No mere wraith or vampire inhabited that zombie flesh... he was a powerful being.

The four of them walked for long minutes in the cold quiet. The catacombs went on for many levels into the ground. They never walked more than a few paces forward before descending more stairs, but sarcophagi lined the landings and passageways led away into the blackness. Tens of thousands of Fallen were entombed here.

Finally the stone stairs descended into a cavern of unworked stone. The cavern was of the same make as the catacombs, but was of rough natural rock. There was no door to mark the transition, only a step into a vast, empty and black space. The chill was palpable, and the Seneschal felt his hair rise on his skin. In all his years he had never passed the threshold of that landing. The Shay'tan often asked him to walk him to the entrance of this cavern, but it was sacred and not for the likes of him. It was a place for the Shay'tan and the Shay'tan alone. It was blasphemy for the others to be here.

"My Lords. Here is what you seek. I have fulfilled my obligation; you have the maps of the tributaries. I request to take my leave."

"Stay a moment. I shall accompany you back. Give me a moment to speak to them." *At least one of them won't be going in and desecrating the cavern.* He nodded in acquiescence to Han.

"Piotyr, old friend. Are you prepared for this?" Han spoke to the man with affection and kindness. Briefly the Seneschal wondered what it would be like to have someone care at all for him in that way.

"I believe so, Han. We are to take the River out of Sheol, and it will take us to a system of tributaries which will all flow inward to the center of Hell?" Piotyr clearly understood the words, but was also clearly not a man of science.

"Theoretical center, but yes. If you can reach Cocytus by any reliable way, the River system should be it. Many texts confirm it, and from many different religions of the old world." *This Han was a learned man. Under different circumstances he would like the opportunity to speak with the man and see just how learned.*

"And you, First?" Han was still polite speaking to the undead.

The zombie looked at Han and answered. "Joshua has asked me to go, and I shall do so. I think your plan has merit, though you might have asked me yourself. You know this journey will require a guide, and that the guide must not be alive. That is why I am going. You could have asked one of the lesser walkers, but I am the greatest of them. This is right, scholar."

Piotyr looked startled and scowled for a moment before turning to Han. "Requires a guide? He is meant to hold my hand then? Han, I have been fighting the damned for well over..." Han's forestalling hand, polite but insistent, stopped the giant.

"Not holding your hand, Piotyr. The Descent you are about to undertake has happened to others, before. Yes we are all damned, but we are here in the flesh and are still mortal. This is not a dream, or a vision, but quite real. I would not risk any of us to the dangers of this journey without taking wise precautions."

A learned man indeed.

"Come, let us go. Seneschal, I shall return shortly. When we walk back, there is a hallway I would like to explore for a moment, if it pleases you."

It does not. Damn this mortal. "As you wish, master Fei-tze."

"Please, just Han. I shall return presently."

The Seneschal watched with dread as the three of them walked into the black. This mortal, Han, knew of the horrors kept in the dungeons. No good would come of this.

chapter ten

And have no fellowship with the unfruitful works of darkness,
but rather reprove them.
- Ephesians 5:11

"Is it just me or did the Seneschal seem worried just now?" Light conversation, meant to distract from the task at hand. Not unexpected, Piotyr was uncomfortable with the unknown.

"Don't worry about him. He means to keep the secrets of Sheol from me, but it is too late. I know enough already. I even know about this river journey you are about to undertake." Piotyr grunted, but also ran his hand through his short cropped hair.

"Worry not, scholar. I shall keep him safe from the depths." The First spoke with no discernible mockery.

"Yes, the depths. I'm sure you know this Piotyr, but whatever you do stay out of the river. The waters you shall ride upon are powerful, and not kind to mortal folk."

"Styx? I have a hard time reconciling this, Han. I do not doubt you but I sort of always thought most of those old stories were just that, stories."

"What, of Achilles? Orpheus and Eurydice? How about Dante and Virgil?" Han had read more than any Templar alive, including the Patriarch. It was a point of pride for him, and of consternation for the old man in Haven. Han knew much.

"The names aren't even familiar, Han. Well Achilles is... medical thing... but I was never one for reading, you know that."

"They are unfamiliar to me as well, scholar. My knowledge is rooted in Hell, though I know a little of the rivers. The waters are not said to be kind to mortal folk here, either." Again, no hint of mockery. Han was briefly jealous of the time Joshua had spent with the First. Such a wealth of conversation.

"The names are unimportant, but I shall tell you what I know of the rivers. Know this; you two are not the first to travel them, though you are in rare company. It is not a journey taken often. Just know that there is precedent here, but all who have come to the rivers of Hell have not emerged unscathed. There are dark terrors waiting, and you must be cautious."

Piotyr stopped and emanated a burst of hellfire from his hand, briefly illuminating the area around them and showing his armor, spear, and sword in stark relief. The darkness crept on for what seemed to be an endless distance. "I don't fear dark terrors. Without my family here, I have nothing to protect."

In the silence that followed, as their footsteps had fallen quiet for the moment, the faint sound of water rushing came to Han's ears. Piotyr was most certainly not boasting. The man was fearless, though the unknown caused him anxiety. Piotyr was not fond of surprises.

"Dark terrors are to be feared, warrior. That is why they are dark terrors. You have a soul to call your own, still. This will not be a good journey to lose it on." The First's words caused Han to frown in consternation. He had always assumed the First *did* have his own soul. This was troubling. He would speak to Joshua on the matter.

"I fear not for your ability to survive the trip. If there were two mightier men... or beings, in all the history of men, I should like to hear of it." That was a half-truth. He mused as they approached an archway at a precipice. This *was* Styx, that was certain, and he also believed that they were not the first men to be here. Han did not believe that such as Achilles were fully of myth; though the tales said he was but a child when taken here. There had been other mighty men in the history of man to come here, he was sure, though he would still place Piotyr, and certainly the First, in the greatest of company.

Rather than argue with the First, Piotyr focused on the archway and the steps descending beyond. "This must be it. The ground is wet and slick and the sound grows loud as we approach."

"Warrior, do you wish to proceed or shall I take the Vanguard?" Han listened again for mockery from the Zombie-King and found none.

"I have never asked another to take risk ahead of me, I shall not begin now. Dead though you may be, you are my brother on this journey, and you will receive me at my best. Guard the flank, and let nothing catch you unaware."

Han was taken aback at Piotyr's words. He had expected some discomfort from the Templar at traveling with the undead, but Piotyr seemed genuine and sincere. He hadn't given him enough credit. Piotyr had grown accepting and wise on his journey in Hell.

"Hold then a moment. It is your custom to pray before such things, is it not? Take my hand, and I shall pray with you, warrior. Pray for success, the salvation of your friends, and woe to our enemies. I stand with you."

Despite himself, Han's eyes watered as the plate-clad Templar and the greatest of Joshua's risen clasped hands and knelt before the archway. In the horror of their arrival, Han had forgotten just how great fellowship could be. He hadn't felt such since before he spoke to the Patriarch about the rituals. The man and the undead prayed, and it was good.

After a time, they rose. Piotyr turned to Han and spoke. "You seek the waters of these five rivers. What else do I need to know, old friend?"

"I need two samples from each river. One separate and one mixed. Take these vials, keep them on you at all times, protected, and safe." Han handed Piotyr a special belt with soft leather clasps and wool padding keeping five large crystal vials snugly in place, and a sixth even larger. He handed The First another, identical to Piotyr's. "Six vials each, for six samples each. I would take Styx water back with me now, but by itself it would do no good and it needs to be fresh. Five vials for Lethe, Acheron, Cocytus, and Phlegethon, and finally Styx when you return. The last is for the combined waters of all the main rivers of Hell. One set for each of you, just in case." He handed them each a measured dipper. "To make the parts equal. Do not touch the waters. Historically, or at least the history of lore, the waters can cause harm to mortal hands."

"Do you wish me to gather the samples, scholar?"

"It matters not, though I suspect with the process involved in making you who you are, the waters may not be kind to you either. Just be careful, and always on your guard. As I said, dark terrors await you." Han said it with a smile.

Piotyr laughed, and spoke with a smile of his own. "Very well, I shall be careful. What else of this journey, other than the samples?"

"That is all, Piotyr. Gather the water, carefully, as you travel from river to river. I don't think you will have any trouble recognizing when you have moved to a new source of water. From my research, the environment will change with the waters. When you reach Cocytus, if the waters are frozen, simply melt the ice with your Hellfire and gather the sample then. Or, bring back the ice whole and we can melt it later. It matters not. Remember, equal parts for the combined sample."

"We are possessed of understanding then, Han. Fare thee well."

Han smiled and held out his hand. The giant Templar laughed and pulled Han into an embrace. "Take care of yourself and of Joshua and Kasim as well. I hope you have an easy time of it here at Sheol."

"I suspect not, but thank you." Han turned to the First, and froze briefly as he didn't know what to do. He didn't want to be rude, though, and moved to awkwardly pat the undead on the back.

"You are a fool, scholar." The First put his hand up to forestall him, and then extended it in a formal manner. "The gesture is understood, and acknowledged. We shall speak again."

Fool indeed. Why would a zombie embrace anyone? "I believe we shall. Good luck, and be careful."

Han looked with pride and hope as Piotyr and the First turned and descended the slick stairs. They would succeed, and with the waters Han *knew* he would heal Kasim. He would help Joshua cure his plague as well. This was good. His smile faded as they descended out of sight. Now to the Seneschal and the horrors kept in the dungeons.

chapter eleven

In all fighting, the direct method may be used for joining battle, but indirect methods will be needed in order to secure victory.
- Sun Tzu: The Art of War

Kasim awoke in agony. His veins were on fire and he screamed as his eyes opened. The world around him was blurred and veiled in red. He could see Dhermina's shape run to him and she placed a cloth to his face. He convulsed as the cloth touched his skin, the sensation spiking his pain into a fever pitch. He never wanted anything in his life more than he wanted to die in that moment. His body wracked with spasms and he choked out a sentence with every ounce of willpower he could muster.

"Kill me... please." The words died on his lips as he collapsed back into darkness.

The first door led to darkness and despair. It called to him.

Ve'kal watched from the entryway to the infirmary. The mortal girl had finally stopped crying, which was good. It was hard to watch a loved one die from the Watcher's Kiss, but it wouldn't take long on a human. There had been, historically, some hale poison tasters in the past who had lived the better part of a week after ingesting food seasoned with the toxin, but Kasim surely would not last much longer than that. The woman was fortunate. Ve'kal had watched Nezmyr suffer for decades. This would be but a moment.

"I am sorry for your loss, child. He was a brave man." The girl looked up at the Ba'alat. Her eyes were rimmed with grief, but the glower she leveled towards Ve'kal was fire given life.

"He lives still, *my lady.* I weep for our friends."

Ah yes, the other mortals from the East who had arrived with Kasim. The ambush in the streets had been brutally effective. Ve'kal could not have imagined a more devious and lethal trap. How the Watchers had acquired that much liquid hellfire and kept it contained was beyond her. When the Watchers decided someone was to die, then die they did.

"Peace, Dhermina. I seek no quarrel. My condolences on recent events, then, if that pleases you more." Truth was as easy to speak as a lie. She had no quarrel with this woman, and Kasim was incredibly valuable as an ally. The attack did not please Ve'kal at all. Oddly, her sincerity appeared to ease the girl.

Dhermina's face softened, and then slackened with fatigue before she answered. "Your condolences are not ill-received, just untimely. He will survive this."

"I hope that is true." Foolish girl. Death would be a gift for the man.

Dhermina sniffed, and rubbed her eyes. "How long will he stay like this without a remedy?"

Ve'kal pursed her lips in thought. No one had ever thought to cure one poisoned by the Watchers. To get in the way of a contract was to invite another one. "Well, I know that Ba'al Maerintor lived a month. That was the longest, to my knowledge." Strictly speaking that wasn't true. Millennia ago Ve'kal recalled stories of a Hellfire wyrm being poisoned near Sheol Am, but it was never confirmed what the beast was stricken with. It had ravaged the area for near to half a year before finally dying. No hunting parties would near the creature for fear of being bitten and infected. It might not have been the Watchers, though.

"So a Ba'al lived for a month. Kasim can best that, to be sure. I have faith that Joshua will come through."

The healer. Ve'kal could not stomach the man. He sickened her. "For your lover to wake, you must trust in Han and Piotyr as well. Does your faith hold strong for them as well?"

To Ve'kal's surprise the girl's eyes did not widen, her breath did not waiver, and her face did not slack in the slightest. "Without question."

Almost, Ve'kal believed her.

Grunting with pain, he backed up slowly and clasped his hand to the gash in his ribs. Foolish man. He had thought the newcomer to the valley would be friendly and welcome a friend. Foolish. He knew better than to assume that, and certainly knew better than to surprise the man. He was paying for his curiosity and lack of wisdom. *Better the makeshift knife that that fucking morning star.*

He grit his teeth and slid his back leg up behind him to shorten his striking area. Old habits. He pulled his ancient knife out of his sheath and held it in a reverse grip as he slowly approached the stranger in a combat stance, his left hand out in front of him open and ready.

The man mirrored his stance but was unarmed. Smart. That sharpened flint was fine for skinning a rabbit, but no good in a fight. His eyes were wide and wary. Surprise favored neither of them. God, the man was huge. Over two meters by a decent amount, with sun-darkened skin and well defined muscles. A fair fight did not favor him.

He had had enough. Curiosity was worth less than peace and safety. He flexed his grip on his knife and slowly circled to his left. As his target matched his pace, the valley dweller flicked his foot up and sent sand flying into the face of his target.

The man cursed as he backed away, but was too slow recovering as his predator closed and sunk his knife into the soft flesh of his throat. Blood pooled and flowed down his hand as the man gasped his last.

As he let the man bleed out, he sighed. "Damned waste."

"Are you sure you want to see this, master Han? There are things here kept locked away for good reason." The Seneschal was not squeamish in the slightest. There *were,* however, any number of places he would prefer to be.

"I think we need to come to an understanding, Seneschal."

Oh, this will be good. The human will now attempt to explain how important he is.

"Please do, master Han. Any chance to increase my understanding is welcome."

"Spare the sarcasm, please. I know what you think of us."

Unlikely.

"Do you know of the account of the Shay'tan slaying the wyrm juvenile at the attack on Sheol?"

"Yes, master Han. Though I did not see it personally, I was told of it. A shame, that." *The words were true, if not the intent.*

"You think it of note that a Shay'tan was able to kill a wyrm in combat yet not live long enough to absorb its soul?"

The Seneschal frowned. He had not thought of that. A wyrm's soul was powerful, much more than that of a mortal. The equal of a Ba'al, though perhaps not if just that of a young drake.

"I suppose with no vessel it would have drifted to the River."

"You are correct, with no vessel it would have."

"I see. Thank you for your illumination, master Han."

"I am here to see the wraiths, Seneschal. Take me there."

Foolish mortal, this is not a menagerie.

"As you wish, though I have stated my concern and caution."

"Yes, you have. Proceed, if you please."

The walk was not overlong, and the Seneschal was pleased that Han did not stop to peer into the cells they passed. There were vile things in the gaol, and the less time spent in their presence, the better.

"The wraiths, master Han. Do you wish to enter?"

"I do. I am prepared with suitable precaution."

"I'm sure. Will it be acceptable for me to remain outside?"

The mortal chuckled, and the Seneschal felt his ears burn. Damn this man.

"Perfectly acceptable. The doors though, if you please."

Nodding, and feeling the urge to rub his hands along his arms, the Seneschal licked his lips and removed the master key ring from his belt. He knew the right one, but lingered as he searched. *I am unsettled indeed.*

Opening the lock, he removed the key and stepped back. "Not to question your abilities, but if this goes poorly I will need to close the lock again."

Han had placed his hand upon the door to open it, and then paused. He looked at the Seneschal and inside his heart quickened twofold.

"Of course. However, if you close the lock without cause, while I am inside, our next meeting will be *most* unpleasant."

The Seneschal swallowed and nodded. "Of course."

Han inhaled deeply inside the cold stone chamber. He Invoked a minor flame to light a pair of torch sconces just inside the door.

The Seneschal was waiting outside the door, his robed form emanating discomfort and anxiety. Han smiled. He knew what he was doing.

The room was dusty and stale. There were dozens of stone slabs covered in smaller stone ovals standing on their end. The tables stretched out into the blackness as far as he could see. To the naked eye, the room was otherwise empty. Han knew better.

He touched the masque hanging on his belt and narrowed his eyes. The hatred flowed through him and surged in the disgusting creature. The whispers crawled in, as they always did when he touched the thing, but he blocked them out. The masque wasn't what he needed now.

Kasim had his inner sight. Han had something else. He had the voice of Hell itself. When he asked questions, they were answered. The voice was sentient, and it spoke to him directly. There were no mysteries for Han Fei-tze anymore, not here.

He opened his mind, and the wraiths flooded the room. Shrieking, rage-filled parasites flitted about on tethers anchored to the stone ovals. Han couldn't see what was within the ovals, but he got the sense that the objects within were unique, and connected to each wraith. He nodded to himself then, and looked down at the vile masque hanging from his belt. *Akin, though not the same.* The parasitic wraiths were nearly identical in shape and form, though not size, and the masque had physical traits whereas the wraiths were incorporeal. The wraiths jerking about on their tethers were greater than a man in size, though not a man as large as Piotyr.

In contrast, the small one connected to the masque seemed a juvenile, perhaps a larva. He shuddered. The pain the thing had caused him had faded, but the memories were still raw. He hated it, yet felt it paled to the power these wraiths could command if given a host to infect.

He turned from the masque, and gazed long at the stone oval on top of the nearest table. He had to know for sure before he attempted his plan. Never again would he let theory or conjecture guide his hand. Though he had been right with the Patriarch and the ritual, the cost was too high not to be sure. This time, he would know beforehand.

Han was not a fool, and was earnest in his claim to the Seneschal that he would take precautions. There was so much suffering in Sheol that Han had to work *hard* to avoid making it coalesce, and down in the gaol it was even thicker. He let the agony pool and then swirl around his legs before he gathered it about his hands and wove it into a lattice web in front of him. The essence was pure pain, but he had learned that most of the innate suffering in a place like this was tinged with the pleasure of those who had caused it. It was especially true in the palace ruins, and underneath it. Depravity had run thick in Sheol.

He stretched the web with his mind, and allowed the traces of pleasure to slowly coat the surface. After a few long moments, he felt the snare was ready, and he used some additional essence of Hell to form a solid rope and bring the stone oval to him through the mesh. He watched the wraith carefully, its black shape pausing for a moment in its thrashing to quiver with hatred and malevolence at Han. Han smiled as he opened the lid to the oval.

The inrush of wind was accompanied by an intense psychic scream that blasted towards Han. His head rang with the assault and his eyes watered. *Idiot!* He hadn't expected an attack on his mind. He remembered his unwitting attack on Mons Montis and felt a great deal of sadness. If he felt even a fraction of the pain he caused those poor villagers, it was a dark deed he committed.

The psychic scream faded, but only into a slavering snarl that lashed out in impotence from the twisting form caught in the web. Han took a moment to gather his wits and recover, closing his eyes and rubbing his temples as he blocked out the mental screeches from the wraith with a powerful psychic shield. *Ok then, now I know.*

He opened his eyes and lashed out at the wraith with his own anger. The thing screeched silently through Han's shield, and to his surprise it grew. The web held, but it *did* stretch. Fascinating. Han wove another web, larger and stronger than the first, as a precaution before blasting the wraith again and with more power. He could feel the wraith grow stronger. He mused for a moment. The hatred was obvious. Han allowed his mind to turn towards his pain, and instead of allowing his anger to surface at what Moloch did to him, he instead focused on the pain and misery itself. Grief and sadness poured out from him, and he amplified it with the essence of Hell. The wraith stopped its struggling and quivered, with what Han could only call ecstasy, growing in size yet again.

Han frowned at the thing, and continued with his experiments. He continually reinforced the webbing, and wove backup snares in case the first failed. He allowed himself to feel jealousy for how powerful Piotyr was, at how skillful Kasim was. He allowed envy for the love they had both found to darken his thoughts. The wraith grew again. Now it near to filled half the space Han could see from the torches. It had ceased twitching and struggling in the webbing, and Han got the distinct impression that it was now watching him with intelligence. Perhaps knowing it couldn't escape yet but waiting for the chance?

Han still felt safe, but wasn't willing to tempt fate. He shook his head and banished his dark thoughts, and instead focused his willpower on the joy he felt when he bound Lokyrg's soul to Eirygaile and the look in Piotyr's eyes when he realized his son was not lost to him. He remembered the smile on Kasim's face when they had all found Dhermina alive after the cataclysm. The warmth emanated from his soul, but when he tried to amplify it with the essence of Hell, sweat formed on his brow and he struggled. He hadn't thought it would be as easy, but it felt near to impossible.

He fought with the essence, and was startled to see the wraith pushing against his web, and straining it to its limits. The first one would break soon. He continued trying to find a way to use the suffering to amplify the positive emotions he felt, but to no avail. The wraith slipped the first web with a psychic backlash and stretched out to reach the second. Han could feel a malevolence and hunger coming from the thing as it swelled to reach out for him.

He wasn't scared, not yet, but he was concerned. Han's destructive powers were rooted in the suffering of Hell, and the emotions associated with them were all negative. If there was a positive association with the essence he wasn't seeing it. He blinked, and noticed the wraith had developed eyes, blacker chasms of despair hanging on an already black form.

Sweat beaded on his brow as he wove another lattice and stepped back. He felt the door to the gaol hall behind him. He was out of room. He thought of escape, but he hadn't learned all he needed to yet. The wraith began to feed on the web still restricting it. It wouldn't be long before it consumed that web and reached the last one.

Think, Han. Hell is suffering incarnate, and these feed on suffering. He ran through options in his mind, before settling on the only one he thought might work, though it was dangerous. The lattice worked to restrain the thing, if only temporarily, because Han had woven pleasure into it. The pain wasn't enough; it had to be the sadism inherent in whatever was causing the pain. He began weaving more pain, though this time not into a web but rather a spear. Once it was shaped, he began drawing more sadistic pleasure out of the essence and coated the spear in it, like a poison.

The wraith snapped the webbing and pressed into the last one. Eyes dripped with malice, and Han could sense a mouth on the wraith, reaching for him to gnaw and devour. Perhaps another minute and he would have to flee.

There was no shortage of the sadism. Much torture had been committed in this place, and much enjoyment had been derived from it. The trick was to separate the purity of the joy, while separating it from the vileness which was the suffering. In a way it was similar to how he had attracted Lokyrg's soul to Eirygaile with the lure. He smiled and set his mind to the task. He was gifted at puzzles such as this.

When the psychic lance was fully formed and coated, he mentally snapped the end off of it on his end and allowed the pain to bleed back into the pool at his feet. It drizzled out at first from the now hollow spearhead of sadistic pleasure, so he pulled on it like thread from a spool. The wraith stretched further and Han could feel the strands of the web about to break. He was out of time.

He took a deep breath as he pulled the last of the suffering from the spearhead and was left with what he hoped and believed was a pure weapon of positive emotion. He yanked on the thread of the last web and readied himself as the wraith stumbled with its sudden freedom.

It recovered its balance and screeched in hatred as it lunged at Han. Han braced himself and brought the spearhead to bear. He focused all of his willpower in his strike and the impact staggered him. The mental screeching from the wraith nearly unhinged him, and he fought to remain conscious and alert. The spearhead stuck out of the wraith about a foot in length, and Han could see the vile essence leaking out of the thing like a sieve. He sighed in relief even as the screeching continued. It was working, and the wraith was shrinking in size.

He allowed it to bleed awhile while he looked inside the urn. His stomach churned as he spilled the contents into his hand. A child's skeleton clattered out into his hands, several pieces spilling onto the floor. He cursed and placed the urn flat on the ground, carefully watching the dying wraith to make sure it didn't have the strength for another attack. He picked up a bone and noticed that the bone was pitted and pockmarked. Han sighed as he imagined the truth behind these things. The child was probably killed as slowly and gruesomely as possible to create the wraith. He imagined if he opened the other vials he would find similar objects. Or if not a physical specimen or remains, some other object linked to intense suffering and loss.

He felt sorry for the wraith, though by now any trace of the sentient being it came from was long gone. It would be a mercy to let this one die, and so he did. He spent a long while watching the thing bleed out, and felt no joy or satisfaction from it. Rather he felt numb, and weary. At times his tasks were so monumental they allowed him to block out the circumstances behind them, but this was not that time. He had wanted to come here to send Piotyr and the First on their way, and thought there might be a way to help Kasim hidden in the bowels of Sheol. If not Kasim, then their cause as a whole. The tasks were mighty, and the details were soul-crushingly depressing. As the thing died and shrunk, he found himself saying soothing words to it.

Over time, the wraith gained definition. Perhaps ten minutes in total had gone by before Han could see the grey form of a lifeless child on the ground, a little girl of no more than three. He was right, and she had not died kindly. His stomach soured, and he fought back nausea. The only thing which stayed him from throwing up was that this had been done ages ago, and there was nothing he could do about her death now. For a time, he had forgotten his hatred of the demons. Lost in the act of moving forward with their plans was the reason for their struggle. He remembered it clearly now.

Sighing, he watched in sadness as the grey form of the brutalized dead child shifted to white, and then his eyes widened as the child spirit rose up and drifted towards him. It smiled. Tears coming to his eyes, Han smiled back.

"Thank you." The only words she spoke were enough to cause Han to well up with grief.

"You are welcome, little one."

He watched as her form grew luminous and then dissolved into motes. She drifted on the air for a moment before flowing gently out towards the door into the gaol. Han opened the door and watched as the child drifted past the Seneschal and out to what he assumed was the river. Her soul would now flow as it should have. Han smiled, and wiped his eyes.

"By all that is wondrous and unwise, what have you done, master Han?"

"I have brought life to unlife, and freed the soul of a wraith." Han was too pleased with himself to let the Seneschal bother him.

"*That* is why you wanted to come here? To liberate a wraith? Truly I misjudged you, master Han. You have courage I have not seen the heights of, and the wits I have not seen the depths of. Why risk all this to free a wraith, or even worse more of them?" Han allowed the Seneschal to speak to him thus as he could detect honest incredulity from the man, Fallen or no. Shock was shock.

He also lost his satisfaction and pride in the freeing of the little girl, as the reality returned to him.

"Because, Seneschal. I didn't come here to free a wraith. I freed that one because I had to after seeing the remains of her mangled corpse." Han looked with his sight at the Seneschal to see if there was any reaction, and unsurprisingly there wasn't. Such things happened by rote here, he was sure.

"I am confused then, master Han. If not to free the wraiths why risk their embrace? Even the Shay'tan tread carefully around them."

"Because I needed to know if they would serve my purposes. Beyond that, my reasons are my own. Forgive me if I have concerns about your loyalty."

The Seneschal stiffened, and to Han's surprise actually looked indignant. "Master Han, you may do or say anything you wish while you are the master of Sheol. I know Ve'kal rules, but I know she does so at your behest and she *is no Shay'tan.* I said I will serve you and I shall."

Han pursed his thoughts for a moment. He detected no lie from the man. Surprising, that. "Very well, then I shall allow you to serve."

"Good. Shall we return to the surface now?"

Han felt a headache growing. He had begun his tasks, now was not the time to stall in them. "Not yet. I wish to visit more dark terrors. Take me to your blood-drinkers."

Whereas before the Seneschal would have led with derision, sarcasm, or outright mockery, this time he did not. "As you will it, master Han."

Joshua let another group of humans into his medical tent. He had a wide array of scientific apparatuses on various tables, desks, and shelves, and he had been collecting samples for the last two days from anyone willing to help in crafting a vaccine. He had acquired vials and vials of blood from his followers, beginning with those from Ithera and ending at Sheol Am. K'had and Ulraen had provided the first, happily, and as word spread of what he was trying to do more of the survivors of the plague had come to him. That was all well and good, but he needed blood samples of those he suspected would die. He couldn't have those people come to him, so he had to send out runners and those that could understand medicine and follow instructions for collecting samples were not common. These were mostly a simple people, not stupid, but not adept at things like gathering blood with a needle, hose, and vial. It was taking longer than he liked.

Still, he was pleased to have any samples at all. Han spoke to him of his plan to cure the plague with the waters of Hell, but Joshua knew that he had to have his own samples for study to work on. He trusted Han in his area of expertise, but this was medicine, and Joshua had no peer.

He had crafted a decent laboratory from the old one belonging to the palace chirurgeon, and had requisitioned the rest of his supplies from the city outside the palace. Flames boiled fluids, liquids were distilled, and Joshua felt alive. From herbs and supplies in the lab, he had even manufactured a basic remedy for his ailment that by no means made him feel healthy, but did alleviate a not insignificant portion of his symptoms. He believed the waters Han was seeking could help him, but he wanted a vaccine for the other denizens of Hell. He would not leave a plague as his legacy in liberating Sheol.

Joshua smiled as a sample of blood brought in from a likely victim putrefied when exposed to his own blood sample. Looking at the hourglass still pouring sand down he felt confident he was making progress. The sample had taken nearly an additional minute to corrupt. Given the time, he could do this. It was enough to give a man hope.

chapter twelve

Terrors shall make him afraid on every side, and shall drive him to his feet.
- Job 18:11

He missed the presence of the stranger. Having killed him, he now truly regretted the exchange. He couldn't shake the look of surprise and anger in the man's face as his blood gushed out over his knife and hand. No fear though, that was surprising. He had killed more demons in his life than he could count, and even desperate, wild men attacking his convoys while traveling from Sanctuary to Sanctuary. He hadn't yet plunged his knife into the flesh of another being and not seen fear flash in their eyes as death took them. He didn't relish that moment in the slightest, in fact he hated it, but he did pay attention.

Sighing, he poked through the man's camp. He had lost count of the days since he killed the Legion at his Sanctuary, but they surely must number in the thousands. Maybe tens of thousands. Time was meaningless. He remembered killing the Ba'al that day, and slaughtering demons by the thousands as if it were yesterday, so etched with fire it was in his mind. He remembered his conversations with his friend and their evening at the tavern so clearly that he felt for sure at times this whole existence in the valley was a dream. Yet if it was, it was eternal.

He never thought he was going to die that night as he approached the portal. He remembered the exhaustion and lying down to sleep, but not to die. He had just been tired. Small wonder given the torrent which had blazed within him and the war he waged against the Legion. When he fell asleep, the last thing he expected was to wake up dead, though that was what had happened. He went to sleep and awoke in the valley. Pleasant enough, except for the sheer normalcy and boredom. He walked and he trained. He drank pristine mountain water and at times, forced himself to eat. The fish tasted better than any he could remember, though he never could muster an appetite unless nearing the border. He still regretted the one time he made himself kill a deer just to eat venison. He had built himself up to it over weeks, and followed through, but in the end felt a profound sadness for the waste. He simply wasn't hungry.

He did things out of habit just to stave off madness, but if it wasn't for his attempts to breach the edge of the valley at times he thought for sure his sanity would have broken by now. He wanted out of there so badly but his body would not obey his mind when he tried to leave. At first he thought it was a matter of will, but over the blurring of time and years, he had come to believe it was something else entirely. His body simply collapsed if he got too far and no amount of desire could make his muscles move him forward. Backwards was always allowed with ease and grace.

He brushed the still warm ashes from the strangers' fire from his hands and stood, turning to look out to the boundary. Perhaps he would try again today. For a wonder, he actually felt a little hungry for the first time in ages.

His eyes widened in surprise as the stranger stood before him, noticing far too late the arcing whistle of a morning star descending on his head. His last thought was that it was strange that he too felt no fear.

Dark terrors indeed, Han. Piotyr shuddered as he lay down, white knuckled, in the small boat as he and the First drifted along the waters of Acheron. He would have gladly faced a dozen Ba'al while armed only with a spoon than listen to more of the screams. Han was crazy; no mortal could have traversed that river and remained sane. Piotyr had a death grip on his terror, and if not for the First stoically rowing and not appearing disturbed in the slightest, Piotyr would never had made it. *Wise to send me with a dead man. Mortals, even ones such as us are not meant to be here.*

Styx had been, by contrast, relatively uneventful. They had rowed along without any real incident, which the First had told him was due in part to them going upriver and leaving from Sheol itself. The transition to Acheron had been abrupt, and unsettling.

The waters had grown completely still, and in an instant silent. Piotyr was not a man prone to fits of nervousness or unease, but he knew in a precise second that they were in a new place. The quiet lasted for hours, as they paddled slowly upriver. The First had counseled him not to retrieve water yet, as it would be diluted, and Piotyr had agreed. They might be on Acheron, but it was not pure yet. If only the silence had lasted.

By God I wish we had taken the damned sample and left. This is beyond my ability to withstand for another hour.

The screams and scratching against the boat were not the worst of it. Those were awful, but mostly incoherent. The worst were the sobs of the voices he could distinguish, and he had been too terrified to even move a muscle to cover his ears. He was lying in the bottom of the boat, concealed with burlap, as the First had first spotted the drowned souls before them. He had told Piotyr to get down and hide... which had rankled the warrior, but only for a moment as the first piercing shriek rose to their ears. He hesitated in that moment, his foolish pride getting in the way of what could only be called wisdom. The First had looked him dead in the eye and spoke so softly though with such intensity that Piotyr nearly felt compelled.

"Get down and hide, now." With haste and a breath released he did not know he had been holding, Piotyr lay down in the boat and covered up, though in his stupid arrogance he had not covered his ears. He regretted it terribly. What followed was so harrowing that he could scarcely comprehend it. This was no war with armed foes that he could slay. The screams of the damned raked across

the inside of his skull without mercy and without end. Men, women, children all shrieked their torments aloud, and he felt a terror so pure and profound that it paralyzed him. If one of the damned crested the boat it would fall to the First to fight them off. Piotyr was locked in place as if rigor mortis had already set in.

Hours went by. His jaw had clenched so tight his head pounded in agony. His eyes had wept themselves dry and cracked with the horror of the river. He had clawed the boards beneath his hands to splinters, the pain keeping him from giving in to madness. Screams bled into more screams, and always there was at least one which he could discern the words behind, one which turned his blood to ice and caused his soul to bleed. Such pain.

Finally, he nearly sobbed in relief when The First stopped rowing, but stopped himself by biting down on his tongue until he tasted salt and iron. The pain was welcome. It was something he knew and understood.

The First casually lowered the oars into the boat and bent to retrieve an empty sample phial from his pack. Uncorking the stopper, he slowly reached his ladle over the side of the boat and Piotyr watched in mute and impotent uselessness as the phial was filled, then another, then a double dose for the mixed samples. The undead man had gathered both sets of the water, as Piotyr was helpless. The screams had not stopped, why had The First stopped here for the samples?

The answer came to him as he heard the slapping of oars coming across the river, their rhythmic motion overcoming even the black cacophony of the screams. *God no, my God no, have mercy, not now. I can't fight!*

He forced himself to breathe, and began to try to steel himself. He must have done something to draw the First's attention, as the undead whispered to him softly. "There will be no quarrel."

He listened, then, as the oars got closer to their small vessel. He locked his gaze to the First, and held his breath and the two watercraft crossed paths. The First maintained *his* gaze with something, or someone in the other boat, and Piotyr would have gasped if he hadn't been holding his breath for all his worth. The First casually nodded as the boat passed, and Piotyr somehow knew it was in response to an in-kind gesture. *Dark Terrors indeed.*

The screams rose in a vile crescendo, and continued for more hours as the boat crept further down the river. *I miss you, Asya. May I live to see you again.*

"Give him this, Dhermina; it will not cure him, though it will ease his pain considerably. I wish there was more I could do, but this poison is beyond my ability to cure with prayer. I must treat him with medicine and patience."

Joshua watched Dhermina look at the bottle with doubt, her eyes red and raw. It was unlikely she had slept last night, or would that night.

"He will live, that I promise, at least for now. This is not a trick; I'm not giving him a sedative that will ease his passing. It's a blood-treatment for the poison. I can't do more without a sample of the poison, at least not quickly. I have Kasim's blood, though a cure is out of the question for now. I promise you, this will help."

She nodded. "Thank you, Joshua Danner. I am sorry for not trusting you; I would not wish my love to die, even out of compassion for his suffering, if there is a way to save him."

"There is, though it may take time. I know not how long my friends will be gone on this task. I will do what I can in the meantime. Han is helping, and I do not question whether or not we can keep Kasim alive for a time. If it came to it, I could force his body into staying alive with prayer, for a little while anyway, though it would be unnatural and tax us both greatly. The Invocation is powerful, but not gentle. I would use it only as a last resort. For now? I can ease his pain with other means."

Her eyes starting tearing up, and nodded to him before turning away. "Thank you again. Would you like to stay with him for a time after you give him the medicine? He has not otherwise changed since this morning."

"I would. I want to see how the philter affects him." She nodded again and led the way into the Sanitarium. It had been a site of horror quite recently, but had been cleared and cleaned into a basic place of convalescence. The blood stains were still there, but had at least been washed and sanitized. It would do.

Kasim lay on a simple straw mattress, stripped to the waist and dressed in bandages below. The stench of burned flesh was heavy in the room, heavy enough that even through his disease Joshua could sense it. He allowed a moment for the sadness, and out of respect for his brother he Invoked Healing for himself. The scent of corruption and blood washed over Joshua, and he steeled himself. It was a mortal wound, even without the poison. Kasim lived by virtue of his incredible will to survive, and also of Joshua's talent as a healer. Hellfire was not a thing one lived through, nor the poisoning on top of that.

He walked to the bedside of his friend and checked the bandages. The flesh was so destroyed that there was no chance he would walk again, let alone be the man he once was. It was beyond hope. Joshua could fashion prosthetics which would allow him mobility but could only hope Kasim would not be too proud to use them. It was a dismal prognosis, but the best one he could give. He peeled back a layer of the bandages to see how his healing had taken and he could only stare.

He must have given Dhermina cause for alarm, as she looked over his shoulder as he knelt and nervously spoke.

"Is something wrong? It looks the same to me."

Something was definitely wrong, but not with the flesh on Kasim's legs. "No, quite the opposite. Dhermina, has Han been in to see Kasim?"

"Yes, he came last night; he said he wanted to check on him and to give me a respite to get something to eat. I didn't want to go, but he said it was important that I eat and keep my strength up."

"I see." *Han, what have you done? Lokyrg, and now this?* "Well it seems Han's visit was good for Kasim. His legs look much improved. Whatever you are doing, keep it up, and make sure he gets the whole philter. It will help."

Dhermina nodded and looked happy. "He said if you wanted to see him, he would be at your laboratory."

"Thank you and God be with you. This is hard, and you are strong. Please call for me at once if there is a problem."

"I will, and thank you."

He left the bedside, and the Sanitarium, and walked in a heated anger to go see Han. By God how could he do this? It was unnatural beyond anything Joshua could have expected from Han.

He arrived at the laboratory and was not surprised to see Han waiting for him in the foyer. Han looked as he usually did, though tired.

His old friend must have seen his mood, for he forestalled Joshua's outburst with an upraised hand. Joshua was angry, but would allow Han the chance to speak.

"I see you've been to see him. How is his health?"

"You know damned well how it is. He should be dead, barring that he should be maimed. I know what you did, Han. Would you deny it?"

Han laughed, but it was not a cruel laugh, nor one containing any humor. It was the sad, exhausted half-mirth of a man worn down, his soul worn and frayed. "I would not. I did what I had to do, and they were dead already. They could not be saved. This way? They can still be of great use to Kasim."

"Han! They loved him like a father! He will weep and gnash his teeth when he learns what you did with them! This is an abomination, much worse than with the drake."

The older man sighed and rubbed his eyes. "You who kill with your mere presence and raise the dead for his armies of the damned would lecture me on what is or is not an abomination?"

In anger, Joshua yelled back, "That is different and you know it! That is not a choice, and barring suicide there was nothing I could have done!"

To his credit, Han stayed calm and did not respond in kind to Joshua's fire. "Suicide, or isolation. Choices were there, though not kind ones. In that we are agreed, and what I did was not without thought, or pain, or regret. It was also a hard choice, but one that I would make again. The monks all served him willingly in life; I choose to believe they would do so in death. Now they can."

"Han, everyone deserves rest. All of them fought at the walls of Sheol and saw the Shay'tan take wing. They have now died because of it and their souls deserve peace. Release them."

"To what end? To have our brother unable to walk? To be useless in the battle to come? We will *need* Kasim before the end, and those from Sagarmatha are dead and no longer of use. However, I did not kill them, and their souls are now doing more for us than ever they would leaving this place to wherever it is they would go.

"Kasim will be furious when he knows of it. Do not mean to keep it from him."

Han shook his head before answering. "It did cross my thoughts, but I agree that it would be better for him to know. He will be angry, to be sure. My hope is that he will look at it rationally and know that what I did, I did for just cause."

Joshua's anger left him. He completely disagreed with Han's actions, but they were done. "You were wrong, Han. You should not have bound their souls to his body. That is something *their* kind would do, not us. We still have our humanity, no matter what shells we are imprisoned in."

"Humanity? I should think not, Joshua. We are no longer human, to say the least. Kasim was perhaps the most human of us, and look what that got him. He may die still, despite all your efforts. Or mine. The souls of Sagarmatha will save his legs, but unless Piotyr and your friend, a walking corpse, succeed, he *will* die. The poison in his veins will kill him yet."

Joshua thought he heard the hint of mockery in Han's use of the word friend, but as they were quarrelling he felt it could be imagined. Even if it wasn't, he had just attacked Han's morality, pointing out the flaws in Joshua's own was fair, if not a logical argument.

"How did you do it? With Lokryg and Eirygaile I understood, but there was no vessel here other than Kasim, and he was away in the infirmary. How did you bind their souls to his body?"

Han smiled wanly at Joshua, perhaps sensing that their argument had dissipated. "I tethered them to my own body for a time. Their souls had lingered in the plaza where they were killed, and were not resting easily. I trapped them, not unkindly, and allowed the tethers to weaken on my way to see Kasim. By the time I was ready, so were they."

"That sounds dangerous, what if you had erred and they remained bound to you?" Despite himself, Joshua was genuinely curious.

"Then I would unbind them. I did not undertake this task lightly, Joshua. I would not have attempted to bind their souls if I did not feel confident I could do so as I intended. I have learned enough about the process that this was not, in my mind, an undue danger. Unpleasant, to be sure, in the larger scope of things, but necessary. Kasim will not only walk, he will be as he was before, if not better. Their souls shall not only heal his flesh, but imbue it beyond what his own strength could be. We shall need him, before the end."

Joshua was silent for a moment, and his rational mind warred with his empathy as a healer. In the end, the cold hard truth of necessity won out, and his anger fled. Sighing, he slumped his shoulders. "So you can bind the soul of a mortal to another man and make him stronger. Why do I sense there will be more to this?"

Han walked to a small table and poured himself a draught of blood red wine before adding a second pour for Joshua. He filled the overlarge goblets near the brim before handing one to the healer. He raised his own goblet to Joshua in a toast. "Lapsis Caelum. Quite the fine quality, I think." Joshua said nothing as he drank, and waited. Han would speak in time. The wine would be murder on his illness, but he would get over it. He needed a drink.

"I know you are quite wise, Joshua, though I would say you are not, specifically, a man learned of war. I mean no disrespect by that, quite the opposite." He paused, to Joshua looking as if he was waiting to see if he had offended. Joshua smiled at him, polite but drained.

"None taken, and you are right, I am not a scholar of war by any means."

"I was not either, though I feel I am now. My journey here has taught me many things, but mostly I see what is coming and what must be done to stop it."

"What is coming? More Ba'al to be sure, but we defeated the Shay'tan... well Jacob did at least. Surely what follows will not be *worse* than that?"

Han looked at him for a long moment before continuing. Joshua was not sure what was behind Han's eyes, but he did not feel it was derision.

"Joshua, it will not be worse in terms of the pinnacle of evil which our brother slew, but the Destroyer is coming, and he is by himself no less dangerous an opponent. You have seen what Ba'al Apollyon is capable of, ruthless and terrible in war."

"Yes I have seen it Han, but Apollyon is nothing compared to his incarnation as Abaddon the Destroyer, and always we drove him back."

"We? By whom do you believe we drove Abaddon back?"

Joshua was silent for a moment before it came to him, and he paled. "The Patriarch. It was always he who with Holy Fire burned Abaddon and forced his Legions back."

Han nodded sadly and answered. "Yes, the Patriarch, and we have no luxury here. Do you feel you could do what he does? Could Kasim? Piotyr? Even with the wyrms I would not wager against Abaddon in open warfare without a weapon of the caliber of our Patriarch wielded against him and hundreds of other priests to fend off the rest of the Legion. Holy Fire rained from the sky for three straight days the last time Haven was assaulted before our journey here, and still the Destroyer was not defeated, merely slowed."

Joshua snorted before drinking more of the wine. It most definitely was fine, and he was definitely going to pay for drinking it later. "*Journey*? Han, that is an interesting way to describe our bodies and souls being torn asunder. Though I understand the necessity I find it hard to wish the Patriarch were here. If he was I might find bloodshed to actually be of my liking."

Han was quiet, and for a moment Joshua got the sense there was something he wanted to say, but it passed. When Han continued it was as if Joshua had not interrupted him.

"It falls to me to defend our walls. I say *our* walls because Ve'kal is not capable of leading the siege defense. Nor am I. That role shall fall to Piotyr when he returns, but it *does* fall to me to repel the Destroyer. The population looks to us as its saviors, and the Fallen look to her as a usurper. It was not she who slew the Shay'tan, and her taking the Throne is a farce and everyone knows it. It serves our purpose for now, but it will not stand in the face of the annihilation which marches on us, and I don't even just mean Ba'al Apollyon."

Joshua was confused, and it must have shown in his face. "But you just said..." Han forestalled him with a hand, and Joshua nodded to him to continue.

"He comes. Make no mistake, and he is the greatest threat, but not the only one. He marches with the entire host of the Legion. Some remain to hold Haven locked down, but not many. He came through the portal once he learned that Ve'kal had claimed the Throne, and not Jacob Merethius, the slayer of the Heir of Lucifer. His hosts came with him, and he now makes ready to cleanse Ve'kal and all other pretenders from the face of Hell."

Joshua's eyes grew wide. His hands shook as he took a large gulp of the wine, finishing it and looking longingly at the bottle. His nose had swollen completely shut. "*The entire host?* Han that must be..."

Han smiled grimly. "My name is Legion," he replied, "for we are many." Han took a moment to fill their glasses again. "Tens of millions march on Sheol. Ba'al from every corner of Hell, and from the front on Earth. The skies will darken with the wings of the Fallen, and the soil will be soaked in blood. We cannot stand against what comes, Joshua."

"Cannot stand? What must we do? Flee? Become fugitives here? We can't just give Apollyon back the Throne. Jacob died to liberate it, and you want to just let something just as terrible take it over? Han, please!"

Han sipped on his own wine before answering. "Peace, Joshua, *we* cannot stand, but what we will become shall. How many of your soldiers would you say you have?"

"My undead? Do you mean actual thinking warriors or the mindless horde?"

"Both, how many of each?"

"I have near two score Zombie Lords. Each of them I would wager against a Ba'al in one on one combat. Below them, perhaps two hundred fast, intelligent, and powerful plague-walkers who on average are the superiors to most Legionnaire. The mindless horde? Maybe ten thousand, altogether. Of course there is also the First, though as mighty as he is he would not turn the tide against the numbers you speak of. There is another, nearly as strong as him. He is called Secundus... his choice, not mine."

"Those numbers will help, combined with what I intend to arm them with. So... ten thousand foot soldiers from you, and perhaps twice that many again if we include out all our remaining Sheol Imperial Guard and Ve'kal's Household Legion, combined with the mortal refugees who both can stand against your plague and can stand in battle."

"Thirty thousand against tens of millions. With those numbers there won't even be a Siege, Han. Provisions and defense of our walls will be of no concern if Apollyon can just swarm our walls like ants."

"Agreed, though we have other means at our disposal. You can command vermin and we have dragons, which I believe Piotyr will be able to call upon again. We will also have hellfire at our disposal whereas Apollyon will not. He won't care for the life of the defenders but he will not want to destroy Sheol. If he razed it to the ground he would lose time rebuilding it before he could return to finish Haven and any other resistance on Earth. We will have no such reluctance on his Legion."

Joshua was listening attentively, but not hearing anything to change the futility of the situation. "Fine, insects, hellfire, undead, and dragons. Still, thirty thousand against..."

"Thirty thousand, half of which I intend to make unkillable by blade, stone, or spear. The other half I have plans to make sure they will fight on... no matter their wounds, with your help and consent."

Joshua was silent for a moment, at first thinking to argue that Han was insane, but he stopped himself and mused for a moment, and allowed that Han could possibly do just that, though he didn't know how.

"Ok, I will allow that you can do that, but the logistics are still impossible. We will be brushed aside like a castle made of sand. The sheer volume of the host coming will smash us like gnats."

"Agreed, our numbers alone would not withstand a full assault, and though we have not the means to kill Abaddon the Destroyer right now, I believe our success lies in one final weapon to turn on his Legion."

Joshua wracked his brain but could not think of another variable that would turn the tide. There were no more troops to be had, at least not enough that would matter, and that left only the Templar to include in the equation. Jacob was dead, Kasim was only one man even if he recovered fully by the time Apollyon attacked, and Piotyr was mighty but not enough to win the battle. That left Joshua and Han. Joshua could heal quickly and triage their forces, and his plague would turn many of Abaddon's forces into undead fighting for them, but the battle would be quick and decisive, and attrition would not happen quickly enough for his walkers to make the difference. So Han must be referring to himself. Having puzzled it out, Joshua was not sure to what extent Han could do what he was speaking of.

"Han, I know that your power is extensive, and you said more so here at Sheol, but are you saying you can single-handedly stop them from breaching our walls?"

"Not single-handedly, but yes. Though I don't pretend I could destroy the host approaching, I believe I can serve Sheol in the role that the Patriarch did at Haven. I will draw upon the power here and rain destruction upon Abaddon and his Legion."

"To slow them, yes, but you think you can keep them off the walls? Tens of millions of rampaging Ba'al and Legion?"

Han was quiet for a moment before answering. When he did, his voice was tired, but firm. "What I think is that we have little choice but to try. Jacob's victory, while impressive, did little in the larger picture to protect our brothers and sisters back home. If Ba'al Apollyon is allowed to simply march on Sheol and take the Throne, a Shay'tan will again stand unopposed and make ready to wipe us off the face of Hell, and Earth."

Joshua rubbed his eyes before answering. "Fair enough, but is this the only course of action? Could we not abandon the city? Find rivals to Abaddon elsewhere willing to join their forces to ours? "

"Joshua, even if we were successful in a guerilla war... and I believe we could be with attrition favoring your undead, it would take years if not decades to change the dynamic of the war here. Abaddon would know that, and would simply take the Throne and ignore us, leaving enough of his Legion to hold the city and going back to Earth to finish us."

"You mean finish *them*, don't you? Hardly seems accurate to consider them kin, after what was done to us."

Joshua was taken aback for a moment as genuine sadness passed over his friend's face. Perhaps Han did think as he did, he was just covering it better.

"Joshua, I will not argue with you that what happened wasn't terrible, but they are still our kin. Our souls and bodies may be altered, but the core is the same. I am still Han Fei-tze and you are still Joshua Danner. No matter what else, who we are cannot be taken from us."

He finished his second glass of wine and longingly wished for another. His health would suffer for it later, but in the moment it seemed to ease the pain in his chest. Han was right, of course. No matter the anger he held onto for the actions of the Patriarch, he still wanted to save Haven. The Templar there hadn't wronged him, and he had friends he would wish no suffering on. If this was their best chance to help them, he would support the plan. "So we don't have the time to wage a war we can win, is that what you are saying?"

Han smiled; again looking tired but not resigned. "Yes, but I also think we can hold Sheol indefinitely. We can't kill Abaddon, but we can stop him from getting to the Throne, which in time may give us the victory we need. All that needs to happen is to keep The Destroyer at bay long enough for support for the war effort to crumble and for humanity to regroup and rebuild. I trust that within hours of Abaddon leaving Haven, the Patriarch was fast at work looking for other survivors and beginning to re-fortify. If we can keep Ba'al Apollyon at bay for a time, perhaps it will be enough. We held Haven against him for years. We will do the same here."

"For a time, Han? How long do you intend to stop the largest army ever assembled to crush a city held by so few?"

"For as long as I draw breath."

chapter thirteen

Is this real compassion that I feel, or only a delusion? My mind gropes about in darkness, I cannot see where my duty lies.
- The Sorrow of Arjuna: Bhagavad-Gita

It had been satisfying to stave in the skull of the man who had killed him, but not wholly. He had hoped for an end to fighting and death, hoped that at last he had earned a measure of peace. It was a pleasant enough afterlife, all things considered, though apparently one not meant to be shared. The surprise on the man's face had not given him any pleasure, though the act of retribution, as it always had, was somewhat soothing to his embattled spirit.

Also, as a side benefit, he was actually hungry for the first time since arriving in the valley and was pleasantly roasting a fresh trout from the stream. He let his mind wander as it cooked and found it hard to want for anything. He wasn't happy, not by any means, but he felt... *content.* The stream was swift, up to his waist in a couple of deep spots, and smelled fresh and clean. It was warm, but not overly so, and a pleasant breeze gently tousled his hair. Soft grasses, fine sand, and plenty of wildlife belied the truth of it, which was that he was dead and in Hell. From all evidence that he could see, it was not an unpleasant way to spend eternity, though he suspected the man with the knife had thought the same thing.

There was something vaguely familiar about the man, though he couldn't place it. It still enraged him that he had been bested by something as simple as sand kicked in his eyes. If his brothers could see him now he would cringe in shame. *Shame enough in being dead, Templar.* His voice mocked him from inside his head. Scowling, he answered. *I did what I came to do, that is enough. I accept my fate.*

The scent of charring fish skin broke his reverie, and he took his dinner off the fire. He let it cool for a minute or so before devouring it. It felt *good* to be hungry again, and even better to sate himself. Truly it was not an unpleasant place for eternity.

He wondered idly if there was any tobacco or similar weed he could find growing in the valley. A smoke after a meal would not be amiss if he was to stay here indefinitely. He stood to go explore a bit when a soft shrill whistle caught his attention before searing pain exploded in his back. He collapsed to his knees, clutching at his spine and in horror felt his blood pouring out over his hands as he found a knife embedded in his flesh. He pulled it out and found no relief as agony grew in a radius from the wound and he collapsed, his extremities becoming numb. He rolled to his side and for some reason, was not surprised in the least to see the stranger from before walking towards him cautiously. He laughed, though for the life of him couldn't understand why it was funny.

The stranger stopped, and stared at the dying man for a long moment, then laughed along with him.

Darkness took him, and he had the strangest, yet comforting thought. *I'll get you next time.*

"I tell you again, warrior, there is no shame in what happened. Mortal eyes were not meant to see such things." The First spoke as he divided the samples among them, giving them each a phial of Acheron's water and carefully measuring a full ladle from the larger container to pour into Piotyr's mixed container. They each had what they needed from the terrible place, now.

It wasn't shame so much that Piotyr felt, but impotence. He had agreed to come on this journey for Han because he wanted to help, and the horror of Acheron had shattered his faith in his own courage. "I am not a mortal, First, not any more. I should have felt no fear passing those waters, yet I was petrified by it. I have faced a Ba'al more than once, and slain more than one, on Earth as a true mortal and also here as what I am now. I cowered like a child before the damned. What good am I to you if I can't control my own fear?"

The First was silent for a long moment before answering. "This is hard to explain, but I will try. You are a mighty warrior, Piotyr. In your own way perhaps the greatest of your brothers. However, you are still of flesh and blood, as are the Ba'al. You are foes in a way that can understand each other. What dwelt on the river Acheron was something foreign, and alien. I am technically flesh, but certainly not as you know it. I was with my kind on the waters, and you were not. It was not a war your body was even capable of waging. Feel no shame in it. There will be other battles."

Piotyr heard the words and even the wisdom in them, and as he stubbornly set his mind to continue doubting his bravery, an admonishing voice came into his mind that sounded like the Patriarch calling him a fool. It was over and he needed to move on. They were not on Acheron any longer and he was unprepared for what would come next. It was time to focus on going forward, no matter his feelings on his cowardice amongst the souls of the damned.

"Other battles. Fair enough. What shall we expect next, First?"

The undead looked uncertain, surprisingly expressive for the usually stoic zombie. "To be honest I'm not sure what waters we will hit next. The others who *may* have historically taken this journey have written a few *possible* accounts, but always it was to Sheol, not away from it. Our destination is Cocytus, but the geography won't be predictable. It could be Lethe or Phlegethon next. We should not be able to reach the center before our journey is complete, if that makes any sense."

"So there is some sort of restriction on our arriving at Cocytus before we are ready?" Piotyr wasn't a simple minded man, and though these planar mysteries were not familiar to him he understood some of the concepts behind them.

"Yes. That is a good way of looking at it. Our journey will take us to all five waters, but I am unsure what shall follow Acheron. Thusly, I shall tell you of both. If it is Lethe, the waters of oblivion, we shall not encounter souls such as we did the last time."

"A relief, that, First. I am unwilling to undertake another such crossing if at all possible."

"Warrior, though I understand your reticence, it may be that we have to cross Acheron again to return to Sheol, though I hope not. In any case, you must take great care once we reach the waters of Lethe. Though you are not wholly mortal any more, you are enough of the seed of Adam that the waters would likely still serve their purpose for you. To drink from Lethe is to forget."

"Ah, I remember something of this I think. It was supposed to be the barrier between Heaven and Hell? Souls going from one to the other had to drink it to forget their past lives or something?"

The Zombie-King smiled now, perhaps pleased that Piotyr, not having been known for scholarly pursuits, was at least familiar with the subject.

"In part, though no souls from Paradise would have ever traversed the waters back to Hell that I know of. In fact, most of the consensus shows that once the waters are crossed out of Hell, the soul is forever lost to the Ba'al."

Piotyr snorted. "Such a pity."

"Derision aside, the truth is that our knowledge, if it can even be called knowledge and not rumor or guesswork, is based on souls going to Paradise. Almost nothing is known of those in Hell who drink the waters, or even traverse them. As the purpose of the water is to forget a past life, I would advise caution, however."

He was silent for a moment as he pondered what it would mean to lose his memory. He would not part with the experiences of Asya and their children for anything, though the idea of losing the memories of the war on Earth was far from unattractive. "Noted, my friend. What of Phlegethon?"

"You would have heard of the waters of Phlegethon by reputation, if not name. The waters burn, or boil, or otherwise exist to cause eternal torment to violent sinners. If we come across those first, I would expect fire and pain."

Piotyr laughed, then, a genuine mirth. "That, my undead brother, is something I can handle."

Ve'kal was haggard. Not even the sight of Nezmyr practicing the swordsmanship Jacob had taught him could lift her feelings of hopelessness.

It is happening, the Destroyer is coming here and I do not have the forces to stop him. The Templar had failed her. Piotyr and the Zombie-King had left on some damned foolish errand, and without Piotyr she had no dragons.

Kasim lay dying from the Kiss of the Watchers and his followers were already dead, except that useless girl who lay over him like a lost puppy. She supposed she should be grateful that the Grigori only targeted Kasim and his fellows. They could have easily killed anyone else in Sheol that day.

Sheol was in ruins. The reconstruction was progressing but even with every able-bodied Fallen, plague-immune mortal, and undead who could form a thought working on it, she feared Abaddon would lay siege to a broken city. Ve'kal tiredly rubbed her eyes and sadly thought it wouldn't matter. The walls could be twice as high and not make a difference. Ba'al Apollyon was bringing his entire force back from Earth.

Initially, when she had called her challenge to the Throne and commanded her house Legion to abandon the front, she was pleased to know that only half of The Destroyer's forces had abandoned Haven to accompany their Ba'al to see Ve'kal either butchered or crowned. That group had been slowly trickling in over the past several weeks. A few had arrived in time to actually fight at the walls of Sheol, though either out of fear, wisdom, or both did not commit forces until the battle was decided. She expected to take the Throne and fight a normal succession.

What happened, Jacob? This was not how it was supposed to be.

She smiled sadly, thinking of the mortal man who had completely changed the course of her House. The line of Ve'kal had been in danger of being broken for some time, but she had been content to hide in her remote corner of the Empire, protecting Nezmyr in his possessed Thrall state. In time, she had hoped that with the final victory over Adam's seed she could find a suitor strong enough to begin starting over but not so strong that she would become irrelevant.

Then he had come. He had been brought to her under guard from her best soldiers, and with word traveling ahead of him that he had butchered an entire village along the larger, upper fork of the Serpent River. *The entire village,* save for a few mortal wretches who had fled. Imperial Overseers, exiled Legion commanders, and all manner of other forces of the Shay'tan had lived there, and had been wiped out by one man, one mortal man.

She had known the human called Jacob for less than an hour and instantly knew he was her salvation. Jacob had been reluctant to help her, understandable given what he was and what she was. His heart was kind, she had found, as he was unwilling to leave Nezmyr imprisoned with his soul a slave to the parasite the Shay'tan demanded take root in all of the still-living firstborn of his Ba'al and Ba'alat.

Jacob Merethius had performed an exorcism and freed her son, and forever changed the course of Hell's fate as well as that of House Ve'kal. In return, she had stalled Abaddon's final push into Haven by challenging the Throne and recalling her forces. Her troops alone would not have made the difference, but the Ba'al were fickle by nature and in droves the other Fallen had also left the front. *Perhaps that is why Abaddon now comes to obliterate me with his entire Host. He seeks revenge for making him wait.*

No, that was unlikely. Ba'al Apollyon was calculating more than wrathful. He came to make sure Sheol was his, and he intended to take the Throne himself to make sure he could concentrate on killing the remnants of humanity with no further incident.

No matter the cause, her options were limited. In truth, she could either choose to stay and fight, and die, or she could flee Sheol and go into hiding with Nezmyr and whoever chose to accompany her. Her own life was precious to her, but she feared more for her child. Nezmyr was a strong boy, but naive. His Thralldom had kept him from being tempered as most sons of Ba'al were.

She snorted and thought of Obistal, the newly ascended Ba'al Geir. That was how most Ba'al treated their offspring. She had wept when Nezmyr was possessed. A weakness she knew, but her consort and other children had been taken from her unexpectedly in the war, burned away in mortal Soulfire. She had no chance to replace him without finding a new mate. The Shay'tan would have allowed Nezmyr to remain free as long as her elder children fought in the war, but her petition to keep him so had been denied once they were dead. He had been an infant.

Now she had her boy back. A precious gift from Jacob, and she had in turn loved the mortal more fiercely than she thought possible. Her own mate, a second son from House Jyrith had been nothing compared to the mortal. She clenched her jaw and ground her teeth in frustration at her fate. She had known Jacob intended to die fighting the Shay'tan, but she had hoped for whatever foolish reason that he could escape with his life and be with her in the aftermath.

She intended to be Shay'tan, but not a weak one with no power, no forces, and no city to protect her Throne. Jacob had done the impossible, and then conveniently left her with nothing when he died. Looking out at the ruins of Sheol and the ragtag group of mismatched zombie, Legion, and mortal troops made her grab her stomach and wince at pangs of discomfort. *Almost nothing, anyway.*

Dragons could have made a difference. Even with the death of one of them, three wyrms were worth tens of thousands of Abaddon's Legion. Even if Ba'al Mirish did possess more Heart of Cocytus, Piotyr would be aware of it now and should be able to protect the brood. It mattered little now. Whether Mirish was alone in possession of the ice or half of Abaddon's army had the stuff was irrelevant. The dragons were gone.

She blinked as Nezmyr grabbed the sword of his sparring partner, pulled him off balance, and struck the unfortunate old Legionnaire in the face with his pommel. Jacob had told her he taught the boy to win, not fight fairly while he fought. No dragons... and no Jacob.

She turned away from her son, so as not to embarrass him with the pride she felt, and looked to the ruins of the Throne plaza. To flee, or to perish.

Can you do anything to change our fate, Han?

Days had passed and Kasim had not recovered, but he had stabilized, as near as Dhermina could tell. His body did not wither away as it did when he was first poisoned, though his frame had grown slight and feeble in countenance. She feared for his health such as she had not since he first traveled the way of death in Sagarmatha. It seemed a lifetime ago, but in reality was less than a year by a good margin. She could not believe it had ended this way for her brothers and sisters, but even worse was that Kasim lay, crippled and near death because he had saved *her*. She knew that the poison, this potent toxin made by these *Watchers* of which she knew nothing other than what they had wrought in the plaza that day, was lethal. Kasim's fate was beyond her ability to influence.

She hated feeling helpless, but at her love's side she knew that any oaths of vengeance were empty and futile. She was alone, knew little of Hell outside of her cloister's walls, and stood no chance in finding let alone waging war against some organized group of ancient Fallen assassins. She wasn't stupid, and knew in her heart that once she started asking questions, she would just disappear. Kasim was her only chance for revenge, and part of her feared he would never be the same.

Stupid girl, look at him, he most definitely won't be the same.

Wiping away tears, she lay down beside the love of her heart and soul, and slept a deep and dreamless sleep.

Things were not the same, and he feared to know the truth of it. The second door again gave him the sense of beasts and those of lesser minds. He turned from it once more, and once more felt a pulling from the first door of incredible longing. He knew in his mind that beyond that door awaited despair and terror, if not madness, yet part of his soul craved to fling it open and move beyond it.

That was why he knew something was wrong. He remembered the attack, and the beginning of his convalescence, and also of Han healing him in some way. That it was Han and not Joshua seemed... *wrong* in a way that he couldn't identify beyond the normal strangeness of Joshua not having done the healing.

He forced himself away from the second door and was taken aback to see that the third door was gone. How could that be? His path had led him to this crossroads for a reason. *To choose that door would be no choice at all.*

It seemed making no choice was no longer an option. He glanced at the fourth door, the one he went through last time, and out of curiosity he tried the handle. Startled, he jumped back as the entire doorframe collapsed into dust. Kasim waved dust away from his face and coughed. That road had been taken before. It would not be taken again.

Despair, or Enlightenment, then. I can't go through and emerge a lesser being. There is no time to learn anything just to die and come here again. A beast or a man with a damaged mind is of no use to anyone right now.

Once more he felt a pull to go through the first door, but he forced himself to turn to the far door, which had been so tempting the last time he was here. He was tired, and had fought long and hard in this war. If his choice was to wallow in darkness or walk in Nirvana, it was not a difficult choice. He turned the handle on the far door and beheld a paradise so perfect it brought tears to his eyes.

Golden light illuminating shores of the purest white sand, being slowly lapped by cerulean waters so pristinely clear gave the lie to calling this place anything other than paradise. Kasim could smell the sea breeze and hear the calling of gulls. Scents of hundreds of flowers and other flora made him smile and with a spring in his step he stepped through, eager to begin the next phase of his journey. What would be would be.

His smile stopped as he was snared by some invisible force that had caught on the doorway. His body had passed through completely, but less than a foot behind him something had snagged as if a large man had stepped on his cloak. Frowning, he turned to free himself but was unable to find anything physically caught.

He turned back towards the pristine shoreline, and smiled to see dozens of his old Templar friends standing on the sands waving to him and grinning. He saw men and women he hadn't seen in nearly a year, as well as Han, Piotyr, and Joshua. He grunted as he tried again in vain to move towards them, an unseen hand keeping him stuck fast.

He surveyed the people again, noting with surprise that Jacob was nowhere to be seen, but his heart soared to see Dhermina standing not twenty paces away wearing flowers in her hair and around her neck, smiling in anticipation and greeting to him.

He smiled as wide as he could and with all of his might forced his way further onto the beach. He made it another several paces before his strength waned and he fell to his knees, the force keeping him tethered back through the door... wherever that door led. Frustrated, he tried to stand and keep going but though his will was strong his body simply could not move any further.

He smiled sadly at Dhermina, and made a gesture behind him as if to say he was sorry. She waved at him as if it was of no concern. Sighing, Kasim stood and pointed back at the doorway, attempting to indicate that he would be back in a moment. Irritatingly, he was able to move back through the door with ease, and startlingly he realized that while on the sands he had forgotten everything about why he was there.

Standing in front of the doorway he felt a longing he could scarcely believe trying to again pull him through, but he knew he would be stopped again. Something was wrong, and it was not his time. Gritting his teeth for what he feared was to come; he steeled himself to just get it over with. He turned to the first door, and taking a deep breath flung it open and prepared to move through.

Blackness greeted him. A cold, crushing, and oppressive darkness which made Hell seem kind and inviting greeted his eyes and soul. He looked forlornly at the wall of emptiness and swallowed. He had traveled through darkness before, but this was different. He instinctively knew that the despair he had felt the last time he died, the depths of pain and suffering he had felt while journeying to these five doors before was a fleeting thing. This would last. Perhaps not for eternity, but not briefly. To step beyond that threshold into the dark would be to test his soul in ways he might not be prepared for.

Perhaps that is the point.

He released his jaw from the clenching he had been doing, and allowed peace to wash over his body and spirit. What would be... would be. He stepped beyond the doorway, and was surprised to feel five distinct threads fling from his body and speed away into the black.

It was as if part of his soul was unspooling like thread, flying away into oblivion. As it happened, he no longer felt that pull to be where he was, instead feeling fear and uncertainty. Instead of joining the threads departing from him, Kasim instead moved back through the doorway to once again join Dhermina, feeling that he had shed whatever it was holding him back from his bliss.

Smiling, he walked through the portal of the fifth doorway into the tropical paradise, and grunted with pain as something yanked his spine backwards as he tried to move forward. Cursing, he stood and gasped in pain as the threads he left in the first door snapped back into him like whips. He took a moment to catch his breath, then cursed again as he once again felt a pull to the first door. Looking from left to right, Kasim had no idea what to do. He left the doors open, and lay down to meditate on his current situation. He was at a loss and needed answers.

Wishing the waters surrounding their boat were roiling with heat, Piotyr felt an unease he found difficult to explain. The cavern around them had opened out into grey, nearly featureless hills, and from all appearances they could have been on any number of unremarkable rivers on Earth. The First had even commented on the relative boredom of their current leg of the journey.

Chiding himself for a fool, he tried to stop fixating on what he expected and instead focus on what was before him. Clearly this was not part of the waters of Phlegethon, which meant they were on, or nearly upon the River Lethe. From what the First had told him, caution must be maintained, but in the context of what he had gone through on Acheron, he *should* have been at ease and at peace on these calm waters surrounded by simple and unthreatening hills.

"Am I wrong, warrior? Or do you wish these waters to be choked with bodies and stinking of charred flesh?"

Piotyr smiled. He felt friendly towards the undead and certainly did not take offense to being mocked in a small bit. "Well it would be familiar to me. This calm quiet makes me feel unease. Are you sure we can't just get a sample here? I worry about forgetting it."

The First actually laughed... which took Piotyr aback and also gave him satisfaction. How many men could claim to have made a zombie laugh?

"Warrior, as long as you don't drink the water, it shouldn't affect you at all. Lethe is known for its properties of forgetfulness... *once ingested.* Don't drink the water and you'll be fine."

The Zombie-King's words sounded true, though he still could not shake his disquiet. Of all the waters of Hell, Lethe was the oddest and most foreign to Piotyr's mind. How could a drink of water simply make you forget who you were? He understood the First's explanation of why... it made sense that a soul leaving their body and traveling to Elysium would need to forget those left behind, but the how just didn't make sense to the Templar.

He put it out of his mind as he watched the hills roll by. The water was not swift by any means, and the terrain was unchanging for hours. He and his companion spoke, but not at length and their journey passed mostly in silence even until nightfall. Not seeing any reason to stop for darkness, as the undead could see as well at night as he could during the day and needed no rest, Piotyr simply lay down in the bottom of the boat to sleep. He slept undisturbed, and the next day passed as uneventfully as the first.

It wasn't until the third day that Piotyr started to feel listless and worried. Something should have happened by now, and the drab, featureless hills around Lethe were as boring and nondescript as they were when they first left the cavern Acheron led them through. How long until they found the source water? Or barring that how long until they found waters leading to Phlegethon? Drifting indeterminably along Lethe would drive him mad at this rate. Piotyr was not a patient man, and three full days on the water had soured what little patience he had, and thus his temper. He kept quiet deliberately so as not to take it out on the First.

He hungered and thirsted normally while on the river, but his hellfire was strong enough to reach the banks. Conflagrating the grass and reeds growing along the edge was enough to sate his stomach and throat, though he longed for a real drink after spending so many hours in the hot sun upon pristine looking water.

He envied the First, who from all appearances required no sustenance of any kind. He didn't drink, eat, or sleep. At night Piotyr would rest in the bottom of the boat, and the undead would simply tell him to rest easy, or the like, and when he awoke in the morning he could swear the Zombie-King hadn't moved.

It was like that on the fourth day, though immediately Piotyr knew that something was different. He sat bolt upright and grabbed Lokyrg.

Finally, Father. I had thought you had forgotten I could be used for something other than trying to stab fish you won't eat.

That wasn't entirely fair, as he had spoken to his son over the days on Lethe, but perhaps the tedium had Lokyrg on edge as well.

Standing up, he noticed that the First had drifted the boat over to the riverbank, where a large stream trickled over stones down to the water's edge. The First waited stoically, nodded his head in greeting to the Templar. *Arrogant undead. When you finally pierce me through his breast, I won't be inclined to eat him.*

He admonished his son and raised his eyebrows to the undead before nodding his head towards the stream.

"I feel it must be, warrior. The water feels... different here, and even the air does. I would have sworn that the current changed before the stream appeared. I was drifting along, and the banks were unchanged, when the boat just stopped moving. I looked down, and the current was gone, then I saw the stream on the riverbank, and it had not been there the moment before, nor were there the sounds of the water moving over the stones. This is the source of Lethe."

Piotyr felt dubious, as there was no way this tiny stream fed this large a body of water, but perhaps the river they had been on wasn't actually Lethe until it joined with this brook. Turning, he looked back at the river they had been traveling on and his mouth dropped in awe. Not a stone's throw upstream the river forked around a giant, black maw of a cavern which he knew had not been there when he awoke. He looked at his companion and though the undead face didn't change in the slightest, he could tell he was also surprised. This was not a place of mundane happenings.

"Look, the waters mix and drift backwards into the cave." Piotyr was sure of it. He was not an expert waterman, by any means, but he could see the current change where the waters met and could follow the different flow pattern easily with his eyes. They mixed, and the flow went upstream into the cave. Looking close at the cavern, he further noticed that the rock and dirt that made up the cavern walls around the entrance were covered in red and yellow flowers.

"You are correct, warrior. I know not what sorcery causes this, but you are correct. This is the water we need."

Piotyr frowned. "Which water, my friend? Where we are drifting? The water by the cave? Beyond it upstream now that it has mixed? Up the stream on the riverbank? I believe you are right, we are here, but which source should we collect? Han didn't say anything about this."

"I imagine he didn't know. I doubt anyone knows, at least not anyone who hasn't been dead since antiquity. I told you, the Fallen don't come here, it's too dangerous and too close to the border with Paradise."

"Well... the only stories I know of men who supposedly came to Hell as mortals are vague, ancient, and considered art rather than history. Admittedly I wish I knew them by heart now, but I don't, and I suspect they wouldn't tell us everything anyway. What should we do?"

They were silent a moment, and a great breathing came out of the cave, as if a giant beast was exhaling. *Not even mother's mighty lungs could expel that much air. Be wary, Father. A mighty foe slumbers in those depths.*

He and The First looked at each other for a long moment before Piotyr shrugged. In that moment, he wasn't sure of what to do, but given the chance that he could be wrong no matter what he chose, he thought it wise to get off the river and investigate the stream. If they were wrong and it didn't pan out, they could always come back and delve the cave. "Let's tie the boat off and go for a walk. We can stretch our legs as we look for a source up the stream."

The First nodded. "I don't see any reason to go into the cavern first, since we don't know. However, once we step off the bank we will be walking towards Paradise, and away from Hell. Things may change in unforeseen ways."

Piotyr snorted. Paradise. Heaven. Elysium. Nirvana. Foolishness. Piotyr believed that such a place existed, he had seen too much stark evidence of its opposite to believe otherwise, but he also believed it was not a place mortals could, or ever would attain. No angels had come when the demons invaded, and for six centuries God had ignored the pleas of humanity as it was ravaged and rent. What good was such a place if you could never go there unless you were dead, and even then only if a demon didn't snatch up your soul beforehand to do with as it pleased?

He had seen with his own eyes the blade of a Ba'al cut a Templar in two. The man had been a friend, Aristan, and as true and kind hearted as a friend could be. The Ba'al had severed his torso from his legs, and Piotyr had seen *something* rise from the body in some sort of white mist. The Ba'al had inhaled it like smelling a roast pig, and laughed as he taunted the other Templar. *"Whose soul shall I taste next?!"*

The battle had been a rout to begin with, and in truth Piotyr thought he was going to die that day, but some other Templar had Invoked the Apotheosis. He never learned who. Only he and Jacob had survived and the bodies of the Templar were too many for the two of them to retrieve. They had left ahead of Legion reinforcements, but he still remembered what he saw. Aristan's soul was consumed by the Ba'al. No Paradise had awaited *him*.

"To Paradise then. Let us see where this stream comes from."

chapter fourteen

Golems are impractical as an instrument of war. They are difficult to make, indiscriminate in their violence, and slow in their movements.
- Patriarch Quintus Salvius Meles

Han had not been kidding when he spoke of the things he had intended. Joshua stood, mouth agape, at what his old friend had created from one of the lesser zombies.

Han had explained the binding ritual, and how he had anchored the wraith to the corpse, but it still seemed horrible, impossible, and yet at the same time incredibly brilliant. Han was not a man of warfare, but he had just created a terrible and mighty weapon.

The zombie was one of the simple-minded ones, created by one of the Sheol Legion falling to Joshua's plague near the end of the battle, mere minutes before Jacob had smote down the Shay'tan. As such, it was dumb, clumsy, and little more than fodder. In time, *if* it survived being hacked apart, *if* it was able to kill another sentient being, it would gain in intelligence, speed, and strength. The First had become what he was through many such encounters, culminating with being the primary zombie that was with Joshua when they killed Ba'al Am, and even that mighty soul had been shared among many of the stronger undead.

There were a few Zombie Lords that were relatively close to The First in terms of development, and of course Secundus who was nearly there already, but by far the vast majority of Joshua's undead forces were like the wretch that stood before them. It could follow basic instructions and could tell friend from foe, but its attacks were clumsy and slow. It took many of them to bring down seasoned Legionnaire, and even when they did it was only the walker who landed the killing blow who absorbed their soul and became stronger.

That was why what Han had done was so brilliant, and repulsive.

"Again, release another one." Han spoke confidently and expectantly. Joshua was surprised to see the Seneschal move quickly to accommodate his old friend.

The strange canine-looking beast bolted forward into the fighting pit and tore into the zombie, which lurched awkwardly as it was mauled, futilely attempting to swing at the four-legged predator. It was a gross spectacle, even considering that Joshua had seen it just a few minutes earlier. The canine ripped at the rotting flesh of the zombie, tearing giant pieces out of it as the undead moaned and flailed about on the sand of the pit.

Anyone watching would have noticed it was a fight that the undead couldn't win, but after a few moments the dog started yelping in pain, then whimpering before finally laying still. Bizarre, yet far less strange than the ruined flesh of the zombie knitting back together and the thing rising... and appearing to move somewhat faster and with more coordination.

"Again, Seneschal."

The ancient Fallen nodded and gave the signal for another one to enter the arena, and again the same result happened, though the zombie put up a somewhat better fight. They repeated the process six times, and by the end the zombie grabbed the dog out of the air mid-leap, and calmly ripped its throat out.

"This is remarkable, Han. You say you can do this with the entire force of undead?" Joshua was still unsettled, but he appreciated the scope and potential in the process.

"Yes, though it will take time. It would be faster with sentient subjects, but even I have limits. Any life will do, but the more advanced, the better the results are. I have already begun, and intend to burn the midnight oil for some time. The Seneschal has already begun searching the remains of the city for intelligent mortals and Fallen to assist me. Without the water Piotyr and The First are gathering, we can't progress further on the vaccine, but we can quarantine those who are susceptible and those who aren't will be put to work helping us in some way."

Joshua was quiet for a moment, fearing what the answer to his question would be. "Do you intend to give people a choice, Han?"

His friend looked at him, and to Joshua it seemed Han was angry to some extent, but also sad. "No, I do not. But they will be fed, paid, and cared for. I wish there was another way, Joshua, but we need hands and bodies to do what needs to be done. I need zombies organized, cataloged, and prepared for the process. God willing I will find at least another man or woman, mortal or Fallen, who can perform the ritual once I show them. If not, I will work myself to exhaustion preparing the city, which will leave me little time or energy to oversee the other details. The surviving people of Sheol *must* be put to work repairing the walls and doing whatever else I need doing. I trust the Seneschal to follow my instructions, but there is so much that needs to be done. I would ask for your help, if you can give it, and if you can understand and forgive me my lapses in morality. I am trying to save us."

Joshua immediately felt bad for bringing it up. In his heart he wished it was as simple as the people being liberated and going about their lives with impunity, but it was not so. Every person in Sheol would die violently if Abaddon arrived without defenses being prepared. It was necessary. Han knew it, Joshua knew it, and neither of them needed to remind them of it.

He cleared his throat before continuing. "I will do what you need, Han, as long as I have the means."

"You do, old friend, though you won't love the work. I need you to supervise a team of engineers who are going to work on a grid of waterways out in the valley."

Joshua was intrigued. "Waterways? Why would you want to create more irrigation canals out there?"

Han smiled, and it was not one of mirth or warmth. It was cold, and to Joshua's eyes, sadistic. He worried about this process changing Han. He was not a cruel man, and this was cruel business.

"The waterways aren't for crops; they are to spread your contagion. I'm going to infect the forces of Abaddon faster and more directly than just proximity to the infected. I'm going to decimate his forces as they approach."

Joshua sighed, but knew better than to argue, not to mention it was a great idea. The more of them killed out there, the more would rise as zombies in their midst and slow down the onslaught looking to swarm the walls of Sheol. It still didn't make it enjoyable to partake in.

"Very well, I shall do what you need. What else needs to be done right now?"

"Everything, Joshua, but one thing at a time."

Chapter Fifteen

First give me a honey-cake, for to descend down there sets me all a-tremble; it looks like the cave of Trophonius.
- Strepsiades: The Clouds

It was no longer interesting for either of them to kill each other. His blade had silenced the breathing of the man several more times, but no more or less than his own brains had been spattered out by the man's flanged mace.

Clearly this was some sort of Purgatory. The two of them seemed destined to fight and slay each other indefinitely. It was a clear waste of an otherwise enjoyable afterlife. *Still, I was here first, damnit.*

He laughed, and enjoyed a bite of wild apple as he waited. He still wasn't hungry, though. This time would be different, and he knew it was coming soon. He whistled an old tune to himself and kept watch on the entrance to the clearing he had relocated to.

He had set traps all around the clearing, and unless the man was a ghost there was no way he could sneak up on him while he ate at the campfire. That left one way in, which had been deliberately left alone so as to encourage the stranger to come that route. He was tired of this game, and wanted an end to it.

For however long it had been, he had been alone here, and he was not interested in spending eternity fighting this man over nothing. True, the valley wasn't huge, but it was big enough for the two of them to share. He would offer a peace, and hoped the man would accept it. Constant, daily resurrection was not appealing.

It was not long that he had to sit and wait before he saw the brushes part at the entrance to the clearing. Sure enough, the stranger emerged after a moment and stopped at the edge of the cleared brush. The two men stared for a long moment, and in that silence it was as if a mutual agreement to cease their fighting occurred. He raised his hand in greeting, and the stranger returned the gesture. They would kill each other no longer.

Asya was short of temper as well as sad, since her falling out with her mate. Ulis and Aruc sensed her being on edge, and stayed far away from her cave on the caldera. She missed them, but they were grown now and did not need her to care for them as they once did. Nor did Piotyr, but his absence hurt and angered her.

Since the raid on the Ba'al with the horrible arrows of ice, she could scarcely believe that her love would wish to continue on with his stupid war. They had *all* almost died, and it was not worth tempting fate.

She loved him with all her soul, but she would not risk her children... her *remaining* children in pursuing the ambitions of mortals or Fallen. She knew Lokyrg was still around, in a way, but it was not the same. He had no flesh, and could not hunt, and though she knew it was futile to hope for her drakes to breed, Lokyrg didn't even have that possibility.

It was abhorrent for her to consider Ulis and Aruc mating, but if enough time went by, she feared they would have no choice. Piotyr was a blessing, but his seed could not restore their line alone. They needed more stock to breed with. It would be centuries before her drakes could shapechange into a suitable mating form for either a mortal or a Fallen, and *no* chance of finding one their hellfire wouldn't burn to ash. A long time for her offspring to be safe and willing to hold off their instincts, and a second source of breeding stock was unlikely. She had *some* time, at least, before she had to worry about that.

For now, the two dragons hunted together without her, and she was fine with that. They were smart, and both their instincts and their father's training had prepared them well for any risks from the Ba'al and their forces. Not to mention, most of the Legion for thousands of miles around the caldera had marshaled their forces and marched on Sheol weeks ago. Aruc and Ulis had the benefit of hunting the dregs and weaklings of the Fallen society. They were better than that, but it still made Asya feel better that there was almost no chance of them facing any real danger.

All that mattered little, though, as she *needed* Piotyr to return to her, safe and cured of his damned foolish ideas about helping the same beings that had hunted her kind near to extinction. *Let* this thing called the Destroyer come and earn his namesake. Hell would be better the more Legion and Fallen that Ba'al Apollyon could wipe out and that that madman Han could kill defending the ruins of the city.

Asya sighed and tried to be fair. Han had saved Lokyrg... in a fashion, and he had done what he could to protect them during the attack at Sheol, but she was still angry with Piotyr for taking them there in the first place. She had trusted him, and it had cost her Lokyrg, at least most of him. It did comfort her that his soul survived in the weapon of Ba'al Moloch, but better would have been for all of them to remain out of the battle completely and living isolated and free.

You know he never could have stayed; he had to go to his kind. Asya hated her own voice of reason, but knew it to be true. Piotyr was not a Hellfire wyrm, and never would be. She loved him as fiercely as any wyrm, but he was still a mortal, if a rare example of one. In truth, until Ba'al Mirish, she was enjoying the diversion and the power she felt hunting with Piotyr.

She didn't want him to come with her because he felt compelled; she wanted him to choose it naturally. Sheol was not a place for their kind... and sadly she hoped that it was not a place for Piotyr either. She could do it by herself, but it was... *nice* having him with her the last time. Placing her hand over her abdomen and wishing he was with her now, Asya silently gave voice to the hope that he would return to her. He was her mate.

Standing outside the tent of him who the mortals called The Destroyer, Ba'al Mirish stood patiently awaiting new orders from the General. When he had first been told of the plan to entrap the Templar Piotyr and his Hellfire wyrms, he was apprehensive, but the boldness and creativity of the ruse made him anxious to try. He wondered if it was simple coincidence that had left as heirlooms in House Mirish a modest supply of Cocytus Ice, or if there was some sort of providence involved. Fingering his bow, and knowing in his heart that he was arguably the greatest archer in all the realms of Hell, he liked to think the latter.

True he had failed to kill Piotyr, or the Wyrms, but Ba'al Apollyon had been more than understanding, and in fact had commended him for grievously wounding the entire group by himself. Mirish was not immune to vanity, but coming from Apollyon it was different. It was like praise from the Shay'tan, but it felt earned.

Ba'al Mirish had always thought Ba'al Apollyon was a more superior leader than Lucifer, and certainly than either of the heirs. He would never have questioned the Morning Star, but privately many of the decisions made by the Shay'tan were too rooted in pride. He was never able to make concessions in looking at the larger scope of things. Not so with Abaddon the Destroyer. Mirish respected the man as a General, but also for his patience and skill at maneuvering the political death field that was Sheol. He smiled. The fact that Ba'al Toly'm still drew breath was testament that Apollyon was a wise ruler. Lucifer, or any of his heirs, would have slain the man the second he opened his mouth. He bet Ba'alat Ve'kal had *not* expected that.

When Lucifer's heir killed his father, everyone with even half a mind for intrigue knew who was responsible, but why question it? It was not even discovered until the portals had opened and the war was joined in full. Mirish remembered the arrogance of Lucifer and how dismissive he was of the mortals' ability to fight back. Not so with Ba'al Apollyon. When the nuclear fire came and incinerated Legion by the millions, Lucifer's heir proved no more patient or adept at understanding war than his predecessor. He raged and screamed and demanded the seed of Adam be rent unto death at once, and it was a calm, stoic Apollyon who had simply told him that he would give him victory in time.

The war had gone favorably at first, but it did not last. Yes, the initial horror and terror of the populace did the mortals no favors, but they recovered quickly and turned an extinction event quickly into a prolonged conflict of legitimate warfare. It galled Mirish to admit it, but it was the Fallen, not the mortals who were more unprepared for the conflict. The War in Heaven had been complicated in origin, but simple in execution. Those such as he, who had sided with Lucifer, warred with the Seraphim who were loyal to the Throne. With Sword and Flame the war was fought, and the side of the Morning Star lost. It was that simple.

The mortals had been completely different. When the Legion came in fire and blood, Lucifer had not planned on organized military resistance, though his son should have. It was not to preserve Legion life that the heir slew the father, it was for pride, nothing more.

Mirish smirked at that thought. Of course it was for pride. That's how the whole thing began anyway. Fitting that it would end that way. Nuclear fire, monstrous machines on the sea, air, and land, and troops in the billions responded to the wave of death that came through the portals. Mirish had been foolish then, and believed Lucifer's lies that it would be a slaughter and that Earth would be theirs in days. Not so Ba'al Apollyon.

True, with the Shay'tan dead and no one knowing it, all they had to go on in those first days was the strategy already set in place. Also true was that Lucifer's Heir was a coward for not announcing what he had done as soon as it was apparent that the war would *not* be over in days and that the mortals were fighting back in a capacity no one could have predicted.

Damned mortals. They should know their place like the ones born here do. Mirish spat on the ground as he waited, not out of impatience but out of frustration for how long the war had taken. Six centuries! Six damned centuries of conflict with the mortals, and Lucifer had said it would be *days* until it was over. Pride was one thing, but secretly Mirish was glad the stupidity of the

Morning Star was finally out of the bloodline of ascendency. If it had been Apollyon leading the battle from the beginning, it wouldn't have been so fucking hard.

He shrugged. *Maybe* it wouldn't have been so hard. He remembered being scared three times in his entire life. For more than ten thousand years of memories, three instances of real fear.

The first was on the fourth day of open conflict in Elysium. He had mistakenly drawn the attention of Uriel in a skirmish and the Archangel had locked his terrible wrath-filled eyes upon Mirish and the Ba'al had known he was going to die. Nothing stood against the seven in those days, save Lucifer himself, and it was not as if Lucifer was able to defeat any of them. He merely stood his ground in battle. The seven were untouchable by the likes of Mirish.

He had fled, and felt no shame in it. His bow skills were legendary among the Host, and he had drawn Uriel's attention rightly. However, he did not follow the Morning Star to die. *No, I followed him to be cast into a shithole for the next epoch of history.*

The second was on the third day of the war on Earth. The first day was an orgy of violence, rape, and desecration. Some of it had even been too distasteful for him, but he understood the hatred. Uppity mortals had it coming, but that was really just the first day. On day two, their unabated wanton destruction of civilization was noticeably harder and the mortals were damned organized and motivated. He remembered clearly what it was like stepping through the portals and carving through shrieking, terrified humans, then all of a sudden facing down a determined *soldier* focused and determined to blow Mirish's head off. Night and day.

That was day two. On day three, he saw the Skyfire, and he nearly shit himself. *Mortals* had created a weapon that made The Sword of Michael look like a matchstick. Of course the Fallen knew of that shit, some had even claimed to have seen it used, but again the arrogance of the Shay'tan had been pervasive and no one was worried about it until it happened and the shockwave was blowing apart their ranks. He knew it was coming when the cloud formed, and he fled that day too. No shame there either. Mirish was not stupid, and he would not die due to incompetence of leadership.

The third time he felt fear was that fateful day in Mexico. They didn't call it that anymore, not for a long time, but it was Mexico, and always would be to him. It was another scorched earth assault, and Mirish had been involved in several. There were several Ba'al involved that day, and Mirish was the only one not vying for control. He was back in the trees awaiting the all-clear that the walls were breached; when the word was passed back that something was butchering the Legion along the walls. To this day it amazed him that he was the only one with any sense that day. *You have been slaughtering the humans in their Sanctuaries for years, with no surprises, and suddenly you are being massacred and no one bats an eye?*

He didn't even wait to hear more. He just returned to the portal and left. If any idiots had survived he supposed he would have been labeled a deserter, but the fact that he was the only surviving Fallen from that engagement did little to increase Mirish's desire to give a damn. He didn't know at the time that the Soulfire had just been discovered, but he did know it was bad for his side, so he fucking left. Now skip forward a few more generations and he was still alive and well. Not many were the remaining original Fallen who fell with Lucifer so long ago, but Mirish was one of them, and piss on the others not smart enough to be here standing with him.

Hence his respect for Apollyon. Also with Lucifer from the start, Apollyon never was one for pride, or ambition. Lucifer used to mock him for having chosen the wrong side, since his primary governing principles were loyalty and justice.

Mirish smiled to remember Apollyon, deadpanning his response some millennia ago... "Justice is why I followed you."

The Destroyer was something else. Mirish knew any of the Ba'al, even to a lesser extent any Fallen or Legion or hell, even a mortal with the right moral inclination could access the latent power of the Shay'tan. Apollyon was something unique. No one else could manifest like he did. Pity he could only do it very rarely and not at all since this bullshit with House Ve'kal had started.

Can you call it bullshit? A mortal bested an heir of Lucifer, and the Shay'tan was cast down. True enough. Mirish couldn't be so cavalier about it, and the fact that the mortal called Piotyr had survived his attack made him stay his own arrogance. Mortals had proven how resilient they were, and these Templar in Hell had done so tenfold.

The rumors were that Kasim had survived as well, which completely baffled Mirish. The Grigori simply didn't fail, and eye witnesses to the attack saw him kissed by hellfire and shot point blank by a Watcher assassin. The man should be dead thrice over, and yet rumors were prevalent that he lived and that the other damned Templar were healing him!

Mirish hadn't been at Sheol, but he had heard of it. They shouldn't take these mortals lightly. Apollyon wasn't, and that was comforting. He had planned the ambush for Piotyr and the assassination of Kasim with thoughtful precision, and though not wholly successful the attacks had not been failures to be sure.

The wyrms had left, Piotyr had vanished, and Kasim... if he actually was alive, was stripped of his followers and likely maimed beyond any ability to fight.

Han and Joshua, the other two, still had to be dealt with, but they would be, in time. In fact, he half-expected that was what this summons was for, and that Ba'al Apollyon would have something for Mirish to do involving the last two Templar threats.

He wished the war was over, but he was enjoying this. He actually believed in Apollyon, and if anyone could finally finish this thing, it was him. He smiled as a herald announced that Abaddon would see him now. Things were moving along nicely.

The grasslands had climbed quickly into hills and then rose sharply into mountains so high that Piotyr got a headache looking to their heights.

"There is no chance we can get up there. We'll be at it for weeks, if not months. We don't have the time, and I know a thing or two about climbing up mountains." He sighed, and looked to the undead for agreement.

"Warrior, I am inclined to agree with you as a matter of practicality, but even beyond that those mountains lie not in Hell.

We look upon Elysium's borders. We must hope the waters we seek are not this way, or we are doomed to fail."

Piotyr cursed inwardly. They had journeyed for three days to get here, following the stream into the hills. The water was a direct line to the mountains, no other water bled into it, at least not aboveground. "Come on, we should get going back."

They turned to leave, and Piotyr fumed at the wasted time. He needed this to be over with. He needed to get Han this water, he needed Joshua to cure Kasim, and he needed Joshua to be cured as well. He needed to feel *useful* and he needed to get back to his family.

He had tried his best not to think of Asya or the drakes, but the First wasn't much of a talker and Lokyrg had grown moody and sullen in the hours upon hours of nothing happening. He missed Aruc and Ulis, and he missed Asya terribly. His guilt over the Ba'al with the Heart of Cocytus gnawed away at him, but he did his best to move past it and focus on the good he could potentially be doing.

If it didn't take three days there and three days back for no good reason, that is. The Templar was trying to think of something funny to say to lighten the mood when he heard something out of place. He stopped to listen, holding up his hand when the First looked to him questioningly.

"Do you hear that? Sounds like a waterfall." The zombie cocked his head to the side, and after a moment nodded his head. "I do. It was not there a moment ago, but yes I hear it as well."

Piotyr had excellent hearing, and he agreed that it wasn't there a moment ago. He got excited. *An intermittent waterfall? Doubtful. A geyser or a spring? Much more likely.* He ran towards the sound, sprinting with enthusiasm.

What is it Father?

Maybe nothing, but maybe our next water sample. We'll see.

Piotyr and the First had run for a couple of minutes when the sound stopped. Frustrated, Piotyr stopped, placed Lokyrg on the ground, knelt, and closed his eyes to listen.

He heard nothing for a long ten count, and becoming angry he opened his eyes to look around, holding his breath with his eyes climbing high on head. He was looking down a sheer drop of thousands of feet to the valley below, and the rock he was kneeling on was slippery from the heavy water vapor dusting the air.

Instinctively he stood and pressed back against the cliff face, and looked around him, not seeing any way up or down from the narrow ledge he was standing on. *What the hell?*

He didn't have Lokyrg with him any longer, and the First was nowhere to be seen. It was just him, wearing clothing ill-suited to a climb like this. Thank God he had left his armor at the boat. He would have plummeted like a stone wearing his plate here. He had no idea how he got there, or how he was going to get down. *I could always jump, as long as the fall doesn't kill me instantly I can use Hellfire to heal myself.*

Looking down, he thought better of it. He hadn't tested a sheer fall since arriving at Asya's caldera so long ago, and wasn't confident that the fall in fact, *wouldn't* kill him immediately. It had to be better than half a mile down.

Sighing, he started inching his way along the ledge, hoping to find a way either up or down. The rock was slick as ice, so he went very slowly. Algae covered most of the stone at his back as well, so he was about as far from sure-footed as he could ever recall being. He was grinding his teeth as he went, nervous about his footing and worried about how he had gotten there. Yet more unpredictability on this accursed river journey.

He had gone perhaps fifty paces, maybe not even that, which took him the better part of an hour, when he rounded a small corner and panicked as he slipped and began to fall. Thinking he was about to find out whether the fall would kill him he was surprised to find that the cliff face behind him opened up and he fell into the opening of a cavern.

Below his feet, dangling off the edge of the rock as he sat down thankful to have more room, was a small slope of rocky debris, coated with algae and disappearing into thin air as the cave and slope met the giant drop-off.

The water must come from inside here before falling down the cliff and forming that stream. Maybe I'm in luck and this is the source.

He stood, and walked inside the cave, sticking to the sides which were dry. Shivering, he channeled some hellfire, carefully, to warm himself while not damaging his sample collection kit.

It was a small cave, only barely taller than he was, so he found himself ducking as a precaution. It was dark but not pitch black as he could see his way fairly well, but he Invoked Night Seeing and was happy to see the cavern light up in a soft green glow.

He had only walked for a few minutes when the cavern opened up into a large room and daylight spilled in from a skylight far above him. Dismissing his Invocation, he walked into the room and was filled with wonder.

It was perhaps the size of a small chapel in Haven. The light drifted down lazily over an array of diverse plant life the likes he hadn't seen in one place in his whole life. Exotic flowers, beautiful plants, and even dozens of types of fungus were all growing over nearly every inch of the cave floor save the channel leading out of the room, and he could see insects and small lizards and mammals scurrying around.

In the center of the room was what he assumed to be the source of the spring, as there was a stone basin, rough but clearly worn down from water, that looked to be natural and not carved by man. More strange, was a chair, table, and cot next to the basin. All three were simple wooden pieces, with a few books on the table and a plain woolen blanket on the bed.

He walked the rest of the way into the room, and was struck by the beauty and sanctity of the place. The sunlight bathed the room in a warm light, and air held a perfect amount of crispness while not cold. It smelled clean, rather than musty, and he felt refreshed and restored. He would be very careful not to accidentally burn any of the flora or fauna in the cave.

His reverie was interrupted by the sound of a vibrating hum coming from deep within the mountain, getting louder quickly. Assuming what it was, he was not surprised when the basin suddenly sprouted a geyser, strong but not explosive, and quickly filled with water before spilling out into the channel and running out of the cave. He could hear the newborn stream rush off the edge before plummeting the thousands of feet to the valley floor below.

He carefully stepped over the water flow, and took a seat on the chair next to the basin, noticing a pair of stone cups sitting on table. He sat for a long time, just watching the water and listening to the peaceful fount in the cave. He smiled, and breathed in the serenity and contentment permeating the chamber. He had not felt so content in a long while. Certainly not as happy as when he was in Asya's arms, but at peace.

The water ran for perhaps half an hour before Piotyr heard the hum stop and his mind was redirected to his task. Sighing, both pleased with how he felt and also wistful that the water was departing, he stood and retrieved the cups and filled them while the basin was still full, having to hurry to get his ladle filled before the water receded. He placed the full cups on the table, and filled two of his small vials from the ladle, one for him and one for the undead, then watched the water level quickly subside and retreat back down into the mountain. He was barely able to get another ladle filled for the mixed phial before the water was gone. At least he got enough for his samples.

He smelled the water, noticing how thirsty he actually was, and that the water's scent was incredible. Clean, crisp, with minerals that made his mouth water. He was glad he filled both cups. One filled another sample for the First's mixed phial, just in case, to take back to Han, and now the other for a deep draught to sate his thirst. He lifted the cup to his lips and was just about to drink deeply when a voice cut through the cave and startled him.

"You would not be the first mortal to ignore the warning signs, but you would be the first I actually interrupted."

Piotyr turned, and surprising even himself, he wasn't angry, or concerned, or even really surprised to find another person here. After all, someone used the furniture.

A woman, older than he was but not by a lot, stood before him. She wore a simple white linen robe and had skin darker than his, more akin to Kasim, and startling green eyes staring piercingly at him underneath long hair the color of copper.

"I mean no disrespect, but I see no warning signs. Of what do you speak?" Piotyr felt utterly at peace with the woman and the cave, and felt no harm in showing deference. It was not his home.

"Do you not know of the properties of the poppy? Or the dangers of the water here? I was led to believe that the five of you were informed men. In fact I was told on high authority."

"Well, far be it from me to argue with a high authority, but who knows of me or my brothers and has come to speak of us to you?"

The woman was silent for a moment, pursing her lips in thought. "I fear that I have a story to tell you that you will not remember when you leave here, unless you are prepared for a difficult journey. I can share much with you, but first I must see that you are prepared to hear it."

Piotyr again mused that he felt no fear from this strange woman. He was not threatened by her in the slightest, though he felt power and confidence from her radiating like the sun. Like Asya, though serene and quiet whereas his love was primal and chaotic. "I shall hear what you wish of me, then, so long as I am free to leave when I choose."

The woman looked at Piotyr for a long moment, and then smiled bemusedly. "How interesting. There is so much blood on your soul that you are half prepared already. Will you do what I ask of you, Piotyr Lamja?"

He nodded, feeling acceptance and no impatience at all, which surprised him, though he couldn't tell why. "What do I need to do first?"

"Pour out that water, you are doing it all wrong."

The First was not prone to worry, but when the Templar had vanished hours ago, leaving his son, the dragon-spear on the ground and not returning for hours, he felt what he could only call anxiety. This was not a place to tarry. The sound of the water had stopped abruptly earlier in the day, and with it the warrior had simply disappeared.

The First had waited patiently, in truth he could wait indefinitely if he so chose, but at some point he would have to leave and attempt to complete their task. Joshua had entrusted them to retrieve the waters of Hell, and so he would, with or without the mortal. As the day drifted into twilight and now into full darkness, his concern in no way approached fear, but he did have a hard decision to make. This close to the border of Elysium he ran the risk of being seen by a Soldier of the Choir. Unlikely, but still a risk. He had no fear of being able to take a lowly angel in battle, or even a squad, but of greater danger would be if they didn't engage him, and instead reported back to a superior.

His own battle prowess was on par with a Ba'al, easily, which would translate to the mightiest of the Cherubim, but it would be impossible for him to remain long if even one Cherubim fell to him in battle. A Seraph would come, with a large contingent of the Choir, and he would be no match.

Piotyr would not be, either, but the two of them together might be, at least he would feel confident enough to attempt such an encounter. The Seraph were not quite the equal of the Shay'tan in combat, but close, probably even better without the power of the Infernal Throne. He checked his thoughts before they ran away from him. What he accepted as truth was only secondhand knowledge from his millennia of amalgamated experience, but enough of it was in agreement for him to believe.

He needed Piotyr to return within a day or he wouldn't risk staying. He would take the water sample he could obtain down at the larger river and continue on to Phlegethon. If it was wrong, then there was nothing else he could have done. He moved closer to the now empty pool at the base of the waterfall, and crept into a dark hollow of shadow against the cliff. He would wait another day.

chapter sixteen

There hath no temptation taken you but such as is common to man: but God is faithful, who will not suffer you to be tempted above that ye are able; but will with the temptation also make a way to escape, that ye may be able to bear it.
- Corinthians 10:14

"So we are in agreement then? No more killing?" He found the actual size of the man unsettling, but he did not think it was a Ba'al he broke bread with. This was a mortal, and he wanted no more bloodshed.

"No more killing. I... I am sorry for my part in it. In truth I thought I was dead, and was not thinking clearly when I acted that way. I will not raise my hand against you."

Hand? He was fine with the hand, it was that goddamned mace he didn't want raised against him. "I am sorry as well. I have been alone for so long I have forgotten how to be human."

The alien-looking mortal gave him a strange look and tilted his head. "That is something I could say myself, but tell me, you *are* human, aren't you?"

"Oh yes, nothing but. Aren't you?"

"No. Well I was, but not anymore."

"How the hell does that work?"

"How does what work?"

"You aren't human, but you were. How did that happen?"

"It's a long story."

He laughed with such genuine mirth that the erstwhile mortal in front of him stopped scowling and laughed too. "You have somewhere to be?"

Dhermina was proud of what she and Joshua had accomplished in a few short days time. She was no engineer, but needed the distraction and Han was pleased to put her to work. The latticework of waterways was complete, and though the water was putrid and stinking, she smiled and thought about how virulent the plague was and how fast it would spread through Ba'al Apollyon's forces.

"Not bad, if I do say so. I was skeptical, but Han is proving to be quite adept at this war business."

As usual she felt sorry for the man; Joshua's wheezing and rasping breath clearly showing how miserable he was. "Yes, I had not known him before, but Kasim spoke of him as a kind-hearted, bookish man. This idea is something more like what your friend Jacob would have devised, I should think."

The man laughed, hacking and spitting phlegm on the ground as he did. "You would think right. Jacob was the best when it came to this. Piotyr could out-chop him in a fight, but Jacob was devious, and cunning. He and a squad of four Templar killed forty seasoned Legionnaire a few years ago with traps, ambushes, and guerilla tactics. Took them two months, but they didn't lose a man. Piotyr loves that story, you should ask him about it when he gets back."

If he gets back. No, don't think like that. He will return, and Kasim will be healed. "I will, when he has time. I expect the three of you will be busy when he does."

"Yes, I suppose we will. The four of us, though. Kasim will play a part, too."

"He may not be conscious. What could he do to help?" She was honestly surprised; she hadn't expected Kasim would need to be awake.

"Oh I can get him up, no fear of that." His chest rattled and clicked, and he stopped for a coughing fit before continuing, gesturing at the fields. "I have a gift for this... vileness, but I'm a better healer than I am plague bearer. Once I have the water samples I will need to bleed Kasim and work quickly. The process Han and I devised is part alchemy, part prayer, and part science, but I think it will work."

She dared to hope, but also didn't want to be rude. "What about your own cure? Han spoke of it healing your disease as well."

"Humph. Of that I am less confident. I believe that the ritual performed to send me here altered my body and soul permanently. Han does not share that belief, and for my sake I hope I'm wrong."

She smiled at him, and placed her hand on his shoulder. "For your sake I hope you are wrong, too."

He smiled back. "Kasim will walk again, I promise you that. I questioned Han at length about the process, and his plans, but he knows more about this place than I do, and though I can't fathom how, he hasn't failed yet. Have you seen what he did with the undead?"

"No, but I heard of it. Something about binding a spirit to the body of the zombie and it consuming opponents even as the zombie is killed... or destroyed I suppose?"

"That's where it started, but he also brought out the juvenile forms of those flesh leeches... wait do you know about the masque he was put in by Ba'al Moloch?"

"Not directly, though I've seen him carry it and Piotyr told me it was a horrible thing."

"To put it mildly. Anyway the masques are the larva, and the juvenile form is a larger parasite that Han has repurposed."

"Repurposed? Where did he find them?"

"In the bowels of the Sheol dungeon. He told me there are terrible things down there, things he isn't willing to share with anyone, not until he has a chance to study them more. He said he almost died twice, and Han isn't prone to exaggeration. I believe him, and he said the masque juveniles are only about halfway up the chain in terms of horror."

Dhermina shuddered. Her life at Sagarmatha had not been unpleasant, but in some ways she lamented how sheltered she was. Becoming wistful, she lamented how sheltered they all had been. She missed her brothers and sisters.

Joshua had stopped talking, and cleared his throat before speaking again softly. "I didn't mean to upset you. I agree that the things are terrible, I just thought..."

She shook her head and smiled again. "I'm not bothered by that. I was just thinking of things past. Go on."

He blinked, and cleared his throat again before continuing. "Right, well he found the juvenile incubation vault and took one up and implanted it into a zombie. He said it wouldn't work without the wraith as well since the parasite would just consume the host, but since the wraith can regenerate the flesh the parasite can feed, and feed, and feed. They will basically live forever as long as the undead can keep finding fresh meat to corrupt."

"How does that help? Won't the parasite just sit there eating?"

"Ahem, well it has a preference for... well... fresh? Yes fresh meat, and if exposed to a living entity the hunger is pretty dramatic. I would suggest going and observing a specimen test, but don't eat first."

That was enough for her, she believed him.

Ve'kal could not believe the developments brought about by Han. Her despair had not lifted, not yet, but it had certainly been mixed with a lot of curiosity. She admonished herself silently. Curiosity was long past, now she had to admit she was impressed. She forgave the man his insolence. He was a gifted scholar of death.

The walls were not complete yet, but the rate at which they rose staggered her. Han's undead were like ants constructing a new colony. She had foolishly thought too many of them to be imbecilic and useless, but Han's willingness to cannibalize the lesser ones to make more advanced walkers was thoughtful. The introduction of the wraiths and the blood leeches was a stroke of genius. Even that was carefully orchestrated, as Han had been incredibly cautious in exposure of the evolved zombies to any other moving creature, living or otherwise.

He had quarantined each of the different populations that he was using, and it was very effective. The humans cleared and sorted non-dangerous debris, the ones not already immune from Joshua's plague having been given some sort of temporary vaccine. She had been told it would not prevent the disease forever, but he said it would prevent infection for the several weeks he needed it to. More to his credit, he had mandated that every able pair of hands join the war effort, not giving anyone a chance to opt out.

She had misjudged him, though she dared not think he was an equal to Jacob in warfare. Still, his mind was incredibly keen, and the preparations were moving forward so quickly that she feared Ba'al Apollyon would march soon.

The valley fields, so recently lush with crops had been turned into a quagmire of decay and pestilence. The waterways stretched to the hills around Sheol's valley, and any siege army would be ravaged in the crossing. The walls themselves would be rebuilt soon, and Han had used his strange power to dig a ten foot trench all the way around the outside of the walls. She had noted, and not pleasantly, that the Seneschal... she checked herself... *her* Seneschal had lost his derision when relaying Han's progress to her. She wanted to be in charge, she felt the need to be in charge, but Han did not answer to her, and he had made that clear. She no longer wanted to kill the man, having proven himself to be competent in surprising ways, but she felt relegated to an unnecessary position.

She had marched on Sheol with Jacob to assume the mantle of Shay'tan herself, not to sit idly by while mortals protected the city. *Protected the Throne, which is mine by right.* Sighing, she remembered her shame as the two mortals looked on when she tried to take the Throne. Not Templar, the men had vanished right after her embarrassing attempt. It wasn't vacant and she feared the cause. *What if Jacob had not killed Lucifer's Heir? What if the Shay'tan was just mortally wounded and could return...*

She banished the thought. Jacob had promised he would spend his soul to kill the Shay'tan, and spend it he did. The cataclysm had destroyed the city and tens of thousands of lives in an instant and if the Shay'tan had survived, she would have heard of it by now. Abaddon would have as well, and would not be amassing an army to take the Throne by force. He would be searching for the Heir. Sheol would be a secondary priority.

Looking out across the plains, she knew she was not a secondary priority. *Other than to Han, that is. He could care less if I knew of his plans.* Abaddon was coming, and he was coming for her.

Kasim had been able to venture briefly into the good door, as he had taken to thinking of it as. The bad door still beckoned and although he knew he was distilling a very esoteric and mystical concept into stark terminology, he still felt that it was a simple matter of good or bad. Unfortunately, it appeared that in his current condition he would be unable to achieve the transcendence he felt awaited him through the far right portal.

He had tried to enter the paradise again, more than once, yet the five threads attached to his soul always prevented him, just as when he entered oblivion, they left him and he felt free to choose as he wished.

He was not prone to fear, yet he could not deny that to truly enter the blackness terrified him as nothing ever had. The contrast between the two was so strong as to defy explanation. His soul called out for the joy and bliss of the sun, his love, and peace to be found through the fifth door. His soul shrank and cowered, transfixed in abject horror at what waited through the first passage.

He had tried to go through it more than once and never made it past the first few steps when the tethers to his spirit let go and he felt free again. He backed up, turned to the paradise, and stepped in as before, yet the same occurred without fail. They snapped back into him, causing pain and disorientation, and finding himself back where he started.

There was something he was missing and he had meditated without success as to what he could not see or decipher. He did not believe in Purgatory, not in the classic sense. He was not destined to simply wait forever. He was needed by his friends and his soul mate.

Guilt and grief came to him often, his arrogance leading to the deaths of the monks from Sagarmatha. It was his pride that led to their murder, and his failure as their teacher to prevent it. Tal and Jio hurt the most, though he knew that was foolish. Ozra, Kishien, and Qor were just as young and had just as much of their life ahead of them, that they were male didn't make them lesser sacrifices in this long and bloody conflict.

He wondered where their souls had gone, now that they were dead. Han was an expert on such things, but Kasim viewed the process of death and where the soul went in a more abstract view since his journey back at Sagarmatha. Of course, there his decision to go through the fourth door, the one next to Nirvana, had happened at the end of his journey. Here it was the first thing he encountered.

He actually didn't think he was dead, unlike at Sagarmatha. There he was sure that his body had actually perished for a brief time to shock his spirit into leaving. Here he felt that he lingered near death, but for the moment was in no danger of slipping over the edge.

With Joshua and Han both watching over him, there were no better hands for his health. Dhermina would be at his side too, though he hoped not all the time. The girl had unfairly spent far too much time watching over him as he lay incapacitated. He loved her, and wanted to be with her whenever possible, but laying in a coma, she would go mad simply attending him. She also would need time to mourn her brothers and sisters from the monastery.

He gazed at the darkened door leading into despair, and again wondered if he simply had to go through there to continue his journey. It wouldn't be so terrible if he didn't have to go alone. Sighing, he focused his mind and willed himself the strength to take the step into the pitch black. Cold, oppressive darkness enveloped him like a suffocating shroud. He found it hard to breathe, and the terror began to force its way into his chest. He felt four streams of spirit release him and disperse into the gloom, and again his thoughts turned to escape and the cerulean waters near the shore of the paradise he longed for.

Except... Dhermina was not dead and would not really be there. Except... paradise though it may be, he was needed here. He would be happy, but it would be at the expense of those he loved. Dhermina would stand at the walls of Sheol with Han, Joshua, and Piotyr, and be swept away like dust. Could any paradise be called that if he only got there by abandoning those he cared for?

He steeled himself. If that door was barred to him, there was only one choice left. He thought about leaving to again gather his will, but feared to do so would be to invite the chance of indecision seizing his mind again. It was past time...

He took another step, and the door closed behind him. Utter, crushing darkness descended upon him.

"The Waters here are not meant to be consumed lightly, or without preparation."

Piotyr felt as if he was being chided for being slow in learning a lesson. The woman did not appear to be angry, but he felt he had disappointed her all the same. "I do not seek them lightly, so I am glad you stopped me. I am here for a water sample, pure and clean, of the River Lethe. Have I not found it?"

The woman looked him up and down, for what felt like the tenth time since he had arrived. "I am sensing no confusion in you, only ignorance, which can be forgiven. Do you know what would have happened had you consumed the water, Piotyr Lamja?"

"No I do not. May I ask your name, and how you know mine?"

"I have no name to give you, but you may call me The Oracle. As to how I know yours, suffice it to say that I had asked you, and you told me, before we had this conversation, and I recall it fully without having had it yet." The Oracle smiled at him, and in a previous life that smile would have enraged him. Now, he smiled back and simply accepted her peculiar answer.

"Well, Oracle, what would have happened had I drunk the water?"

"Those who drink the water but once cease to exist. Their minds are washed clean by the Mnemosyne."

He blinked, and frowned as he looked down at the water. "By cease to exist you mean it kills me?"

"No, Piotyr, I mean it washes your mind clean, and the man who you were up until the moment the water touches your lips vanishes in an instant, annihilated forever and left an empty vessel with no idea what once was."

"Well, then thank you for stopping me, Oracle. I meant no harm; I am here to help those I care for."

"Ah yes, you seek the Waters of Death for Kasim and Joshua, hoping that the Rivers of Hell can restore their life and health."

"I suppose I told you this in a conversation we also haven't had yet?"

"No, though you did confirm as much. I knew it beforehand, though, told from a traveler come to call on me not long ago."

"A traveler who knows of my companions and our plans? Not to sound threatening, but I would know of such a traveler." He finished speaking, and was alarmed when the woman laughed, not in a quick, bemused way, but a full, deep laugh which caused her eyes to sparkle. He frowned again, not accustomed to being laughed at, though in no way did he want to hurt this woman. He opened his mouth to respond but was forestalled by a raised hand.

Finishing her laugh and smiling at him, she raised her eyes high before speaking. "Piotyr, I mean no disrespect, but you are as far from threatening as possible in this cave. There is no being alive, from Heaven to Hell to any realm in existence which can harm me here. It is law. Nor should you have any concern about the messenger which told me of your journey upon the Rivers. I am not of your kind, nor was he, and your comings and goings mean very little to me other than idle entertainment."

Piotyr found himself becoming angry, despite his every attempt not to. He was not a plaything to this Oracle. "Now look, I will not be..."

The woman stepped towards him and raised a slender finger to his lips; his breath died in his throat as her robe fell open, exposing her beautiful form beneath. "Quiet, mortal, and I shall show you a better way to spend time in here."

Panic welled up within him, and shame. He allowed Hellfire to gather about his body and engulf his form as he moved away from the woman. "That is quite enough, witch. You call yourself an Oracle but I know a succubus when I see one."

The woman laughed again. "A succubus? Would that I was interested in consuming your soul! I am sure it is quite tasty, but I actually just wanted your flesh. You label me a demon for having a carnal desire? Your church hasn't changed much over the years."

Again he was confused, but still guarded. He did not trust this woman. "I have a woman already. I am flattered, but not interested, Oracle."

"Ah yes, the dragon. I must admit, that is tough competition. Tell me, have you spoken vows? Words of commitment? Are you... *spoken for*, Piotyr?"

He already knew how this would go. He was no man of words, and she would be able to twist anything he said around to make him confused and feel foolish. "I have no interest in this game. I say again, I came simply for the water of Lethe. I sense you can help me, so instead I ask if you will."

Sighing, the woman covered her body, and Piotyr for a moment hated himself for feeling regret. "You owe nothing to Asya, Piotyr. She left *you* if you recall. I will help you, but you've already wasted the easiest way for you to drink this water. Laying with me would let me extend my protection against the water to you, and is the easiest and safest way to survive the water with your memory intact. You have declined, foolishly I may add, and so now there lies only sacrifice."

Seeing her robed and no longer pressing upon him, he felt less guarded. He dropped his aura of fire and tried to relax his muscles. It was not easy. "What manner of sacrifice?"

She rolled her eyes at him and snorted. "Again, typical of you men of faith. Sex is abhorrent... yet bloodshed means nothing."

For a reason he couldn't explain, her derision shamed him again. He *was* faithful to his mate, and he loved Asya. He wouldn't just sleep with this woman to make things easier. He was better than that.

"I shouldn't have to explain myself, Oracle. Tell me of the sacrifice."

The woman shrugged her shoulders and spoke. "In times past, you would have had to purify yourself for days in a shrine of good spirit and fortune, abstaining from all things save a cold, cleansing bath in a sacred river. Then you would have had to sacrifice some *beasts* merely for entrails to be read to see if you would be allowed inside."

Piotyr did not like the way she said beasts, but allowed her to continue.

"For days the purification and sacrifices would last, then once your body was pure, on the night you were to descend another *beast* would be sacrificed and its entrails read again. If the signs were fortunate, if you were to be allowed in, you would be taken again to the sacred river, bathed and anointed in holy oil, and led by pure acolytes to this shrine."

Piotyr was confused, and spoke up. "You said descend, however I climbed to get here."

The Oracle looked annoyed at his interruption, and Piotyr again felt foolish. "Yes, in times past this shrine was not as you find it today. Things have... changed... over the long years. It is where it is, now. May I continue?"

The Templar ground his teeth and nodded. It was just a simple question, was she so petty as to hate him now simply for rebuffing her advances?

"Once here. you would drink from the Well of Oblivion, to forget all of what and who you are. Then, from the Well of Recollection, to recall the vision you would receive. Once the waters were consumed, you would fall into terror, lost, confused, and unable to remember anything about your life, even where you were and why. You would have been led to an altar, and made to pray to a figure you would not recognize nor understand, and then taken to the Oracle."

He frowned and opened his mouth to speak but a harsh glance from the woman silenced him. "I am but one of many kinds of Oracle, some are flesh, some are but places. The one I speak of now is both, and neither. Once led to the Oracle, the supplicant would lie down and vanish, returning some time later having seen the future, and been driven mad by it."

He became angry and yelled out before she had a chance to stop him. "I am to be driven mad for achieving a water sample?! Enough of this. Give me the water sample and I shall take my leave!"

"So often with mortals, it must be the hard path. Sit down and be silent." She spoke the words, and the cavern expanded into infinity for a moment as her eyes smoldered with intense inner fire. Piotyr closed his mouth and sat on the cavern floor.

"You will not speak until I am finished. If I so choose I shall have you against your will. If I so choose, I shall have you leap from the cliff to your death. If I so choose you will leave this place and murder your love and your children. If I so choose you will join the forces of Abaddon and wage bloody war against your friends and family. You will do whatever I wish, because I wish it. Do you understand, Piotyr Lamja?"

As she spoke, for the first time in his life, he experienced perfect clarity. The Oracle was telling him the absolute truth, and he was finally in understanding of what it meant to know something, unquestionably and unwaveringly. Her words were his law.

"As I spoke earlier, when you first arrived here, that you have already been deemed worthy of entrance by forces you simply have not the means to comprehend. You have shed so much blood in your life that it has stained you, and I can read your aura like a codex of suffering. You wear entrails to read like a bird has feathers."

Why had he been angry with this woman? She was to Piotyr as Piotyr was to an ant. This was no woman, she was something else. Not a god, that blasphemy was still known to him, but certainly no mere human. He listened patiently, as she had asked.

"You *will* be allowed to drink the waters, but not without a price. As you would not partake of my flesh, for your own protection, an event you would have enjoyed beyond any you could imagine, I instead offer you an alternative. You shall drink the water with no buffer, and no protection. Your sacrifice will be to lose all of whom you are, and as a price for your hubris, I shall not allow you the means to find it again. When you leave, you shall have your Lethe Water, and you shall know of your task and your role in the battle to come."

Piotyr nodded as she spoke. She was being fair, and just. He had refused her, and he was wrong to do so.

"You shall have your vision, and you shall have what you came for. I shall keep everything else. That is your payment. That is your sacrifice. I so choose. So shall it be. Rise."

He stood, patiently awaiting instruction from this incredible being.

"Follow me, it is time."

chapter seventeen

Still I can see it: a doubt that lingers deep in your heart,
brought forth by delusion.
- Renunciation through Knowledge: Bhagavad-Gita

"Funny. I hadn't thought names would stay the same after so long." He had some weird ideas in his head that far in the future humanity would have strange names and wear white jump suits or some shit like that... from some book he read. "I actually knew a couple Jacob's. They both went by Jake, though. Do your friends call you Jake?"

"No, they don't. Do your friends call you something other than Markov?"

"Actually that's my last name. I don't think I can remember anyone calling me something other than Markov." He knew Luis hadn't spoken it for at least ten years before that day on the wall.

"So did all of you Templar call each other by last names? It seems an odd custom."

Markov looked at the stranger, at Jacob. They were nothing alike, yet he could sense a bond in the man far beyond anything he could see. The man was bigger than Markov by well over a foot, and probably outweighed him twofold. Markov wasn't huge, but he wasn't a shrimp, either. Jacob was nothing like any human Markov had ever seen, yet he could sense nothing infernal at all about the guy. Hell, he liked him, and Markov had fought the

Legion long enough to know a Ba'al when he saw one, and Jacob was no Ba'al.

"No, I called most of my friends by their first names, I was just Markov. Probably because my first name was hard to pronounce or something."

"Hard to pronounce? What was it?"

Markov felt uncomfortable, which shocked the hell out of him. Memories of being taunted by other kids at the Sanctuary for having a funny first name came flooding back. He was one of the only kids around with a Russian-descended name, and the other one he hung out with was a kid named Vlad who was twice Markov's size and nobody fucked with. It was ridiculous for him to feel awkward telling Jacob his name, he was a grown man.

"Vasily. Vasily Markov." He said it, and it even sounded weird to him. God, how long had it been since he said his own name aloud?

"Vasily Markov. Jacob Merethius. I am honored to meet you." The huge, angelic man offered his hand to him, and Markov reached out and took it. Human contact felt strange. "You too, Jacob. I'm glad we aren't killing each other anymore." He laughed, and felt good about meeting this fellow Templar, even if he was from hundreds of years later.

"I as well. If I had known I was attacking our savior, I would have stopped much earlier."

Savior? What the fuck? "What was that?"

Jacob had expected to find oddities when he awoke here in the valley, but in no way expected to meet Markov... *the actual* Markov, here in this purgatory. Sadly, the man did not appear to know of his legacy and what it meant for humanity.

"Our Savior. We call our most powerful Invocation Markov's Gift... The Invocation of the Sword."

The man blinked before responding to Jacob in his strange, thick accent. "Get the fuck out of here."

Jacob blinked, and then scowled. This man was incredibly rude. "Sorry to have disturbed you, Markov." He stood to leave.

"Where the hell are you going?"

"You just told me to leave."

"No I didn't... oh hey that's just an expression. I didn't want you to leave...uh, it means that..."

Jacob stood and stared at the man in general confusion. What was he talking about?

"It means, well hell it's hard to explain, but it doesn't mean literally leave. Well sometimes it does, but only if someone is really angry and the person is being... shit never mind, ok it's a stupid saying. What I meant is, you call it Markov's Gift... and that was really hard to believe."

Jacob sat down, and tried to remember that Markov had been dead for centuries, and was unlikely to speak the same way he and the other Templar did. "I shall try not to be offended or confused by things you say. Perhaps you can try to speak plainly so that I understand you?"

"Of course, of course. Sorry, meant nothing by it. So why do you call it Markov's Gift? I'm just a soldier who died defending his Sanctuary. It probably fell after that."

Jacob knew that the Bastion on the Divide still stood up until the very end, before he made his report to the Patriarch and ended up here. He didn't have the heart to tell Markov that humanity had probably lost by now.

"The Sanctuary survived that day, and many more. It was a beacon of hope... of prayer for all of us, and you are the reason why."

"How? I just killed some demons and then died."

Jacob blinked, how could he not know?

"Killed some demons? Markov that battle is *legendary* in Templar History. You didn't kill some demons... you killed *all of them*. The entire invading force was wiped out, and you are the one who did it! Thousands of demons, Ba'al among them, all killed by you. Your Invocation became the basis of our faith and allowed us to push them back to Hell. You are our savior... at least in a way."

Jacob sighed, sadly. Hero worship was more fun, it seemed, then following it up with the aftermath.

"Unfortunately, there was more to it than that."

"You did it, Joshua. You did it. A working vaccine."

Han smiled at him, and clasped him on the shoulder. In truth he actually did feel really good about it, and was proud of using his knowledge and experience for healing purposes.

"For now anyway, it won't last forever and constant exposure will weaken the vaccine, but until Piotyr gets back with the water it's a workable buffer for anyone in the area. It should give about three weeks of protection without a booster."

"Fine work, my friend. Fine work. If ever there was a finer practitioner of medicine, I haven't heard of one, and I've read about quite a few."

Joshua felt it was flattery, but indulged it. It had been some time since he had been acknowledged for his skills as a healer. Not since the battle at Sheol Am, and Ryrig. "I'm not making it in quantity. It would be disastrous if it got into the hands of Abaddon's forces, so I'm only going to be making enough for a couple of dozen shots at a time, and I'll keep it on me until administered. Not very efficient, but I can make two batches a day for the time being."

Han sighed, and rubbed his eyes. His friend looked exhausted, like he hadn't slept well in weeks. "No, not very efficient, but you are right, it would be disastrous for it to fall into The Destroyer's hands. Perhaps three dozen and three batches a day with dedicated help? We did find some capable folk among the mortals and Legion alike."

Joshua pursed his lips in thought. One hundred a day versus fifty. It was very appealing, but with so many doses he feared theft. "Agreed, as long as the ones needing the vaccine are kept right nearby in the quarantine area and you give me sufficient forces to defend the lab."

Han smiled, and held out his hand. "Agreed."

Kasim felt colder than he had in his entire life. It was not a cold of the elements. When he arrived in Hell on the slopes of Sagarmatha, the wind, snow, and ice had chilled him to the bone and would have killed him without shelter.

Here, in the blackness, it was a deeper cold. His soul was being attacked with icy razors, and with each step, each agonizingly difficult step, he felt the cold penetrate deeper inside of his essence. He looked behind him, but knew that the door was shut. There was no way back.

"This is not forever. Darkness is not eternal, and while I still live, no matter in what form, there is hope, and eventually warmth." As he said it, he felt a little better, and was able to take another several steps before the cold deepened so starkly and powerfully that it took his breath. He stopped, staggered, and fell to one knee.

There was a time when he thought himself fearless and walked amongst his enemies, killing their infernal masters with ease and grace. Never in his life had he feared for his life, and never for his soul. Not like this. He tried to rise, and failed. Sharp, bitter terror rose in his throat. The deep dark around him thickened, and he could sense the oppression like a freezing fog. *You are lost, he was once Death.*

Kasim shivered violently as he knelt, unable to stand. The forces around him were crushing him, trying to bring him to the ground. He grit his teeth and shook his head. *No! It will NOT END LIKE THIS!*

He pushed against the darkness with every ounce of strength he had and smiled in painful triumph as he stood and walked another several steps. He had overcome death itself before and would do so again. This place of despair would not claim his soul. He was Kasim, and he was Death.

He finished the thought and stopped, poleaxed, as the cold sapped his strength completely and the force of the hopelessness dropped him to the ground. He lay there, unmoving, frozen in body and spirit. He tried to summon his strength and courage again, but could not, simply laying there unmoving, shivering in paralyzed terror.

His thoughts were left to him, but constantly ran from him like roaches in the light. *Cold, so cold.* He tried again and again to focus, to concentrate, but the deeper gloom crushed him without mercy and always he returned to dwell on the cold, and the misery.

Thrice now he had failed catastrophically. Once as a man, once in Hell, and once in death. The clarity caught him by surprise, cold as he was. His thoughts dwelled on his defeats, the unkind memories filling his head undistracted by the icy black.

In decades of assassination missions for the Templar, he had only failed one time. The memory was still vivid, and he relived it in perfect detail now cowering in the darkness.

The walls around Haven had been cleared for months, which made stealth harder, but Kasim was a master. Invoking Camouflage and Concealment, Death crept from shadow to shadow under a moonlit sky, making haste across the scorched and ruined former forest. The Patriarch and The Destroyer had danced many times over the last several weeks, and the damage to the earth was extensive and deep.

Smoke filled his nostrils from that day's reign of fire, both Holy and Unholy. As always, the Legion had pressed, and Haven held. Kasim had not been in Haven long, only a few days since returning from his last ranging southwest to the Ancient Grove. It was gone now, and he had gone to Haven.

He crossed the field silently and unseen. Kasim's senses were keen, but he Invoked Dark Sight and Far Hearing as well. Legion patrolled sporadically, always in two, but though these were disciplined troops... The Destroyer tolerated nothing less... Kasim was a master to their mere proficiency. At his whim he could have silenced them all, but killing sentries was not his purpose tonight. Tonight he was meant for a greater prize.

The Patriarch's summons had surprised him, as he assumed that whatever breaks he had in the near constant warfare would necessitate sleep for the old man. When the acolyte had brought him to the cornerstone of the Order, Kasim wondered how he still stood. Such exhaustion behind those eyes, yet eyes still focused and alert.

The mission had been simple. The Patriarch had told him Haven would not survive the month, and that unless The Destroyer was killed it was over. He didn't have the strength to fend him off any longer. That simple. Kasim understood.

He crept unseen and unheard to the outer edge of the Legion Camp. Order and discipline kept the Legion in check here, though Kasim could see the effects of morale here as well. The siege had taken the lives of tens of thousands of Legion troops, and exhaustion was not unique to the Templar.

Kasim searched quickly from the darkness outside the reach of the soldier's fires, finding what he sought in a few minutes. Hiding in the night, he listened with his enhanced senses for the barely audible sound of faint snoring coming from within a tent. He made his way inside, sneaking past the sentry at the fire with ease.

One lone Legionnaire slept on his bedroll, and Kasim moved to him with grace and ease, silencing him with a blade inserted in the demons ribs with a hand clasped over his mouth. He quivered briefly as Kasim expertly slide the seven inch blade horizontally between the demons ribs and wiggled it gently on the way in, piercing his lung and slashing into his heart. Kasim knew his work well, and severed the artery he sought. The Legionnaire never regained consciousness. He gave it a long ten count, then staunched the wound and rolled the body over. It would be discovered, but not for a time.

He quickly dressed in the Legionnaire's armor and clothing, his Invocations allowing him to see in the darkness with ease and hear any potential danger outside the tent. Finished, he moved to the back of the tent, and right at the corner seam made a quiet incision and left. Quietly Invoking Mending, he fixed the tear and moved back into the night.

Kasim knew from experience that various Invocations of Stealth were not always reliable, and his costume was meant to aid his efforts should any Legion be possessed with particular focus and attention. With his Prayers, disguise, and natural talent for avoiding being in sight, Kasim made his way easily into the center of the camp.

The direness of the Patriarch's assessment gave Kasim courage. An assassination attempt on Ba'al Apollyon was not unheard of, but nearly impossible to try. He rarely left his command tent unless manifested as The Destroyer, and though there were other assassins in the Templar Order, none had Kasim's skill. Kasim was not surprised that the Patriarch had tasked him for this, but he did know why he had not tasked others.

The sight of the command tent was a welcome one. Kasim felt an anticipation he had not felt in years. There were three banners flying in the wind over the tent. He recognized the sword with the complex triangles on it as that of the House of Lucifer, underneath was the seven-headed black dragon of House Apollyon, and on the bottom was what would be the symbol of whatever Ba'al currently had the honor of providing the additional guard of the fortification. Kasim did not recognize the flaming Bronze Bull on the banner. Perhaps Han would know, but demonic heraldry was not a subject the assassin knew well.

Kasim walked in a slow patrol outside the circle of guards within the tents immediate visibility. Nearing the back of the tent he veered off into the night, away from the light given off by the torch sconces. Finding a stack of crates, he made sure he was still unseen before ducking behind them and removing his Legion armor and garb. There was little hope in moving silently wearing the metal armor of the Legion once inside the tent. He walked a few paces before doubling back to the canvas wall and making an incision at the corner behind a darker section that from experience he expected to be behind a wardrobe.

He was correct, and made his way inside Ba'al Apollyon's tent, unseen from eyes without or within. He silently repositioned himself behind the solid wooden furniture, and listened for the sound of sleep. A long ten count he waited, before the sound of a page turning caused him to curse inwardly. It would have been far easier if the Ba'al was resting.

He stilled his heartbeat and crept to the edge of the wardrobe, seeing the Ba'al standing above a table covered with maps, books, and figurines Kasim took to be representative of troop movements. Another time, such information would have been part of his mission to obtain. Not tonight. He was tasked with blood, nothing more.

Kasim was the best the Templar had at this work, and in his mind he envisioned his blade twisting in Abaddon's back. One slice, severing the spine, and Kasim would be on his way back to Haven to give the Patriarch the good news.

He drew his blade and slid without sound from behind the wardrobe, his cloth Templar vestments making not even a whisper against the fabric of the tent wall. Two paces from him, the Ba'al gazed intently at a document held in his hands. Twelve feet tall at the shoulder, wings furled behind him and wearing a simple silk robe, Abaddon was not the terror he was when attacking the walls manifested as The Destroyer. This was the best chance the Order would have at killing him.

He positioned his dagger and stilled his heart. Moving forward, he plunged the knife deep into Abaddon's back.

He shook his head as the memory faded. He still didn't know what went wrong. His blade had struck true, or at least so he thought. He recalled clearly the resistance of his knife sinking into the flesh of the Ba'al, and remembered just as clearly turning the blade just as Abaddon spun and leapt away from him over the table, screaming for the guards. What did he do wrong? The war could have been, if not won; at least the tide turned that day.

"You believe that, don't you?"

Kasim gasped and looked around in the darkness, but saw nothing.

"Who is there? Show yourself."

"I'm right here, master, you just can't see through the blackness."

"Ozra? Ozra are you here with me? How can that be, this is my death and my penance."

"I am here because we all lingered after the attack. You were weakened and unaware, but we are here. At least I am. The others have gone somewhere else. When you finally went through that door, they went further in, but I stayed."

"Ozra... I am so sorry. It was my arrogance that led to your death. All of your deaths."

"Yet you saved Dhermina."

Kasim was silent for a moment. Yes she had been closer, but his instinct had been to help her above all else. He knew the truth that he would not have even tried to help the others unless she was safe.

"Yet I saved Dhermina."

"At least you are honest about it. For what it is worth, I would have done the same for Jio."

Kasim felt tears come to his eyes. He had failed them all.

"Master, enough of that. You did not kill us."

"It was not my blade, but my failure that led to your deaths. It is my fault."

"Stop. What's done is done. I bear no ill will, nor do the others. We chose to follow you, do not bear this sorrow without cause. We free you from it."

"You speak for the others?"

"No, but they will seek you out in time. You have long to journey, master. This is a place of sorrow, and pain."

Kasim sighed, and thought back to his first journey through such a place. Surely it could not be worse.

"Guard your thoughts, master. I can hear them, and so can the others here."

"Others? You mean Kishien, Qor, Tal, and Jio?"

"No, though they can hear them as well. This will not be as your last walk with death. That journey had a different purpose."

"What is my purpose here?"

Ozra waited for a long moment before answering, and Kasim felt the air grow heavy.

"You are here to suffer, master. When you have suffered enough, you will be allowed to leave. I am sorry, and I do not wish it on you, but I feel I must speak truly. You exist in this place now to feel pain."

"I see. No other reason?" Kasim felt the question of why rise to the surface of his thoughts, but he felt the answer rise just as quickly.

"Yes master, you must atone. Fortunately, your scales will be weighted in your favor. I journey with you, until such time as I can be released."

"How is it that you are here, anyway?"

Kasim heard a good natured laugh in the black, the warm emotion feeling alien and strange in the darkness.

"Han bound us to you. I don't know how, but he did. For some reason, he felt our souls and yours were not yet finished in our association, it seems. You will have to ask him, once you are finished here."

"Very well then, I shall proceed. Do you know what to expect?"

"Yes, as unlike you I am actually dead. You merely linger on its door. What will follow will not be pleasant. Know that I take no pleasure in it, and that it is necessary. Suffering comes."

Kasim mused for a long moment on Ozra's words. Suffering comes. To him, it seemed just. Kasim had caused so much suffering in his life, justifiable or not, that his soul was marred. Purification through pain. It was not a foreign concept to the Templar, though not widely used. Hell as an eternal torment was simply an extension of the concept.

"Then I shall suffer."

He stepped forward, and the dark shards of icy terror shredded his soul. Torment came to him, and assaulted him without mercy. *This is just, I have earned this.* The thought comforted him, as suffer he did.

The day had come and gone, and it was time to leave. The First had stayed the night, and remained hidden all the next day, but would not risk a second night by the intermittent falls. He gathered up Lokyrg and Ba'al Am's War-axe and left the rocks surrounding the pool.

I hope you are not thinking of leaving my father, walking corpse.

"I am, dead dragon child."

You may not. You will stay until he returns, whether one day or one thousand.

"I will not."

If you leave this place, I will...

The First tossed the spear unceremoniously in the dirt and walked away five paces. He turned and stared at Lokyrg for near to a minute, his War-axe propped against his shoulder. Nodding to himself, he walked back and retrieved the spear.

"I hope we are clear, now. I mean no malice."

I was once capable of things I no longer am. If this is my fate, I ask that you sunder me and free my spirit.

"No."

Your cruelty runs thicker than mine ever did, corpse.

"There is no cruelty in it. Your father may still be alive, and if so I shall return you to him. I must act, however, on the possibility that he is not. There are events at play that are larger than you, than Piotyr, than me. I will not tarry."

I can't stop you, and my words won't either.

"Correct."

Lokyrg did not answer him, and he took that to be a good sign. If Piotyr did return, the zombie-king would prefer no ill will, particularly over dealings with the dragon-spear. In his memories, he recalled many parents lacking wisdom and perspective when it came to their offspring.

Either way, Phlegethon awaited.

He awoke unclothed on the cold stone, gasping in terror as the visions swept through his mind like a hurricane. Time after time the battle played out in his mind, and thousands of variations of each individual outcome sprang into being and fell away just as quickly.

He groaned in pain, his headache pounding in rhythm to his heartbeat, great hammers slamming into the inside of his skull.

"Breathe, Piotyr."

Piotyr? Was that his name? The battle took every possible piece of thought in his head, hundreds of thousands of troops, millions... smashing into a great walled city.

"Breathe, child of Adam."

Child of Adam, Piotyr. The Legion, he was here to get something for someone. Water. He had to get water. It was critical to the battle.

"Breathe, and still your mind, Piotyr. The visions will still be with you, but will lose intensity soon. Just breathe."

The woman was startlingly beautiful, and her words soothed him. Her voice had a strength that belied its sweetness. He listened, and inhaled deeply, placing his hands on his temples and gently rubbing them.

"Good. The pain will fade, in time. Just breathe."

He did so, and as minutes passed the pain did lessen, and the visions slowed and were easier to discern. What battle were they from? He had not been in anything like it, he was sure, but he remembered it all the same.

"You are not remembering a war you have fought. You are remembering a war you are going to fight, soon."

"Who are you, what is this place?"

"I am the Oracle. You are in the Oracle. We are one and the same, Piotyr."

"I don't remember my name, how is it that you know it?"

The woman smiled and slid behind him on the rock, gently running her hands over his shoulders and back of his head. Tension melted out of him.

"You have tasted the waters of Oblivion. Who you were before coming here is gone. Now you are simply Piotyr, and you have something very important to do."

He sighed in pleasure as her hands soothed away the pain in his head. The pounding subsided and his heart rate lowered. She was gifted. "Water, I must return the waters of Lethe to a man named Han."

"Yes, you must. You shall have your water when you leave, but two more samples must be collected. You know from where?"

Phlegethon still awaited. "Yes, the river of fire." *Cocytus.* "The great pit of ice."

"You know what awaits you there?"

"I do not, Oracle. I... I believe I have spoken of it before, though I can't remember."

The woman laughed, and Piotyr felt chills dance over his skin. Was that malice in her voice?

"Many things will be lost to your memory, but not what is important. You must take the water with you, and then I will send you back to the river on the way to Phlegethon. You will know it when you get there. Leave the vials I marked at the shore, you won't need your extras, but another could make use of them... *just in case*." The woman giggled as she spoke.

Her hands had descended from his shoulders and she was now running them down his chest. Her voice lowered as she spoke, and he felt his pulse rise again.

"When you get that water, the way will be open to Cocytus. There your journey will end, likely in death, or if you happen to succeed... return to Han in Sheol. Give him the water, and tell him you are ready to lead the battle. He will be confused, but tell him Hell speaks to many people, not just him. Your knowledge of war not yet waged will be enough to convince him. Answer him truthfully, and your task shall be complete."

Piotyr felt innately that he was in danger, like an insect about to be preyed upon by a mate. His body responded as she gently rubbed his torso and abdomen.

"I can send you on your way whenever you wish, Piotyr. Is there anything else you want before you leave?"

He sensed a hint of mockery in her voice this time, though he thought perhaps it was good natured. He turned in her grasp to embrace her, and placed his lips upon hers.

The kiss lasted mere moments before he was surprised to find her smiling. Stopping, he pulled back to look at her, and scowled as mild amusement was the only emotion he could detect on her beautiful face.

"I'm afraid I am no longer interested, Piotyr. Too bad. Let me gather your things, it's time for you to be on your way."

She stood, and left him alone on the rock. Somehow he knew that something was wrong.

chapter eighteen

The art of war teaches us to rely not on the likelihood of the enemy's not coming, but on our own readiness to receive him; not on the chance of his not attacking, but rather on the fact that we have made our position unassailable.
- Sun Tzu: The Art of War

Markov felt sick. Jacob's words cut him to the core. To learn that he had killed the Legion force that day, that was incredible, but to learn that he had ignited his own soul to do so... worse was that others had done so after he paved the way. He was responsible for the death of tens of thousands of Templar men and women. Hundreds of thousands, perhaps millions. He said as much to Jacob, and was surprised at the response.

"Markov, those Templar sacrificed themselves at a cost of untold death among the Legion. Markov's Gift..." he shot Jacob a look which said he wasn't going to accept that name "... The Invocation of the Sword, rather, saved us. We were dead, without it."

"But you just said it cost you far too much, that after a Templar used it they died. Too many... extinction through salvation."

Jacob sighed sadly and rubbed his eyes. "Yes, that is what happened, but that wasn't because of the Invocation itself, it was the fervor and excitement of winning. We were careless, and too many of us burned our souls without real cause, because we were ignorant. No one knew... and by the time it was discovered it was too late. There weren't enough of us left. I don't know how it was in your time, but a good Templar warrior, not even the greatest of us but merely a capable warrior is worth any ten Legion."

"Maybe not quite that, but we had firearms. Most of our marksmen could drop a Legionnaire at half a klick and early on we even had artillery. Shit ran out fast though."

"Firearm? Klick?"

"Sorry, guns, do you know what a gun is?"

"Yeah, ancient ranged weapons. They are in books; they used controlled explosions to propel a metal projectile fast and far."

"Pretty much. We had ones that would blow the head off Legion from way the hell far away. A klick is 1000 meters."

"We didn't have anything like that, just bows and crossbows. We did have artillery though, catapults, ballista, trebuchet."

Markov laughed, and smiled in good nature before clapping Jacob on the arm. "Well that's fucking great! We had howitzers, but I think I like yours more. Anyway, yeah we were better pound for pound than the Legion, but they outnumbered us exponentially."

"Well after you won at the Bastion on the Divide, or San Luis as you call it, the balance of power changed. We were winning for a change, and if we had been more careful, we would have been victorious. We just got careless, and too many of us died from the Soul's Last Fire. Not that we can totally be blamed I suppose, no one knew the consequences until it was far too late. We were lucky enough of us lived to even keep going, though population totals were far too low to survive for long."

"Sounds like it just prolonged our end, then. I don't know you or your people Jacob, if you've been fighting for as long as I've been here, maybe it wasn't worth it?"

"Well that gets a little complicated."

To the man's credit, he listened to Jacob's entire tale with wide eyes. Jacob told him everything, from losing slowly over the centuries in between Markov's Invocation and the Patriarch's ritual, to the acts of Jacob and his brothers here in Hell.

"So you killed him, huh? I'd buy you a drink if I could. Well done, Jacob."

Jacob blinked in surprise, and then smiled back. "I hadn't really thought about it much, but yeah, I guess I did. I killed the Shay'tan, but I had to use your Invocation to do it. Burned my own Soul, but it was worth it. We won."

"I suppose we did, Jacob. Well, do you mind if I take some of the credit, since as you say it was my Invocation? Not trying to steal your thunder, but I never thought of Markov as a hero."

"Take all the credit you want, and you were a hero. I know you hate the name, but Markov's Gift is a weapon all Templar were taught. We were just taught not to use it unless it was a last resort."

"Bah, you killed him, you swung the mace. I just like that you used my Invocation to make it happen. Sorry it killed you though, though since it killed me too I'm only a little sorry."

Both men laughed, and Jacob felt a friendship beginning. He liked Markov, and if he had to share eternity with someone, well he would have preferred Ve'kal, but at least he and Markov had a lot in common. They sat and talked for hours, swapping stories of the war, and of their friends, and of their lives.

It wasn't what Jacob would have chosen as his reward for victory, but it was better than being alone.

Ve'kal had seen such strides being made that when the news came that Ba'al Apollyon had broken camp, she felt anxiety, but not terror. She requested Han's presence at the newly opened Salt and Sear, her Palace Chef overseeing the restoration and serving fine food again. Priolt was a treasure, and though she had not had cause to visit Sheol often in recent years, she had come before and knew the food to be without peer.

Sheol was not as it was, but the city had been cleared of debris and bodies and the restoration was progressing quickly. Han was a master and her Seneschal had learned from him. Her people were truly motivated, and not with terror or bloodshed. The commoners respected, even liked, the Templar, and although her pride smarted at admitting it, she looked better because of Han and Joshua.

Han. The things that man had done with Sheol were astounding. She had to admit humans had an industrious and resourceful quality that The Fallen simply lacked. Lucifer and his heirs had not been what Ve'kal would have called lazy, though perhaps complacent, but with limited time and resources the Templar had spurred a level of response and preparation that she could scarce believe.

Apollyon would be there within the month, but Sheol would stand when he arrived. The fields had been prepared for the contagion, and zombies not slated to be imbued with the blood drinkers or spirit reavers had been secreted in hidden pits and hollows, ready to kill Legion as they passed and increase their own strength and intelligence.

The Walls had been restored, through Han's strange sorcery in part and also with the sweat of honestly devoted mortals, Sheol and Ve'kal Legion, and even begrudgingly from other noble Houses who had hitched their fate to House Ve'kal and not House Apollyon. Ba'al Geir had been devoted to her, even after what had happened to Kasim, and though the boy was young he was apparently better liked than his father. Ba'al Geir was a wonder, in truth. If Ve'kal didn't know better, she would swear some of the Templar seeds of virtue had taken root in the boy. She had seen him praise his Legion, and bend his back to work at their side. The positive results were immediate and stark. The Legion of House Geir would count among her best troops.

Even the Legionnaire left by Ba'al Toly'm worked their hands to the bone in her service. She did not expect to see that lecher again, but on the off chance he was spared by Ba'al Apollyon his Legion was now hers anyway.

She rose and smiled as she saw Han enter the inn. Wine and bread would be brought to them, tasted first, of course to be safe. Priolt could be trusted, but she would not casually risk Han's life with the Watchers still a threat.

Han waved at her and they both sat down at the table. "Welcome, master Han. I thank you for taking the time to meet with me."

"It is no trouble, Ba'alat Ve'kal. To what do I owe the pleasure?"

Right to it then. Another refreshing quality of the Templar was their aversion to social banter or political maneuvering. These men from earth spoke plain, and it was a challenge to become used to it.

"I wish to speak to you about your preparations. Specifically have you made any attempt to reach out to Piotyr's dragons?"

Han shook his head. "I have not, nor will I. Asya has made her decision, and in her condition she would not come anyway."

"Condition? What has happened to her?"

Han frowned, looking as if he regretted speaking. "I should not have said anything, as it is not my place, but Asya is with a second brood. There will be more drakes soon."

"That's fantastic news, Han! How long until they can fight?"

"Months, but that is not the point, they will not fight without Piotyr and Asya asking it, and there is little incentive for them to do so."

"Little incentive? Do you think Ba'al Apollyon will be merciful to those who ended the line of Lucifer?"

"Do you think the dragons care much for our wars or which faction will end up hunting them?"

Ve'kal was silent for a moment, hearing the wisdom of Han's words. Why would they care, other than for Piotyr's sake? He wasn't there, and Ve'kal herself had enjoyed a wyrm hunt in her youth.

"I shall offer the protection of the Shay'tan to Asya. Hellfire wyrms will be against my law to hunt. I doubt Apollyon will extend the same protection."

"I agree, and it is a good idea. I will send word to Aruc and Ulis. They will hear a message from me, I hope. Asya will not come, but perhaps the others will."

Good, it wasn't a guarantee, but at least it was an attempt. Two mature Hellfire dragons would make a significant difference. A second brood?! If they could be kept as allies... "What of a general to lead?"

Han laughed before answering. "What, you don't trust myself or Joshua to take charge of the siege?"

She blinked, not knowing how to respond at first. "Master Han, by all accounts, including yours, you are not...."

"A warrior? Yes, I know. Worry not, it was in jest. My place will be on the walls, but it shall fall to Piotyr to lead the actual battle."

"You expect him to return then?"

"Yes, I do. I expect Kasim to recover as well, but he is not a general either. It must be Piotyr; he has experience that no one here can match."

She was inclined to agree. Though many Ba'al would claim to be possessed of military prowess, the truth is their society was a decadent one, and most of the seasoned campaigners from the war on earth would be with Apollyon... though even they would be inexperienced at fighting large groups of Legionnaire during a siege. The Templar had been doing it for centuries, and Piotyr by all accounts she had heard was among their best students of battle.

"So what of our chances then, I want your honest assessment?" She hoped Han's optimism would be honest, and not blind.

"We are all going to die, Ve'kal."

The shock of his statement fell into a heavy silence, as their food had arrived. "What do you mean? All this work you are doing? The upgrades to our defenses, the undead you have created? The plague distribution? How can you say we are all going to die?!"

Han calmly picked up his knife and fork, waving away the food taster. "It's safe. There was a Watcher assassin trying to harm me here, but I killed him on my way here. They are unable to hide from me."

Carving off a piece of his hart venison, he chewed and swallowed methodically and without any apparent distress before answering. "Compliments to your chef, Ba'alat. I've never tasted finer. Ve'kal, the preparations I have made have only turned a complete and utter annihilation into a brief pause of resistance before being crushed. A month ago, The Destroyer would have needed to do little more than walk inside and sit down to win the city. Now he will have to actually enter into a battle, but it is one that his numbers will assuredly guarantee his victory in."

"But in a siege, his numbers won't be fully..."

"Ba'alat Ve'kal, you need to look at this rationally. I don't have an exact number, but I would estimate his numbers at well over ten million Legion. That's just Legion, not including the untold Fallen that comes with them."

"Fallen, yes, but only a fraction of that are true Ba'al."

"Fine, but even a fraction of ten million is significant, and it's at *least* ten million. It could be fifty for all I know. Our records indicate that over one hundred million fell with Lucifer, if even half have died over the millennia, which I doubt, then fifty could stand with The Destroyer now."

"Some stand with me, instead."

"Yes, I'll grant you perhaps one in ten. I'll even grant twice that, for the sake of argument, and leave us with impossible odds. The plague won't touch the Ba'al, and Joshua's undead can't reach them. I expect to absolutely slaughter the Legion Ba'al Apollyon brings to Sheol, and I'm sure he expects that as well. That leaves us with potentially tens... *hundreds* of thousands of Fallen to descend upon us from the air. If even one in one hundred is Ba'al? More than enough to take the walls, and if even every single one of Abaddon's mortals or Legion other than a Ba'al dies in the siege, we will still have lost, and our enemy won't care about the casualties."

"That is not true; he will need the Legion to finish wiping out humanity."

"I'll concede that, but he is patient, and if needs to wait another century, or even two, he will."

Han was right. Apollyon could outwait a stone. All that mattered was victory, it did not matter when.

"What of your power, Han? I have seen you do incredible things with sorcery. You are a force unto yourself."

He sliced off more of his hart-steak and chewed, washing it down with wine before responding. How could he eat when talking about their own destruction so casually?

"Yes, but there is a problem."

"What problem?"

"The power I use is finite. The more I use, the less is available. I had thought the depths of suffering here endless, and that I had no cause for concern in using as much as I could draw. That is not the case. There is a lot of it left to draw upon, but it is diminishing by the day."

"I don't understand, what is the power you are drawing upon?"

"The suffering of Hell itself, and there is an ocean of it, but as I draw it from the soil and use it to bend to my will, it does not replenish. I feel that without the innate cruelty of the Shay'tan causing more of it, the power will subside, in time."

"But surely not before the battle? You said there is an ocean to draw upon."

"An ocean there is, and it will be at high tide when The Destroyer comes. Have no fear that I will bring death in waves upon his forces, but as I do so the supply will dwindle, and I fear that there will not be enough to matter when it comes time to face Abaddon and his Ba'al."

"You know this for fact? You say you fear, but in conserving the power for the Ba'al and Abaddon could you not be mistaken about the supply?"

"Ba'alat Ve'kal, all things are possible, I am merely telling you my sense of our chances. I expect to wipe out his land infantry, but only with the walkers, the plague, possibly the dragons, and with me raining death where the enemy gathers most strongly. With Piotyr to lead us, and if everything goes well, I would be pleased if we could even make the Ba'al stop long enough to face us on the walls. I think in a prolonged battle we could whittle their numbers down enough to make it a contest... except for Abaddon. If he manifests, and I don't see why he wouldn't, then the battle is decided. All of us combined could not stop him, though I will do what I can. I shall rain fire upon him, as my Patriarch once did on Earth."

"Why do you expect him to become the Destroyer? His power comes from the Shay'tan, and Lucifer's Heir is slain."

"Yet you do not wield the power of the Throne. That mystery is kept from me; I know not why the Throne lies vacant, absent a Ba'al to grace it. However, I know that the power is not barred to Abaddon, and we will face the Destroyer come the siege. I cannot slay him with my power alone, he is too powerful."

"So, if it is so hopeless, what can we do to help even our odds?"

Han had finished his meal and smiled at her over a long drink of wine. "Pray."

Joshua exhaled deeply and rubbed the exhaustion from his eyes. The vaccine was a success, and he had been producing it as quickly as he felt was safe. He had allowed himself a break for some strong tea and fresh air outside his laboratory.

K'had and Ulraen had come to visit him earlier to check on him, which for some reason warmed him.

"How are you holding up, Ba'al Joshua?" K'had smiled as he said it, a far cry from their first encounter at sword point over the corpses of a dead city.

"Fine, just a bit tired. How goes the training of the conscripts?" He spoke to both of them, and not surprisingly it was Ulraen who answered. The two caravan guards were of like minds and answered for each other as often as not. He had not met friendlier mortals in Hell.

"Well, though most of them know they have no chance in battle against seasoned Legion. Yes I know that the idea is for them not to be on the plains in open battle, but we also know that the odds of the battle not reaching the walls of Sheol are non-existent. Many of us will die, Joshua."

"I know, my friends. Would that I could do something about that. Death comes swiftly for many of us." He had offered them a drink as they spoke of things horrific and not. "How is Ryrig doing?"

"He is fine; if he remembers his encounter with Ba'al Am he has hidden it. It is as if nothing ever happened to him." Ulraen spoke calmly of that terrible day, and if Ryrig had forgotten being ripped limb from limb by the Ba'al, so much the better for him.

"It is still a subject of worship for your followers, Ba'al Joshua... how you restored him after such a thing." K'had was not prone to exaggeration unless it was of his own actions. If he was speaking of the other mortals Joshua's retinue had gathered on their march north from where he arrived in hell, he would speak truthfully.

"In the moment, it did not seem very important, more like simply what I needed to do. In hindsight, however, I could see how it could be misconstrued as miraculous."

The two of them stopped mid-drink and looked at each other in the eyes before laughing. "Misconstrued?! Joshua you are a damned fool at times. It *was* miraculous, don't be absurd." Ulraen nodded to K'had's words.

"Well, in any case, I'm glad he is doing well. I am fond of you all, you know."

It was a friendly exchange, but it wasn't until after they had left and he returned to his vaccine work that he got to thinking about how many mortals would soon be rent asunder just as Ryrig had been. The Legion would storm the walls, of that Han had been crystal clear, and Joshua agreed. His plague, and the walkers would answer for many of them, but it was expected that the force would number in the tens of millions. If one in a hundred of the Legion survived the plains and made it to the walls, their pitifully small defense would be overrun in hours, not days. The bulk of the forces they had would be held in Sheol, the risk versus reward erred against staging the more intelligent and effective undead out in the plains.

Even so, their thousands against the hordes of Abaddon simply didn't equate to a battle. It equated to a slaughter. Joshua had wracked his brain for ways he could help, and after talking about Ryrig with K'had and Ulraen he had an idea. It wouldn't turn the tide, but it would help, if he could pull it off.

Rubbing his eyes again, more vigorously, he eyed his sleeping cot wistfully. Sleep would have to wait.

Deep violet shadow surrounded him as he stumbled forward. He felt Ozra as a comforting presence as he moved further into the oppressive gloom, though that did nothing for the physical and mental agony he felt. The torment finally abated for a moment, leaving him feeling worn thin, parched, and his body throbbing in pain.

Suffering. He supposed this was to be expected, this enduring assault on his body. He could not physically touch Ozra, but he clung to his presence like a log in a swift moving river. He lurched forward into the gloom as again pain swept over his flesh. It was not any specific sort of pain, not that he could see and attach a name to. It was simple, pure suffering awash over his skin. He forced himself to keep moving, and as time crawled by for him, he began to put images to the pain, and was rewarded with the gloom showing him in stark black and indigo the sources of his enduring torture.

Blades. Blades of every size and shape pierced his flesh, slashed his skin, and severed his limbs. He knew it would be thus. He had made his life upon sword and dagger, and had entered the flesh of his enemies for decades in such ways as he now experienced. He grit his teeth with every wound, gasped with every skewering, and grunted in agony with every spilling of his life blood.

He couldn't die here, that was not the purpose of this. He simply endured the process of being killed, ongoing and unceasing, as he stumbled forward. The blades from the gloom did not come from Legion or Fallen, he simply *knew* they didn't. They came from a Templar, they came from him. Time went by with only Ozra for comfort as he saw himself through the eyes of his victims, over and over again. The death he visited on them was not just, or unjust in this particular experience. It simply was, and he needed to experience it to balance the death staining his soul.

He acknowledged this, and felt an approving pulse of positive energy from his former disciple. He was glad; he did not think he could have endured this without Ozra. The pain went on for hours, perhaps even days, he could not tell. His thirst, unnaturally worsened from the blood loss he felt constantly flowing from his arteries, drove him near to madness. He stumbled, fell, collapsed, and finally was unable to rise again. He felt the blades plunge into him faster than a tailor mending a cloak. Over and over his body was pierced, and finally he surrendered to the onslaught. He had administered death so often, and only now was he beginning to understand what it had done to his soul.

Piotyr walked along a river, crossing peaceful plains as he did. The Oracle had been true to her word, as if there could be any doubt, and had sent him on his way with the water samples. Upon leaving, he had thought some sort of traversal would be in order, but he had simply said farewell, blinked, and found himself at the base of a cliff with waterfall drops gently drifting in the air. The serenity of the moment was ripped from him in a haze of battle not yet waged.

His thoughts were a chaotic torrent of warfare, and he knew that none of it was from any battle he had ever fought in. He saw minute pieces of a life he didn't recognize, of sword and armor and the blood of men and demon alike always present. Names were lost to him, as was any understanding of why he was doing what he was doing, but images flashed of familiar sights. The war was crystal clear, though. He saw a great host of Legion spread across the horizon, their marching was deafening even across the plains.

A winged host that blacked out the sky flew above them, and in their midst he saw a dark angel at least twice his height and a wingspan that made him swallow in fear. *Ba'al Apollyon.* That name he knew, and with it came dread. He saw The Destroyer lead his armies against the city where he, Piotyr, stood. He saw the Legion advance slowly until the plague started, then explode into action as the siege truly began.

In his mind he saw every movement, every decision Abaddon made, every section of the Legion that fell to the undead, and every battalion that held fast. He knew that it was his destiny to command the forces at the siege, but there were pieces missing. He saw his own forces as insubstantial. He moved to give orders to troops he did not have, and shouted commands to those that he felt *should* be there, but were absent in his visions.

He trusted the Oracle, though. She had told him he would lead the battle, and needed only to provide the water to the man called Han. He simply needed to go on... *"You would have heard of the waters of Phlegethon by reputation, if not name. The waters burn, or boil, or otherwise exist to cause eternal torment to violent sinners. If we come across those first, I would expect fire and pain."*

Someone had spoken those words to him, and recently, though he could not remember who or when. He mused on his lost memory as he walked, and finally came to the river. It was familiar, and he recalled coming this way before, though it was hazy and the details were lost to him.

There was no boat, which he found odd since he thought he had taken one to get here, but it was no matter, there was driftwood around and plenty of reeds. He could fashion a decent raft, certainly good enough of one to traverse such calm water. He thought he should have armor as well... though at least he had his sword. Of the waters of Phlegethon he had no fear. Burn, or boil, he knew it didn't matter. That, at least, he did remember.

I still think we should have waited, corpse.
"Noted."

I am not arguing without purpose, I know your concerns and they are not invalid, but a day at the shore would not have been unwise.

The First did not bear any ill will towards Lokyrg, as he now felt was right to call the being imbued into Eirygaile. He had proven to be a reasonable companion on the journey back to the river and along its waters.

"As I say, I am aware of your opinion, but if he had not shown within a day, we would risk discovery by the Choir for naught, and now we are well on our way to Phlegethon. I trust your father to be able to find his own way, unless he is dead, which I doubt. Your concern, then, *is* noted, but I did not feel to delay was wise. Of greater concern is whether or not the water I gathered beneath the falls is, in fact, of Lethe."

Lokyrg was silent for a while which allowed him to think about what had probably happened after the Templar had vanished. The First knew that even more than the other waters of Hell, Lethe had a strange and mystical reputation. He feared that somehow Piotyr had been exposed to the memory sapping properties of Lethe and now wandered aimlessly in the darkness. Frustrating, yes, but there was nothing he could do about it.

As they passed the giant cavern he stopped rowing and watched in silence as the river took the boat away from the giant maw.

Something horrible is in there, corpse. I can sense it.

He did not respond, but he felt it too. Palpable dread came from the cave, and the First was in no hurry to investigate. The current took them away, and the memories of Lethe faded for even the Zombie-King. The heat slowly rose, and Phlegethon came closer. He hoped Piotyr had fared well.

chapter nineteen

He spake, and there came divers sorts of flies, and lice in all their coasts.
- Psalm: 105:31

They sat in silence at the campfire after Jacob had finished recounting his tale. He liked the... at least *chronologically...* younger Templar. Jacob looked to be several years his senior, but he was born a couple of centuries later. *Fucking weird.* He liked Jacob. He thought they could be friends in other circumstances, were they not forced into spending eternity here in purgatory. Without another option, he was grateful that he did, in fact, like the man.

"I think we should try to leave."

Markov looked up to see Jacob looking away towards the edge of the valley. "We can't, I've tried for, apparently, hundreds of years. The closer I get, the weaker I become."

"I tried too, and felt it as well, but I think the two of us can do it."

"Why do you think that?" The hunger was too great to overcome; it always rose to a point of incapacitation.

"I think, perhaps, that this is a prison meant only for one, and that two could escape. I know you have no reason to believe me, having just arrived, but hear me out."

Markov's eyebrows rose. Of course he would hear Jacob out. What, he should be angry that Jacob was suggesting they leave just because Markov had been there for far longer? That was petty. "Sure, what do you suggest?"

"I think perhaps we are unique in that we both called the Apotheosis in Hell. Well, at least I did, but from your words you say you reached the portal before succumbing. What if you actually didn't succumb until you were *through* the portal?"

"Hell if I know, but I suppose that could have happened. I only remember the portal, and falling asleep."

"Well you might have fallen forward. If you did, then your soul didn't burn out on Earth, but rather like me you were in Hell when the Tether burned away."

"Look, I don't know anything about it, but it sounds like you do. Sure, whatever you say, that could have happened." He wasn't irritated, but he also wished Merethius would just get to the point.

"Well if that is true, then I believe we two are unique in being the only two mortals to have done this in Hell, and coincidentally I think that is why we are both here instead of wherever else mortal souls should end up in Hell. I knew a... a woman who told me some of the workings here and she indicated to me that souls consumed in Hell are simply gone. Ours still exist, and feel relatively intact. Why is that?"

Ok, now he was getting annoyed. He was no philosopher. He was a soldier. He killed things. "Jacob, I don't want to be rude, but seriously, I don't know or care about this shit. Spit it out."

The other Templar scowled for a moment, but seemed to get over it quickly. His face softened and he spoke again.

"Ok, well I believe that we are stuck here together because of the Apotheosis occurring for us in Hell, and that our souls were supposed to be destroyed but weren't because of that. I think we can leave any time we want, but we will have to do it together."

"Fine, I'll bite. How?"

"Are you familiar with Invocations of Sustenance?"

"Yeah, but I don't think that would work. I've tried before, but the hunger gets too strong and I can't think, let alone pray."

"Agreed, but what if I were to Invoke for you as you moved forward, and then you could do the same for me?"

Markov sat still for a moment and thought about it. No way could it be that easy... but... he *hadn't* ever had the possibility of a second person helping him before. Fuck it, it was worth a try.

"Let's go."

"Now? You are ready to try now?"

"You want to stay here? Look, it doesn't change. I've been here for goddamn ever, and it's going to be the same tomorrow as it was fifty years ago. If you think this will work, let's try it now."

"Very well."

🛡️☪️📜⚕️📖

"Watch carefully, Han." Joshua nodded for the man to move forward, smiling reassuringly. It had been hard to convince himself of the ethics of what he asked the man to do, but he believed in the elixir and the man had been willing to assist with very little prodding.

The man was nervous, but Joshua hoped that was more to do with being intimidated by Han than worried about Joshua's competence. Han's reputation had grown somewhat fearsome as of late. He smiled at the man again, Olrig was his name, and motioned to go ahead.

The man appeared to steel himself, and nodded back at Joshua before drinking the elixir. "Go ahead Ulraen, he will be fine."

"Ok, but I absolve myself of wrongdoing if it goes poorly."

"That's not how absolution works, but fine." Joshua watched with rapt attention as Ulraen almost gently took out his knife and slashed a long gash along the man's forearm. Olrig winced in pain as the blood welled in the wound, but before it could spill Joshua let out a shout of joy as the flesh knit, closed, and healed in seconds.

"Pay him, Ulraen. Olrig, your bravery and assistance will be noted. Thank you."

"Anything to help, Ba'al Joshua." Olrig smiled, accepted his payment, and left.

He left, and Joshua looked to Han. "Well?"

Han stood without answering, and walked over to the now empty vial. "Do you have more on hand?"

"Yes, I have another sample. It isn't hard to make, just taxing on the mind. I can produce it in quantity, now that the vaccine production is well in hand."

"Might I try the other sample?"

He blinked for a moment before his eyes dropped to Han's torso. His friend kept it covered, but now it made sense. "Of course, Han, I'm sorry I didn't think of it." Joshua went into his laboratory and retrieved a second vial and handed it to Han. "Drink in good health."

Han smiled and raised the vial. "Longevity and Heath." He drank the vial, and opened his robe to expose the red, raw looking scar that he had earned at Sheol Moloch, when a ballista bolt had impaled him. The Ba'al had him healed, but it was not like what the Templar did and the wound had remained as fresh as the first day it was sealed.

To Joshua, it did appear that the wound began to knit together somewhat, but the process stalled and ceased before any real progress was made. He frowned, but Han's laugh forestalled him. "Don't worry; I didn't expect it to do much. It was worth a try, though."

"It must be a residual effect of what Ba'al Moloch did. Without some understanding of their methods..."

"Really, Joshua. It's fine. It doesn't even hurt that much, it's just uncomfortable. I keep it clean, and even my novice knowledge of healing allows me to stave off infection. Perhaps someday."

"Maybe someday, if we win the siege and any Ba'al survive, I'd like to question them. I would imagine at least one of them would be willing to help, if they thought it would increase their chances of survival."

Joshua honestly believed that. Certainly not out of the goodness of their black hearts, but self-preservation was a powerful motivator. If a Ba'al caused the wound, then a Ba'al ought to be able to show him how to heal it.

"We'll see. How many of those can you produce in the next couple of weeks?"

"Several hundred at the least, but I hope to make well clear of a thousand. It should make our lesser troops far more effective."

"Agreed. Good work."

Joshua smiled. It truly was just another small thing, but enough of them added together might mean something.

The blades had stopped plunging into his flesh for some time but he let the agony fade for far longer before he stood. It was a deep and profound sensation, standing without injury. He could not have guessed at the number of wounds he had suffered but he had the sense that for every cut and stab he had given the Legion in his lifetime, he had been given one in return. More. He had killed men as well, in his long career.

Ozra was still with him, and Kasim smiled to see the young man talking with Jio quietly a short distance away. He wondered when Jio had arrived. They both turned to him as he righted his posture and smiled back. "Are the scales balanced, honored students?"

"Not yet, master." Jio spoke as Ozra stood by. "You have felt the physical pain you caused over your life. That price has been paid. Before you move on to your next trial, we merely wished to thank you and wish you well."

"I see. You will not be joining me any longer?" He had hoped that whatever Han had done could be undone. They deserved better than to be bound to him.

Ozra touched him lightly on the shoulder as he spoke. "It is time for us to move on, master. We have assisted as we can, and our time in this place is near its end. Our own journey must continue."

Kasim felt a bittersweet lump in his throat. He would never escape the guilt over their deaths, but he did have an intimate knowledge of death's journey and knew that greater possibilities awaited them. "Peace be upon you, honored warriors of Sagarmatha."

Jio and Ozra smiled as one, genuine warmth and affection coming from both of them as they answered in unison. "And on you, honored teacher."

Kasim held their gaze as they dissipated and faded away, leaving him alone in the gloom. He was happy for them, in a way, though sad at the loss of his friends. He calmly accepted that it was simply more death he had caused. It clung to him like a lover's embrace. He longed to escape violence at some point, but also knew that day was not coming any time soon. He shook his head from the uselessness of wishful thinking, and resumed his journey into the twilight. He knew there would be more. He steeled his courage against the dread he could sense still awaited him.

Piotyr snorted as the water rose in bubbles and steam. His raft had begun to smolder so rather than wait for it to burst into flame he had put ashore and now walked along the river's edge, in tattered rags slowly smoldering into ruin. He did not know if this was Phlegethon proper, in fact he suspected it was not, but certainly it was the right direction.

The heat didn't touch him in the slightest, though he did have concern for any denizens of the water seizing him. He kept a good three paces away from the water when he could, and carefully watched the surface for any sign of movement when terrain forced him closer. Few were the beings in Hell that could withstand the touch of his flames, but if there was such a place that was likely to have them it would be here. He kept his sword drawn as he moved along the water's edge.

His journey was not taxing, though his mind fought him at every step with distraction. The siege of The High Sheol played out over and over, with variations each time depending on what he chose to do. It was almost like a chess match where he knew what the opponent was doing not only on their next move, but the next five. Always the moves changed though, as he and his opponent countered each other's decisions.

He had a hard time focusing on what he was doing, but the hours passed without incident, and then the night did as well. He did notice every now and then something rippling below the surface of the water, but never did anything breach the surface or try to bother him on the water's edge. Perhaps they thought he was kin. Snorting, he realized that perhaps he *was* kin.

His thoughts and battle planning kept him occupied and the heat roiling off the river became hotter and hotter, which kept him energized and causing him to feel no need for rest. For two days and two nights he traversed the riverbank, and the water boiled. It was without surprise he saw ahead as the water, bursting and bubbling, plunged into a great cavern. Heat always came from within the ground. Without fear he entered the darkness, though noted great vents of red light would make it easy to see once his eyes adjusted.

For another hour he walked and noted with dismay that the water disappeared underground. He would not be able to go any further without plunging into the burning water. He stopped where the riverbank descended into the rock and sighed. Touching the scalding water, he at least was pleased to not feel any pain or discomfort. He would be fine from the water itself.

If there were creatures under the depths, he would deal with that then. It would not be the first time he had faced a beast with nothing but his bare hands. There was little chance he could use his sword underwater, at least not effectively. He was thankful for the leather scabbard for it, though he didn't know what sort of reptile had skin tough enough to withstand the heat he radiated. His head swam for a moment with strange images of red scales and roars of pain. Placing his hand upon the cavern wall to steady himself, he shook his head free of the strange images. Something was definitely wrong, but he couldn't place it.

He could think of no reason to delay. He needed the source water, and that meant a plunge. The river disappeared under the rock swiftly, leading Piotyr to believe that it would not be underground for long.

Wishing himself good luck and taking a deep breath, he dove into the river. He hoped he would breathe air again soon.

Ba'al Mirish couldn't help but smile. Since he had been given special orders from Ba'al Apollyon, he had been anxiously awaiting the call to arms and the signal to break camp. It was time, and his excitement was bursting. *The mortals had no idea...*

He had been instructed meticulously, but it was not to begin until Abaddon gave the order and the Infernal Host left the portal to Haven to begin the march back to Sheol. Now that camp was broken, one month would be about how long it took to march, and Mirish spared a self-indulgent perusal of the might of Abaddon.

Legion indeed. The Destroyer had called nearly the entire combined forces of the Ba'al back from every single front in the war to join him in marching on Sheol. Of the few Ba'al whose Legion was not called, strict orders had to be given for them to remain to keep the mortals at bay, lest the rest come of their own volition. No one wanted to sit on Earth to await the results of a challenge, especially one involving the end of Lucifer's line. Only a few token, weaker Ba'al remained at some of the critical areas, including Haven, but not any real force. If the humans weren't almost dead already, it might have given them a chance to regroup.

The logistics had taken time and more time would pass before the forces would find their stations again and finish the war. Months at least, perhaps even a year. It was a certainty that the mortals were beaten, but extermination took time. Haven was the last Sanctuary, but they were not the only humans left still drawing breath. Mirish had a lot of respect for the roving, nomadic guerilla fighters who had survived for so long without the walls of a Sanctuary. Most were gone, now, but not all. Mountains, in particular, were where many of them hid like rats. To finish would take longer, but the destruction of House Ve'kal came first.

With a smile, he gazed out at the forces, so massive that he couldn't see their end on either side of the horizon. Tens of millions of Legionnaire were breaking camp and beginning the slow movement that would take them to Sheol. Ve'kal would flee, or surrender, within moments of seeing the force Abaddon commanded, of that Mirish was sure. Or she wouldn't, he laughed as he thought. Maybe the stupid bitch would actually allow The Destroyer to live up to his name. Mirish didn't care at all for Sheol. Let it burn.

He had heard Abaddon calmly detail the opposition he expected to face, as if it was a real threat. Mirish checked himself. Ba'al Apollyon was his better, in every way, and if he chose to treat Sheol as a real obstacle to overcome, Mirish would respect that.

Still, listening to the Destroyer list the counters he had prepared for what Ve'kal and her human pets could bring to battle was comical. He expected the plague and knew much of it from information gathered from all over the Empire. Alchemists from House Apollyon had worked directly with the Grigori and the finest minds in the Infernal Host to craft salves and injections which while certainly would not inoculate the Legion, it would most definitely slow down the process significantly. Ve'kal would expect the Legion to die within seconds, while in reality it would take minutes, if not the better part of an hour. Abaddon's Master Alchemist had even theorized that if a Legionnaire could survive being exposed to the pathogen for long enough, they might be able to fight it off themselves.

It had been tested, of course, and while the results were erratic, there was some evidence to support that some of the Legionnaire would live much longer than others. They all died, eventually, after exposure, but the time spent healthy and hale before succumbing varied wildly from subject to subject. Not that it mattered, they could all die and Abaddon would still win the day. It would make coming back to earth and finishing the scouring take much, much longer, but so be it. Legionnaire were useful, but ultimately a secondary weapon.

Millions of Fallen angels had answered Abaddon's call as well, more than he wanted, in truth, but the flood was so vast it would have taken longer to sort out who shouldn't be there than just to accept all comers and move as one giant battalion. More than one hundred million had fallen with Lucifer after the Seraphim won. Though the millennia had taken a toll on those original true Fallen, the majority of the Host was intact. Betrayal, dissention, schism, civil war, and involvement with Earth had

189

culled many, but not since the followers of Lucifer stood against the tyranny of Michael had such a force been united. Ve'kal had no chance. Let her summon her plague, and her Templar Invoke the Soul Fire. Looking out at the vast and invincible infernal Legion, Mirish knew it mattered not. The end was upon them.

Do you believe that fate is unavoidable, corpse?

The First thought about Lokyrg's words carefully, as staring at the cavern inexplicably in front of them again caused him, uncomfortably, worry.

"Unavoidable is a powerful word. I do not think anything is unavoidable, though often we lack the knowledge and wisdom to avoid."

That seems an expedient answer. Philosophy is abhorrent to me, and I only know of its toxic existence from that fool, Han. Do you think we must be here?

He didn't want to argue, and although Han was certainly no fool, Lokyrg in many ways was. Cunning, vicious, and quick to learn, yes, but brash, reckless, and simplistic as well.

"I do not mean to speak in circles. I think there is a way for us not to enter the cavern, but I do not know of it, so perhaps in that sense, yes, *our* fate is currently unavoidable."

So what do you think is in there? This is our third time circling back on it, and I sense something terrible within.

He could sense it too. Deep within that cavern was something powerful. What purpose did he serve in being here? What was his reason for being diverted here, time and again, instead of seeking Phlegethon?

"I believe we are meant to find out. Are you with me in journeying within?"

There does not seem to be another choice available to us, corpse.

There was always a choice, but he didn't feel it was a viable one. With no understanding of an alternate route to take, he suspected choosing to leave would only result in finding their way here repeatedly. He knew that Hell had strange and mysterious things... and none stranger perhaps than near Lethe.

He stood on the raft staring into the maw of the cavern for a long moment before raising the oar and drifting into the blackness. What would be, will be.

⛨ ☪ ♟ ⚕ ⛰

Joshua didn't feel comfortable with what Han was doing, but he knew it could be potentially devastating to Apollyon's Legion. He sighed, and grudgingly admitted that it wasn't Han's actions he was uncomfortable with, but rather his own innate ability.

The room was in a vast, lower chamber beneath the Sheol dungeons. Han had taken him there to show him yet another of his newly designed siege defenses. Well, perhaps not designed, but certainly repurposed. The stench was overpowering, but Joshua was used to such things. Han was now, too, he supposed.

Since the battle at Sheol Am, when Joshua had learned to control insects and make them do his will, he had largely avoided the issue. Beyond that, one of the primary goals in the weeks following the defeat of the Shay'tan was hygiene, which demanded that the rotting carrion outside the walls had been cleared and immolated. At least that is what Joshua had thought, anyway. It turned out that Han had a different use for the decaying meat, and had it transported down in the bowels of Sheol.

Objectively, Joshua could identify it as distasteful, but smelling the putrescence and hearing the skittering and swarming in the darkness, he knew why Han had asked him here.

"Yes, I can do it. Have you created an effective vector for getting them to the plains?"

Han nodded, and clapped Joshua on the shoulder. "Yes, I've had Dhermina supervising the engineers. Her descriptions of the light panels where she comes from gave me the idea. There are tunnels, about a pace wide, that lead up from this cavern right into the fields."

"What about getting them to move there quickly? I can help, but I need to be close enough to see them as well as where I want them to go. I had thought to be on the walls."

"Yes, Joshua. I think that would be best as well. I can get them out of here and into the fields quickly, without you directing them from down here. When they are amongst Abaddon's Legion, will they follow your orders without constant direction?"

He thought about it for a moment, but he really wasn't sure. He sent out his thoughts, carefully, as the swarm was a chaotic storm of different sensations. He gave the order to fly in a circle before going back to eating and reproducing.

A myriad of thoughts assailed him. Hunger, lust, fear, devotion, rage... all poked at his consciousness like tiny needles. He struggled to keep the sensations out, and with great effort, he was successful.

"Yes, I think they will. How big do you think the swarm will be?"

Han frowned a moment before answering. "I'm not entirely sure. I can't communicate with them like you can, but the swarm is growing. I know this is disgusting, but I thought of it shortly before Kasim was attacked. I thought it was a waste to just burn the corpses, and the flies had already laid so many eggs in the bodies..."

"I don't disagree, Han. It is disgusting, but you are right, we can use them. The ones that didn't rise were just wasted resources. I'd prefer the plague-walkers, but this is a good idea. I won't waste resources just because it's unpleasant."

Han smiled at him. "This is all unpleasant, but I want to win, which is highly unlikely. The chances do not lie with us, but everything we can do to make victory even somewhat more possible is a smart decision."

"I agree. Lots of little things can add up. I just wish we had Piotyr back. I would feel much better with him, the water, and a healthy Kasim."

"As would I, my friend. As would I."

chapter twenty

Great in soul are they who become what is godlike: they alone know me, the origin, the deathless: they offer me the homage of an unwavering mind.
- The Yoga of Mysticism: Bhagavad-Gita

The gnawing in his belly threatened to tear out his spine. He felt the ravenous hunger like a wound. Jacob grit his teeth and tried to take just one more step but collapsed to his knees, nauseous and light-headed.

His thoughts were overwhelmed with the desire to flee back the way he came and he made to do so when the waves of sustaining vigor washed over him and his hunger faded into nothing. Grinning, he stood and waved Markov forward. The other Templar smiled and quickly ran up to and past Jacob before he too slowed, then doubled over with hunger pangs, and fell to his knees as Jacob had.

Jacob gathered his willpower and Invoked a powerful Prayer of Sustenance, completing it just as his own stomach once again began to grumble and churn. He sustained the prayer while Markov stood, barely able to keep chanting as his hunger grew. Markov waved him on and Jacob ran quickly forward, barely getting two paces beyond the ancient Templar before once again collapsing.

The pattern repeated, for how long, he had no idea. All of his attention was focused on moving forward or Invoking Sustenance for Markov. He spared no glance behind them, focusing instead on moving ever onward. Strength, Invocation, movement, weakness. Again and again the Templar traded Invocations, while the sun fell behind the mountains and darkness slowly entered the valley.

They made their way ever onward up the sloping hills, navigating around trees, streams, and rock. They covered less and less ground as the terrain grew more difficult. Eventually only a few steps were being taken by the Templar before the hunger forced them to sustain themselves with prayer. The effort grew harder until it felt to Jacob that every step was gut wrenching. The night grew black, and Jacob wove an Invocation of Dark Sight into the rotation. He feared for the loss of any time for the Sustenance, but if one of them fell and was injured all their progress would be lost. An actual Invocation of Light would have made it easier but it would have taken more time and required more energy, neither of which Jacob thought he could spare.

Markov must have feared normal exertion as he Invoked a simple Vigor Prayer. Likely he felt the same, that Strength would have been more useful, but also more taxing and time consuming. Jacob was running on fumes and he doubted the other man was faring much better. They had to ration their stamina. Almost every ounce of energy they had went to moving forward and Invoking Sustenance.

The moon grew high and then dipped low again, and still they trudged upwards. The air grew cold and thin, and frost crunched under their boots as dawn slowly inched towards them. The rhythm took over, and Jacob spared little thought for anything other than the journey. The only sounds were their footfalls, labored breathing, and the occasional broken branch. Dawn broke and the warmth of the sun was welcome.

Hours more must have passed. He couldn't tell from his own perspective, but the sun climbed high in the sky and then crested the zenith. The hunger, he was sure, would have killed him by now if not for Markov. They were long past the point of no return. If they faltered, their bodies would fail long before they could get back to the valley, and after having gone this far, Jacob would rather die than return. He had earned freedom and he would have it.

He would have bantered with Markov, or at least spoken to help the time go swiftly, but he couldn't spare the breath. Invoke, move, falter, and receive sustenance. It went on for the rest of that day. The two men neared what looked like it could be a summit. He smiled weakly, but forced himself to keep at their same pace. Push themselves too hard now, and exhaustion could get them before hunger.

It was the longest hour of his life, that last leg of the journey to that last point on the mountain. He did not know why but reaching the summit felt important to him. With a final, mighty effort, he crested the rise and gasped in relief as the hunger left him and he looked down the other side of the mountain across a wide expanse of plains. Not Sheol, of that he was sure.

He turned to help Markov, and stumbled as his legs buckled. He cursed his weakness and crawled forward to reach a hand out to help the other Templar. Markov grabbed it, and the two men collapsed, exhausted but alive, on the summit. No words were exchanged, just a broad grin from each as both fell into exhausted slumber, having escaped their purgatory. It was as sweet a sleep as Jacob could recall having.

"I fear this may break him, Tal. This is too much for one man to overcome, even our Master."

"No, Qor. He will survive this. He must. His soul demands balance, and this is part of it."

Kasim heard the words through a hurricane of chaos. The blades had torn at his flesh and he longed for that simplicity. The torment he endured now carried no pain and no physical discomfort, yet was all the more disturbing. He *felt* his sanity being rent, his mind unspooling. Thoughts were taken from him like thread pulled from a garment.

He fought against it, but was only successful in placing a few errant strands back in place as more and more spun off into oblivion. He screamed only for a moment before stopping, confused at his own actions.

He wept as everything he knew was taken from him and then ceased that as well, wondering why he was so sad.

"*He* will survive nothing, what remains will be a husk, a shell. Our Master is ceasing to exist before our eyes."

"Qor, we are here to guide him back to himself. He won't do this alone. I believe in us."

The woman who had just spoken was familiar to him, but only for a moment. In short order, there was nothing, only the sense of sitting and waiting and for what he did not know.

"I hope you are right, Tal. Let's do what we can." The man was not familiar to Kasim, though it sounded like he should be.

He let himself be helped to his feet by the two people standing near. Both were young and Kasim felt strongly some kind of connection to them before that too dissipated into confusion.

His mind made feeble, he let himself be led away from the twilight and towards a brighter, though not very, light some distance away. For what, he did not know, and did not care.

Gasping for breath, Piotyr broke the surface of the steaming water as the outflow pressure shot him far out into a ruddy grotto. The red cavern wall glowed hot as he sucked in the precious air. This had to be the source water for Phlegethon. He tread water lightly, filling his lungs as his eyes took in the sights surrounding him. The stink of sulfur was powerful and he wrinkled his nose at the stench, but it was barely noticeable against the sheer awe he felt in looking at the massive cave.

Never had he seen such a place with the scope being, he guessed, dozens of miles across. The subterranean room was immense and the red glow which he thought at first to be coming from simple fissures in the rock was instead writing... in a script he had not seen since... since something long ago.

"To destroy that which is darkest, I freely sacrifice that which burns brightest. May our greatest fire purge all that is black."

His head reeled in dizziness and he sputtered as his head went back underwater for a moment. Spitting out the thick, brimstone tinged water, he coughed and swam to the side of the cavern. The pressure from the under current diminished quickly, leading him to believe it was a deep pool he was in, and if the size of cavern was any indication, the pond was more likely a lake, with incredible depth. Placing his hand along the wall, he was pleased to feel the solidity and warmth of it. He was not sure how long he had held his breath and swam along the current, but with his Invocation of Air and how out of wind he was when he surfaced, he guessed over ten minutes. Perhaps more than a quarter-hour. The speed at which he had been swept along meant he was far, far away from the currents of Lethe which had led him here. The scent, the sights, and his gut all told him he was in the right place. He had found the source water.

Attempting to climb out of the water was pointless where he was at, it was sheer rock, but he was able to swim along the edge towards what he hoped was a landing further in. The cavern was beautiful, in a dark and forboding manner. The writing was Angelic Script, he was sure of it, though he knew not how. *The Tongue of Babel.* It was distinct, and though he couldn't read more than a few words, he still knew it when he saw it, though he had no idea why. That much writing was incredible. Even at this distance he could tell the letters were large, but not so large as could be read easily from where he was. What could possibly be written over the entirety of the cavern?

He conserved his strength as he swam, steadily moving along the rock face on his back in the water and gazing in wonder at the writing. No, not just writing, he saw etched pictures as well. Demons, Angels, and other incredible beasts he had no name for all graced the cave surrounding Phlegethon's source. The heat would have been unbearable, had he not been endowed with the gifts he had. Steam hissed and poured from the writing, and he knew without question that the blood of Hell itself flowed in those words; hellfire, magma, and molten metal pumping in time to the pulse of Hell.

He felt something brush his leg, startling him, and he looked down from the cavern ceiling and tread water again. The outflow had stopped completely and he was surprised to see hundreds... no thousands of burning skeletons drifting lazily in the scalding water. Scalding? The water must have been so hot that it boiled the flesh off the bones. He swam back a pace to see if a nearby skeleton noticed him, and even as the eyes of the corpse followed his, he could hear a whispering hiss escape the charred mouth. Piotyr cursed inwardly as it closed to him, then more so as dozens of corpses nearby saw the commotion and swam towards him.

He couldn't go back, that was out of the question, so he Invoked Strength and struck the hissing skull in the teeth, grunting with satisfaction when it shattered. Just bones. More rushed him and he fought them off as best he could in the water, though eventually was overwhelmed and grappled. He flailed and struck out in the water and destroyed the skeletons by the score. Athough they were light and his strength mighty, eventually he was overcome and slowly sank. He knew it was coming and did not panic. He held his breath and allowed them to take him down, not allowing himself to struggle. He held his breath for perhaps a minute, nodding with satisfaction that the skeletal hands and teeth did nothing to antagonize him further, and instead he assumed were content to just drown him.

He allowed his body to go limp, and inwardly smiled as he was released and the skeletons swam away. *Mindless creatures, or near enough to it.* He gave it another ten seconds or so and swam back to the surface, catching his wind and Invoking Air for more breath. He might need to do this several times. He watched in curiousity as the skeletons drifted away, leaving a wide circle around where he currently was. *Perhaps they keep to their general position, and the ones I destroyed here won't be replaced for a time?*

Perhaps. He swam away from the cavern wall taking great care to not exert himself and to keep his breathing even and steady and his Invocations strong and refreshed. He was not left alone for long, but it was much as before. He was slowly swarmed, taken down, and then after a minute or so, he feigned death and was released. The hands never tore or grasped at him, or his sword, other than to keep him under water.

Surfacing again, he spared a moment to look towards the center of the cavern and saw, way in the distance, an island of some sort, or at least something solid surrounding a white pillar. Distance was hard to judge, but it might have been several miles away. Sighing, he started the process again and kept at it for what felt like an eternity. Strangely, he felt a strong sense of deja vu while swimming across the burning liquid.

He knew it could not have been more than a couple of hours, and he was a very strong swimmer, but his muscles burned and his lungs ached as he drew closer to the spire of white and the blessedly solid rock surrounding it. He had lost count of the times he had struggled with the skeletons, but at least they hadn't adapted to his methods. God he was tired. He panted with effort as he dragged his wet, aching body onto the island.

As he sat on the warm stone and dried off, he smiled in weak satisfaction and filled up his sample containers with Phlegethon's life blood. *Only one left.* He lay back on the stone and basked in the warmth as his skin quickly dried. The white pillar was the only prominent feature on the island, and looking around at the enormous lake, Piotyr could see the water curve around a corner to his left and his right, far in the distance.

Perhaps its not really a lake, then, but merely an immense river. The waters barely flowed at all, but he still felt sure this was the right source that he needed. He stood, noticing more of the Angelic Script etched all over the stone island. He wished he could read it.

He moved to the pillar and stopped, so startled at the sensation he felt that for a moment he couldn't place it. The air around the pillar was cold. Freezing. It had been so long since he felt it he had almost forgotten. Frowning, he reached his hand forward and touched the white stone, cursing in pain as he realized it was no stone, but solid ice, unnaturally cold.

He blew on his hand, but as sure as he could possibly be, it was a frost burn. Not a bad one, but it did sting. Moving away, he placed his hand in the waters of Phlegethon and the pain was soothed.

He frowned again. "Cocytus. It must be from Cocytus." His head swam again, and he grabbed at his chest as he felt freezing barbs, for just a moment, pierce his flesh.

Growling, he moved to the pillar and walked around it in a circle. It was at least two paces in diameter, perhaps closer to three. It was completely frosted over. The ambient temperature must have been well over the hottest temperature he could imagine in Hell, so the only explanation for the frozen pillar was that it led to someplace much, much colder.

He went back to the water and dove in, swimming out a ways until he drew close to one of the burning corpses. He grabbed the thing hissing and reaching for him, and hauled it back to the island. By itself, it was a feeble opponent, and Piotyr had no trouble manhandling it and forcing its searing bones up against the pillar.

High pitched steam and screeching assaulted his ears, but he held the thing in place as the ice melted away from where the skeleton was pressed against it. The bones slowly lost their flames, and the thing fell limp, even more lifeless than it was a moment ago.

Tossing the pile back into the water, he was surprised to see the thing twitch a moment before swimming back out to its former place in the lake, or river. The opposing forces must be somewhat in balance, he thought. Briefly able to cancel each other out, but not overpower each other for long.

He looked closely at the pillar where he had melted the ice away and saw that it was in fact, stone underneath, and was also covered in Angelic Script. He peered intently at the edges and saw the frost begin to encroach back over the rock, albeit slowly. Someplace cold indeed, but the ice was not strong enough to force its way further into the cavern. Not somewhat in balance, then, but perfectly in balance.

He looked closely as the frost crept back over it and one of the carved phrases in the Tongue of Babel burned brightly and caught his eye. It was a word he knew. *Hellfire.* The word ignited on the pillar and Piotyr felt a surge of power familiar, yet confusingly foreign, arc into his veins as fire from Phlegethon leaped over the stone Island, into his veins, and burst from him over the Icy Pillar.

He fell to his knees in rapture as the ice melted away and flowed over the stone to join with Phlegethon. Steam rose around him and Piotyr felt renewed. He stood and placed his hand upon the now completely thawed stone pillar. It felt neither cold nor warm. He laughed, and climbed up the carving on the outside of the pillar. It was not an easy climb, but he managed.

He reached the top with some effort, and without surprise saw that the stone was hollow and led down far into blackness. Cold air rose from the depths, and he could feel ice crystals form on his eyebrows. He snorted, and spoke the word again. "Hellfire." Another powerful burst of fire came from Phlegethon and poured into him atop the spire.

It was clear that this was a barrier to someone other than him. He knew now where to find the last source, and he hoped that his journey was near to completion. If he descended into the cold, and found Cocytus to be too far removed from Phlegethon to draw upon hellfire, he would die and his quest would fail.

The fear of failure was greater than the fear of death. He was no coward. He believed he would be successful. He had come this far and would not fall to the ice of Cocytus any more than the fires of Phlegethon. He steeled himself and Invoked Voice with all of his willpower. Screaming for Hellfire as loud as he could, he cast himself into the pillar, immolated like a falling star. He would see this through to the end.

"Fuck me, would you look at that?"

"I don't think I will ever get used to how you speak, Markov."

The centuries older man looked over at his apparent elder and smiled.

"I never thought I'd get out of there, Jacob. You have to understand that, I thought I would *never* get out. It feels incredible. You coming here was a gift from God."

"Well, I wasn't there as long as you were, but you might not thank me when we get down off of the mountain. This is Hell, Markov. I don't know what is different between this piece of rock and the one twenty feet back the way we came, but that wasn't Hell, and this is. I can feel it."

Markov scowled and looked down the other side of the summit. Desolate plains stretched as far as they could see, with not a single sign of civilization. "I don't doubt your word, my friend, but I don't feel anything."

Jacob was silent for a moment before answering. He had thought about this conversation only a little. The man had a right to know but it would not surprise Jacob if Markov hated him after. Still, he had a right to know.

"Markov, I told you briefly of how I came to be in Purgatory with you, but not of how I came to be in Hell to begin with. I will tell you now, and I ask only that you allow me to finish before you cast judgement upon me."

"Uh, sure? Its none of my concern, Jacob, but I will listen if it makes you feel better."

Jacob smiled at the younger, yet far older, man and told him. It was not a long story but the sun was setting as he finished. "That is how I came to be part demon, and cast into Hell."

Markov was silent for a while, then responded by clapping Jacob on the arm. "Done is done. You are no more demon than I am, and I'm not any part. What he did to you doesn't change who you are, Jacob. Let it go. What say we get out of here and find something to eat. I feel a normal hunger, and I would love to get out of this place."

Jacob felt relieved. In truth, he expected Markov to turn his back on him at the least, or attack him at the worst. Markov seemed genuine in not caring about Jacob's past, which meant he was a true friend. Piotyr wouldn't have judged him either, but then again the same thing had been done to Piotyr. The others as well. Markov had not been damned, and still did not judge him. He was a rare man, then.

"I agree, and I would like to eat something as well. It is getting late, we should take care climbing down in the dark."

Markov nodded and both men began their Invocations for Dark Sight. It felt good to be out of the valley and back in the lands of the living, Hell or not. He finished the Prayer and gasped as his soul ignited in a torrent he had felt only once before.

NO! NO! NO! He screamed internally as the Apotheosis burned through his veins, just the same as when he had brought Duskfall down atop the skull of the Shay'tan and liberated Hell from the House of Lucifer. His divine tether, his connection to God burned with holy fire and Jacob noticed that Markov had also fallen to his knees. Both men knelt on the ground in pained ecstasy as their souls burned away.

NOT AGAIN, I WILL NOT GO INTO THE DARK AGAIN! Jacob railed against the injustice of it, having done his service a thousand times over and paid the ultimate price. Now he was to relive it again?! He screamed defiance and rage into the sky and noticed with surprise that he was on his feet and then floating in the air. Immense golden wings erupted from his back, a nimbus of white glowing in the air around him.

Markov changed before his eyes as well. The smaller man had clutched at his skull for a moment before he too stood and metamorphosed into a golden winged form of his own. The two Templar hovered in place above the mountain summit, two mortal angels in the throes of the Soul Fire as it washed away their very spirits in a deluge of righteous wrath.

He raged for long moments, screaming invectives into the sky and blasting white lances of holy destruction into the valley below him. He would not go back! His hatred for the injustice of his life threatened to consume his mind even as the Apotheosis consumed his soul. He watched Markov, at first surprised at the man's lack of anger, then he felt his own anger give way to sadness and futility as the reality sunk in. He was already a dead man, there was no escaping it.

He lowered himself back to the summit and waited for it to end. "Not with a yell, then, but with a whimper." His voice was as pure, strong, and soothing as a silent snowfall in the dead of night. The gravity of the loss was not lost on him, and his voice brought a great and heavy sadness upon him.

"What are you talking about, Jacob?"

"This. Our souls flow out of us like a wound. The Apotheosis consumes us even as we speak. Minutes are left to us, perhaps less."

Markov looked at him intently, then up to the sky, closing his eyes and inhaling deeply. "At San Luis I felt this, but only briefly before the sense of loss became urgent. I knew then, when I did this thing, this thing you call the Soul Fire, that I was on borrowed time and had to hurry. I rushed to kill the attacking Legion, Ba'al and all, as I knew I did not have long."

"I am sorry you had to be the first, Markov. Would that it didn't have to be so, although I feel if it did not, we all would have died long ago. Sorry that it has caught up with you here, and me for that matter."

Markov smiled and placed his arm on Jacob's shoulder. "Stop thinking for a moment and *feel*."

Jacob frowned, but something in Markov's face gave him pause. He was short on time in any case, and what use was arguing about it going to do them. He closed his eyes, and allowed the sensations to wash over him.

The Apotheosis was supposedly somewhat different in each Templar it had manifested in, but there were some typical similarities, always reported second hand. Time appeared to flow differently for those in the midst of the Soul Fire, and Jacob found that to be true. Both now and when he had battled the heir of Lucifer at Sheol, he could sense a stillness about the air around him that belied a simple calm. Wind was slower, the light shined differently, and the sights and sounds of the environment were more stark, easier to distinguish. Markov did not appear to be affected, at least to Jacob's senses, but he was within the Soul Fire himself.

Other things were also typical and easy to see once a Templar manifested. Strength, speed, stamina, all of those things which Templar frequently Invoked in battle all were magnified tenfold, perhaps more. These things he felt as he stood on the summit, eyes closed. He could sense the power in his arms, his legs, even his voice as he did as Markov asked. His fatigue and hunger were distant memories now and if a batallion of Legion were to appear on the fields far below, he could wipe them out without straining himself at all. These things he knew.

What he also knew was that the power was finite, and would fade quickly. It was the nature of the weapon, and the fuel to use it was a Templar's own soul, their own divine connection to God. Once ignited, it would burn away until nothing remained but a husk. The Final Invocation exacted the ultimate price.

But... as he stood there waiting, he did not feel the tether diminishing. He was not an expert, but he knew what he had felt last time and clearly his experience now was not the same. The tether was staying strong and Jacob did not feel an oncoming doom. It was as if the ashes his soul was turning into had been *banked.* It was the only way he could describe it. He felt the connection, as strong as ever, and he felt it burning, but not burning away. He opened his eyes, and Markov was standing there smiling.

"It burns, but remains strong. Watch." Markov then Invoked Dark Sight as they had intended, and then with a shuddering gasp his wings dissipated and his golden aura vanished. He was Markov, as before, alive and well.

Jacob did as well, and gasped himself as the holy power fled from his body, though he could have easily grabbed it back. Time snapped back into place, his enhanced body became normal again, and the only different thing he felt was that he could see into the dark, as intended, and he could feel the tether within him unbroken and strong.

"I don't understand... we should be dead, or dying. This cannot be."

"Well, looks like it can. It is there... not out of reach, not running out, not anything except... there. I can feel it waiting."

Markov was right. Jacob felt it as well. The Soul Fire was accessible. If he wanted to, it was within his grasp. He had no idea why, but it had to have something to do with him... with *them* being in Hell, or perhaps the demon imbued into his soul... *no, that can't be it, Markov has no such essence within him and I had that demon in my soul already when I slew the Shay'tan.*

He shook his head in wonder and his night eyes could see clearly for leagues. He smiled at Markov. Answers could wait. Food could not.

A child trusts without question and accepts their environment with no skepticism, and it was thus with him. Kasim walked with the strangers Qor and Tal with wonder and appreciation and a smile on his face. He walked in silence, content to follow the strangers and their smiles and encouraging words without question, fear, or cause for worry.

They smiled back at him often and told him he was doing well and was strong. He did not know who they were, not really, but their names sounded kind to him. Kasim could not remember his parents, nor any siblings, but the two kind strangers were much as he imagined a brother or sister would be like.

The shadowy gloom within which they walked was strange to him. It was thick, like a hot fog falling on a jungle, though the temperature was cool, bordering on chilled. The smell was odd as well, cloying like a sweet tea, yet acrid like a salt flat under a broiling midday sun. He shrugged his shoulders and smiled. He was not worried and nothing ill would befall him within the presence of his newfound friends.

They stopped in a small stone circle, the indigo and violet hued mist drifting in and out of the ring lazily. Strange characters adorned the stones, glowingly black with sparkling energy which meant nothing to him and caused him no concern. What possible threat existed with his friends to protect him?

"Master... Kasim, you are... you have done things in your life which you do not remember. Vio... difficult things which we need to show you. It will not be easy, but you must heal your mind. Purification does not come easily..."

"Qor... no words will prepare him. He must be shown. It is time."

The two of them shared a long glance and Kasim smiled at them. He was not worried. "I trust you, show me what you need to show me."

"Very well, master. Be strong, know that you will not enjoy this, but it must be. Know that we love you, and we would change nothing about our journey. We do not blame you, and as always, we honor you. Peace be upon you."

The woman called Tal finished speaking and gently grabbed the arm of the man called Qor before they stepped out of the ring and into the gloom. The quiet grew deep and heavy, and Kasim felt his ease slipping. He was not afraid, but without his friends, the gloom was not comforting. It was ominous.

He waited, rubbing his arms with his hands and anxiously peering into the twilight mist to see his friends. He felt a restlessness grow within his breast and he moved to enter the fog where Tal and Qor had vanished. He moved not even half a step past the stone circle when he gasped and fell back upon his backside.

A malevolent figure peered back at him from the gloom, human in many ways, but insidious and evil. Immortal eyes glowed red beneath a black helmet of wrath and spite. A mouth full of too many teeth leered at him where he sat paralyzed with fear upon the ground. The mouth split wide with a terrible facsimile of glee and Kasim felt horror descend upon him. He made to scream but as his mouth opened a slender blade of metal quietly slid out from the mouth of the horrific visage and blood poured forth as the being died beneath a rictus of shock and agony.

Kasim's scream died in his throat, a lump of terror and paralyzing fear choking him as he sat on the stone. The image of the monster dying faded and he saw more, similar beings rush into the gloom to shout alarm at the death of the first. Four of the beings drew blades and yelled in a language his childlike ears could not understand. They all, one by one, saw him sitting on the stone and smiled in pure evil satisfaction as they raised sword, axe, and knife to murder him... and one by one all fell as the same slender blade opened their throats, ribs, and groins.

The horrific images played out slowly over what felt like days. As they continued, knowledge crept into his mind. Demons, the beings were demons. *Legion.* The Legion had terrible fell beings among their ranks, and he saw dozens... hundreds of them turn murderous eyes upon him as he lay helpless. He saw their screams, tears, and coughed up blood endlessly displayed in front of him. The slender blades tore flesh and pierced the demon's veins for what seemed an eternity. Thousands of them died.

The bloodshed turned his stomach and he vomited upon the stone until only dry heaving and tiny amounts of yellow bile were squeezed from his abdomen in agonizing cramps as he still saw murder after murder play out. The creatures were not real, he could tell, because their bodies didn't accumulate and as soon as the evil eyes were drained of life, the corpses vanished only to be ever replaced by more carnage. The visions felt real, though.

Kasim fought his stomach convulsions and sat with his knees clenched to his chest, arms wrapped around them as he stared, wide-eyed at the neverending torrent of murder. Hours passed with the only change being the shapes and sizes of the victims. Legion, Fallen, Ba'al, and even what looked like true mortals fell to the slender blades. Uncommonly, other methods of death visited the unfortunate souls, here and there a Legion axe or an arrow or bolt, but the vast majority died to the silent, slender metal. The cascade of murders slowed, mercifully, as the time wore on, and eventually he saw an end to the death. He shivered violently and whispered softly to himself that it was over.

He saw more beings then, some Legion but also some mortals. He was relieved at first before he started to hear bones break and screaming from the myst forms. He was confused, as he didn't see any weapons, but soon came to understand that the demonic entities were not being killed, they were being maimed and crippled. The avalanche was not as overwhelming as the death visions, but it was still hard for him to watch. No blades erupted from flesh from unseen assailants, but he saw knees shatter and elbows snap, occasionally a throat crushed as well.

The images played out somewhat more quickly than the murders and once they were over, Kasim sat in silence on the stone circle as the horror and nausea slowly dissipated. Long minutes passed, until eventually the mist thinned and coalesced into a single shadowy figure who moved into the stone circle and knelt in front of him. He didn't flinch as the form moved slowly and did not threaten him in any way as it moved to within arms reach. Kasim smiled at the figure, but noticed with some disquiet that the figure was completely veiled in shadow and had no features that he could discern.

He waited for a short time for the creature or being to interact with him in some way, but when it just knelt there, unmoving, Kasim spoke. "Hail, friend. Did you see the horrors in the mist as well? Unsettling, and I am glad it is over. Do you know why such an image exists here, and why I needed to see it?"

The mist figure nodded, and Kasim took that for permission to continue. "Will you tell me? I have no idea why I am here or what is going on, though I would suspect you do. You look as if you belong here, and I don't mean that in a bad way."

The figure nodded again and beckoned Kasim closer. Kasim smiled and rose, moving towards the shadowy figure as it lifted its hands and lowered its now apparent cloak. Kasim's smile dropped in confusion before realizing the figure before him wore his own face.

Startled, Kasim voiced his confusion. "I don't understand, we are the same?" The figure nodded and rose, and handed Kasim a pair of scabbarded blades. Kasim took them, still confused, and gasped as the figure turned into insubstantial vapor and vanished, leaving only the blades.

Frowning, he grasped the hilt of one of them and drew the weapon. He shook his head as the images began to rush back in, of death and dismemberment and of the slender blades he now held piercing the flesh of the Legionnaire and Ba'al he had witnessed be slain.

"I still don't..." the words died in his lips as his mental acumen began to gather and then swiftly form. Yes, the mist creature had killed and maimed all those beings, but the mist creature was him. He had done those things. The realization came with the resurgence of his thoughts and awareness, and no horror took him, and no sadness. Regret was something that he reserved for acts he would change.

Did he like the killing? He mused for a moment but he was honest with himself and he did not enjoy it. He didn't hate it either, but he was not a cruel man. The death was necessary for the time and place he lived. The mist drifted further apart as he reflected on all the pain and suffering he had caused. He had caused them to vile beings and vile men, save for his true regret at hurting the monks at Sagarmatha when he arrived there.

That did bring sadness to him, though at the time he didn't know any better. Perhaps he *was* a violent man at that point. His instincts had been honed to kill or incapacitate, though he would consider himself a merciful assassin. There were those who enjoyed the crippling or a slow death for a mark among the Templar, but he was not one of them. No, he was not perfect, but he was a weapon forged out of necessity for the time in which he lived. No regrets and he would do it all again.

"Well, master, that went easier than expected. I feared a harder transition."

"I told you, our master is strong, he is ready for the last trial."

Kasim smiled at Tal and Qor. "Yes, I am ready. I am also ready for you to continue on your journey, honored warriors. May you find peace in your journey past death." A deep quiet descended upon the three of them.

Tears came to the eyes of his students, and it was Qor who spoke to him first, for the last time. "May you find peace as well, Kasim."

Kasim embraced both of them, and smiled with genuine warmth. Their fate was unkind, and they had earned a respite. He hoped they would be granted the peace and warmth he had declined when last he was here.

He turned and left the stone circle. One more trial, was it? He was ready.

"Stupid man, you knew it would be like this!" Piotyr cursed himself through clenched teeth as he pulled as much warmth as he could through the funnel from Phlegethon. The hellfire still came, but it was a stream, not a torrent, and the bitter cold of Cocytus was slowly winning the battle of fire and ice.

He couldn't see more than two paces away, the blizzard was so powerful, though he had the impression of a vast and empty ice field. Wind tore at his flesh, sapping his muscles of heat and strength. Snow came down in such thickness that it barely melted away as his hellfire bathed skin fought to keep the cold at bay.

Darkness surrounded him and he had no inkling at all about where to go or what to do. The hellfire was melting the ice though, and if nothing else he would gather a sample from the forming rivulet before returning through the chute to Phlegethon.

That won't work and you know it, fool. He hated the truth in his thoughts, but he feared that he had no alternative. The ice here was simply stronger than hellfire. He laughed then, through chattering teeth. A smarter man might have mocked his ignorance. *Of course the ice is stronger, Piotyr. It is solid, and fire is not. Would you deflect a rock with wind?*

"You have a point, o' learned one, though I hoped the *wind* I control was strong enough to deflect this cold." Wishful thinking. Yes, a hurricane could pick up a rock of a certain size, but generally ice would win out over fire just as stone would win over air. A truth he wished he had spent more time thinking about.

If the water he created here was only by virtue of the hellfire he brought from Phlegethon, he doubted if it would work for a sample. Somewhere here had to be the source, and he would find it. *If you can live long enough, idiot.*

He channeled downwards into the ice and was rewarded after several paces with rock. It was also out of the wind, and felt substantially warmer. He drew more of the stream from Phlegethon and melted some of the rock into slag, but eased off once it was liquid. It cooled quickly in the ambient frigid environment and he scooped it up and covered his torso first, then his abdomen and legs. It wouldn't protect him indefinitely, but it would certainly insulate him more than nothing and his own inner reservoir of the hellfire would serve to keep the stone at least somewhat malleable. He would not be as mobile as if wearing a full suit of plate armor, but he wouldn't be a statue either. It was also a damned sight better than being naked, which he was only moments before. His hellfire aura disintegrated his clothing except for the odd leather his scabbard and vial belt were made of and the crystal of the vials themselves.

He was also pleased to see that the fires of Phlegethon did not seem to be stopping. There would not be enough for him just to melt everything he wanted, but he felt confident he could channel enough of it ahead of him to melt the ice and keep the flow coming from the chute. It would be slow going and certainly not optimal but at least it was something, and he could progress.

Wearing his carapace of slag, keeping only his head and arms clear, he began the slow journey of melting the ice ahead of him and waiting for Phlegethon to flow up to the newly cleared section. He felt like a mole. He went no faster than a slow walk, though it wasn't wholly miserable. His inner reserves did keep him warm enough that, while not comfortable, he felt he was not in danger.

It was perhaps not even a league from when he began that he found the first intersection, and was unnerved. The ice he had bored through was smooth, but not as smooth as the round, nearly perfectly round from what he could see, tunnel he found himself inadvertantly breaking into. It was taller than he was, though not by much, and stepping into it he could not see either end of it, the empty space stretching off into the darkness as far as he could see.

It was not natural, that much he knew. It had been carved, or bored, just as he was doing. So Cocytus was not barren of life, then. Something, or someone, had been through here, though he couldn't tell how long ago. The thought comforted, rather than scared him. If something lived here, no matter what or when, then it was likely it lived near running water. This tunnel probably led to either a settlement, if the creator of it was intelligent, or a den or warren if it wasn't. Either way, he would far more likely find the source of Cocytus there than wandering aimlessly through the ice hoping to stumble across it. He smiled, and pondered briefly which direction to go.

The tunnel sloped, ever so slightly, and Piotyr imagined that if there was water here, it was likely to be underground, heated from within the ice and stone. Down it was. He felt that his journey at last was coming near to its end, and it felt good to be in what he perceived to be the last leg. He would have the last sample shortly and could make his way back to the man called Han and do whatever else he must do before his fate unfolded.

His spirits uplifted, it was still rather slow traversal as even in the tunnel the fire from Phlegethon did not flow very quickly. It still took considerable effort, but by this time at least he was actually feeling quite warm, though he was anxious to move along. The stone armor he was wearing was getting very soft, more akin to mud than to the clay he had been utilizing. In another quarter-hour it would melt off of him completely, but for now he kept it on. He wished he had some real armor as the stone really wouldn't protect him from any serious threats other than the cold. He made and discarded a dozen full battle plans, for the siege, in his mind as he walked.

He kept traveling past the point where the armor lost cohesion and dropped off. He abandoned the idea of making more for the time being, assuming that if he needed to go back up to the surface, and he was hopeful he wouldn't have to, he would address it then. Down in the ice tunnels he was relatively warm, if he started to feel chilled he could always alter his plan.

He did his best to stay focused but the cold and monotony caused his thoughts to wander constantly to his visions of the battle in his future. He felt no apprehension over what was clearly an immense siege. Instead, inexplicably to him, he felt excitement. Battle plans, troop deployments, city defenses. He felt without question that he was accustomed to such things, he just couldn't remember any specifics about his forces or the details of the city, castle, or walls he would be defending.

He knew that was bizarre but he didn't have any answers as to why, other than that he felt the woman from the cave had something to do with it. He couldn't remember much of their interaction at the fount and even the brief conversation they had was muddled and confusing. It also didn't help him in his current situation at all. He put all thoughts other than focusing on the ice, Cocytus, and the source water out of his mind.

He spent the better part of what he assumed was the rest of the day slowly traversing the ice tunnel. Hard to tell, as it was dark in the passageway. The only light was a small ruddly reflection from the fires of Phlegethon he kept slowly advancing down the frozen surface. His body had lost all sense of time both from the cavern of fire and now his journey through ice. Day, night, it made no difference to him at the moment and his inability to tell them apart did not concern him... to the point where he was pleasantly surprised when the ice began to slowly illuminate and lighten with what he hoped could be daybreak. Warmth of any sort would be welcome.

Another hour went by as he traversed and he could sense dawn had fully come to the ice above him. He smiled and decided to spare some time to bore a hole upwards and feel the sunlight on his skin. If it was still bitter cold he would not spend long.

He took his time, and etched crude steps going upwards at an angle into the ice. Perhaps half an hour was spent on the incline, the normally quick work made slow by the glacial pace of Phlegethon flowing along the tunnel floor and the almost nonexistent supply of of his own hellfire in the place. If there was any organic matter at all for him to consume with flame he could replenish his stores, but the ice would yield less than it took to melt it in the first place. Cocytus so far was lifeless, and he had to rely on what he brought with him from the last river he had visited in Hell.

Cold wind pierced the hole he slagged as he broke through to the surface, as unwelcome as the sunlight bathing the tunnel was welcome. He climbed up to the top of the ice shelf, and gazed across the beautiful, though completely lifeless expanse of white. Subtle hues of blue, black, and purple highlighted upswells in the ice, but it was a pale vista before him that stretched as far as he could see, with the only notable landmark being a lone mountain rising tall above the ice several leagues further in the direction he had been going. He smiled through the fog his own breath wreathed his head with. At least there was that, and he had been going in the right direction. That was where he would find Cocytus' heart, he was sure of it.

Climbing back down into the tunnel and the proximity of Phlegethon's stream was welcome. He scooped the magma into his hands and rubbed it into his skin, warming his chilled flesh and exhulting in the heat. He stood, refocusing on the continued journey towards the mountain, when the tremor hit and he stumbled to the side of the tunnel.

It ceased and he righted himself and scowled. "That was no mere trem..." The words died on his lips as another tremor shook his bones and rattled his teeth, vibrating his brain as he fell to his knees. He cursed in the rumbling quake as he was unable to steady himself and get to his feet. It went on for several moments, his frustration growing until he realized, panicked, that it was getting closer seconds before the ice beneath his feet erupted in an outward explosion of stone, frost, and screeching noise.

He had words only for a terrified scream as he was launched upwards out of the tunnel and into the freezing air above, rock and snow blinding him in a skin shredding chaotic blast of debris and pain.

The roar coming from beneath him froze his blood and swelled his throat shut. A ravenous maw of flashing teeth and fetid breath gnashed below him and rose up to engulf him completely as his ascent upwards slowed and he fell back towards the glacial ground. *He was going to die.* He acted without thought, expelling every ounce of hellfire he had in his veins in a desperate plea to fend off his predator.

Nowhere to run, his instinct had led him to attack the monster beneath him in pure primal terror, and it worked. Piotyr fell to the ground away in an arc from the beast as it reared back, roaring in surprise and pain and disappearing again beneath the ice.

He landed hard, and grunted in pain as his cold joints landed awkwardly and stiffened. He was not safe, not at all. He had exhausted his reserves and had nothing to defend himself with. If the creature came back... he was doomed. He steeled himself, drawing his sword, and waited in fear for the beast to reappear.

The first few heartbeats were agonizingly slow, but when they counted more than ten, he took a deep breath and started to relax the tension in his shoulders. Perhaps he had been...

The thought died as he heard movement beneath the ice. His footing was completely unstable and he stumbled back and forth as what had to have been a beast at least twice the heighth of a draft horse dug up through the frozen ground underneath him and surfaced several dozen spans away from him. His first thought was that it was huge, but as he noticed it continued beyond his eyesight down into the ice in a sinewy mass of flesh he felt completely minuscule. He was an insect to this thing.

The body was shaped like a worm, bluish white but with massive red patches of steaming skin on the outside. The head was shaped more like a snake than an actual worm... *flashes of red flailing teeth and roars of hatred and rage again caused him dizziness and confusion in his mind...* this ice creature having a definite triangular shaped wedge ending in a hissing, steaming mouth at the center of a series of more of the red patches of skin spiraling down its jaw and neck like a malevolent sunburst on a flag.

The creature continued to clear its body length from the ice and Piotyr was horrified to see that it dwarfed anything he could imagine in size. This beast would have towered over any city walls with ease. He stood there, shivering in the cold, as it drew up and wove back and forth like a serpent, watching him with the obvious interest of a predator observing prey. He had no way to defend himself short of running back into the ice tunnel. His blade would be akin to a needle against something this large, so he dropped it in futility. He would not die in terror though. There was no chance he would outrun this thing in its own terrain. He was finished.

He laughed then. Though his memories continued to elude him, the laughter felt right, like it was something he *would* do in the face of his own death coming for him. What was left to do other than laugh about it and embrace it? He would have chosen something other than being devoured by a giant worm if he had his pick, but dead was dead. He was reluctant to fail on his quest, but it was out of his hands now. The strange woman from the cave would have to find someone else to finish his work.

He watched the gigantic ice worm for a moment to see if death was imminent, but it appeared to be content to observe for the moment. Perhaps his fight or flight hellfire blast had been enough to teach the beast caution, at least for a moment. He hurried to detach his sample belt and pack and gently laid them in the snow. It might not last long in the elements, but certainly longer than in the stomach acid of that thing.

His small hole was woefully insufficient, but he laughed again and realized what would he care once he was dead. He noticed a large, flat rock laying in the snow and decided it would do for a marker. It must have been blasted out in the eruption of the ice worm. Gazing cautiously at the worm, he retrieved it and etched a simple epitaph as fast as he could on one side.

Here fell Piotyr. I brought the waters of Lethe, Styx, Phlegethon, and Acheron here to Cocytus. Please gather a pure source of the water of Cocytus and return all to a man named Han at the High Sheol.

He finished placing the stone gently next to his satchel and walked slowly away from the marker. He knew death would come swiftly, and painfully. His body was beginning to shut down from the cold, and the worm would have an easy time of it once it attacked.

The moments stretched into a minute and still the beast looked at him without moving. Piotyr shivered, but began to feel perhaps the thing was going to let him go. He flexed his hands and feet for warmth and circulation, and made slowly to retrieve his pack when the worm roared and must have risen another five paces high, rearing up so high as to blot out the sun.

More roaring accompanied the first and Piotyr's chattering jaw dropped to see half a dozen more of the worms burst through the ice and snow, ringing him in an unpenetrable wall of blue and red flesh.

It was to be a feeding then. Bad enough to be eaten by one, but now he was to be torn apart like scraps tossed to wild dogs?

He thought of grabbing his sword and ending his own life, but that was the coward's way. It was too cold to run anywhere, not to mention futile. Where could he go? These things could easily outpace him, digging through the ice and snow, and he guessed they could probably sense him through the ground anyway. It was over. In that moment, he wished for nothing more than a drink. He sat down, and closed his eyes to await his fate.

Words came to him then, over the cold wind but clear as day to him. Words he hadn't heard in any life he could remember, but the effect was soothing and peaceful, yet carried the weight of ancient power. The Tongue of Babel, spoken, though not to him. He opened his eyes and was astounded to see the newly arrived worms each crowned with a single rider, all with golden wings and a nimbus of light surrounding them.

"What brings you here, half-breed?" That *was* spoken to him...in the common tongue that he knew.

The words came from a winged, golden form that hovered over the first worm that had burst from the ground. He was freezing, confused, and the cold was making him dangerously tired. He shrugged his shoulders and gestured at the marker he had made. He couldn't stop them from taking it anyway as he was just about out of strength.

The being lowered himself from above the ice worm in a graceful dive and banked gently down to the ice, drawing what for Piotyr would have been an oversized hand and a half blade but held lightly in one fist by the huge, beautiful creature. He couldn't call it a man, not even the most flawless man alive could have been compared to the grace and stunning perfection of the face of the creature, a face which was all he could see as the rest of its body was wrapped in thick cloth. The elements here must harm even one such as he in a place like this.

The golden aura'd man kept his blade drawn at Piotyr, but it was obvious the mortal was fading and little threat. He spared him minimal attention as he retrieved the marker, satchel, sword and looked at them.

"Well then, *Piotyr,* why don't you come with us for warmth, food, and an explanation to this. You are merely the third of your kind to come see us here in Cocytus, and the first with demon blood mixed with the seed of Adam within you. Never let it be said that the House of Sammael is not without social graces."

Piotry sighed as he tried and failed to rise. "A Ba'al is it? After all this, a Ba'al shall kill me anyway. Pardon my rudeness, emmisarry of the House of Sammael, but I'm tired, weak, and don't have the strength for this any longer. I ask for an end to it if it is to come to that. I don't know why, but I feel I have earned that much."

The stranger sheathed his sword and picked up Piotyr in one hand as a child would with a doll. "I shall forgive you once for calling me Ba'al. Once. The second time and I shall kill you slowly over a brazier while keeping you fed and watered for weeks. You shall have my hospitality then, as well. Shall it be the mead cup or slow death by burning, mortal?"

Well, when he puts it that way...

He smiled as best as he could through the darkness coming for him from the icyness. "Pleased to meet you, whoever you are of House Sammael."

chapter twenty-one

Now you need fear no more, nor be bewildered, seeing me so
terrible. Be glad, take courage. Look, here am I, transformed, as
first you knew me.
- The Vision of God: Bhagavad Gita.

The water flowed over the edge of the pit and as far as The First could tell, into oblivion. The sound roared at the edge. As he gazed over the side, the water faded into blackness that, even with his unnaturally enhanced eyes, lasted for miles.

"What could this be, a pit such as this in a cavern we can't escape on the river Lethe? What possible new challenge could this deliver us to?"

I know not. I do not feel that my father passed here, but again I feel that we are unable to avoid this place. This pit has summoned us, and I feel our answers await at the bottom.

He was not capable of fear, though of late he had come to experience what he could only call anxiety. He was the equal of almost any being in existence when it came to combat but he had agreed to come on this journey with Piotyr at the request of Joshua. Since the warrior's disappearance and his strange new relationship with the spear Eirygaile... Lokyrg, he felt little ease or comfort in his situation. Gazing down into the maw of the Abyss, he knew in his mind that if he was capable, fear would be wrapped around him like a viper.

He steadfastly paddled in place, his tremendous strength allowing the small raft to stay in place easily even in the powerful current. At the moment, he really couldn't think of what else to do. Retreat and start over? Was that even possible? They had found themselves at the cavern repeatedly even after leaving it behind. He doubted leaving would even work, and why should he try? Joshua had said the water samples were critical to healing Kasim, and himself for that matter. If he returned now, without Phlegethon and Cocytus, he would have failed and the whole venture was a waste not even considering the loss of Piotyr.

He didn't broach the subject with Lokyrg. It was natural for the offspring to refuse the idea of the death of a parent, but in this case with no knowledge about the subject in any capacity, such a conversation was fruitless anyway.

He sighed, as close to a human form of exasperation as he could muster. "Should we see this through, then?"

I say yes. The River of Fire will flow beneath us, and this leads down. If my father was able to continue this task, he will be below Lethe.

The First was quiet for a long moment but came to the decision that he may as well attempt it. Returning to Sheol empty handed was not an option for him, not for pride, but for the reality that without all of the Templar weapons brought to bear, Abaddon would obliterate the city and all who defended it, himself included. He did not fear death. He did not fear anything, but he had grown fond of his semblance of life and wished to do all he could to help.

"Then let us see where this takes us. I'll see you at the bottom, Lokyrg." He lifted his oar and allowed the raft to approach the precipice. The two of them disappeared over the edge and fell into the abyss.

Jacob knew the settlement from conversations with Haj'ur Ve'kal. The man was ancient and had taught Jacob much of the little he knew of Hell from his brief time at the Ba'alat's Estate. The province where he and Markov now found themselves was called Tyana and was known for wheat. It was ruled by a lesser Ba'al named Zagan. His knowledge was minimal but it was a relatively prosperous province with many lesser Fallen houses providing food and spirits. It would suffice for the two of them to get a fresh meal and hopefully find an inn.

Both men were exhausted from their ordeal getting out of the valley and over the mountain and had to stumble more than walk the majority of the day. Jacob felt more than once the loss of Jezebel, his infernal horse from Red Bank here in Hell, or any of the many horses he had used in his time as a mortal. He smiled slightly to himself. *His time as a mortal.* It no longer seemed strange to think such things.

Markov was quiet on the journey, but it suited Jacob. He did like the man, but it was all he could do to keep walking. Conversation would have been ill tempered and unwelcome. It was without fanfare that they arrived on the outskirts of what appeared to be a wealthy farming community, passing several mortal workers far off in the fields and large manor houses in the distance. Ve'kal could have told him who lived there he was sure, but he had no idea.

His stomach was screaming at him by the time he and Markov found an inn with a wooden sign in front depicting a smiling demon with black claws draining a pint of something to drink. Perfect.

They passed the carriage and horse posts and shambled in, looking he was sure like vagabonds at best.

It was near dusk and thus near mealtime. The inn was mostly full and there was some unpleasant dissonant music playing. Most of the patrons didn't stop drinking or eating or talking for more than a few seconds as they entered. Fallen, mortal, and even a couple of ancient-looking Legionnaire made up the clientele. Jacob was grateful his entrance was uneventful. He felt tremendous satisfaction sliding into a booth with Markov doing the same across from him and resting his aching body.

"My God this is going to be nice, I can't wait." Markov appeared to be almost giddy, even given his advanced case of exhaustion. Jacob was just hungry, but for Markov, this had to be even more incredible, given how long he had been sealed in the valley.

The barmaid came by their booth and Jacob opened his mouth to request a bottle of wine when Markov jumped in front of him, whistling lowly and smiling at the woman with so transparent an expression Jacob had to laugh. "Well aren't you a pretty one? What's your name, love?"

Jacob looked at the woman, definitely a woman and not a girl, at least twenty years Markov's senior, but not unattractive. Certainly nothing on Ve'kal, but there were other factors there, he supposed. The woman's dark green eyes climbed high on her forehead before answering.

"Ah, Jora, my... " she stopped for a moment to look at Jacob briefly before returning to look at Markov, then back at Jacob. "My lord."

Jacob felt bad for a moment, remembering how broken these people were. Markov wouldn't have any context for it, to him she was just another human, and one of the right gender that he hadn't seen in centuries. He raised a hand slightly to Markov, who was scowling at him.

"Jora, it is alright. My friend speaks for himself, and no harm will come to you for it. My friend and I have a mighty thirst, and a terrible hunger. What say you bring us back a bottle of Lapsis Caelum..."

"Ales." Markov broke in sternly, still scowling at him.

..." two ales and a bottle of Lapsis Caelum then, and whatever delicious meal I smell cooking, and then come on back and tell me all about yourself and this place. The price of our meal and accomodations shall be paid in full by Ba'al Zagan." She nodded at Jacob, then shot Markov a brief glance before hurrying back to the kitchen.

"Look, I don't know what game you are playing, Merethius, but in my time that was about as much bullshit as..."

"She is all yours. Markov, be at ease. You need to know something though. Everyone here, and I mean everyone, will defer to me because of how I look, and will assume you are a slave at best. We look like we were robbed. No one will assume a free mortal traveling with a Ba'al has any freedom, will, or really anything."

"You are no Ba'al, and I am no slave, Jacob. I won't play some part that..."

Jacob laughed and Markov's face started to redden so he quickly raised his hands again to calm him. "Markov, be at ease. You don't have to play any part, my friend. I'm happy to explain things twenty times a day if you want, I have no fear of this place, not any more. I just told you *this* time so that you know why she only had eyes for me, and it was not out of lust. They are all terrified of the Fallen, of a Ba'al in particular, and I *look* like one of them now. You don't, so they assume you are my servant."

"That's fucked."

He chuckled again softly, but Markov wasn't angry with him any longer. "I agree. This is Hell though. Everything here is. We'll set it right, with time, but it is complicated. The battle at Sheol may have changed things. With the Shay'tan dead, there may be a succession war, though I hope Ba'alat Ve'kal was able to consolidate and hold her power."

Markov's expression changed from scowl to suspicious glare. "Ba'alat Ve'kal, is it? I take it the two of you were..."

Jacob sighed, and shrugged. "Complicated as well, though I did care for her, and her child, in a way that was unexpected. Keep in mind at the time I had been here less than a fortnight, had just been condemned and damned by the Patriarch, and wanted nothing more than to die in battle as soon as possible. The demonic essence flowing through my body did quite a lot to blur my morality on such things."

Markov made a strange gesture in which he raised a hand and quickly made as if Jacob were a fly to shoo away. "Morality nothing. I give two shits about all that. You weren't making a play for Jora, and that's enough for me. Just do me a favor, tell her I'm not your servant? Can't abide that shit."

He smiled, again genuinely liking the man. "Fair enough."

They didn't have long to wait for their drinks and was pleasantly amused and surprised to see that Jora had brought four ales, as well as the bottle and glasses. Frothy beer fizzed over the top and despite himself he felt his mouth water. He could wait a brief moment longer, though. "Jora, this is the best Legionnaire I've ever served with, Vasily Markov."

Halfway finished with his first ale, Markov wiped his mouth with his arm and interrupted. "Fuck, just Markov, please."

Jacob cleared his throat. "Though he prefers to just go by his last name. Anyway, we were set upon by a pack of dragons and our belongings were destroyed, though we did drive them off. It has been some time in the wilderness for us both though, what news have you?"

At ease now, Jora smiled at Markov and nodded to him before returning to Jacob's attention. "Glad to hear of your survival with the dragons, though I hope you didn't kill any."

Surprised, but intrigued, Jacob looked at Markov and shrugged. "We didn't, but why is that, Jora?"

"Ba'alat Ve'kal issued a proclamation that no Hellfire dragon was to be hunted, under penalty of death. The word spread quickly, even out here, that they are protected. No one may kill one."

He smiled inside. "Ah, this proclamation comes solely from House Ve'kal then?"

"No, my lord. The Templar who fought at Sheol rule there, with Ve'kal as regent in the absence of the Shay'tan. Truly you have been in the wilderness for a time, to have not heard such momentous tidings."

Markov joined in. "Jora, love, I'm sorry but did you say in the absence of a Shay'tan? So he's dead then?"

She looked at Jacob, who nodded and smiled, before she turned to Markov to continue. "Yes... ah, Markov. Lucifer's line has ended, at least that's what has been said. Ba'al Apollyon marches on Sheol to punish the usurper Ve'kal and put the humans who stood with her to the sword."

Both Jacob and Markov were quiet for a moment, but it was Jacob who continued. "The humans, what news of them, Jora?"

"Little. I have heard that The Knight of Hellfire has gone, the largest of his dragons as well. I have heard that the warriors from the mountains in the East are all dead save two, and one lay dying, the one called Kasim. I have heard nothing of the other two." Jacob felt his heart sink, and was glad Markov interrupted.

"What of the fifth, the one who fought the Shay'tan and stood at Ve'kal's side?" Markov only knew what Jacob had told him, but what Jacob had told him was true.

"He's dead. Both he and the Shay'tan. More than half the city, too. Travelers passing through here were calling it The Cataclysm. It is said when the Shay'tan fell the palace exploded and nearly took half of Sheol with it."

"I had heard of these men and their deeds before the battle, though again, we have been isolated in the wilds for weeks now. If these men could kill Ba'al with the ease the stories tell of, what has happened since?"

Jora appeared to have lost all of her unease, and was now speaking conversationally, and to Jacob's eye, actual friendliness. He attributed it to his voice. Since his transformation here, it had a strange affect on people.

"My lord, I'm sorry but I am unsure. I had heard the... " her voice dropped to a whisper as she said the next word... "Grigori... were involved, but just stories from travelers."

Both men looked at each other. The name was familiar to Jacob, more in passing than any deep knowledge, but he was familiar with them. Markov looked to be as well. He thought to ask Jora, but if she was afraid to speak of them it wouldn't be very productive to ask.

"Thank you, Jora. I may lose myself in thought for a time. Feel free to converse with Markov, though. Your news is appreciated, as will be the meal, I'm sure. Compliments of Ba'al Zagan, again."

Jora nodded and smiled at Markov. For his sake Jacob hoped she was either the innkeeper's sister or daughter, rather than wife. He'd wager the younger man had a decent chance. "Of course, my lord. He has guests frequently, and this happens quite often. I'll return with more ale and your food shortly."

He watched her leave, then turned to Markov. "Something is terribly wrong. Piotyr gone? Kasim dying? Attacked by the Grigori? What do they have to do with any of this? My knowledge of scripture is sorely lacking, but the Grigori weren't assassins that I know of."

Markov had drained his ale and was working on his second glass of wine. "Asking the wrong man, Jacob. I'm a soldier, not a scholar. They were just one of the groups that came down the first time... took a liking to our women, right? Can't blame them for that. Thanks for the in with Jora, by the way."

"Sure, it's nothing. Oh, speaking of by the way, Ba'al Zagan will probably hear of us by morning at the latest, and come investigate. Be prepared for a fight, he won't like his hospitality being taken without having been offered."

Markov snorted, and drained his first glass. "Assumed as much. You worried at all?"

"No, he's a lesser Ba'al under any circumstances. Far more concerning is Abaddon the Destroyer. Have you heard of him?"

"Can't say that I have. I didn't keep up on the names much at San Luis. Just patrolled the walls, fought, drank, got laid when I could, repeat. We were lucky though, we were pretty isolated and didn't see a lot of combat until... until, well until whatever happened when I was brought here."

Until the Apotheosis. Until you changed everything. He shook his head. The morning would bring change and purpose again. "Well, enough of dark thoughts for now. Eat, drink, and be merry."

Markov smiled at him and raised his glass. It was a good night.

Truly, Kasim had not expected this. He remembered the Throne from last time, fleeing from it in fear while dying his second death in the bowels of Sagarmatha. Far more pleasant than the death at the hands of the Patriarch, it had been a death more of confusion and effort rather than simple pain and suffering.

Something was wrong, though. The clear bright light emanating from the Throne had been so powerful and piercing that it had shook him to his soul when he last saw it, but now it looked wrong... like the light was muted, and coming from a deep place within the Throne and only barely escaping.

"You see it too, master? After the attack I came here to meditate, and saw the crack. I feared something had gone wrong." Kishien was alone when Kasim arrived here at the top of the stairs. No angelic beasts this time, no swords swinging towards him. It was just all so different.

"I see it, my friend. I'm going to look closer, do you want to come with me?"

"No, Kasim. This is your trial. Your last one, if I understand things correctly. I... met a man here, who said you would come, and that something must be mended. He seemed kindly, if that means anything. I shall wait here, though."

Kasim smiled to Kishien and nodded. A very promising student, just like the others. He wished him well on his continued journey through the afterlife. "I shall see you when I return, then."

Kishien smiled back. "I shall be here."

Kasim moved towards the Throne yet found it hard to look directly upon it the closer he got. It was immense, and what first appeared a small landing atop the stairs was in truth a large courtyard, or plaza he supposed since it was open to the clouds above. Could it be considered either? The clouds went on forever as far as he could see, mixes of blue, white, and hints of the reds and oranges of sunrises and sunsets flaring occassionally from all directions, though he could see no sun.

The Throne itself was white... he thought, or at least mostly white. Glowing golden sigils covered it to such an extent that it was easy to confuse at a distance for gold, but up close he saw the white stone... or perhaps silver? He shook his head and as he approached, his eyes ached and he had to avert them. Perhaps mortal eyes were not meant to gaze directly upon it, no matter the mortal.

He crossed the stones leading to it in a few minutes, not hurrying overmuch but moving with purpose. Other than the Throne upon the dais, the plaza was empty. No columns, no buildings, just a simple cleared area of white stone. He closed to perhaps twenty paces and could no longer just avert his eyes, but had to do that as well as actively squint and place his hands in front of his face. *This is muted? This light would have blinded me when full.*

He closed to within a few paces and he could not bear it any more. He turned his head, closed his eyes, and ripped a piece of cloth from his shirt. He quickly wound it and wrapped it around his eyes, and that helped immensely. He couldn't see, but at least he wasn't in pain. He smiled, took a deep breath, and closed the last couple of paces slowly, taking care not to trip.

The dais itself was higher than his head so he had to run and jump up to catch the lip. He chuckled briefly at the thought of misjudging the distance and running face-first into it and knocking himself out, so he waited until he could touch the dais, then turned and ran parallel to it before jumping. He caught the lip and pulled himself up, pleased that he wasn't so weakened that simple fitness was beyond him.

The light felt like it was infusing him with energy, and even without his eyes, or his third sight, he could sense the raw power emanating from the Throne. This *was* power incarnate. Stepping forward, he could also sense that something was very wrong. That crack in the stone was causing a gap in the light so that it shone unevenly, a shadow which felt like the embrace of the grave in its absense. He felt no evil from it, just a profound lack of its presense as it passed over his face as he approached. He passed under the shadow, and the light returned again to his face and he smiled in deep contentment.

He knew exactly when to stop, his eyes simply not being needed in the awesome radiance of the Throne. He felt a brief moment of apprehension as he thought about touching it, but then shook his head and willed himself to it.

"You should wait a moment, Kasim."

The voice was definitely that of a man's, and he sounded younger, though not by much. There was no tone of malice or violence, just warning. He lowered his hand and turned towards the voice.

"I am a patient man. Why do you caution restraint?"

The voice spoke again, but did not sound closer. Kasim had the sense that the man was perhaps a pace away, and not moving.

"Your patience is recently learned, as is your wisdom, but I see they have both taken firm root. That is a good thing. I fear for your companions, and you may be a necessary tempering for the weapons you five from Adam's seed have been forged into."

Kasim smiled towards where he thought the man was. "I am a patient man, though I am also an observant one. You did not answer my question. Was I wrong to ask it?"

A soft chuckle came from the voice, and one that put Kasim at ease and seemed tantalizingly familiar. He knew this man, but he couldn't place it.

"Wise, patient, observant. Kasim, your virtues are too many to list. It is only a possible vice that concerns me. The real question is whether you are proud."

Kasim pondered the man, and internally was somewhat unsure. Pride was a difficult quality to measure. He felt pride at times. He was proud of what he could do as a warrior, as a Templar, as an assassin even. He was proud of the victories he and those of Sagarmatha had won en route to Sheol. He was proud of their victory there upon the walls, and was proud that not one of them had fallen to the forces of the Shay'tan.

A faint flicker of the shadow caught his hands as he ran them through his hair. He had been proud on the day when they all died in the plaza, burned to ash by the hellfire of their assailants. *Are you proud, Kasim?*

A sadness took him then. "Not any longer. I was, and it led to ruin for those I love. I once would have called myself a proud man. I now call myself a humble one."

There was silence on the dais for a long moment. When the voice spoke again, Kasim felt it was softer, quieter than before. "Do you remember the last time you were here? The words you spoke?"

He did. Not the exact words, but he had freed God from any obligation to him, or from him. He had offered freely a break in the contract he had kept with the Father, and though it had pained him at the time, the despair was so overhwelming that he could no longer utilize his faith as a strength.

"I remember the intent, and most of the words." Kasim had prayed since that day, but not as he used to. His pursuit of justice had been his own, his goal was light and pure, not vengeance.

"Do you still mean them? Do you feel forsaken?" The voice was but a whisper, and Kasim felt a tremendous gravity wash over the dais. He knew, then, that the sundering had been his doing. Yes, it was a vision and a mental creation in his state to help him understand his journey into death, but it was in a sense also very literal and real. His faith had been broken that day, and thus had the Throne been rent as well. Guilt began to take hold of him then but he refused to let it. Anger then reared up from within his chest. Who was this man to question him? Where was he when Kasim was left to die after both his parents had been killed by the Legion? One by the sword and the other by the Soulfire. Where was he when the Patriarch damned him to Hell? Where was he when they burned on the plaza?

His anger began to swell but as he opened his mouth to rebuke the man on the dais he stopped. It was done with. He had said the words and had meant them. He had felt abandoned, betrayed even, but he did not slight the Father, nor did he work against him. He took up the sword, even after dying, and with his rebirth and then with his companions Kasim had done more than he ever had as a mortal Templar, full of faith, youth, and devotion.

Why be angry? The voice didn't ask him if he regretted his words, he asked him if he still meant them. An apology was not being sought from him, simpy an ascertainment of what he felt now. He felt the anger drain from him, and his muscles relaxed.

"No. I do not. I know now that there is far more to life than the small facet I knew as a man. I learned it most convincingly as I saw the children of Ba'al being kept in imprisoned torment to satisfy the power lust of a madman, and ever more so as I saw the innocence still present in those children of evil beings freed from the tyranny of their environment."

"It sounds like wisdom has indeed found you, Kasim. I fear that in time, soon, you will have great need of it. A hard, dark path lies before you and your brothers." The voice spoke not unkindly, though Kasim had to try not to chuckle.

"I mean no disrespect, but our path has already been brutal, and horrific. If you mean to say there are worse things coming, perhaps there are, though our mettle to this point can not be said to have been untested. We Templar are forged already." Kasim spoke the truth, and did not feel hubris in his words.

The voice did not rebuke him. "A forging is never complete, and I will not trivialize your journey nor your decisions. I merely want to warn you that if you survive, Abaddon, if conquered, will not be your last test. You have the temperance and fortitude to do what is right, your brethren may not."

Kasim sighed mildly. *If we survive Abaddon... that is a very large if.* "I trust my brothers. Even after what happened to bring us here, we have all perservered and emerged, though scathed, to stand against evil. Hell did not break us."

Another long silence greeted Kasim before the voice answered again, very quietly. "Fear the Shay'tan, Kasim. Pride, once it takes hold, is nearly impossible to dislodge."

Ve'kal must have taken the Throne after he was attacked. Or perhaps another Ba'al did and ruled in her place? In mattered little. He would stand against Abaddon because it was what he needed to do. "Your warning is noted, and I thank you for it. When my ordeal is concluded, my body will be weak, but my spirit is strong. I shall fight Hell until my life is taken for me."

The man moved closer, Kasim could sense it, though he still felt no danger or malice. He even smiled as he felt an arm placed upon his shoulder. "Only one more death shall ever be asked of you, Kasim. No more tasks, no more tests, and no more waiting. When next your mortality is laid bare, rest shall finally be yours, and you will have earned it. It is my sincerest hope that you die an old man, surrounded by your children and theirs."

Unbidden, he felt his eyes water. Such a thing would be... more than he could ever have wished for. Unlikely, but he did still dream of a time where he and Dhermina could live in peace somewhere. "Kind words, and after The Destroyer comes to Sheol, one way or another, rest shall be first on my mind."

"No, Kasim. I said you will not be tested in death again. Life will not be so easy. There is more to this tale, and it shall fall to you to see it end well. 'Ware the Shay'tan, and all who stand with the Throne of Hell."

"I shall." He again felt the person was unimportant, whatever Ba'al held the title, he *and* the other Templar would be ready for them. Now that Jacob was gone, it was simply what they would do. He felt the light of the Throne shining wholly again, unbroken by the rending.

"Your words and heart have mended it. I could not be more proud of what you have become, Kasim. I long to see you in happier times, with a ready smile on your face. Either here or there, I wish nothing but joy and peace upon you."

It was true, he could feel that the flickering shadow had passed, and strangely the light felt less intense, though whole. Almost as if the fissure had forced the light out unevenly, and now that it was repaired it could emanate as it was meant to. "I feel like I know you. I get the sense that my time here nears completion, but before I go I would like to know if we have met?"

"You are correct, your time here is measured in heartbeats. We did meet, once. It was only for a moment, and right after a battle. There wasn't time for a proper introduction, but you did make an impression. Fare thee well, Kasim. You have done well, today."

Kasim smiled and removed the cloth from his eyes, wanting to look upon the man, but frowned when he found the dais empty. The light shone perfectly from the Throne, bright, but no longer hurting his eyes as it now shone evenly from every part of it. He yawned and felt as if his body was being pulled from someplace very far away. He was waking and he felt sad. Sad to be leaving this place, and also he knew agonizing pain and rehabilitation awaited him upon his waking. Still, this was not yet where he belonged, and he knew that. The voice knew it as well, and Kasim shook his melancholy with a smile. He had gotten what he needed here, and learned what was required. Gratitude filled his heart... and, beyond any of that, he *knew*.

"Goodbye, Father."

chapter twenty-two

And there, all in their order, are the sources and ends of the
dark earth and misty Tartarus and the unfruitful sea and starry
heaven, loathsome and dank, which even the gods abhor.
- Hesiod: Theogeny

Another two of the beasts lay slain at The First's feet, their serpentine bodies and grotesque heads twitching and spurting blood. Lokyrg spun in his grip, quickly flinging acidic residue from it's barbed head.

"I still wonder how this Moloch was able to continually draw acid out of Eirygaile. I do not understand enchantments like Han does."

When Piotyr's son responded, the words were not audible any longer to his undead ears. It had surprised him, then he came to believe that they had bonded over the flesh of the beings they slew, and the telepathy innate to his kind had taken root.

There were other souls here when Han bound mine into the weapon. The Ba'al know ways to bind a soul eternally to material things, giving various qualities and properties to them in exchange for eternal oblivion.

"There *were*, other souls?"

Yes, I consumed them.

"Fair enough. What do you make of these things?"

They aren't demonic, that much I know. Some other beast or monster, but not of the Hells or Heavens. This place feels wrong, somehow.

The First felt it as well. Their descent into the darkness had seemed to go on forever, but his surprise when they finally landed in a pool at the bottom grew quickly as it seemed an ordinary lagoon in an ordinary cavern. Ordinary that is until he looked up and felt as if a tremendous hand was poised just out of sight to smash him down if he should dare think to ascend. They were fortunate that the raft had survived the fall.

This was a prison. How he knew, he could not tell, but he felt it as sure as anything. His intelligence and intuition had grown exponentially in his journey with Joshua and he did not need to see the first of the bizarre creatures to know that this was a place things did not escape from lightly. "I fear there will be no way to Phlegethon here."

Piotyr did not speak of anything like this from his world, though we didn't talk about Earth much at all. Mother never spoke of things like this either, but we have limited generational memory. This is alien to me.

There were steps ascending in a spiral from where their raft landed, though he could sense such a level of oppression and forbiddance pressing down from above that he didn't even bother going up. There was a way out, but there was another piece of the puzzle somewhere. His thoughts were given truth when he saw the first of the creatures.

He must have surprised those first two, as he had walked not very far down the cavern when he saw them slowly slither around a corner and almost in a daze approach him in serpentine movement. They watched him for several heartbeats as they approached before hissing and charging, enough for his eyebrows to climb slightly before he had impaled one and bashed the other's skull into the cave wall.

The second pair had been more alert and he wondered about pheromones or some other death effect. His hyper sensitive ears could pick up sounds of movement coming from deeper in the cavern and he feared he had caused a stir.

Like wasps. I believe you are right, corpse. They don't look like insects, though.

"No, they don't, but these don't really look like snakes either. They just move like them. They are also different. That last one had tendrils on its face that moved. We are not dealing with one type of beast, but many."

Demons are similar in that. An aspect can change appearance, though at the risk of arguing, they can do that even though they would be considered the same type of being.

"A reasonable argument, Lokyrg. We'll see how this progresses."

They made haste as the alarm grew, and with a certainty, The First was sure the monsters had either a hive mind or could detect their own deaths in another way. At first a trickle came, then a flood. Snake bodies were the most common, but certainly not the only bizarre combination. He saw birds with human female torsos, men with bovine heads, and all manner of hide, feather, and skin in grotesque combinations. He even saw a few creatures with more than one head.

He used Lokyrg to great effect in keeping the swarm at bay, stabbing and thrusting with the great spear that was almost weightless with his incredible strength. Ba'al Am's war-axe was just not as practical in the close space of the tunnels. As he killed them, their souls left their body. As with every other being The First had killed since Joshua's plague took him, each soul absorbed into his and made him grow more powerful as the battle went on.

The corpses began to pile up and made a natural choke point for him to exploit, and his only concern was that were so many that the cavern would be blocked off if this kept going.

Kill until there are no more, then worry about moving the corpses.

"I know, I just wonder why they don't fall back and fortify their position. This is a slaughter."

It was not an infinite slaughter, though. The tide did slow, then stop, and The First reckoned his own power had grown considerably in the process. Perhaps an hour of constant skewering, and more than a hundred slain. If such things bothered him, the sight and smell would have been unpleasant.

You are skilled, I'll give you that, corpse. My own father would have been hard pressed to match you in battle before, and you devour souls much as I did when I received this host. When this is over with, you may rival Ba'al Apollyon in strength.

Immune to pride, the words nonetheless gave The First a positive sign that Lokryg had warmed to the undead wielding him, finally. "I don't think it possible to equal him in combat. I overheard Joshua and Han discussing him over wine one night, and they both seemed sure that he can Invoke the power of Hell much as the Templar do the power of God. They even suggested that he could be using something similar to the Apotheosis when he manifests as the Destroyer."

If you are right, then why bother to come on this errand at all? Why would you and my father risk your lives to heal Kasim if what comes to lay siege to Sheol is too terrible to conquer?

A fair question, but not one he could answer easily. "I owe Joshua much. Everything, in fact. Yes, he killed me, but what I am now is so far superior that I can only consider him my own father, or creator I suppose. He suffers because of his illness, and there is a chance that the waters of Hell could heal him. Kasim I know not and care not about, beyond his interest to Joshua, but if in coming here I can assist him as well, I would if only to please Joshua. Han too, I suppose. He has been kind to me."

That one is soft, and mad. Don't trust him.

Continuing to pull bodies down and make a slow path through the slaughter, he smiled at Lokyrg's comments. "He is neither, though I understand that he was, at one time. Joshua tells me the defense of Sheol will fall to Han in great capacity, if not as much as Piotyr."

How, shall he command his army of quill and parchment?

He chuckled. Lokyrg was fierce, cunning, and had a certain feral intelligence that was pronounced, but lacked wisdom in any capacity at all. He also had little knowledge of tactics beyond what he and the Lamja family had utilized as a cavalry unit. "It will take a lot of parchment to repel Abaddon's Legion. It may number in the tens of millions."

I can't put an image in my mind to a force that large. My father will have to make no mistakes. Provided we find the fool, that is.

"Indeed, Lokyrg. Though I do not think we are going to find him here, I do think there is a point to all of this."

Finally, after clearing what seemed a small mountain of bodies, the undead and his wraith-spear were able to continue deeper into the cavern. He still carried the war-axe though he left Piotyr's armor back at the raft. He could wield both weapons if he had the room to maneuver them. His strength was not constrained by the weight or size of the weapons but rather the size of the tunnels.

Shortly, the unworked stone gave way to smooth cave wall only briefly before becoming completely crafted stonework. The First had several genetic memories of stonemasons in his collective soul, and he knew the level of craftmanship evident on the tunnel complex was incredible.

Perfectly chiseled archways supported the tunnel while total symmetry greeted his eyes from the torch sconces to the pillars to the curved supports where the tunnels branched. Checking the sconces, he was pleased to see them prepared for use already and every other one even held a paraffin soaked torch. This was not some long forgotten crypt, then, but a series of tunnels in use by more than swarms of monsters.

He took a moment to strike a spark into one of the sconces, and it lit instantly. A warm glow spread outwards from the fire, and The First retrieved the torch and began to lite the sconces as he walked, Lokyrg in his right hand and the axe secured on his back. Lokyrg was silent, for which the plague walker was glad, as the images on the walls were very strange, and he was in contemplative mystery as to what he was seeing.

He was familiar enough with the ruling powers of Hell from his memories that he knew what he was seeing depicted on the walls were not in accordance with how things really were. He saw in black and red paint, bas relief, and mosaics of all manner of shapes and sizes depictions of what he could only describe as a war, but it was not a war he was familiar with.

The beings depicted were different in many ways from the Angelic and Demonic inspired artwork that one would find at an estate of any Ba'al or Ba'alat. For the most part, the beings depicted here looked human, though with the scale depicted by trees and mountains in the artwork they were huge. There were also two distinct sides in the conflict, and from what he could tell, it looked to be in some way a familial conflict.

Strange. Some ancient death cult or something that predated the war in Heaven? Was that even possible? He frowned as he saw one particular section of wall showing a woman splitting open the head, and climbing out of, a man. Another showed a man tied to a flat rock while a horrific looking bird tore at his abdomen.

Certainly the themes were the same, he supposed. Bad people do bad things, get bad punishment. What was strange was that the trappings were all different. This was not the artwork of a people who were familiar with Heaven or Hell.

The corridors stretched for miles and he walked for hours. He and Lokyrg did speak occassionally when a particular piece of painting or artwork was of mutual interest, but mostly it was silence. When he did finally hear an outside noise it was startling, but not of immediate concern. His eyes and ears were supernaturally acute, and when he heard the murmuring he could tell it was from far, far away.

Nor was it approaching him, he could tell, as he stopped to listen for a span of minutes. The volume did increase, slowly, as he continued on, however. After another half hour, he could tell quite clearly that he was listening to a crowd, and one that was not small.

I had not thought we were done with combat. I sense tension and apprehension in you, corpse.

"Not tension, just anticipation. My curiousity is piqued. This is a strange place, and I hope to find answers soon."

You can have your answers, I'll have my bloodshed.

"I would wager we shall both emerge sated."

The volume increased until it was near deafening. He passed archway after archway leading off into the darkness, the sheer size of this place was incredible. Millions of those monsters could live here. The First tried to make some sort of rational theory about what the place, or its denizens, were, but was completely baffled. The artwork, the strange, twisted forms of the monsters they had slain, and the twisting architecture were a mystery.

The sound was so loud he could feel it pounding against his body like a drum. He rounded a corner and entered a large chamber with statues depicting men, mortal men this time, but all in a manner of distress. One was being crushed under a giant rock, another was pushing a huge boulder up a hill, another was having his eye plucked out by a raven, and other morbid carvings.

The chamber led to a wide set of stairways going up, and dust shifted in the air from the noise resounding within. He traveled across the chamber and up the stairs, which went upwards perhaps five hundred paces, emerging finally into a giant arena with sand for a floor, and surrounded by what he could scarce believe.

There must be hundreds of thousands of them. What is this place?

He didn't think Lokyrg could hear him above the din, but even if he could, The First had no idea. Blood sport of some kind? Did the beasts have enough intelligence to be entertained by violence? This was bad. He came here for answers, not to butcher for the amusement of insane, deranged freaks.

He stood on the sand searching for anything he could learn in the stands, finally seeing a box that looked different from the rest of the arena. It was lined in red fabric and contained two large thrones on a dais. Some sort of nobility among the beast people? He made his way there, grinding his teeth against the onslaught of noise. He wasn't prone to anger, but the sheer volume was making his brain vibrate against his skull.

I think they mean for us to fight something, or many things. I long for death, not this much though. Corpse, we could be here for hours... days even. We can't delay this long.

"WHAT WOULD YOU HAVE ME DO? GO BACK INTO THE TUNNELS?" He shouted to be heard, not because he was upset with Lokyrg.

No... I suppose not.

He was relieved the conversation ended. Speech was difficult and became harder the closer he got to the stands themselves. He was quick with visuals and numbers, and by a fast estimate, he put the numbers at close to a million, but on the far side of that number rather than the near. Nothing close to what Abaddon was bringing to siege Sheol, but still far more beings in one place that he could ever recall encountering in all his years and memories.

He approached the stands and was close enough to see those who were in attendance clearly. Much as the beasts at the entrance to the tunnel complex, he saw all variety of monstrous life. Men with lion heads and scorpion tales, women with writhing snakes for arms or hair and glowing eyes. Children were in attendance as well, though deformed and twisted like the adults were. Not demons that he could see, but not human either, not by any stretch.

All manner of beast parts were mixed with human features such that the variety was astounding. Serpent scales, canine heads, bat wings, even shells like a turtle or snail on some of them. He had never felt more normal in his short life, or long memory. He stood perhaps twenty paces back from the first tier of arena seating, and was further dismayed to see food and drink being consumed by the attendants. It was blood sport then, and he was of a mind to assume he would be a participant, willing or not.

He would have sighed if he thought there was even a chance he could hear himself. Small chance of that, though, so he instead placed the haft of Lokyrg into the sand and stood patiently looking up at the empty red box with the thrones. What would be, would be. He drew Ba'al Am's axe with his free hand, dropping the torch. He stood ready.

Minutes passed, and finally a tremendous gong sounded, and a hush descended quickly in the crowd. It wasn't instant, but it was certainly rapid. The silence that followed was staggering. He did sigh, then, in relief that was quickly replaced by apprehension. Something was coming, he could feel it.

A small retinue of less deformed beings than the others entered the red box, carrying what he assumed were refreshments. He saw platters with pitchers on them, carafes, and what he guessed was meat and cheese, though from this far he wasn't sure. Fruit, he thought he could see as well, though how fruit could make its way down here was beyond him. Five men and five women eventually were inside the box, or male and female forms he supposed. Definitely not men and women, not with those features.

The attendants made their way to the outside of the box, and then his eyes widened as a hulking brute came into the box, not even vaguely a man at all but some sort of walking bull-creature that was at least twice The First's height. He dwarfed the other forms there, and carried an axe that made his own feel like a toy.

The bull creature moved to sit in the throne to The First's left as he watched, and the zombie could feel the heat from its glare even from this distance. He was prepared for some degree of oddity, given the rest of their strange journey, but what came next caught him unexpectedly.

A woman, by all appearances normal and human, came into the box and took a seat next to the man-bull. She was not even half its height, but looked to command his respect or his loyalty, as he nodded to her. She wore a white robe that left one shoulder bare, and a metal crown of what looked to be very intricately cast snakes.

It appeared that she was in charge, as the silence lingered as she sat and seemed to hinge upon her. She smiled and waved to the crowd, and The First was sure of it. This was some sort of ruler to these people, though probably not a Ba'alat, given that he was not seeing any demonic overtones.

Does she rule with the cow?

"If so, I would wager that he rules with her, more accurately. The power lies in her." He had thought he was speaking quietly, but she must have heard him, as she leaned forward and spoke in a clear and powerful voice.

"It does indeed, stranger. Welcome. What brings you to Khthon?"

Khthon? Never heard of it.

The First shrugged his shoulders. "No directed purpose, I assure you. I was traveling upon the Rivers of Hell, trying to find the source water of Lethe. I traveled with another man, who has disappeared. I sought to resume my journey in the hope of finding him, but the River kept taking me back to the cavern above us. Hell brought me here."

The woman suddenly stood up and pointed down from the gallery. "No! Hell did not bring you here! I brought you here! Kill him Asterion!" Her shrill shriek had barely enough time to register before the roar of the crowd rose up like a tide.

His eyebrows shot up but he didn't have any time to wonder what was happening, as the giant bull-man grabbed his axe and leapt down onto the sand. Bellowing and lowering his head as he charged forward.

Bloodsport it is.

The First dashed to the side and ran outwards in a circle around the charging beast. He wasn't faster than this Asterion, not at full sprint anyway, but he was able to stop the momentum of his run and force him into swinging his axe sideways, just slow enough to roll underneath. The wind from the axe passing above him cooled him. By Hell if that thing connected...

Asterion roared as he flipped the axe and swung backwards in another arc towards him, this time downwards slightly at an angle. He rolled backwards and got to his feet, thrusting Eirygaile out at near full extension to force his foe backwards.

That was the intention, at least, but he was surprised when Asterion instead of falling back outside of his reach turned his body and pressed forward. Eirygaile glanced off his torso, with the First noting with apprehension that the spear barely scratched the thing's thick hide, not even the dripping acid from it slowing him as he brought the haft of his axe up in a blindingly fast riposte that smashed into his jaw and nearly ended the fight then and there.

Careful! You might not bleed but you'll have a hard time fighting without a head!

Noted, he thought wryly as he focused intently on being on the defensive. He was not used to being unable to press the fight, but with the strength and speed of Asterion he would not be able to trade blow for blow. This obviously was not a normal beast he faced, there was a supernatural quality to his foe that dwarfed that of any Ba'al he had seen. Am would not have been able to best this beast, he was sure of that.

Asterion snorted hot steam out of his giant nose and swung his axe in fast arcs that The First was able to deflect relatively easily, but only while constantly falling back and unable to mount any offensive of his own. Frowning, he knew that if Asterion was able to force him all the way back into the wall it would be over. Shifting tactics, he feinted a parry then instead dashed forwards at at angle and slashed at Asterion's legs. The blade struck true, and the beast bellowed in pain.

The First leapt back immediately, barely dodging out of the way of the axe's counterswing, and then dashed in again this time forward but at the opposite angle and thrust at the other leg. Blood welled in Asterion's other leg and the acid from Eirygaile made the wound sizzle. Asterion howled in pain and roared up to the cavern ceiling in rage.

Stupid cow.

The First agreed, and while his opponent bothered with his useless display of frustration, he was graced with another small gash across his stomach as Eirygaile struck home. Not a killing blow, not by any chance, but if it took him a thousand cuts to fell this beast, so be it.

Asterion recovered from his pointless howling and attacked again, more ferocious and even faster than before, but as The First danced backwards and thrust Lokyrg at him to keep him at bay, it was clear the beast was losing control. Rage might make him more powerful, but it would make him impatient, clumsy. The First might not be as strong as this thing, but he was certainly smarter, and could outwait a stone. He longed to land a solid hit with his war-axe, but the speed of the beast relegated the slashing weapon for parrying.

Cold, calculating, the mightiest of the plague-walkers deflected attacks when prudent, dodged when necessary, and mercilessly gashed Asterion with minor cuts and stab wounds for the span of long minutes. The First suffered a few close calls with that wicked axe, but blood loss and exertion took their toll quickly. It was not long before the chest of the bull was heaving, great clouds of steam bellowing out of his mouth and nose. The fur all over its legs and chest was matted with blood and then, finally, he stopped moving and rested his axe on the ground, falling to one hoof, kneeling in pain and exhaustion.

The roaring crowd once more grew quiet and still. He assumed this outcome was unexpected.

Yet another failed attempt to best us. Do you think this sport will continue?

He wasn't sure, but other than what he guessed was a dislocated or fractured jaw, he was fine. One of the benefits of being undead, he mused. He could do this forever. "What happens now, mistress of Khthon? Am I to kill Asterion? Is your champion meant for death this day?"

Murmurs arose in the arena. Not loud at first, but clearly audible as more voices joined in the whispering. The woman in the white robe was silent for a long moment while he waited for an answer. Asterion stayed where he knelt, panting and from all appearances unable to move.

"Would that bring you joy, mortal? Would it please you to kill him?" Flat, no tone in her voice. Was this woman sane?

"Joy is beyond me, as is pleasure. I will kill him, or not, at your request. The respect due my hostess is not lost on me."

The murmurs died down as he waited for her response. Did they mistake his response for flippancy?

You should have told them sarcasm was beyond you, as well.

He thought of clarifying his comment, but decided against it. If they thought him being flippant, it was too late.

"It would please me to watch you kill him, but it would not please me to have him dead. He is a comfort to me, even in his failure. The Warden grants a stay of execution." She clapped loudly then and called out in a language that he had not heard before. He turned at the sound of gates opening across the sand, and a dozen smaller human and animal hybrids came scurrying out with a giant stretcher.

The First watched with genuine curiousity as ape, bird, and lizard-men picked Asterion up off the sand and lay him down on the canvas before lifting him in tandem and carrying him away.

What now?

He thought the circumstances were now right to broach what he was doing there. He chose his words carefully, fearing that this Warden was mentally unstable. "I see now that I was mistaken, and that it was you who brought me here. My apologies. Might I inquire as to why you brought me here?"

The woman waved her hands to quiet the crowd, now murmuring again after his words. "You must be tired after your battle. Come, be refreshed and we will speak." She gestured to a set of doors on the far side of where he entered the arena, loudly creaking as they began to open.

Tired? She must not know that you are a corpse.

"Indeed." He didn't say anything more as he walked over to the other entrance. The eyes of the aberrations were upon him as he moved, but he was hopeful he was about to get some answers. The woman had to have some reason to bring him here, after all.

Piotyr's eyes were well conditioned to look for practical use in all things, and he was impressed with the halls of House Sammael. The ice of Cocytus was hard and unforgiving, but here below the surface, warmth and protection from the elements had been well applied and engineered to create an amazing fortress.

The angels, *not* Ba'al, who had found him topside, were only a few amongst many, it seemed, as the halls were home to many other male and female angelic beings who all shared the wings and nearly flawless features of the ones who had rescued him from the worms. He had a hard time wrapping his mind around what they were, though it was painfully obvious. Angels lived here, and it was difficult to accept.

The fortress was well protected from the surface and vents of some kind of geothermal heating kept the place relatively warm. The air was chilled, but no more so than a cool day. Carpets lined the hallways as well, soft, silken, and luxurious. Tapestries depicting battles between angels, demons, and all manner of beasts hung in the halls, and alcoves with intricate and bejeweled statuary pleased his eyes as they walked.

He could even smell fresh bread being baked somewhere close and his mouth watered. This was as close to an inviting place he could remember. Even in his muddled and foggy mind, his memories did not give him any sense that he had been in such a place before. This was new, and incredible.

He had been given a heavy cloak for warmth and he walked with it wrapped around him in gratitude. He had nearly set the first one given to him ablaze on accident, which caused much laughter amongst the six hunters who had first found him. One of them then grabbed the cloak from him and replaced it with another, saying it had been treated to resist hellfire, and would serve Piotyr better. In truth he liked these men, and the women he saw looked at him not unkindly either. He could not have any idea where he was or what was happening, but it was all much better than being eaten by giant worms or freezing to death on the surface.

They came to a large set of double doors which the lead angel opened and then walked through. Piotyr followed at the direction of the others and he found himself in a great hall with tables, fire hearths, and a raised dais with a stone chair upon it, simple and unadorned. The hall was cold, but the angels spread out and quickly lit the fuel in the hearths. He did not smell wood smoke, but instead a hint of Phlegethon's sulfur came to his nose and he assumed it was more engineering and not simply burning wood that created the warmth which soon filled the room.

"Have a seat, Piotyr. Mead and food will be here shortly. Be warmed, and take your ease. No harm will come to you in my Great Hall."

His Great Hall? It must be Sammael himself, then, who greeted him topside. It was hard to get used to the man. His voice was powerful, resonant, clear. His face was beatific, and though Piotyr felt no attraction to him, he could feel a magnetic pull when Sammael spoke. This was an incredible being.

He sat at a table and sighed in pleasure as warmth moved from the hearth through his cloak and warmed his flesh. Nothing he could recall had felt so satisfying. He sat in quiet, looking around the Hall, and was pleased to see that while he was certainly a subject of interest to the other angels moving around, no one looked at him with hatred or mistrust. A casual nod here, a small smile there, and he felt if not welcome then not unwelcome either. When the mead came, he felt truly satisfied.

A flagon which required both hands to lift brought a huge smile to his face as he drank deeply. Sweet, frothy, and strong. He tasted clove, and nutmeg, and precious alcohol as his legs and stomach warmed even more. He couldn't remember anything tasting so good before, and he had the sense that it had nothing to do with his memory being awful. It was delicious.

Food was brought as well, black bread and yellow cheese. He was going to be allowed to refresh himself, it seemed, before he was questioned. Whatever else happened, he decided for the moment that he liked angels. These ones, anyway. His eye kept being drawn to a banner which hung over the stone chair over the dais. He saw two beautiful figures, angels, locked in combat high above a battle. One carried a flaming greatsword and held the advantage over another who held a glowing one. It was a masterpiece, and the battle was as detailed or intricate as he could imagine.

He was deep in reverie, enjoying his warmth and the mead, as well as the bread which was also mildly sweet and incredibly good. So deep that he started slightly when he was spoken to. It was not Sammael, but he thought it was another of the six who saved him from the worms. "When you are ready, Sammael would like to have a word with you."

Piotyr wiped his mouth clean of his drink and brushed his hands off before standing. "Of course. Lead the way."

The man looked at him oddly for a moment. "He will question you here... you don't need to move."

Piotyr colored slightly. Damned mead. "Of course. I thought perhaps I was being taken to a cell or the like."

"No, we aren't barbarians. Custom and courtesy shall be yours for as long as you return the gesture. Be at ease, he is seated."

He hadn't noticed while speaking to this other man, but Sammael had taken his seat on the stone dais and raised his hand in an informal greeting.

Not really knowing what to expect, he sat there patiently while waiting to be addressed. He didn't know much of anything about custom, or even courtesy, really. He could be polite, though.

"So, Piotyr. You travel where men cannot. I do not mean that men are forbidden, I mean that they physically cannot. How do you come to have the blood of the fallen in your veins, such that it heats you enough to walk amongst the ice fields of Cocytus?"

He cleared his throat, hoping that his ignorance would not be taken for insult. "I, ah, thank you sincerely for your hospitality, Sammael. I do not know the answer to your question, though. I awoke recently, perhaps a week or more ago, I'm not sure, in the presence of a woman calling herself the Oracle, and my mind was not clear. She told me some things, but who I am or what I am is lost to me."

Sammael frowned, and spoke again. "The Oracle is known to me. She has interfered with mortals before, but I find it strange she would send someone here merely for water. Your marker, and the water samples. She sent you here merely for that?"

Piotyr shook his head. "No, that was my task from before I encountered her, I believe. I can't recall for what purpose, but I at least remember that there was a purpose. She allowed me to continue here to resolve the task. I was trying to do so when I encountered the worm on the ice."

"Yes, this Han you spoke of in the High Sheol. He is another man like you?"

"I do not know. I am sorry but I truly don't. I know what I was supposed to do, but little else. I remember pieces of things, but nothing whole or clear."

Sammael leaned back and pursed his fingers together. "Peace, I believe you. The Oracle has great power over the mind. We avoid her altogether unless the need is dire. She doesn't owe us any favor currently or I would send for her, though fortunately we don't owe her any favor either. It is not wise to be in her debt."

"What is she? Some sort of witch?"

The angel smiled down at him before answering. "All I know is that she is ancient, and was here when we arrived in Cocytus. I've spoken with her a few times, and I don't trust her. She is something much more than a witch, and is no mortal."

Piotyr frowned. Not human. "Not to offend, but is she angel or demon, then?"

The angel's smiled broadened, and Piotyr felt a warm glow he hadn't felt since he was a child and his father had praised him. "Neither, Piotyr. She is something else, but far more important... what are you?"

The question confused him. "What do you mean? I'm a mortal."

"Demon blood flows through your veins. You could not survive here otherwise."

"I can't survive here as it is, I would have died on the surface if you hadn't intervened."

"Yes, though even arriving in Cocytus is impossible unless one is attuned completely to Hell. Arriving from Phlegethon is the only way, and the hellfire there would kill anyone traversing it, including us. Yet here you are. So I say again, what are you?"

Piotyr frowned, and was upset that he didn't have an answer that would please Sammael. He wanted nothing more at the moment than to make him happy. "I... I don't know."

The hall grew quiet for a moment, and all eyes looked to Sammael. The angel stood, and his wings unfurled behind him as he spoke in a loud, clear and booming voice. "You do know, somewhere in your mind. I do not think you a liar, yet the knowledge is there. Will you submit to our reading?"

All around Piotyr, the other angels, every man and woman in the hall, also stood with wings unfurled. "Will you submit?" They all asked in unison, and it was like a thousand horns in perfect harmony all piercing his mind. He gasped.

"Yes... yes I will submit."

It was quiet in the hall for a long moment, then Sammael first furled his wings and sat, followed by everyone else. "Good. Then eat, drink, and be merry, for a reading is taxing, and will be hard. Great care will be taken in your well-being, however, until this mystery is resolved."

Shaken, but relieved that they weren't going to just kill him, Piotyr smiled and resumed eating. He was at their mercy anyway. If they wanted to read his mind, he couldn't stop them. Maybe they would share enough with him that he could figure out what was happening, and why he was really here getting these samples.

The mead was good, the food was good, and the angels were congenial, if somewhat aloof. This was a sight better than being eaten by worms he could say.

Markov had spent the night with Jora to Jacob's approval since it was, in fact, the innkeeper's sister and not his wife. He wasn't sure if Markov would have cared, but now he didn't need to ask.

It was dawn and Jacob was downstairs in the common room sitting by the fire. He had no more than half what Markov drank the night before, as he and Jora had sat late into the date drinking and laughing. Jora was pretty, smart, and for a wonder, kind. Jacob a few years ago would have fancied her himself, but certainly not any longer. She felt almost like a different species to him.

The fire was warm, and he sank into a mild reverie as he sat beside it. Warmth and ease seeped into him and he felt his spine relax and tension flow from his shoulders. He tried very hard not to think about the circumstances, but it was impossible, so he tried to remain detached, calm, and think clearly.

What was he going to do? The Shay'tan was dead, but Piotyr was missing and Kasim lay dying. What had happened? Could Ve'kal have been so incompetent? How could she have let this happen? The Destroyer marched on Sheol with his *entire* force? It would be a slaughter more than a siege, especially if the only command fell to Han and Joshua. Good men, but not military minds.

He had to return, that much was clear. He didn't want to. Painful memories of death accompanied his thoughts of slaying Lucifer's Heir. Duskfall falling upon the Shay'tan amongst a sea of fire and death, the stench of burned corpses and diseased undead... no good memories were of that place, but he couldn't leave them to this fate. It was tempting to stay. To find a quiet corner of Hell and settle down. Maybe even here, it seemed nice.

He sighed and smiled as tension crept back into his neck. Ve'kal, it was about Ve'kal. He feared that he actually had grown to love the Ba'alat, and now that he wasn't going to die he had no excuse for their tryst. Would he still feel affection for her now that the Shay'tan was dead? The assumption for both of them when they fell into each others arms was that he was a dead man. The

Apotheosis would claim his body and soul in exchange for slaying the Shay'tan, and so it did... or so he thought.

Jacob lived, when no other man except Markov had before. He was supposed to be dead, had *told* her that he would be dead, and if he returned now, would she call him a liar and spurn him? Painfully, he also thought of Nezmyr. He had grown fond of the boy as well, and would like to see him again. Exorcising him from the parasite Iz'reth'kal had been a pleasure and after that Jacob had come to think of him as a son in some ways.

He shook his head. He had to go back, so the worry was meaningless he supposed. If they hated him for living, so be it. He could always start over later. He hoped for some sort of happy reunion, but that was stupid. He couldn't leave them to die at the hands of Ba'al Apollyon and his Legion, but he couldn't expect smiles and embraces from them either. When someone died, you moved on. Abaddon. Could he slay him as well?

He looked up as he saw the innkeeper enter the common room, carrying a flagon of chilled milk and fresh bread which he brought to Jacob. "Good morning, my lord. Will you be staying with us another day?"

"Probably not, though your hospitality has been much appreciated. I will go see Ba'al Zagan today and be on my way."

The innkeeper nodded, then smiled as he went on. "Not to be prying, but will your man, Markov be going with you? I only ask because usually Jora is awake this early and helps with the preparations."

Jacob laughed. They had been up quite late. "Yes, I believe he will. Sorry for last night, he hasn't had the chance to spend much time around a woman for some time."

"It's no trouble my lord, I just wanted to know, so as to know what to expect. Enjoy the breakfast."

He bowed his head and left Jacob alone by the fire. Another hour or so went by and Jacob tended the fire by himself as a few patrons went up and down the stairs or left to begin travel preparations. God, he was tired. He hadn't slept well, not just because of how late it was when Markov and Jora finally shut up, but his back was itchy and hurting and his thoughts were running rampant all night.

He reached under his tunic to scratch at his back and was alarmed to feel his skin raised and hard. *Great. All I need is a skin rash or a parasite.* He would seek out an apothecary or herbalist for a salve today. Travel would be hard enough without that to deal with. His thoughts... those would have to be sorted out on their own. He would return to Sheol, and if it was to warmth and affection, he would appreciate it greatly, but if it was to a cold glare and an expectation that he should be dead already, he would accept that, too.

He was surprised to see Markov come down the stairs, bleary-eyed but looking quite happy, if disheveled. Jacob waived him over and flagged down the innkeeper for another flagon and cup.

"Rather early still, isn't it Markov?"

"Aye, but I feel better rested than I have in years. Who knew all I needed was a woman and some booze?" He laughed then, and Jacob shared in the amusement. The man had certainly earned a good night, not only in causing the salvation of their race, but in then consequently paying for it with centuries of purgatory.

"Speaking of which, is Jora asleep?"

"Not really, but I figured I'd slip down early and let her sleep in if she wanted. I didn't get the sense that she got a lot of time off."

"Fair enough. Are you up for Ba'al Zagan today? We could wait for him to come here, but I thought it wise to be on the offensive."

"Whatever. You mean to kill him? I'm game."

"Probably, depends on his actions. If he is hostile at all, then yes I will kill him. He may be against Abaddon though, and if so I'll just conscript his house and take his Legion with us to Sheol."

"Well as I said, I'm game for whatever. I don't really understand the politics here, but I'll follow your lead. I trust you."

Jacob smiled and raised a glass in thanks to Markov. He was about to ask about the other man's night when the door opened and three men walked in dressed as simple peasants. Jacob, just by looking at them, would never have guessed anything off, but each of them had horrific visages on their faces and his spine quivered at the sight of them.

He calmly set his glass down and watched as the three men entered the inn, to all appearances, disinterested in the patrons. Jacob stared intently at them as their eyes swept over him, and though their human faces merely glanced at him and moved on, the visages snarled, hissed, and locked onto the two Templar sitting there.

"Markov, those three men are Fallen, and we won't have to wait for Ba'al Zagan to make a move. Steel yourself." He whispered, and smiled in greeting as he nodded at the three men. He could see them, but could they really see him?

They took a table across the common room and ordered food and drink. Jacob felt it was time. He nodded to Markov and stood up, making his way over to their table. Markov followed.

"Good morning, what news, travelers?" Jacob felt their hatred burning into him from their true forms, but smiled politely at their human faces.

"Seems you are the ones new to Tyana, stranger. What makes you think we are travelers?"

Jacob shrugged his shoulders. "You didn't greet anyone when you came in, and no one else here appeared to recognize you. Are you so hated that even the few patrons at this hour wouldn't greet you?"

All three demonic entities snarled and hissed at him and he could feel their hatred in a palpable wave of black energy. The mortals still smiled. "Tyana is not so small that everyone is known everywhere. Can three uninteresting workers not enjoy a breakfast in peace?"

"Not so small indeed, yet you know we are strangers. Tell me, does word travel so quickly of Ba'al Zagan's guests staying here? Come to meet us out of curiousity?" He smiled throughout, not betraying any sign of his awareness of their true nature.

The three men looked at each other before the one who had been speaking answered him. "Aye, word spreads. Perhaps I was asked to see what the fuss was about... just as a favor to someone."

"Well, as I'm sure Zagan is a man of action, feel free to pass along that we would be pleased to make his acquaintance as soon as possible. No reason to send the three of you to ascertain our intent. We will wait on his convenience."

The lead man laughed, and the other two continued to stare hard at Jacob. "Stupid man, who says we are from Ba'al Zagan?"

Jacob smiled wider and laughed himself before speaking loudly. "Get out, everyone. Murder is coming."

The sounds of chairs scraping and boots hurriedly retreating barely registered to Jacob as the three men stood up and their visages manifested in their mortal faces. Jacob opened his soul to the inferno of holy fire that lay smoldering within him, and gasped in ecstatic pain as the burning in his back intensified in a piercing release as wings shot out of his skin.

He blinked as he grew at least a foot in height and laughed as the three men slowly, almost as if in honey, slowly reached inside their cloaks for daggers. He stepped forward and flipped the table onto the lead man, and grabbed onto the left man's head with one hand, snapping his neck like a dry leaf. He reached with his right and crushed the throat of the man to his right.

He followed the table's momentum forward and stepped on it with his boot, pinning the man underneath it in less than a single heartbeat. Eyes wide with shock, the man yelled in fear as Jacob stood over him. He again felt no ebbing of the power at all, and knew for truth that the Apotheosis was not draining his soul in the slightest. The rules had changed.

Jacob smiled down at the would be assassin, and casually looked back to Markov. "Gather their daggers, if you please?"

chapter twenty-three

For ages you have come and gone, courting this delusion. For ages you have run from the pain and forfeited the ecstasy. So come, return to the root of the root of your own soul.
- Rumi: We Can See the Truth in Your Eyes:

He awoke from his vision with a calm ease of someone truly at peace, and he smiled. Then he tried to move. Agony shot through him like a arrow, but it was within his veins, not his legs. He had been asleep for days at the least, possibly weeks, but he hadn't felt any physical evidence of his burns. Stupid to hope that they miraculously had healed while he was asleep, yet he felt no pain at all in his legs. He lay still in the darkness, only a small candle was lit as far as he could tell. He gently flexed his muscles to see how bad it was, and he sighed in frustration as even a slight movement caused waves of pain to course through him. He was useless, as he had feared.

"Is... is anyone there?" He hoarsely whispered.

"I am here, my friend." Han answered in the darkness, and Kasim feebly tried to raise his hand in greeting.

"I should tell you that I am not pleased at what you did to heal my legs." He said it truthfully, but without malice.

"I know. I should tell you that I was not pleased to do it. Tell me, when you were unconscious, did you release them? I had hoped their souls would imbue you with their strength, but I felt them depart, not all at once, but in three groups."

"More or less. They helped me, and it was time for them to move on. What you did was immoral, but I understand it. It is good to be back, Han."

"It is good to have you back, though I fear your health is a matter of great concern."

Kasim smiled weakly, and had to stifle a laugh. Laughing would hurt like hell. "I can imagine."

Asterion had joined them while The First was still being annoyingly fawned over by the beast people. He wanted to get to the point with this Warden, if that was even her, but he was reluctant to do anything to risk offending her. Seeing her up close, madness was assuredly a part of her, and not a very deeply covered one.

So he sat patiently while tray after tray of food was brought to him and he politely waived them all away. The woman in the robe and the crown of serpents just stared at him, saying nothing, as he did so.

Maybe you should just choke something down. Pretend you aren't dead for a moment.

He didn't answer, both due to the difficulty in explaining his telepathic link to a spear, and also that he didn't feel like informing anyone that he didn't have a digestive system and couldn't process food. It was his own body, and his own business. If she said something, then so would he, but until then he was content to sit in silence.

The giant man-bull had been cleaned up, and had gained his wind back. He came into the room with a hush from everyone as a greeting. Snorting, he grabbed several handfulls of food and sat next to the woman. Hopefully, the social graces were over.

"You refuse our hospitality, after having bested our greatest warrior. I'd say that was a lack of a proper upbringing."

This is absurd.

"I didn't have an upbringing, proper or not. I was created, not born. I decline refreshment not to slight you, but because I don't eat, or drink."

"You kill well. Many of my subjects lie slain because of you." The woman spoke without inflection.

"I was attacked when I arrived. I had thought this place was hostile, and reacted accordingly."

"It is most certainly not hostile. Khthon is the most wonderful place in all of creation. We are just unused to visitors from the topside." A smile, that time. Pride in her voice.

"I meant no disrespect. As I said I was attacked, my response when that happens is to defend myself. I apologize for the loss of your subjects." While not entirely true, if he had not been attacked when he arrived he most certainly would not have drawn first blood.

The foot does not apologize for stepping on the ant, corpse.

"I do thank you for sparing Asterion. It would have pained me to lose him, though he certainly deserved death for such a miserable performance." The look she shot him, the undead could only describe as lustful, or longing. Consorts? Bizarre. He was at least twice her size, and a different species. Khthon was a very, very strange place.

"He fought well. I mean no ill will. I will respect whatever customs you have, as I can. I am ignorant to your laws and ways here in Khthon. I have not heard of it before."

She laughed, at least to his eyes an honest and merry laugh. "Of course you haven't, you simple man. We are a secret kept from everyone!"

Asterion snorted again, and the look she shot the bull was withering. "Fine, everyone except that damned Sammael. Everyone else though, knows nothing of us."

Great, this is where she tells us we can never leave.

The First wanted to get to the point, and if she was going to try to bar him from leaving to protect the secret of the place, the blood may as well start flowing now. "I hope my arrival and leaving won't distress you. I don't need to tell anyone of this place."

"Leave? Impossible. No living being may leave Khthon. It is simply impossible."

Here goes, he thought to himself, and smiled at her. "Well then we are in luck, as I'm not alive. In fact, I'm not even really one being, but an amalgamated grouping of souls all slain by one guiding intelligence. I am called The First, as I am the greatest Zombie Lord of the Templar called Joshua Danner."

She stood quiet for a moment, then hissed and glared at him. She walked towards him slowly, and he noticed her eyes glowed a deep red to match the ruby eyes of her serpent crown, which also glowed. She thought to beguile him? "The First... chosen of the *human* Joshua. You *will* remain here in Khthon, and you *will* be my champion and consort."

Well, this just got weird.

He put his hand up as she closed enough for him to feel her breath on him. Not an unpleasant looking specimen, but he really wasn't interested in such things. He not so much as pushed her as allowed her to press into his hand. Amusingly, it was her breast that made contact with his hand, and he supposed this was some sort of human sexual power thing. Her eyes glowed like fire and the serpents on her crown matched, hissing and sparkling their jeweled facets as they moved in a hypnotic pattern.

Pressing gently against her, he did his very best not to smile, or otherwise offend her. He did remember, clearly, that women in power did not take kindly to being rebuffed. "Warden, if I may call you that..."

"You may not, that is a title, not a name. If it pleases you, call me Ekidna. I am the Warden, but my name is Ekidna." She rubbed herself further against his hand, and fearing it would become ever more awkward, he gently pressed her away.

"You mistake me, Ekidna. I truly am not alive, and the pleasures of the flesh do not interest me, no matter the attractiveness of the source."

She blinked at him, and took a step back, looking him up and down. "My form does not interest you?"

"No form in existence interests me. Not man, woman, beast, or any other conceivable object. Carnal wants are not part of my being."

"Pity, I've never lain with the dead. I looked forward to broadening my horizon. It looks like Asterion can remain in my service in that capacity... for now."

She shot the bull a glare, and for his part he only snorted and continued to eat.

No... now it just got weird.

"Will you allow me to leave, then?"

"Yes, yes. In time. The rules are clear that no living being may depart Khthon, but you aren't alive, so you can skip all those silly restrictions. Wait, you aren't a god are you? Gods can't leave either."

"No... not a god. Wait, *a* god? Is this a pagan place, believing in many gods? That would explain the murals."

Her laugh was lyrical, light, and beautiful this time. Madness truly must run deep in her. "Oh, my dear zombie... you are a delight. You actually think the way things are on the surface is the truth? There are FAR older and more important things, great and terrible, than that silly conflict those so-called angels and demons have up there. Your Shay'tan is a gnat. Your "god" is a sparrow."

Careful, she is mad. True madness is dangerous, I've seen it in Han, before.

"I see. Well I won't pretend to understand the complexity of this place, then. May I inquire why you brought me here to Khthon?"

"Well, I had thought to keep you here, but since you are dead I guess that won't work. The dead actually aren't supposed to be here. Every now and then one of them floats in, or falls down from above. No, not supposed to be here at all. Barring that, then, I guess I will do as I was asked."

He was intrigued. "Someone asked something of you in regards to me?"

"Yes, yes. The Herald visited me recently, drunk as usual. He said the Oracle was going to ruin everything, and could I *please* undo the damage she was going to cause. I don't like The Herald very much, but I *really* hate the Oracle, so I agreed. Oh how I wish it had been the Keeper... I do love his conversations. Not the Herald, though. He's a boor. A beast, really."

Asterion bellowed in the strangest laugh The First had ever heard.

"That will be enough, Asterion. Don't forget that your blood *should* be staining the Colosseum sand right now."

I really can't wait to get out of here.

"So this Herald asked you for something on behalf of me?"

She looked at him and glowered. "Please don't interrupt. It's rude. No, not on behalf of you specifically. He didn't say anything about a walking corpse, especially not how handsome you would be. You sure I can't entice you into a tryst?"

"Ekidna, I am simply not..."

"Fine fine, your loss. No, The Herald asked that I intervene on behalf of the other Templar, the Hellfire Knight."

If she somehow has something to do with father missing...

"Piotyr? You know where he is?"

Ekidna wryly smirked before answering. "Not any more, but I know where he *was*. The Oracle had him, and probably destroyed his mind before sending him on his way. She does that, you know. She probably tried to mate with him first, but whether he did or didn't I doubt she let him leave with his mind intact. She does that. She is sort of a bitch."

"Destroyed his mind? What do you mean?"

She means I'm going kill someone, and soon.

"Destroyed his mind, as in she lives at the Mnemosyne, and anything that has to do with Lethe or the Mnemosyne is incredibly dangerous. Piotyr went there, recently, and though he did leave, I seriously doubt he has any idea who he is, or remember any of his life. That, is why I brought you here."

I will kill her for that. Ask her how we get to the Oracle.

"So where is Piotyr now, is he in danger?"

She laughed and drank her wine before answering. "A mortal, no matter how powerful, wanders in Hell with no knowledge or wisdom? Yes, he is in danger. Are you a simpleton?"

"Please, Ekidna, I'm trying to help a friend. Tell me what you know."

She stopped, and looked at him wide-eyed. "Courtesy. How... unexpected. Asterion, why can't you speak more like this gentlemen?"

The beast snorted again, and bellowed in what sounded like anger. The servants cleared a large space around the thing.

"Oh stop your sulking. At least you are still alive. Its not your fault, you know, this one doesn't fight with the strength of one man. More like a thousand. Anyway, he is now in Cocytus. He found his way through Phlegethon and is now either dead, or at the Halls of Sammael, who will either kill him, or help him."

Useless.

"Will you release us and allow us to go to him at Cocytus?"

She laughed again, a highly musical laugh that he supposed mortal men would find alluring. "No, but I will send you to the Oracle to retrieve his memory. Oh she will *hate* that! She dislikes uninvited guests more than anyone. Well, save the Archivists."

I tire of this folly. Tell her I'm going to kill all of them if this is a trick.

"I would appreciate that, Ekidna. Once I get Piotyr's memory back, how am I to find him in Cocytus?"

"You aren't, if you try, you will freeze solid. The path to Cocytus is barred to everyone with hellfire flowing through Phlegethon. Your friend, this Piotyr, I'm told... has a unique gift for traversing it. No, you can't get to him, but worry not, either he is already dead and you couldn't help him anyway, or he is in good hands. Sammael is a finer host than you could imagine in a place like Hell."

I haven't heard of him, but I doubt any Ba'al is a fine host.

"So what am I to do then? Abandon him to the clutches of a Demon Lord? He is important to us, I can't just leave him."

"Demon Lord? Now you really should be glad I didn't send you there. Sammael is no Ba'al, he is not even technically a Fallen. He refused to take up arms against the Seraphim in the War, but he sided with Lucifer before the Throne. When it came to bloodshed, he and his loyalists left on their own. They came here as Lucifer fell, and found their own quiet corner where they have lived for aeons. Lucifer didn't even know they were there. If you call him a Ba'al, he would slay you without pause. It is a grave insult."

Even if what she says is true... I have my doubts of that as it is, but even if it is true, he will need help getting back.

"Still, I would like the chance to..."

She sighed in overly dramatic fashion, almost like a teenager in some of his memories. "I *told* you that you can't go there. It's too cold, and you would freeze solid in minutes. I'm not sending you, and that's that. I will send you to the Oracle, and that is enough help from me! When you are done, get whatever you need from Phlegethon, and then get back to whatever place you call home. Your quest will be complete. Don't argue, that is how it will be."

Corpse, let me slay her. We can find our own way to this Oracle.

The First pursed his lips in thought, and decided that Lokyrg was wrong. They probably couldn't find a way to the Oracle, and that Piotyr was likely summoned to her in the same way that Ekidna summoned them repeatedly to the immense cavern on the river.

Finally, he decided to just accept her peculiarities and take her assistance. He was curious about the place, though. "You called yourself the Warden. What sort of beings are imprisoned here?"

The room became nearly silent when he spoke. The only audible sound for a long moment was Asterion's deep, loud breathing. He feared he had said something wrong and would have to fight just to get out of the place, now. When Ekidna spoke, he was relieved.

"Older things than I care to explain, and more powerful than you would care to learn of. Suffice it to say that they are kept here for the benefit of all. Their release would only happen should humanity die completely and Heaven and Hell not continue their war with each other until there was a clear victor. The Warden has said all she will say on the matter. Are you ready to visit the Oracle?"

I am ready to leave, that is for certain.

He was still curious, but it was as clear a dismissal as he could remember. "Yes, I'm ready."

He awoke in a daze, though physically unhurt and apparently cared for. He lay in bed near a fire in some room that was not the Great Hall. He was covered in furs and was for the most part comfortable, though his head hurt and he was disoriented.

The process of reading his thoughts had, he assumed, been completed, though he couldn't remember anything after sitting down and seeing the eyes of Sammael's consort. What was her name, Lilith?

He got up, slowly as he was dizzy and out of sorts, and noticed that he was unclothed. He didn't smell burnt cloth, but it was a safe assumption that he had burned through whatever garments he had previously brought, and the special cloth Sammael had provided would have to suffice going forward. His sword was scabbarded and rest against the wall of the room he was in. They must not consider him a threat. He was at once comforted at that, and mildly offended for some reason he couldn't fathom.

Other than the hearth, chair, bed, and a small wardrobe, the room was mostly spartan, though it did have an ajoining water room with a stone wash basin in it. He stepped into the room and was surprised to see water spigots along the wall as well as buckets.

He laughed in joy as the water came out of the wall, splashing into a bucket as he turned the spigot. "Why not?" he said aloud as he filled the basin. He assumed any other guest would heat the buckets over the hearth fire in the other room, but he didn't need to. As long as he was careful he could heat the water right in the basin.

He couldn't remember the last time he had soaked in hot water, *really* soaked and not struggled to swim while fighting off undead... though to be fair he couldn't really remember anything more than a week or so previously. It was luxurious. His muscles soothed and unclenched, and other than the gaping hole in his memory, he felt truly at ease.

He bathed for perhaps an hour, and feeling refreshed and invigorated, got out and dressed. Clothes had been set out for him earlier, and he assumed they had also been treated to resist his gift as they stayed intact and were quite comfortable. He retrieved his scabbard and blade, and left his room, looking for someone to speak to.

The halls weren't bustling, but were certainly not empty either. He saw male and female angels in various dress, most of whom gave him a polite nod but nothing more. Their faces were beautiful, and as far as he could tell, ageless. He couldn't place any of them at an age other than appearing between twenty or sixty, except almost universally they had flawless physiques and not a wrinkle on a face to be seen.

Their builds did vary, and greatly, but only in general size and shape. There were short angels, tall angels, lithe angels, muscled angels... male, female, all were more or less flawless in whatever shape and build they were in. Piotyr was in excellent physical condition, but it seemed strange to him that not one angelic being in sight was fat, or frail, or gaunt, or aged. He had no recollection of any other society or city... but it still felt like it was aberrant. Easy on the eyes, though.

He followed the hallway for awhile, marveling at the beautiful sculptures, tapestries, and engineering of the place, and came to a junction. He stopped a passing angel, a woman, and asked politely where he could find Sammael.

"He is in the barracks, Son of Adam. Do you know the way?"

Son of Adam. He still didn't remember anything other than his task and his destination, but smiled at the title as he supposed it was a positive one. "I do not, might I ask you to direct me there?"

The angel nodded, and led him for a good quarter hour. This place was immense. He marveled at the number of people who might live here... in this frozen land of Cocytus.

The barracks was huge, he learned upon arriving. The woman leading him nodded to the guards outside and they opened a set of ornate stone double doors. Immediately a sensation of familiarity washed over him as the scent of sweat, metal, and leather greeted him. He heard the sounds of combat before his eyes confirmed it, and smiled as he observed perhaps fifty winged forms engaged in various training exercises, sparring, and other mock combat.

He knew, then, that he was a fighting man. It was too familiar. He actually grinned as he watched, and though it was frustrating that he couldn't remember his past, he innately knew that he was at home in a barracks.

"So, this is not unknown to you, Son of Adam?"

Piotyr turned to see Sammael walking up to him. He was dressed down to a leather cuirass, leaving his arms bare, and basic linen clothing and sandals. The armor was moulded, and lacked the muscle definition he had seen on the earlier metal cuirass Sammael wore.

"No, it is not unknown. Though I can't remember, this feels like home. I feel that I was a warrior of some skill among my people."

"You don't know the half of it. Come, spar with me. I wish to see what the best of the mortals can do."

Piotyr frowned. He couldn't remember fighting... though he innately knew he was good at it. He sized up Sammael, and though the man... the angel... was nearly twice his height, he felt no malice from him. More importantly, Piotyr felt no fear. He felt a rush of excitement.

"Weapons?"

Sammael laughed before clapping him on the arm. "That's the spirit! Sarus, training sword!" He bellowed loudly and Piotyr noticed with wry amusement that the training in the barracks stopped. A slightly shorter angel ran to a weapons rack and fetched two wooden blades, handing one to each Piotyr and Sammael. This would be a spectacle, it seemed.

"Hmm... I'm not sure if we have any leather that would fit you..."

"We can fight without?"

Sammael grinned at him again and stripped to his waist. A section of the training area was cleared, and Piotyr found himself facing off against the man who was hosting him in this strange and wondrous place.

Sammael raised his sword above his head, pointed towards the mortal in a guard position that Piotyr instantly recognized, though he couldn't place why. *The Ox. It is called the Ox.* The words blossomed in his mind as Sammael lowered his blade to point at Piotyr's face.

Piotyr mirrored him, though slightly off angle to compensate for the larger size of his opponent, then frowned as something clicked and he changed his stance into a lowered blade stance. *Meet the Ox with the Plow.*

Piotyr felt... right. This was who he was. Sammael smiled at him, and attacked. The angel was fast enough as it was, but Piotyr could barely blink as his opponents wings unfurled and he burst forward with a beat of them and closed to him in a beat of his heart.

The Plow instantly switched to the Fool as he stepped back. Sammael's practice blade thrust down but Piotyr deflected it and whipped it instantly up in a counter which nearly connected before Sammael deftly parried as well.

Piotyr felt the sting in his arms and knew Sammael was far stronger than he was. He would not be able to overpower him. He dropped again into the Plow and awaited the next strike from the angel. Sammael was testing him. Not attacking at full strength. Frowning, that lack of respect angered him. He was not an opponent to be taken lightly.

He switched his stance to the Long Tail, his blade jutting out behind him at a sharp angle downwards and feigned a strike at Sammael's legs. The angel brought his blade up to parry, but Piotyr abandoned his strike and switched to the Ox as he sidestepped Sammael and closed. Sammael turned his body to meet Piotyr's new angle of attack, but Piotyr had no intention of striking with his blade again and instead kicked low at Sammael's leg, causing the angel to grunt and shift off-balance.

Piotyr closed again, and punched Sammael in his exposed kidney, the angel was now on balance, and turned to strike at Piotyr from a Roof Guard position. The mortal again shifted back and worked his stance changes to keep Sammael off balance and unable to overpower him.

He wasn't smiling now, Piotyr noticed with satisfaction. They switched stances and parried strikes for several minutes, with neither man landing a clean hit. Sweat poured off both of them, and Piotyr felt incredibly good. He felt alive. It went on for several more rounds of back and forth before Sammael stood up and lowered his practice blade.

"Enough. Well fought mortal." He raised his blade in front of his face in what Piotyr took to be some sort of honorific.

He returned the gesture and answered. "You as well, Sammael."

"I at least take consolation that you are counted among the greatest of your kind. Come, let us be refreshed while I tell you a tale that will be of great interest."

"Thank you. Refreshment sounds good. What tale is that?"

"Why, Son of Adam! The tale of Piotyr Lamja, of course."

Markov didn't have the stomach for this sort of grisly work. Blood didn't make him squeamish, but interrogating a prisoner with blades and the like was just not his preference. The inn had been cleared, at least, including Jora. He was glad. No one should have to hear this.

Still, Merethius had been quite effective. Only one of them survived, but the man had to be unnerved as Jacob had killed the other two so quickly and easily. It was odd. He would have wagered money... well if he had any money... that the remaining demon would not talk. He had seen their kind before. Hard sons of bitches, and they would die before breaking.

Merethius had a way with words though. The first time he spoke, Markov could feel the power coming off of him. That Soul Fire thing. The wings still hadn't gone away from his friend, and Markov was in awe as he spoke.

"You could live, in comfort and splendor for the rest of your days. Or you could suffer without end until your heart gives out. I shall give you a moment to decide which fate you desire."

Again, Markov had seen their type before, and so it was with a spluttering shock that Merethius removed the gag and the man gushed out everything. He was so surprised that he forgot the beer he was drinking and just watched. It wasn't grisly at all.

So these were the Grigori. Three of them, anyway. The survivor couldn't speak quickly enough to get his words out, tripping over his sentences in a mad rush to give Merethius what he wanted. The Ba'al had nothing to do with their arrival. Zagan apparently still had no idea he was paying for their stay here, or if he did he didn't care. These men knew of his arrival because they have spies everywhere and had been contracted by that asshole Abaddon to kill all of the Templar in Hell.

Wild. The Grigori told him their structure, their locations, they communication system, their methods, everything. Markov couldn't believe it, and looking from his face, neither could he. He had to laugh. Was it his voice? Surely he wasn't breaking just because of the threat of a little torture. He checked himself, no torture was *little* he supposed, but Merethius hadn't even done anything to him yet... just killed the first two.

Hell, Markov himself wouldn't have talked yet. He would have at least made his torturer honest. Make him at least sink a blade or two before getting into it. This was incredible. He drank his beer as the Grigori told Merethius everything as fast as he possibly could.

For his part, the interrogator even looked taken aback. His eyes seemed wide, to Markov, as he looked from the man to Markov and asked question after question about their leadership, the contract, drop points for messages, everything that Markov could think of asking, Merethius asked.

It probably took a couple of hours, but by the time it was done Markov could have written a book about these guys. The information was staggering. The questions finally slowed, then stopped, and Markov watched Merethius intently to see what he was going to do with the man.

"That was appreciated, Watcher. I will now reveal to you your fate. I keep my word, but in this case I feel that you were so earnest that I will gladly allow you to live out your days, on the condition that I am voiding your contract with Abaddon and you shall never raise your blade again to a Templar. Do we have an accord?"

The man looked at both Templar in what Markov could only call relieved joy. He nodded to Merethius, and for a wonder, he smiled and let the man go. "Markov. I think Ba'al Zagan can do without our presence for the day. Have you any desire to visit these Watchers in their home?"

"Hell if I care, but do you have a plan? Sounds like something big is happening soon at this Sheol place."

"Yes, I have a plan. It is time to go home."

Dhermina smelled wonderful to him, though he smelled a fair amount of sorrow about her as well. She had been crying, and recently. Kasim knew she had been working with Joshua and the engineers quite a lot, but his recovery from death had jarred her back to the pain of the attack. The deaths of the others had hit her hard and now it was all too raw again.

He embraced her and inhaled deeply into her hair, not minding the salty scent of her tears at all. She was his love and he had missed her.

"I am sorry to have left you again, Dhermina. I promise you it was the last time. You won't stand vigil over my body again in this life, I swear to you."

"Kasim, I don't mind standing vigil, I just wish there was some peace for us. The others... they burned and died and all I have left is you. I want an end to this."

Secretly he wished for that as well, though he knew there was more death to come. "The others have left this place of suffering. I visited with them in the afterlife, and they all wished us well and were looking forward to moving on."

"So what Han did... it is ended?"

Kasim was uncomfortable, but there was no use ignoring it. "Yes, though my legs work because of what he did. I won't condone it, but now that it is finished I won't harbor him any ill will."

"They deserved better."

"I agree, but it is done, and they are free now. I think, in a way, Han knew that it was necessary, and it is a hard thing for me to say that I would rather him have left me crippled. I feel weak enough as it is, and my insides are still turning to stone. That poison will kill me yet without an antidote."

"That's why you aren't able to leave the palace ruins?"

Kasim hesitated but knew that if he didn't tell the complete truth, she would know it anyway. His empathic link with her was not one-sided. "In truth I fear for my safety, and yours. The assassins failed to kill me, so I would assume they will try again. I am not fit to defend myself yet, and I am not comfortable assuming they will simply wait for the poison to finish what it started."

"Joshua said he feels confident that his treatment will give you weeks longer before you succumb. Surely Piotyr will return by then."

"If he is not dead. It has been long already, he should have returned by now unless something happened."

He felt her beginning to dig in for an argument. "Kasim, there is no precedent for what he is tasked with doing... he could be making his way back here now, but how could you possibly know how long the journey would be?"

Smiling, he released their embrace reluctantly and looked down at her beautiful green eyes. "I don't know, I only suspect. Piotyr is more than capable, and that undead of Joshua's... he is as well. I simply worry that ill fate has befallen them. I hope I am wrong."

"Well, fortunately the battle preparations are nearly complete. Ba'al Apollyon has already marched, and is headed here now. Our scouts report that his army reaches both ends of the horizon, and the last man marching is three full days behind the first. Millions upon millions march on Sheol."

He sighed. He would like nothing more than to sit with her, talking of more pleasant things, but in truth oblivion was coming for them all. "Yes, I haven't had the chance to inspect all the changes, but I had the chance to speak to a palace servant about them. I'll speak with Han at more length and Joshua as well as soon as I've rested again."

"Sorry... I could send for them now, I just wanted a moment with you first."

"And I, you. I'll be fine in another few hours, I'm just weak. I saw Han already, but he let me rest. The burns are healed, but the poison saps my strength. Joshua did well, but so did the assassins. Might you stay with me for a time? I know you are exhausted as well."

She smiled at him before answering. "I could use a short rest as well. The door is still sealed, and only Han or Joshua can get in. Sleep would be welcome."

Curling up on the ground, he smiled as his love lay next to him and they both closed their eyes to rest. Sleep would be welcome, a deep and dreamless one, he hoped.

chapter twenty-four

The wild beasts of the desert shall also meet with the wild beasts of the island, and the satyr shall cry to his fellow; the Screech Owl also shall rest there, and find for herself a place of rest.
- Isaiah 34:14

The First blinked as he stared down the precipice at a drop that would surely shatter his bones. Ekidna had been true to her word, and had sent him here shortly after a final command.

"You shall speak of this place to no one, ever. The Vault is a secret that only my kind know of, and it shall remain that way. This price I demand from you in return for calling you to me and setting you on the path to help Piotyr."

"I am a man of my word, but it surprises me that you would trust a secret to me. How can you trust me?"

"I have enchanted you. If you speak of this to anyone, you will return to my side. I will not allow you to leave a second time. The Vault, and its secrets, shall remain hidden from everyone except you. Do you understand? Eternity locked away with us will be your punishment for betraying this secret."

He had nodded to her, and said he understood, and then she had given him a draught to drink off of one of the serving platters some bizarre looking girl with arachnid eyes had carried.

Asterion had snorted loudly and nodded to the zombie in respect. The First had returned the gesture before drinking the draught in one long gulp. He didn't drink, not really, but his body could absorb the liquid in time.

He had blinked, and the room collapsed on itself in a rush of air and he found himself transported to the cliff top overlooking the waterfall he had lost Piotyr at. So, that was what had happened. He suspected this Oracle had done to Piotyr what the Warden had done with himself. These beings must be able to summon others to their domain.

Quite the drop. My father can't fly, this could have ended badly.

"If it did, we'll know soon enough. Let's find this Oracle person. We should have answers there."

I hope she is saner than the last one. I've had enough madness for two lifetimes.

He carefully made his away along the slick rock face. The way was treacherous enough that he took great care and went very slowly. The mist from the waterfall was intermittent, but definitely enough to give the algae every chance to kill someone walking across it. He was far more agile than most, but slick was slick, and he had no desire to take the quick way down.

He found his way to a small cavern, well lit and teeming with flora. Flowers of every color and shape imaginable mixed with ferns, mushrooms, and plants he was not familiar with. He carefully made his way further into the cavern and was surprised when he found a chair sitting next to some sort of fount. He was even more surprised to see a woman standing next to it, one arm resting on the back, staring at him.

"I told him he wouldn't need to collect both sets of samples."

She did help him then, at least with the water.

"Greetings, Oracle. I take it to understand you met with my companion, Piotyr Lamja?"

The woman smiled and walked around the chair to stand before him. She was attractive, he supposed, though not to him. She actually looked like she could be related to the Warden. Sisters, perhaps?

"Yes, he was here, but you already know that since you are here. Who am I to blame for this intrusion? Not the Keeper... and no Archivist would dare... so it must be that witch. She stop fucking her cow long enough to meddle in my affairs?"

Not knowing quite how to respond, he decided not to address her comment directly. "I was looking for my friend, out on the river. I came to a strange place, and a woman told me of you and sent me to you on behalf of Piotyr."

She smiled in a way that he could only call predatory. "Oh, and what of this place... tell me of it."

Manipulative bitch. She must know of what Ekidna spoke of.

"I am not to speak of it, so I won't."

The woman laughed and stepped closer to him. Her eyes became very intense and she locked gazes with him. "I *insist.* Tell me of this place you visited."

This one uses the same tricks as the other. Perhaps you should wear a sign informing these fools that you are immune?

He wanted to laugh. Lokyrg could be funny when he chose. He didn't want to insult her, though. These beings were alien, and who knew how unpredictable they could be. "Oracle, I must insist as well. I am not to speak of it, so I won't."

She scowled at him. "You aren't alive, are you?"

"I am not."

Her expression softened, and what could only be called a pout crossed her face. "Pity. The mortal was easy to bend to my will. I am unused to those who aren't."

Bitch. Let me kill her!

"I apologize. My unique characteristics make me immune to such things, as well as... *other* types of persuasion." Best to be clear about that beforehand.

Her eyes widened, then she laughed again. "She tried to seduce you, didn't she? God, that one would mate with anything... but the dead?"

Curiously, he felt offended. He *was* dead, but he wasn't a corpse. Well, not a real corpse anyway. He could move better than any mortal alive, was intelligent, had *more* than one soul even, and his flesh was unmarred, perfect even. "Well, suffice it to say I don't resemble most corpses. In any case. she sent me here so you could help me find Piotyr. I was told he made it here, and departed for Phlegethon and Cocytus."

"Oh I could help you find Piotyr, but it wouldn't help you. Cocytus is barred to you. Barred to anyone. Piotyr could travel there because of his unique physical traits. The Keeper and I remarked on it, actually."

Who is this Keeper? How does he know my father?

He quieted his thoughts to concentrate on what the Oracle was saying.

"She also told me as much, but I would go at least as far as Phlegethon. Perhaps I could meet up with him on the way back. If nothing else, with the water I will collect here and the additional sample from Phlegethon, I would only be short Cocytus to give Joshua what he needs."

She snorted and looked at him with what he supposed was derision. "You assume much, that you could traverse the River of Fire safely and retrieve source water. I allowed Piotyr to continue with his fools errand because of what he is. You? Your flesh will burn like any other corpse."

The First felt the stirrings of anger, which was not a familiar sensation with him. He didn't get angry, not even in combat, but the words of this Oracle were mocking, and he would not be mocked.

"Did you destroy Piotyr's mind?"

Finally, thank you.

The Oracle's eyebrows climbed high upon her forehead. "She told you that? That surprises me. I don't divulge her ways and secrets."

Other than saying she fucked Asterion. She evades the question.

"Did you destroy Piotyr's mind?"

"This conversation is boring, and is now over. Leave this place, or I shall send you over the precipice. I doubt your body will survive the impact."

"I will ask one more time, politely. Did you destroy Piotyr's mind?"

The Oracle stood, stunned, before glaring at him and hissing. "Die, fool." She spoke in some language unfamiliar to The First, and gestured at him. He felt a tingling in the air around him, and that was all he needed. He leaped forward as fast as he possibly could, and struck her square in the face. She cried out in pain, but rather than collapse, she danced backwards in a blur and began to incant again.

The First had no idea what sort of powers she possessed that didn't prey upon his immune mind, but he didn't care to find out. His memories held stories of witches and sorcery, nothing good would come from the Oracle. He spun Lokyrg in a close, tight circle, no chance of hitting her but acid dripped off the barbs and splashed her in the face and neck.

She screamed in pain and the incantation stopped. *Good, keep interrupting her.*

He pressed the attack and was surprised that she was able to dodge as well as she could, particularly while wounded, but he was no mere mortal. His speed was greater, and so was his mind. He feinted to one side, deliberately slowly, and when she again spoke he accelerated to her body and struck her with his fists three times rapidly in the head, chest, and stomach. They were telling blows, and though he expected they would kill any normal woman, they were only able to stagger the Oracle. She lost her wind, though, which was as he intended.

Doubled over and gasping for air, she had no resistance to offer as he brought his knee up into her stomach twice and grabbed her into a choke hold. He applied enough pressure that her breath would not easily come back to her, though he did not expect to kill her with it.

"You will answer me, witch, or by all that is holy or unholy I will break you. The next time you refuse me an answer, I will tear off your hand. Know that I take no pleasure in this, but I will not play your games. You may find mere mortals to be beneath you, but Piotyr is my friend, and I find you to be beneath me. If I have to rip off all of your limbs to get the truth from you, I will, and without hesitation. This will be your last chance. Don't waste it."

A far more enjoyable conversation, corpse. Well done and well spoken.

He slackened his grip somewhat, but did not release her. It would take much longer, but it would also be painful and she would feel like she was suffocating. He allowed the air to slowly come back to her, her breath coming in what had to be agonizingly insufficient spurts. Minutes passed, and when he felt that she was close to being recovered, he spoke.

"Now, did you break Piotyr's mind? Don't bother to speak, just nod." It was all for show anyway, he already assumed she had done as much, and given where they were, he assumed it was the water.

The woman nodded in his grasp, probably still unable to speak anyway.

"Can you restore him?" Again she nodded. He gathered that she probably gave him the water, or some variation of the water and had him drink it without any protection or guidance. Lethe was known to do that to mortals anyway, and stranger still were tales of this Mnemosyne.

"Here are my sample containers. Prepare me a sample of Lethe water, two in fact, one in an empty vessel and then add that to the larger one, refilling another. I shall at least return to Han and Joshua with these and the waters of Phlegethon. As to what you gave Piotyr? I care not for the other water for myself, but you *will* prepare a draught for Piotyr to restore his memory. I will know if you attempt subterfuge, and it will not go well for you. Perhaps I won't cut off your hand, but I will remove your tongue. I will release you now, do not tempt my wrath."

I do not compliment you enough, corpse. I approve.

He released his grip, but stayed right next to her and casually allowed Lokyrg to pass in front of her face. The acid gathering down the barbs was close enough for her to smell as well as see. She would be a rare woman indeed if she attacked him again. He would be surprised if he actually did need to remove her hand.

He gave her the minutes needed to get her wind back. When her breathing deepened and sounded normal, he moved back slightly, not showing that he was less of a threat, but indicating that he now knew she was ready. "You may proceed."

"So that is your story, Piotyr Lamja. Templar, Hellfire Knight, and father to dragons. Quite a tale, though I regret you had to hear it from me and do not remember it truly for your own. I'm sorry if the reading was disorienting. Lilith is thorough."

"Indeed I am, husband." Lilith spoke in a high voice tinged with authority.

Piotyr said nothing at first. He had been disoriented when he awoke but the bath and subsequent combat had cleared his mind. He didn't remember anything, but he believed Sammael implicitly. *He was a father? His mate was a dragon?*

"I don't remember any of it, though it rings true. This Oracle has much to answer for."

Sammael gently laid his hand on Piotyr's shoulder. "Let it go. She is impossible to reach unless she summons you. Her shrine lies on the border of Elysium, and the cliff can not be scaled without alerting her... to fly is to invite the attention of the Choir. I know you are angry, but it will end in pain and death if you try to find your way to the Oracle again."

How can you possibly know how angry I am? I have children. "I am limited in options at the moment. I would ask your leave, though, to bring some Heart of Cocytus back with me to Sheol. I can't remember anything else, but that much is clear to me. I was tasked with it."

"Yes, I will allow that. We have plenty." The man laughed, and Piotyr managed a half-hearted smile. He wasn't angry with Sammael, but he certainly felt no mirth. "I can send you with what you need. I'm sorry I can't do more, but at least I could tell you of your past. I know it is not the same as actually remembering, but I hope it is small comfort."

Can't do more? Or won't. "I thank you for your hospitality, and for the Heart of Cocytus. Could you take me there? I am anxious to complete my task."

"Of course, Son of Adam. Walk with me."

Piotyr went with Sammael through the palace for what felt like forever, though probably was not even an hour. He saw more grandeur, but the revelation from his host had taken all the wonder from his eyes. How was he supposed to lead the army when he couldn't remember anything about the war? Being told that he cared for people wasn't the same as actually caring for them.

Sammael made idle conversation as they walked, though most of what he spoke of was the war in Heaven before Lucifer fell. Sammael was clearly a kindred mind when it came to military matters, though Piotyr again felt no stirring at the names spoken. Without passion, everything seemed meaningless.

The air grew colder and heavy as they walked, and when they came to a doorway leading into a narrow staircase, it made sense. The palace, or fortress, was built right into the ice, so Piotyr assumed that if they went down far enough, they would reach both the source of the geothermal heating as well as a pure sample of ice frozen at the source.

Sure enough, after perhaps half an hour more of cold descent, they arrived at a landing with two doors, both completely walled in with ice. "I could chip away at it, but it would be faster if you would do the honors. The left door, if you would."

Piotyr nodded, and channeled a tiny amount of hellfire, just enough to quickly melt the ice covering the door. It warmed him slightly, but not like it did when his fire consumed flesh or even organic matter. Ice was just water, and it did little to provide him with strength or sustenance.

"That will do, we don't need to completely uncover it, just the seam."

"May I ask what is behind the other door? It doesn't appear that this is an area well traveled."

"Nothing of much use, I'm afraid. We have long memories. Visiting the past is less productive for us than staying in the present."

Piotyr didn't press, as he actually didn't really care. It was just conversation. "How much further?"

Sammael managed to shoulder the door open with a grunt. "Not far, it's past the birthing chamber, but not very. Speaking of that, I don't think the wyrms will view you as a threat, but your scent won't match ours, so be on your guard."

"From what you tell, I have an affinity for these creatures."

"Possibly, though hellfire and Frost wyrms are merely similar. Related, but distantly. I just want you to be alert, in case they take a dislike to you."

"Lead the way, I think it will be fine."

Entering the room beyond, the first thing Piotyr noticed was the smell. A strong scent of earth and musk hit his nose. He then realized the temperature was noticeably warmer. The room was dark, but not the pitch black he had expected, and his eyes quickly adjusted. Luminous crystals shone in the darkness, not of white, but of deep blue and purple. Vents with steam gently pouring out of them dotted the cavern wall and he saw lichens and fungus clinging to the stone around each steaming fissure, but no more than perhaps two feet around them.

Sammael walked into the cavern and Piotyr held his hand out towards one of the vents, which was about as wide as his torso. The steam was hot. "I had thought the wyrms would like the cold."

"They do, once they mature. The larvae don't have the carapace of the older ones yet, so they can't survive away from the heat. It also helps with their feeding. Without the food grown here, they would either resort to cannabalism or attack our livestock reserves."

"Are they intelligent?"

"Somewhat. They can follow commands once trained. They spend decades being conditioned as mounts. They were rampant when we arrived here, but we got their population under control when we domesticated them."

Visions of the war ripped through his head again, though this time he clearly saw Frost wyrms on the field of battle, doing as he bid. "How many are down here?"

"About a hundred juveniles, twice that many eggs. We count twenty full grown and trained war-wyrms, and another twenty in various progress in their training. Quite a lot of mouths to feed as it is, so we cull the unborn young so as not to create a shortage of food."

"Is there a queen, then? Or some other brood mother?"

"Yes, but we stay away from her chamber. They get very aggressive if she is approached. The eggs get moved from there to the steam vents to hatch, and not often. "

"What about food for her? Do you leave food down here?"

Sammael stopped for a moment and turned to look at him. "You seem quite interested in all of this. Is this because of your connection to Asya, to the Hellfire wyrm? They are related, as I said, but not the same."

"Asya is more than just a wyrm, she is my mate, at least that is what Lilith saw in the reading, right? She is also highly intelligent, as are our drakes, if what you say about our cavalry formations are true. I ask because I have had visions of a great battle at Sheol, and in that vision ice wyrms followed my orders."

Sammael frowned, clearly visible in the ambient light from the crystals. "I would doubt the possibility of that, Piotyr. As I said they spend decades being trained. The only way that they would be effective would be if...

Piotyr stopped walking, and Sammael did as well. "You saw us in your vision as well? Following your orders?"

"I had thought you would have seen all of this when you read my thoughts."

"Lilith is quite accomplished, but she said nothing of this. She has no reason to keep it from me, so I must assume that it is a vision given to you by the Oracle. She would not have seen a gift from the Mnemosyne."

"A gift? It's like a hurricane inside my head. They are memories that haven't happened yet, and they aren't fixed... it's like thousands of possible outcomes are constantly ripping forward and backward across my mind."

"I use the word *gift,* rather lightly in Hell. Your hellfire is a gift. That vision from the Oracle is a gift. Our isolation from the rest of hell is a gift. I would take notice of what you have in your mind, Piotyr. It is not a mere vision of what could be. The Oracle gave you the truth of how that battle *will* play out. That is not something to be discarded lightly."

"I told you, there are so many variations that I can barely make sense of it. Troop movements, siege developments, hell even what units are where... they aren't fixed, they are fluid. Sometimes I see an entire section of the siege play out completely differently than it did previously. How can it be a vision of what will happen if there are so many variables?"

Sammael pursed his lips in thought for a moment before answering. "I haven't fought in a true battle in millennia, but the one I did was chaos. Things could have happened differently at any moment, I think, no... I know. Perhaps it is your charge to sort through the chaos and formulate plans from them? I only know what Lilith could discern from your past, and that is certainly not a complete picture of the man who is Piotyr Lamja, but from my limited knowledge of you it would appear that you are the best candidate to general the forces there at Sheol."

"That may be, I can't remember, but accepting that it is true... would you join forces with me against Abaddon?"

Sammael looked at Piotyr in silence for a long moment. "So you did see us?"

"I did. I saw your angels, and the wyrms, in units of heavy cavalry."

"How many did you see?"

"Not as many as you say are here, perhaps three dozen, though only about half were on the front lines. As you said, twenty trained and ready for combat? That is close to the number I saw, ridden by your forces."

"You saw this clearly, then. What of the forces we were engaged with?"

Piotyr snorted. "A force that could not be defeated by any force we could muster. I saw millions upon millions of Legion, and Fallen as well. In the skies, true Ba'al darkened the air with their wings. I saw a force meant to annihilate, and no matter how I try to change decisions in my strategy, we always lose, and decisively."

"You ask us to join in suicide, then?"

The question enraged him. "I am answering your damned question! I saw you in my vision, and your wyrms. I was sent here for the damned ice, not to recruit angels which I had no knowledge of!"

"Kindly lower your tone, Son of Adam. There is no cause for discourse here. I bear your kind no ill-will. I am not like Lucifer, though I did stand by him before the Throne."

I don't care, I can't remember any of this anyway.

"Sorry, lets just get to the ice."

"As you wish, Piotyr."

At least the damned itching had stopped. Jacob had been surprised when his wings had broken through his skin on his back, but incredibly relieved. The painful scratching had been maddening. They were useless, vestigial things, but at least they didn't hurt. They made clothing on his torso uncomfortable, to say the least, but still better than the itching.

He had kept the Apotheosis burning in his chest for some time after releasing the Watchers. With no fear of it consuming him, he allowed it to stay for nearly an hour as they reprovisioned at the inn and departed. All on the generosity of Ba'al Zagan, of course.

Markov hadn't joined him in it, which he found strange, but perhaps the man wasn't comfortable with it yet. When he finally released the power, he had sighed in regret, but then felt the relief as his wings burst through his skin. He was changing, and not just in the wings. His hair had grown out, mostly, now falling in soft curls to his shoulders. His scars and injuries from battles new and old had faded and healed, and his body had filled out even more than when he had arrived in Hell.

He didn't need to see a mirror to know that he would not see the man who had first arrived in Hell near the river so long ago. That man was a burned and broken mess. He was flawless, or at least nearly so. The wings were a problem, but he hoped they would grow in time.

The two had journeyed mostly in silence across the fields of wheat and then uncultivated prairie. Markov had kissed Jora goodbye, had given her backside a grab and laughed with her as they departed, but had remained quiet as they traveled. Jacob allowed the silence to remain. If he wanted to talk, he would.

The Grigori had told them exactly where to find the nearest cell, and it was two full days journey by foot. The headquarters were in Sheol, though. He could walk there in a couple of months, but he didn't think they had that much time.

"Markov, we can use the Soul Fire to fly. Would you be willing to join me in making haste to the Grigori headquarters near Sheol?" They hadn't been speaking much, other than a few small comments, so Jacob appeared to have caught Markov in his own thoughts.

He didn't answer right away, but instead looked up at the sun and back down the road before answering. "Jacob, I think you and I are playing with different rules here. I'm glad that you seem to be able to pull an infinite amount of power through this thing, but I'm pretty sure I can't."

Of all the things Markov could have said, that was about the last thing Jacob was thinking about. "What do you mean? You didn't die when you used it, and you had that same experience on the mountaintop outside of our shared purgatory, didn't you?"

"Not in the way you did, it seems. You say that when you use it, it is a bottomless ocean, and you don't feel any different while it burns within you. I don't feel that. I feel more that... well... that I can turn it off or on, but it still feels like it is running on a limited supply. I think maybe in coming here, that the Soul Fire... mine anyway, was banked. I can stoke it up, and keep using it, but the fire it burns with won't last forever. I can't just do what you do, or eventually it will get me."

Jacob of course didn't have any answers, but that didn't seem right. "How can that be? We are the same. We both used it, both felt it consuming our souls, and both ended up in Hell wasting away in an eternal prison. Why would I be any different than you in that way?"

Markov laughed quietly. "Oh come on, the valley wasn't that bad. You can get used to it over a few hundred years. Anyway, I don't mean to cause any distress, but we aren't the same, Merethius. Have you looked at yourself in the mirror? You look a lot more... and I again don't mean this as an insult, but you *look* like them. Not me."

Jacob scowled, but checked himself before he got angry with Markov. It was true, and he *had* seen himself in the mirror. "Are you suggesting that I am able to do this because of my physiology? I'm not a Ba'al, I am just a man..." He stopped. He couldn't finish the lie. Of course he wasn't a man any longer. The Patriarch had taken care of that months ago, and since killing Lucifer's Heir it had become more pronounced. He might not be a Ba'al, but he certainly didn't look like a mortal any longer.

"See what I mean?" Markov wasn't mocking in the slightest, in fact there was genuine friendship in the man. Jacob was grateful for the kindness.

"Ok, so do you think it is my body itself that allows for this? Or do you think my soul somehow tapped into something deeper here? That's the only alternative I can think of, the only variable."

Markov shrugged. "Hell if I know. That sounds both mystical and spiritual... both of which are things I know fuck all about. There is another variable though... I burned mine on Earth. You burned yours here. That might have something to do with it."

"True. I hadn't thought of that. I wish Han was here, he loves these sorts of things. I'd like to ask him."

"We will... and I'd be happy to fly with you to Sheol... but I'm afraid you'd have to do the heavy lifting. Good thing I'm not very heavy."

Jacob blinked for a moment before realizing what Markov was getting at, then he laughed. "Ah. You want me to carry you. I can do that. Do you think you could use the Apotheosis if you had to, if we were attacked?"

"Yes, I could. I would just rather not unless it was life or death. You can keep it burning all day it seems, so I'd just assume you take over the transportation duty."

Jacob smiled and clapped Markov on the shoulder. "Done."

He Invoked the Sword, now it was second nature, and again felt an infinite torrent of power cascading through his body. Markov slowed down, as did everything around him. Flies hovered in mid flight. Birds hung suspended in mid-air high above. Even the wind seemed slow to him. As before, great golden wings burst from his ignited soul, and because he was thinking about what Markov said, he closed his eyes and concentrated on his pool of energy.

He was sure of it. It was infinite, and there was no sense of losing strength or power at all. It felt nothing like when he killed the Shay'tan and every step he took felt like he was a sieve and the torrent was constantly bleeding out of him. He flapped his wings, and noticed that his own real wings on his back had grown some more. If he kept this up, he might have them for real by the time he landed in Sheol.

He slowly held out his hand for Markov to take, which in the slowed reality of the Apotheosis seemed to take forever. Finally, they were ready, and Jacob took to the skies. It would not take months. He would be at the Grigori within a week, he was confident, and could resolve that nightmare before Abaddon arrived at Sheol.

He could still fix everything.

"The first scouts have been sighted a days ride outside of Sheol? We don't have long, then." Kasim spoke with more energy than he had the day before. Joshua had been working with him on an extensive healing regimen.

Kasim sat with Han, Joshua, and Ve'kal at a small table adjacent to the convalescence room he had been recovering in. Outside, Kasim knew that Dhermina and the Seneschal waited, as well as several of Joshua's followers from before the Templar had rendezvoused at Sheol.

It was Ve'kal who answered. "Perhaps a week until his vanguard begins to appear on our doorstep, though five days is just as likely. Perhaps another five after that until he is gathered in force. The hope is that he will at least wait until his strength is here in totality before he launches an attack. He could just send wave after wave as soon as they arrive, though that would waste troops and Ba'al Apollyon is no fool."

Joshua cleared his throat, several times, and joined in. "They will be slowed and mired by the swamps we've created outside Sheol. The walkers and the plague will infect them in haste as they enter, so I would imagine once the sickness starts, they will move quickly. If the vanguard were to just move in and attack, we would be able to kill them all before the rest of the troops got here, but the defenses would be spent. It wouldn't work twice."

Han nodded before interjecting. "I imagine The Destroyer will make the plan he best thinks will win him the city, and the Throne, with the minimum amount of resources used. He will hold his vanguard outside the valley floor until he gathers in strength. I am sure of it."

Kasim stood, and was grateful for the work Joshua has been doing with him. He felt tired, and his veins hurt, but he could move. It was a far cry from the agony he felt when he first awoke after his most recent ordeal. "So, what of our current defenses? The Seneschal told me that the palace walls are complete as of yesterday, and the city walls will be complete within two more."

"Yes, that is true." Ve'kal spoke with authority, though Kasim detected a hint of anxiety in her voice. He could sense it within her as well as fear. She stood to lose more than any of them if they should fail. "It is true, and the walls will hold. We have troop placements completed. Nothing extravagant but Ba'al Apollyon won't find any weak sections of the wall. It will be manned and fortified evenly."

Han spoke up this time, and Kasim noticed a great weariness in his friend. Beyond just the dark circles under his eyes, Kasim could sense an exhaustion in the man. His work with his strange power was taking its toll. "The provisions have been prepared in secret. I won't risk the Grigori finding out about the regeneration elixirs or the vermin repellant. Everything will be distributed the day he marches on us in earnest. I have also enchanted the siege ammunition with as many souls as I could spare from the vaults. We are as prepared, at least as far as provisions and equipment go, as we can be."

Kasim did not like that Han had used the Shay'tan's stockpile of captured souls, but he didn't say anything. Desperation was in the air, and if those souls were simply released, they wouldn't help their cause. "How goes the training of the men?"

A minor fit of coughing was all that stalled Joshua from answering. Apparently his own treatment was at least somewhat effective. He sounded much better than before the Grigori had attacked them in the plaza. "Good, actually. K'had and Ulraen have been at it for twelve hours a day since we arrived here. The mortals are competent, our Legion are killers, and the Ba'al forces loyal to us that we have here are brutal. I'm no Piotyr, but Han and I have done a good job teaching them Templar siege tactics. Between their training, and their bolstered bodies and equipment, our forces will be more than a match, man for man, for Abaddon's Legion."

It was left unsaid that Abaddon's Legion was not the real threat. Properly defended Sheol could hold against the tens of millions of infantry that was coming for them. The real threat was in the air. The true Fallen that came with Abaddon, not even including the thousands of Ba'al he commanded, were what they couldn't counter. "What of Piotyr, any news? You say he left the day after I was attacked, and it has been nearly two months. Should we consider the possibility that he won't return?"

"He will return. I have foreseen it." Han's voice was strong, if his eyes betrayed his fatigue. "He will return, and he will be successful. I don't know about the First. His unique composition eludes my scrying. Well, Hell's scrying anyway. I'm just the vessel."

"Ok, so he will return, will we have his brood?" Kasim asked Han, but it was Ve'kal who answered.

"We will have the two younger dragons. Ulis and Aruc. Their mother, Asya, responded to my granting of protection for them, though she is with child, and will not join the siege."

Kasim blinked. More of them? Pity the timing was off, another three dragons, four counting the mother, would be immensely useful, especially against the Fallen and Ba'al. "They are well trained in taking winged foes, but I fear they will be overrun and annihilated. You are sure the vermin will obey you?"

Another rattling cough indicated that though he may be better, Joshua was still far from hale. "Oh they will obey. Have no fear of that. They also are far too difficult to control. I can direct them out into the battle easily enough, but to give orders? Out of the question. Once they are loose, it will be like trying to give a tornado orders. If I concentrate I could give a single, simple command to them at a time, but there will be no fine maneuvers or quick adjustments. We are relying on the repellant to keep them away from our troops, and the heat of the dragons or the stink of the grave on our corpses. Abaddon's Fallen should be their chosen targets once released, and I will send them out with those instructions."

Kasim was quiet for a moment, thinking about their chances. "I feel that the amount of preparation accomplished in these short weeks is nothing less than extraordinary. I am humbled by the craftiness the three of you have displayed." He smiled as he said it, and it caused him joy to see how proud Joshua was of his part in it. The healer radiated confidence that he hadn't seen in him, ever. Han was harder to read, but Kasim still felt a sense of accomplishment and conviction in his old friend. Han had probably changed the most out of all of them that had survived. Even Ve'kal, surprisingly, was emanating a complimentary aura of pride and contentment. It didn't negate her fear or worry, but Kasim was sure she felt a kinship with Han. Fascinating.

"We have done what we can, Son of Adam. The rest will be up to fate. Tell me, have you seen one of Han's creations? We have kept them a closely guarded secret, but I thought he might have shown you." Ve'kal smiled as she said it.

Han gave a small blush before answering. "I did not show him. I am keeping them locked up below us in the dungeon, and it is a long and cold walk. I know he is still healing, and without the water Piotyr is bringing he won't be able to be fully restored. I did not want to cause him any undue stress or pain."

Kasim gave a weak smile before nodding. "I am afraid I am not now, nor will be of much use in the battle. I can walk, but barely. A trip to the dungeons would not be easy, or advised, for me right now, I'm afraid. What creations, Han?"

Joshua broke in and gestured at Han. "I'll explain it. They are unpleasant, to be sure, but Han was brilliant in their creation. We are calling them wraith-walkers and leech-walkers. Han created new undead from creatures that were already down in the Shay'tan's dungeons. The new ones feed on flesh and soul both, and can absorb them from their enemies. We have about a thousand of each of them, and they can't die. We experimented at length, and it would take an explosion powerful enough to completely eradicate one to remove it from combat. We cut one up into small pieces and it still grew back together once... fed."

Kasim was not squeamish, but Joshua's aura took a minor turn towards sickly, even more than his usual illness. "What do you mean, fed?"

Han looked at Joshua for a moment before he took over answering. "As Joshua said... they feed on flesh or blood, or souls. If something dies near them, they heal, almost instantly. We tested them extensively, and even torn apart, a freshly killed body, and before you say anything we used dogs... but a freshly killed body will cause them to come together in seconds. A thousand wraith-walkers, and a thousand leech-walkers. They are imbued with this above and beyond their normal growth as undead, like with The First. As the battle goes on, they will become more and more powerful, and barring something unforeseen, they will be able to withstand anything Abaddon throws at them. They should be nearly invincible."

Kasim pursed his lips in thought. "Pity they can't fly, then. Is their regeneration better than the one you created for the living, then, Joshua?"

"Yes, though it pains me to admit it, living flesh is much harder to keep functional once you cut it apart. It does work though. All of our defenders will be instructed how to maximize their chances of living once we distribute them... again we worry about the Grigori discovering too much... but the live tests we have done are incredible. Don't say anything, but we used humans for the tests... but strictly volunteers. Styx water is amazing, incidentally. I have no doubt that with the others, I can heal you completely Kasim. Anyway, as long as any weapon can be removed from a wound, the flesh will heal within about ten seconds. Decapitation is harder, as the head has to be more or less held in place for those ten seconds to work, but we did test it and it worked."

Kasim blinked. "You found someone who volunteered to be decapitated?"

"Ah, yes. Actually several. We told them it was safe, and if anything went wrong their families would be provided for. We actually got more volunteers than we needed... the culture here is quite distinct. Anyway, dismemberment works the same way, but a person can hold their own severed appendage to the wound. A head... well not really, but we will instruct them that if they happen to see a companion get beheaded, if they have the chance... within about ten seconds it isn't fatal. After that, well the flesh might knit together but I doubt the mind will be intact. Maybe fifteen, but I wouldn't push it, personally."

"I had just always thought that when the head leaves the neck it would be a rather rapid death." Kasim had killed many that way. To think that it wasn't necessarily a killing wound was... strange.

"Oh it is definitely fatal, Kasim. What I've done is just create a philter that causes the flesh to heal so quicky that the body could recover from the initial trauma fast enough to ignore it. As I said, I wouldn't push it past ten seconds. After that, I would think the body would not be able to recover from the injury. This is also very potent stuff. Alchemy imbued Styx water with very strong Invocations of Healing fortifying it. I doubt the Legion could have even theorized how to make these, let alone actually create one. They also don't last long, either before consumed or after. Maybe a week of potency before it goes inert, maybe a few hours once consumed. It isn't a cure for death, by any means."

Still, it was an incredible creation. "You have done very well. All of you, actually. I wish there was more I could do. It seems the preparations are mostly complete, and I don't have a task myself. Do you have any instructions for me, Han?"

Han looked exhausted. "No, old friend. There is little for you to do right now other than rest. Once Piotyr and the First return, Joshua and I will focus all of our attention on creating a cure for your poison. Hopefully it will act swiftly, as I fear you will need your strength before the siege lifts. I expect to call on you before this is over."

It was Ve'kal who joined in to pointedly speak to Han. "You also need your rest. I know you have work to do, but you said yourself that it will come to you to hold off Ba'al Apollyon if he manifests as The Destroyer. You also said yourself that when your Patriarch held him off at your Sanctuary, it took a great toll on him physically and spiritually. You look exhausted already, and that puts you... and us... at a great disadvantage. Will you heed this request?"

Han sighed and rubbed his eyes. "Yes, yes. I will rest today. Nowhere safe, really, but I suppose I could stay here in the infirmary with Kasim. Can I trust the two of you to oversee the rest of today's preparations and to alert me right away if there is a problem?"

Joshua hacked for a moment before answering. "Only a problem that we can't resolve. I think we are done for now, get some sleep you two."

The group stood and the three Templar embraced, while Ve'kal made her exit. Joshua followed, and Kasim was left with Han to return to convalescence.

"Do you think we can win, old friend?"

Han curled up on another of the cots and covered himself with a sheet and blanket, yawning. "No, but there is hope if we can at least break them enough to give Haven a chance to rebuild. Maybe, just maybe, I can actually kill Abaddon. No chance of us surviving the siege, however. The Ba'al alone will sweep us from the walls. We need a miracle, and I believe our last one went with Jacob."

Kasim was quiet as he listened to Han's breathing deepen as he drifted off to sleep. He thought about getting up to go see what he could help with but abandoned the idea as his body stiffened in pain. He was just no use with the poison running through his veins. As much as he hated the idea, he really did need to sleep as much as he could. Sighing, he also lay down to sleep. He had never felt so useless.

chapter twenty-five

He casteth forth his ice like morsels: who can stand before his cold?
- Psalm 147:17

"Take it and get out."

The Oracle had been true to his expectations and had prepared his water samples without further incident. He didn't know if it was because she was humbled or because he followed her at a pace length with a spear raised if she so much as twitched in a way he didn't like. Either way, she did as he bade.

"I shall. What are the side effects of this? Once he drinks it will he be incapacitated?"

"Of course he will, idiot. This will restore his memory loss, but it will not be pleasant, nor easy. It will hit him like a volcano in his thoughts. I hope he chokes on his tongue."

I hate this woman. I trust you will kill her once we are done?

The First was tempted, but if something went wrong they needed her alive. "No Lokyrg, we aren't going to kill her. If she tricks us somehow, we will need to return. I hope that isn't necessary, though."

The Oracle looked at him and blinked. "Are you mad? Who are you talking to?"

I grudgingly agree, though every instinct I have tells me she should die.

"Split personality. Most of me wants to kill you. I'm trying to reason with myself."

The Oracle muttered and cursed under her breath but handed him the container of the Mnemosyne water that she swore would restore Piotyr's memory.

"A fortnight, you are sure?"

"Yes, he has that long to consume it. If he doesn't, it will become inert and won't work. I don't plan on allowing anyone back up here... ever, so for your sake I hope you can get it to him by then."

"I have no wish to return either. We are in agreement, then. Two weeks. You also didn't answer my question about side effects. What else will this do to him? I implore you again to speak the truth."

She laughed, then. "Why would I lie? I offered him a chance for salvation, and he threw it back at me. I gave him what he came for, and I got nothing. I hope you *do* make it back to Sheol, with Piotyr, and offer this to him, and he drinks it graciously. If you give him this, he will lose the gift, and his knowledge of the battle will be lost. You will lose your commander, Abaddon will raze Sheol to the ground, and you will all die. That is the side effect."

She lies.

The First looked at her for a long moment and pondered her words. It was possible that what she said was true. The properties of the waters of Lethe were strange enough, and if she was truly an Oracle in the tradition of the ancient Oracles he knew little of, then what she spoke of was possible. Piotyr could have been given a vision of the future, perhaps even a very detailed one, that he would be able to use at Sheol. If he drank a restorative, he might get his memories back, but he could also lose his foresight.

"Why do this to him at all? How had he wronged you? Why not simply help him and send him on his way?"

"Your ignorance is telling. A mortal simply can't drink from the Mnemosyne without preparation. They can't even touch the Mnemosyne without being purified. Piotyr could have chosen one path to the vision, but instead he spurned my offer. He still had to be prepared, and the only path left to him was to cleanse his mind... so cleanse his mind I did."

"What was the offer he spurned?"

She snorted. "Unimportant, since he declined."

He frowned. Something wasn't right. Piotyr didn't come here for a vision, he came here for Lethe. "He declined an offer for something he didn't seek, it sounds like. My friend came for Lethe, not the Mnemosyne. Why offer it to him at all? It sounds like you tricked, and trapped him."

She shot him a glowering look, but to his relief did not give voice to a lie. He did not want to strike her again. "I so tire of you mortals and your stupidity. No, he didn't ask for it, but without it you are all dead, and maybe that is for the best. You dying can rid the rest of us of your intolerable idiocy."

"Why is the vision so important? Why would Piotyr not just lead the siege defense with his memories intact?"

"Do whatever you want with it, I have no interest in furthering this inane banter. You will live, or die, by the whim of the fates, and I care not. You have the restorative, do with it what you will. Leave me."

He opened his mouth to speak again but a tremendous rushing of air accompanied a feeling of rapid movement, ceasing as he arrived at the river he and Piotyr had walked from what seemed a lifetime ago. He was pleased to see his raft was there, intact, as was Piotyr's armor. A kind parting gift from the Warden, it seemed.

Back here again. At least it saves us the trip downstream from the cliff.

"True enough. Come, lets get going back along Lethe. I think our journey nears its end."

The chamber was large, though not so huge Piotyr could not see the sides. It was freezing, a much deeper cold than he remembered feeling topside, though that could just be for the contrast with the warmer keep.

"Sorry for the chill, the geothermal vents are blocked off in here. This is the coldest place in the entire inner ring. We need to move quickly, the cold will sap our strength quickly."

Piotyr agreed. The sooner they were done, the better. He channeled a trickle of hellfire into a torch on the wall, retrieved it, and walked into the cold dark. It was perhaps fifty paces until he reached the edge of a shelf which plunged down into darkness. Perhaps a stone's throw to the other side was a huge block of dark, nearly black ice which towered away up into the upper reaches of the cavern.

"Is that it? Is that the heart of Cocytus?"

Sammael walked up next to him and nodded. "Yes. Ice so cold it will peel the flesh off your hands if you hold it long. Come."

Sammael had his own torch which helped light the way, though Piotyr was more concerned with his footing. The ice they walked on was slick and he did not like the look of a fall in the chasm. Curiousity got the better of him, though.

"What is at the bottom of the pit?"

Sammael chuckled before answering. "Eventually? Back the way you came. It is a long fall through darkness and freezing despair, then it warms and you would end up back in Phlegethon. The rivers here circle each other, in a way. If you survived the fall, you would hasten your journey back to Sheol greatly."

If he survived the fall. That did not sound encouraging. He couldn't think of a worse way to go than slowly freezing to death while falling, though perhaps his nature was to blame for that.

They walked for only a minute or so when Piotyr saw a frozen bridge leading across the chasm. The bridge was a pace wide, and looked to be stone underneath the frost. One could easily grab both of the guardrails on either side, and it looked sturdy enough. Sammael stood next to the bridge and set his torch into a sconce built right into a support pillar for the bridge. He then took something out from under his cloak.

Piotyr stood and watched as the large angel produced a large canvas, or burlap sack of some kind. "Here, Piotyr. It has been treated much as your clothes have. It won't stave off the cold forever, but it will prevent the ice from burning you for a time and will keep the ice safe, briefly, from heat. Be wary of hellfire, though. It would melt it quickly enough with prolonged exposure.

"That doesn't sound right. Your tale of this Ba'al Mirish and his attack on me led me to believe that Heart of Cocytus is stronger than hellfire. It barbed my flesh and kept me from both healing and channeling more hellfire."

"Your flesh isn't made of flame, though. It isn't stronger, just sharp and acute. With time, it will melt. Even the waters of Phlegethon, though not pure hellfire, will make short work of it if you aren't careful."

He nodded, and took the cloth from Sammael. "How much should I take?"

"Take however much you think you need to fill those crystal vials you have, with a little extra as insurance for spillage, I would think. You wouldn't want to have to come back here." The angel smiled and, despite himself, Piotyr smiled back. He liked the man.

"Come now, Sammael, your hospitality wasn't so bad that I wouldn't return. Might be a long time, though. I fear I might be busy for the foreseeable future."

Sammael lauged and clapped him on the arm. He then produced something else from under his cloak. It appeared to be a wineskin. "It will help with the cold, Son of Adam. Just a fortified draught of mead, but Cocytus is a cold place."

Piotyr took it from him, then frowned. Why would he give it to him now... "I'm leaving by the chasm, aren't I?"

Sammael gave him a wry look, but answered him directly and honestly. "You don't have to, if you want you can walk back through the keep and across the ice to the vent from Phlegethon you came through. My scouts found it shortly after we found you, but it is frozen solid again. You would spend hours, perhaps a day just unthawing it from this side. It is up to you, but if you leave from here, you'll emerge in Phlegethon right at the Lethe border. Your journey is your journey, however."

Piotyr sighed, then secured the skin to his flask belt. "Fair enough. Anything else, Sammael?"

"Just one." Sammael was silent for a moment then shrugged his shoulders as if bracing for something. "I know you don't remember anything, but indulge me for a moment. I have something I need to say."

Piotyr wondered what else could possibly be of import, but was patiently quiet while Sammael gathered his thoughts.

"I have lived a long time, and I have only two regrets, both of which I will confess to you now. Maybe it is easier since you lost your memory, but you are here, and my confession should go to a child of Adam. First, I need you to know that I am sorry I stood with Lucifer before the Throne."

Piotyr understood the basics of what Sammael was saying, and had been given an abbreviated history of the war after Lilith read his mind, but the context was lost on him. Still, he was polite, and Sammael had been a good host.

"I was angry at how the mortals were being treated, jealous of how you were raised up and given praise over us. I listened to Lucifer when he argued for our place above yours. I nodded and shouted encouragement when he spoke out against you, and called for you to be put in your place. I say this because it was the second gravest mistake I ever made. I was naive, foolish, and prideful. For that I am sorry."

Not knowing what else to say, Piotyr simply decided to speak for the entirety of his race. "Apology accepted."

Sammael blinked, then nodded and smiled. "The second thing I am sorry for is not taking up arms against Lucifer after the Fall. We were shamed. *I* was shamed. I would not take up arms against the Seraphim with Lucifer, because it was madness. I was angry at the mortals, and at the Throne for choosing you over us, but never would I take up a blade against my brothers. I would have rather died then shed the blood of my fellow Seraphim, but once Lucifer lost and all those who stood with him were cast out of Elysium... my choice was to hide here. It is my shame."

Piotyr nodded again, and began to accept his apology again but something in Sammael's eyes stopped him. The angel had water in his eyes, which slowly slipped out and slid down his face in a single frozen tear. Piotyr was taken about by the intensity of his gaze.

"No, Piotyr Lamja, son of Adam. This is something you cannot forgive me for. I could have stood with you against the

Legion on Earth. I did not. I cowered here, hiding in my shame and self-pity while you and yours were scoured from your home. The ban did not affect my House, as we were no longer of the Choir. We *could* have come. I did not allow it. That is something I cannot ask forgiveness for, but I tell you now I am sorry."

Piotyr swallowed, feeling the emotion himself from Sammael. The man was certainly sincere. He raised his hand in acceptance and smiled. As Sammael took it, he said the only thing he could think of. "Stand with me at Sheol against Abaddon, and your debt will be paid."

More tears leaked from Sammael's face, his already beatific visage made ephemeral in the cold gloom. "I will stand with you at Sheol. The Seraphim fight at last with the seed of Adam."

Man and angel clasped hands and the accord was struck. Sammael wiped the frozen, salty water from his face and cleared his throat. "Now get out of here. We have arrangements to make, but it won't take us forever. It wouldn't do for us to show up before you. Farewell, and Godspeed, Piotyr Lamja."

Piotyr smiled at the man. "You as well, Sammael, Seraphim of the Choir."

The angel grabbed his torch, turned on his heel, and left, leaving Piotyr before the bridge. He waited a moment watching him leave, then placed his own torch on the other pillar. *Damn it was cold.* He took a moment to grab the wineskin and take a long drink from it. Fortified indeed *This was mead?* It didn't taste like it, though he *could* taste the honey. Much stronger. He felt a warmth in his belly match his cheeks. It was much appreciated.

He replaced the wineskin and crossed the bridge carefully. It was slick, but had been carved smartly, with sharp edges to increase footing. He moved slowly, deliberately, and safely reached the other side. There were more pillars there with torches on the landing, so he lit them. He whistled as he looked down the chasm, and noticed with surprise that the block of ice in the middle of the cavern didn't sit on an ice shelf as he thought initially, it went through it and on into the blackness below. It must be huge, thousands of feet tall.

He looked up and away from the pit, back at the immense block of Cocytus; the Heart of the frozen center of Hell. Piotyr walked up to it and carefully placed a hand right next to the surface. It radiated a deep cold that chilled his arm just with being close. This was it, certainly.

He carefully laid out the canvas Sammael had given him on the frozen ground and channeled a trickle of hellfire in a large triangle. It was slow going, but he was methodical. When he grew chilled, he paused a moment and had another drink of the strong mead. This was not a fight he could win forever, but he could win it for long enough to get what he needed.

It took perhaps an hour, but eventually he had two large chunks of ice removed from the otherwise smooth, mammoth chunk of ice. He took a moment to admire his handiwork then gasped as his throat caught. Deep in the ice he thought he saw an immense eye looking at him. He blinked and it vanished from his sight. He sought to find it again, but couldn't. His heart was pounding in rapid fear, and he took a long moment calming down and convincing himself it was nothing and that he imagined it.

Eventually, his heartrate returned to normal, though it took several minutes and several more draughts of the mead. Silently he thanked Sammael again. Very useful, that stuff.

Taking a deep breath, he bundled the chunks of ice and secured them in his pack, which was also treated with whatever it was the House of Sammael used to proof against hellfire. It was time, and his journey was complete. He felt a sense of pride that he had been successful in getting the water, now he just needed to get back to Sheol.

He turned away from the ice block and walked to the chasm. He was cold and it wasn't going to get any warmer standing on the edge. He rubbed his arms together, took another drink of the mead, and then secured everything on his body.

"No time like now." He said the words and didn't allow himself a second thought, casting himself into the black. Freezing wind whipped past his ears, shrieking and making him deaf as he fell. The cold air was too much for his eyes, making them freeze as they watered. He blinked as quickly as he could to clear them, but had to keep them closed as he plummeted into the depths.

The fall was indeterminate to him, but frost gathered on his arms and face as he fell. He kept his eyes closed, only opening them for a split second every now and then to see if anything was coming into view below him. He couldn't have put a time on how long he fell, though when he finally began to warm he would have guessed an hour.

Opening his eyes he was relieved to see red glowing far below him. *Phlegethon.* The river below was a welcome sight. He kept his eyes open as best he could as he fell quickly towards the burning waters, not worrying about trying to slow down until he was very close. He was surprised as the chasm he was falling down abruptly flared at an angle and he found himself sliding on the ice. That was actually to his benefit, as it slowed him considerably and allowed him the chance to shift his position.

The ice flanged again, and he found himself briefly shunted sideways, slowing his momentum almost completely before shifting downwards again. Good. He had feared he would hit the river hard and be forced to heal in it. Better not to have to worry about it at all.

It was almost gently that he slid out of the chasm and into the open air of the cavern he remembered from Phlegethon the last time. The script was still etched into every surface he could see, burning red from the lifeblood of the river of fire. He landed with a splash in the water and took a moment to gather his bearings. He didn't see the white pillar he saw when he went to Cocytus, but more importantly he felt a strong current pulling him away from where he was. That was new. It should take him back to Lethe along the other side.

It would also be much faster than walking, he supposed as he allowed the current to take him quickly along the cavern. He saw several fiery skeletons slowly turn towards him and stretch their arms out, but he was moving far too quickly. His journey was swift out of the cavern of Phlegethon, perhaps only another hour. His arms were tired from swimming but the current had done most of the work as he neared a solid rock wall where the water disappeared under. Smiling and knowing he was close, he held his breath and ducked underneath.

Long minutes went by but he was not worried. He expected parity at this point. Indeed it was not long before he was shunted out into midday sun on a normal looking river which looked identical to Lethe, save the current flowed the other way away from the rock. He swam quickly to the side, and tiredly crawled up onto the rocky riverbank to catch his breath. He laughed and hollered in excitement, taking his wineskin off his belt and happily draining it. It had been an ordeal, but he made it and he had what he came for.

He ached for rest, but forced himself to stand. Hearing a quiet hissing sound, he looked up behind him and saw a steaming, spurting vent of fiery water shooting out of a narrow fissure perhaps not three paces above him near a ledge. Phlegethon indeed.

"To the river of fire!" Piotyr shouted as he smiled, greedily getting the last few drops of his mead out of the skin.

He turned to begin walking along the river when he heard his name called out.

"Piotyr!"

He looked where it came from, and was surprised to see a man on a raft rowing upstream next to a bend in the river, a wicked looking spear strapped to his back along with a huge greataxe. He frowned, but the man appeared to know him and was certainly not threatening him at the moment. He also had a raft. This was fortuitous. He waved and walked quickly to meet up with him at the bend.

"Hail, and well met!"

chapter twenty-six

This matter is by the decree of the watchers, and the demand by the word of the holy ones: to the intent that the living may know that the most High ruleth in the kingdom of men, and giveth it to whomsoever he will, and setteth up over it the basest of men.
- Daniel 4:17

Jacob landed a mere twenty paces from the village where the Grigori made their home. He let Markov drop gently to the ground and flexed his newly complete wings. No longer vestigial, they had formed completely while en route from Tyana.

Markov dusted himself off and stretched his arms out above his head. "Hell of a way to travel. Did you know back in the old world they had giant machines that hundreds of people could get in and fly all over the world?"

Jacob hadn't heard that but he wasn't very interested in the old world. It was much farther removed from him that it was for Markov though, so he was polite. "No, I didn't know that. Sounds fascinating."

"Yeah, lots of cool shit back then. We didn't get to see much of it at San Luis, but there were some old magazines and pictures and stuff. Supposedly there were movies, but the machines to play them on didn't work very well. Too bad."

"That is a shame. Are you prepared for this?"

Markov nodded. "I'm a little worried that this is a town of assassins, but as long as you've got your Soul Fire on hand and I *can* use mine, I think we'll be ok. You still plan on killing everyone?"

Jacob nodded. It was the most practical way of dealing with the threat. The Destroyer's Legion would be upon Sheol within days, now. The two Templar had even seen signs of the devastation that those many marching troops caused as they flew over the countryside. He needed to tie up loose ends and get to Sheol to help.

"Yes, I'll spare children, and perhaps the women too though if they don't raise a hand against me. I don't doubt that there are plenty of female Grigori now, though."

Markov nodded. It was grim work, thinking about it. "Lets get to it, then."

Jacob nodded to him. "Ok, stand ready, I'm calling them." He felt his Soul Fire sitting just out of reach, but decided to wait. He might not need it. Invoking Voice to let his already mighty words work with maximum effect, he bellowed at the top of his lungs.

"Grigori! Jacob Merethius summons you! Come join battle with me or I will kill every last one of you with shared blood to the last babe!"

The words cresendoed outwards from him, astonishingly in a visible cone to his eyes, and blew apart the first two houses they reached. He blinked as the wood, straw, plaster, and cloth fluttered in the air after the impact, leaving only stone and metal framework behind.

He saw a family inside cowering under a heavy wooden table, and he drew Duskfall. "Come face Merethius, Watchers!"

Markov spoke softly as Jacob stood there on the road. "They are coming, look."

Dozens of men emerged from their homes, looking at him and back at the destroyed house. Most of them had weapons, but it was clear he had caught them unprepared for war. He checked himself. These were assassins, not soldiers. They did not fight in open conflict, he wagered in his mind. They didn't need arms and armor whilst just living in their homes.

"You wish to gather in strength? So be it. I command you all to come face my wrath! *I say again, Grigori, come face Merethius!"*

"Seems slightly theatrical, but as long as it works I guess."

He glowered at Markov briefly but didn't say anything. The end was the important thing, not the method. The crowd gathering grew in size quickly, as more homes emptied, and then from the ground itself poured more of them. Plants opened over hidden ladders, tree stumps gaze way to steps leading down, walls shifted and more of the Grigori emerged. In the short span of a few minutes, the force had swelled to easily a few hundred men and women.

"Might be half a thousand of them. You prepared for this, Jacob? Going to be a nasty fight."

Jacob didn't feel the need to correct him. His could obliterate them without breaking a sweat if need be. He needed answers first, though.

"You have one chance to live. One of you recently poisoned a Templar at Sheol, a man named Kasim. The poison is killing him. Fetch me the antidote, now."

No one moved right away, but an older man, perhaps half again as old as Jacob was, stepped forward and cleared his throat.

"Jacob Merethius, is it? The kill order was given by Ba'al Apollyon. It was carried out in good faith."

Jacob blinked. Was he arguing about the details of his contract?

"I don't care if Lucifer himself gave you the contract. Kasim lives, and he will live on. Give me the antidote. Now."

The older man nodded to another of the assassins, who ran into a hidden bolt-hole in a tree and disappeared. A few minutes passed, and the man returned with an apothecary's satchel.

"Give it to my man."

Markov glared at Jacob, but didn't say anything. God why was the man so prickly? It was just how things were done here.

"Thank you, for that, I assure you death will be swift and merciful, and I shall spare your young."

A murmur arose in the Grigori, and as Jacob stepped forward the old man spoke in a language that Jacob recognized, but didn't know. He was speaking in an ancient dialect, but before Jacob could Invoke Tongues, to a person the entire gathering had dropped prostrate and were bowing to him.

"Hah, bet you can't kill them all now. That's fucked up. Never thought of that... though I doubt the Legion would have cared."

What was happening? Did they just want to die without resisting? They were not soldiers, but he hadn't expected them to be cowards. Damned Markov, he was right. He would have a hard time killing hundreds of defenseless people bowing and scraping on the dirt. This wasn't right. He had expected a fight, a battle, something. Briefly he flashed back to a family in Red Bank that he had almost executed while they cowered before him. He couldn't do it, then, even though he thought the whole town was demonic.

"Get up! Will you not defend yourself?!" The prostrate Grigori didn't move. The sound of wind blowing through the streets made little impact on the depth of the oppressive silence. "Answer me, damnit! Will you not stand and defend yourselves?!" When again no one moved, Jacob moved to a man a few paces in front of him and grabbed him by the scruff of his neck, picking up and staring into his face. There was no fear on it, or hatred, or anything. It was a blank expression, devoid of any feeling at all. "What is wrong with you? I'm going to butcher this entire settlement, and you don't care? Will you not defend your women? Your children? Your elderly? Will you stand idly by and watch as I destroy everything you hold dear?"

The man looked him in the eyes, no spark of feeling whatsoever, and answered him. "The will of the Shay'tan is absolute."

Jacob blinked. That wasn't the answer he was expecting. What, Lucifer's heir had ordered them to die? Why, and for what purpose? No, that couldn't be it, those Grigori at Tyana had meant to kill him. So what had changed?

"I killed the Shay'tan, his will is as absolute as any other corpse. If he ordered you to die, then you are a fool for following the command of a dead man."

"We knew the Shay'tan had been killed, and now he who killed him stands before us. The circle is complete."

Disgusted, Jacob dropped the fool and looked for someone older and wiser. He found another Grigori prostrate in the dirt and Jacob moved to him in haste and picked him up as well, though more gently than the younger man. It wouldn't do to break his neck.

"Do you lead here?"

"I do not, that honor falls to Sav the Small..."

"Show me."

The man walked down the street perhaps twenty paces, amongst the hundreds of men and women of all ages, and found a young boy of perhaps twelve years. "Sav the Small, master..." Jacob shoved him away and commanded the boy to rise.

"You are the one in charge? You are but a boy."

"It is our way, the leadership of the Watchers is protected this way. No one suspects a child."

"I don't care. Why will your people not defend themselves?"

"We would against any foe."

"I am your foe, I mean to slaughter you. Command your people to take up arms."

The boy smiled weakly. "Grigori, raise arms against this man."

No one moved. Jacob grew incensed. "Are you mocking me?! I said command them to defend themselves!"

"I did, master..."

"Then are you in charge or aren't you? Do you lead these people or not?"

"I do, master..."

"Then why won't they follow your orders?"

"They will."

"I swear on my own life that I will crush your skull in my hands if you mock me again, boy."

"I could no more mock you than raise a weapon against you. The will of the Shay'tan is absolute."

"He's dead, you simple fool. I slew him in the palace at Sheol."

"You did."

"So stop following his damned orders! Do you not have your own free will?" Jacob stopped as soon as he said it. He understood.

"We do not."

They couldn't. If they had been commanded not to fight him, for whatever reason, the choice was barred to them. Han spoke to him about this several times. Humanity was given the ability to choose, most of the Fallen were not. Ba'al could, but they were the only ones. Fallen and Legion simply did what they were told.

"I see. So if I kill all of you, not one of you will stand to defend against me?"

"The will of the Shay'tan is..."

"Absolute." The boy, this child called Sav the Small... actually smiled at him.

Jacob released him and the boy dropped back into the dirt, lowering himself.

"This isn't what I expected, Markov."

"No shit? Look, it is what it is. You can't leave them alive, they will kill your friends. You heard him, they just follow orders. If you value the lives of the other Templar, especially Kasim, you can't leave here until they are dead. You don't have to like it, but it needs to be done."

"Markov..."

"No. Now look, I will help you, but don't ask me to do it alone. This is terrible work, but you *can't* leave them alive. You heard them!"

Jacob sighed, feeling tired and drained. Markov was right. Arguing wouldn't change anything. He had *wanted* to kill the Grigori, but not as they lay helpless in the dirt like worms. He was a soldier, not a murderer. He flashed again back to the memory of slaying the Kariev brothers on the River outside of Red Bank. *It was an accident. I am not a murderer!*

He Invoked the Sword, and let the Soul Fire consume his flesh. In the midst of the Apotheosis, he let loose his voice with as much force as he could.

"I command you to stand. Rise and face me." To a man, the entire village stood and stared at him. "If you are going to die, you will do so on your feet, as men and women. You will not die like a dog." *He had killed those too, here in Hell.*

"My name is Jacob Merethius. Know that your deaths bring me no pleasure." He raised his burning, glowing morningstar and closed his eyes. *This will haunt you, more then Red Bank. This will haunt you to the end of your days.*

"As you will it, Shay'tan." Sav bowed his head, and closed his eyes.

Jacob blinked and looked at Markov, who gave him a confused expression. "I am not the Shay'tan."

Sav opened his eyes again, and looked upon Jacob with what the Templar could only call adoration. "Seek whom you may devour."

"What the hell does that mean, Sav?"

The boy cocked his head to the side and gave him a puzzled expression. "The will of the Shay'tan is..."

Jacob lowered his mace. "Stop it, Sav. Why did you call me the Shay'tan?"

"If I have offended you, slay me with pleasure. Consume my soul as would a roaring lion. I welcome it."

Jacob grabbed the boy and shook him, not terribly hard, but not gentle either. "Sav! Stop this and *speak* to me! Why did you call me the Shay'tan?!"

"Because you are the Shay'tan, you fucking idiot. Look at them. They know what they are about."

Jacob stared at the Grigori, who had not moved in the slightest. He looked at Markov, who gave him a sad smile and a shrug of his shoulders. "It isn't all bad, Merethius. It's just a name, right?"

He released Sav, who dropped back prostrate to the ground. "Then why did those attack me at Tyana? These people didn't raise a hand against me, why did the others?"

"Like I know. Maybe you didn't look the part, then, and you do now? You've got a twenty foot wingspan and are almost twice my height, now. Hell Merethius, if I didn't know you, *I'd* call you an angel. Wasn't Lucifer the prettiest of the bunch anyway? Look in the mirror, man. No one would call you a human at first glance."

Still raging with his own Soul Fire, Jacob Invoked a Reflecting Glass and gazed at himself intently in the mirrored surface. A beatific face stared back at him. A familiar face, but also an alien one. He saw hints of the man he once new in the pristine image before him, but he saw just as much of the horror he slew at the gates of Sheol's Palace. He agreed, there was little of humanity left in his appearance.

"So that makes me The Adversary? I am the Shay'tan because I look this way?" Jacob was not angry. If anything, he was confused.

"You are asking the wrong man, Merethius. Here, I'll talk to the Grigori, maybe I can get a straight answer."

Markov walked to the older Watcher that had fetched the satchel for Kasim's cure. "You, my friend is somewhat confused. Why do you think he is the Shay'tan? None of that bowing and scraping, just tell us plain."

"I can't answer why water is wet, Voice."

"The fuck did you call me? Voice? What is this shit? Merethius, you better not have just made me another of your bullshit subservients!"

Jacob sighed and felt truly tired, but he felt something inside him shift slightly. He had fought for so long, and hated for so long, that he just didn't want to at the moment. He thought for a change he would try accepting and not rail against what he was being told.

"So I am the Shay'tan? I am The Adversary, now? Can you tell me how that happened... anyone?"

Markov glowered at him and mumbled something under his breath. Jacob gasped as two Watchers leapt to their feet and drew daggers on him.

"STOP!" He shouted and dust flew away from a cone of powerful wind bursting from his mouth. The Grigori froze in place and, for a wonder, so did Markov.

"He is under my protection and no one here will harm him!"

"The Will of the Shay'tan is absolute." Hundreds of voices answered him in unison.

Whistling to himself, Markov looked at Jacob with wide eyes. "Well, I guess that's that."

Ve'kal looked out from the completed ramparts and sadly remembered how impressive the lands around Sheol had been the last time she had been here before she and Jacob had come to lay siege. It was early-evening and the sense of incoming doom was growing by the hour.

It was a muddy, ugly mess out there now, not that it mattered. The ruddy glow coming from beyond the hills gave every indication that the vanguard would be here tomorrow, or at least could be. It looked as though Abaddon was content to gather his forces in totality before committing any to the siege. So even though battle could begin on the morrow, it would probably be another four days before blood was shed at Sheol.

The expectation was that once the invading forces had gathered in strength just beyond the foothills surrounding the valley, they would all march as one massive group the thirty miles to Sheol's walls and smash the defenders in one prolonged assault. Ve'kal was not a great student of tactics but she did her best to envision the battle and how it could play out in their favor.

Her head hurt before long and the spiced wine she was drinking did little to help matters. Sighing, she poured the rest of her cup out, went back inside the city, and made her way to the tent set up in the Plaza of the Throne.

The city had been cleared of all debris and the main structures had all been repaired. There were still dozens of missing buildings though, giving the city an unfinished feeling. Still, it was night and day from when the cataclysm hit. Thousands had died that day so the city was slightly down in population, even allowing for the influx of the Ba'al loyal to her cause and their respective forces. She frowned, thinking of Ba'al Geir. Not many were, in fact, loyal to her, and the ones that were numbered far too often among the old or the young. Abaddon had not only the numbers, but the experience.

It was a struggle not to despair, plus she *had* come this far. Failure meant death for her and Nezmyr, though she would never let Abaddon's forces touch her or her son. If the battle went poorly, she would make the decision to end both their lives quickly and painlessly. She did not long for death, but the quick embrace of poison would be much preferable for both of them than the continuous torment they could expect should they be captured.

She shuddered. It would be worse for the Templar, she imagined. Ba'al Apollyon was not known for his atrocities, not above and beyond any usual degree, but the circumstances here were unique. His surviving army would scream for the blood of the mortals. Ve'kal frowned and shook her head. This line of thought was not helping her at all.

Victory. She needed to think of victory, and of all the steps they had taken to ensure theirs. Han was competent, Joshua and Han both were inventive and their defenses had come around full circle from when Jacob had felled the Shay'tan. They had a chance and she needed to focus on that.

She had resisted the temptation of having a grand feast before Abaddon's forces arrived. She had discussed with Han the benefits of raising morale before the siege began. He had told her to use her best judgment, but to also consider the chance, however remote, that the siege *would* be prolonged. Food stores *could* matter.

None of them really believed that, but it was possible. She also considered that a feast may have the opposite effect. If there was no hope that the siege could stand long enough for food to matter, her forces could interpret that as a sign of futility.

Her mind was not used to thinking of such things and she suspected neither were the minds of the three Templar left to her. She did her best not to curse her luck but the fact that none of the three remaining was an actual experienced commander rankled her. Kasim was a killer, but knew relatively little about the tactics of siege warfare. Joshua was far, far less knowledgeable than Kasim, and Han was well-read, but that was not a substitute for experience. She would have felt much, much better if Piotyr had returned already. She would have felt better still if Jacob had lived.

Stop it, Ve'kal. She admonished herself. *You fought war with the weapons you had, not the weapons you long for. It was enough. It had to be.* It couldn't all have been for nothing, just for her and her child to drink essence of poppy and sleep eternally. They could hold the city. They had to.

The Plaza of the Throne was a bustling bee hive with all the mortals, Fallen, and Legion running around. The command tent was large and stood directly in front of the actual Throne of the Shay'tan. No one seemed to care, and neither did she. Inside the tent, tables with maps of the valley and figurines representing troop movements took up most of the interior. A massive wedge of painted figures was moving slowly towards the city, with the slow inevitability of fate.

Han was standing over one of the maps and looked up as she entered, giving her a nod. She walked over to him and spoke in an even, controlled tone. She was very careful not to let fear begin to take root. "Four days, then?"

"Four days. Possibly three, though they would have to accelerate significantly to make it here in three. No matter, we are ready now... at least our defenses are."

She stood with him for a time, looking over their own defenses. From above, it looked like a game. She pondered briefly how her Legion would feel, knowing they were represented by painted metal men, to be simply removed from a cloth map as they died screaming on the battlefield. *Probably wouldn't care. That is the strength, and weakness, of the Legion. Not mindless, certainly, but no will of their own. They would die as she saw fit.*

The Seneschal came into the tent, surprisingly winded and moving quickly. Ve'kal cocked an eyebrow as he moved in haste towards where she and Han stood. "Master Fei-tze, Mistress Ve'kal. They have returned."

It all seemed very busy and important to Piotyr, though his memory still wouldn't allow him any reasons why. The six of them walked briskly through the dank tunnels leading away from the river landing quietly, not speaking of him or his journey. His amnesia hung like a pall among them. He and the undead man had traveled back from Lethe uneventfully, with the man called The First accepting his memory loss with a nod and no further questions. Pleasant enough company, though he hadn't appreciated his insistence at traveling through Archeron laying down on the raft with a blindfold and wax in his ears.

When they had arrived at the landing of Styx underneath Sheol, there was a messenger boy waiting for them at the top of the stone steps who had run off to fetch the other four now walking with them, at least that was what Piotyr assumed had happened. He had tied off the boat at the docks with the undead and walked quietly across a vast and eerily quiet cavern before reaching the steps going up. The liveried boy had been sitting there waiting. When he saw the two men walk out of the dark with a torch, he had grown wide-eyed and ran off into the dark. The two men waited at the request of Piotyr. He wanted to see Han before he went anywhere else.

When the other four arrived, the undead man had interrupted any greetings with a brief explanation. Piotyr didn't mind, as The First told the truth. He explained to the other four that Piotyr didn't know any of them, and that his memory had been taken by the Oracle at this place called the Mnemosyne. Piotyr just stood, somewhat uncomfortably, as the corpse said he would explain everything in detail soon, but for now Piotyr should be taken to the command area.

Piotyr was in agreement on that. He wanted to see what he had to work with and he felt uncomfortable around people that he didn't know... yet knew him. Han and the man called Joshua had accepted the undead's explanation, though this woman, Ve'kal, and her Seneschal had scowled throughout the First's words.

No matter, the quest was complete. They stopped briefly at a laboratory where Joshua and Han remained with the water samples Piotyr and The First provided them. Two each for Archeron, Lethe, Phlegethon, and now Styx since they had returned, and the two large combined sample vials which lacked only melted Cocytus. At Han's direction, the group waited patiently as Piotyr carefully melted measured amounts of the ice into glass beakers.

The samples properly gathered, Han had spoken to him with great enthusiasm, though Piotyr couldn't generate any affection or excitement himself. They all seemed very pleased to see him, but he simply didn't know them. Their words rang hollow, not because of insincerity, but because of his own disassociation with them.

The First said he would stay with Joshua and Han in the lab but asked that Piotyr be shown to the command center, which the Seneschal gratiously offered to do. The three of them, along with Ve'kal, departed the lab. It all felt awkward and strained to Piotyr, but he had a battle to plan and a siege to command the defense of. Their words felt as if they came from a great distance away. He barely remembered what was said as he walked to this Plaza of the Throne.

When he arrived, he breathed a sigh of relief. *This is one piece.* His visions included a lot of him standing right there above the maps and unit representations. He looked carefully around, and smiled. *Time to get to work.*

🛡 ☪ 🏛 ⚕ ⛰

"As I said, I didn't tell him about this philter, because I wanted to talk to the two of you first. She was quite clear that it would restore him, but I see no reason to believe she lied about it destroying his vision of the future. It is not a choice I wanted to make, and not one that I thought he should make either in his current state." The three men stood in Han and Joshua's laboratory, discussing the water returned by Piotyr and the First.

I know why you didn't tell him of his past, but I still think you should have told him I was his son.

The First didn't deign to respond. Lokyrg was still a child in many ways. That knowledge would have been a needless complication at best, at worst it may have unsettled Piotyr more than he already was. He was right to have told him next to nothing on their return trip on the river.

"So this is a pure draught from the Mnemosyne? This Oracle lives there?" Han spoke with obvious fascination, not unexpected given his nature. The man was a curious sort.

"Yes. We have time before he needs to be given it, a fortnight from when we left three days ago. If you are correct and the siege will begin four days hence, you will have a week for him to command the defense before he needs the philter. On the seventh day of battle, we need to either have won, died, or he will need to be given this."

Wheezing and rasping brought a smile to The First's face as Joshua spoke. He had missed the man. "A week should be enough, one way or another. It would be unfair to deny him his past."

"I agree, I just wanted the two of you to be involved. I worried that by giving it to him on our return journey, whatever insight he gained from this Oracle would be lost and wasted. He is a good man, but right now I would wager a good general is more important."

"Agreed." Joshua smiled at him.

"Agreed." Han placed the vial on his desk, carefully. "For now, the far more important elixir is the one Joshua and I need to complete for Kasim. Would you be so kind as to let us get to it?"

The First nodded to Han and clapped Joshua on the shoulder. It was an odd sensation he felt, but he was sure he would have called Joshua a friend, having been away from him. "Good luck, the two of you. I hope the alchemy goes well." Having exchanged farewells, he left the lab and walked for a time with only Lokyrg for his company.

I don't wish to quarrel, corpse, but I do not wish to be ignored, either.

"Lokyrg, I know this is difficult, but Piotyr is of a single focus right now, and since he doesn't have his memory in any case, I will not complicate things for him. Han will tell him about the elixir, which is for the best as Han is actually *in* his memory to some extent... at least in that he was supposed to trust him. That is more than can be said for anyone else, including his blood. I haven't told him details about Asya or your siblings, either." He continued walking the halls with Lokyrg and Ba'al Am's huge axe, their conversation passing the time as he walked below the now cleared ruins of the palace.

Mother would flay his skin if he forgot her.

"So much the better the reasons for not telling him. He will know soon enough. Far more pressing for us is preparation for war. Have you not seen and felt how dire things are? Even with the preparations made..."

I must admit, Han has done well.

"Yes, I agree, but even with those preparations morale is not good. They seem confident that they can hold the Legion outside the walls, perhaps even win that battle over time, but they do *not* share that confidence about stopping the tens of thousands of Ba'al and other lesser Fallen who will be flying over the wall to sweep the defenders away like gnats."

You have a plan for that?

"Not so much a plan to stop it, but yes I do have some preparations I'd like to make, with your blessing and the blessing of Aruk and Ulis if and when they arrive."

I can't speak for them, but in terms of battle I trust you completely. What do you propose?

Having arrived at the armory, The First nodded to the Legionnaire guarding the front and went inside. "I'll show you. What do you know of harpooning?"

Kasim sat up in his bed as Joshua helped him drink the entire elixir while Han and Dhermina looked on. The sensations from the water were incredible. Freezing cold mixed with burning hot, sweet and salty, heavy and effervescent. He gasped as he finished it, and then shivered and wrapped his arms around his body as he started to convulse.

"What is wrong?! It's hurting him!" Dhermina dashed to his side, not quite pushing Joshua away but forcing him to extricate himself quickly to avoid her.

"He's fine, Dhermina, it will not be without discomfort, this healing, but it will work, you must trust me. We did our work well. Medicine, prayer, and mysticism are all at play here. Kasim will be healed."

She held his legs as she looked on helplessly but Kasim couldn't spare her more than a pained look. His veins were on fire. He tried to muster a weak smile but it was ripped from him as the torrent of razors and needles ripped through his vascular system. He grit his teeth in pain and embraced the agony. His experiences had taught him much about enduring. This was a real, physical pain. Nothing compared to his journeys through death.

"It is working, Han. Come, join me in the healing." Joshua began to incant in the High Tongue. Kasim knew healing Invocations would be following soon. It was Joshua's voice that was loudest and most clear and, in his distracted and pained state, he still knew that Joshua had healed himself first. It would not last, but it would make him physically stronger for a short while and would ease the diseased corruption in his chest. The healer must have expected a long process if he spared the time and spiritual energy for his own well being in the beginning.

His thoughts turned once more to his own body as the ripples of divine energy washed over him. Waves of intense healing power and restorative command accompanied Joshua's voice. The water in his veins was purifying his poison and Joshua's Invocations were regenerating his flesh.

He focused on the feelings of relief he found, though fleeting, rather than the pain of the poison being diluted and washed away. Cascade upon cascade of regenerative energy flowed over him and he could do little more than hold on. He felt like he was being drowned under a giant waterfall.

Another voice entered the torrent. He recognized Han Invoking alongside Joshua. His mind was too fragmented to hear what was being done but he trusted both men implicitly. The Invocations bombarded him for what seemed an eternity, but he endured. His body was frozen with tension as he held himself in a tight ball. Dhermina tried to soothe him, but he could barely hear anything outside his own ears. This too, would pass.

It was harsh, but did not last overlong. The candles in his room had melted perhaps a few hours worth by the time the pain started to recede. He was exhausted, but not nearly as much as Han and Joshua were by the looks of them. Both men sat slumped in chairs, drenched in sweat.

He tried to sit up, but Dhermina placed a hand upon his chest. "Not yet, my love. Joshua was adamant, you must rest. Sleep, and when you wake, eat. Your task for the next three days is to regain your strength."

He smiled at her and nodded. "Thank you, I will listen." He turned to the two Templar. His friends. "Thank you both, as well. I can feel the absence of the poison. You have saved me."

Joshua bowed his head to him. Han smiled. Kasim hardly even noticed the two of them nodding off as he did as well. Sleep had not felt so deep and well earned in a long time.

Markov was impressed with Jacob's ability to cope with what these Grigori had told him. For Markov, the entire war had been fought without a great deal of knowledge about what went on beyond the portals. Hell was just the place the Legion came from, and no one gave any real thought to how things worked over there.

For Jacob, Hell had become an actual front that he fought on and, from all appearances, had been victorious on. What the Grigori were now telling him, that he was their leader, was a large and bitter pill for anyone to swallow. Merethius was doing pretty damned well with it, though.

The two Templar sat in the home of Sav the Small, drinking mint tea and listening to various Watchers detail their missions, locations, and organizational hierarchy. There were about a thousand of them, though only half did assassination work. Like any society, they needed craftsmen, logistical support, and many other jobs that didn't require a blade or poison.

Of those five hundred actual assassins, many were older and had been out of the trade for a long time. Retired, though, and not withered. Apparently it was a trait of the Fallen to live forever, or near enough to it.

He and Merethius sat listening to report after report from Grigori about contracts they were currently on or had recently completed. It was impressive that so much control of the infernal empire was exerted by so few. They were feared across the land, and the previous Shay'tan... really all of them before Jacob... had made liberal use of them.

"So why was Kasim targetted in Sheol?" Jacob asked Sav, who had mentioned that it was best to speak directly to him. These guys were a particular sort about respect and propriety.

"Shay'tan, we had been contracted by your predecessor to eliminate all the Templar with all haste. It was a new contract, one that only arrived shortly before your army attacked Sheol. Abaddon sent missives after your victory to maintain all outstanding contracts, which we would normally laugh at... no one commands the Grigori save the Shay'tan... but we knew the Shay'tan lived and hadn't heard anything otherwise. We thus continued as we were."

"I did slay him, though. He died." Merethius wasn't arguing and Markov didn't detect even a hint of anger in his voice. This was idle conversation from someone who was curious, nothing more.

"Yes, Shay'tan. The resulting cataclysm took the lives of most of Sheol and leveled the palace. Some of us were in Sheol when it happened."

"So if I killed him, why wouldn't you know of it then? Why would you not cancel your contracts with him, and return home to your families?"

"Most of the true Fallen can feel a connection to the King of Hell. How deep that connection is varies, but usually the more devoted to the House of Lucifer, the deeper that bond. The Grigori were birthed by the will of the Morning Star, so our dedication was more than most. We would feel lost without a connection to the Shay'tan, and on that day, I swear to you, not one of us felt that our Lord had died."

"But you just said you knew of the explosion."

"Forgive me, Shay'tan, I would not dream of arguing with you. What I mean to say is that our bond didn't give any indication of his death. There was no break, no pause, nothing. Whatever happened between you and Lucifer's Heir was instantaneous, and we didn't notice anything wrong. We assumed he had lived, at least long enough for another to take his place. Hell must have a King, and now that King is you."

Markov looked at Merethius for any kind of reaction. He didn't know how he would take it if it had happened to him, but he wasn't Jacob, and they were different men from different times. For his part, Jacob didn't appear bothered in the slightest.

"Who did you think was ruling?"

"At first, we didn't think the Heir had fallen. Once it became common knowledge that Ve'kal was ruling in Sheol, we thought perhaps she had taken the Throne while the two of you battled. Up until today we still thought that was a possibility, though unlikely.

We thought perhaps Abaddon had preserved the soul of the Shay'tan for a time, but ultimately we didn't really care. There *was* a Shay'tan, somewhere, and we had our contracts. Without hearing otherwise, it was not our place to cancel them or question them."

"I'm glad I showed up here, then. If I hadn't ordered you to cancel all contracts against the Templar, would you have kept trying?"

"Most assuredly. Be at ease though, our ravens are flawless, and the message will be received across the empire. No blood of the seed of Adam will be spilt by us. The real question is now, what do you want to do with us? We are yours, Shay'tan."

Markov knew what kind of a tool these Grigori were, though in an abstract way. The Church had used assassins at San Luis, but really they were just glorified snipers. The concept of infiltrating the Legion to assassinate officers and Fallen was something this Kasim had done, according to Merethius, but that must have come about centuries after Markov was gone. In his time, their assassins simply hid and fired upon likely candidates from stealth.

These men and women, children too he supposed, were a far more refined and effective weapon. They looked like the Legion, though he understood that they all were Fallen and had wings, unless they had removed them. They could go anywhere in the empire and pass unnoticed. If they truly believed Jacob was their master...

"How fast can you get to Sheol? I am headed there after our business is concluded here."

"It is a few days journey for us, master. Do you mean to send us there?"

Markov had a sudden thought. "Merethius, these are assassins, no?"

"Yes, Markov. What are you getting at?"

"Don't send them to Sheol. Send them to Abaddon. Send them to kill his Ba'al."

Jacob looked at Sav before speaking. "Could you kill Abaddon?"

"No, master. Though we would be happy to attempt for you, he is too powerful. He has a powerful connection to the Shay'tan, more powerful than any living Fallen. As long as you live no blade wielded by any flesh save yourself can kill him. Wound, perhaps... but not kill."

"That would be why Kasim couldn't kill him. Damn."

"What do you mean?" Markov had heard a lot of this Kasim from Jacob, but nothing about an assassination attempt on The Destroyer.

"Shortly before we were... sent here by our Patriarch, Kasim had reached Ba'al Apollyon and managed to get his blade into his back. He swore his knife was true, but Apollyon didn't die. Kasim fled the camp, lucky to escape with his life, and soon after, the attacks continued unabated. If what Sav says is the truth of it, he didn't have a chance."

"Ah, could be then. Would be nice to let him know."

"Yes it would, he took it hard. This is just from what he told me, but Kasim wasn't prone to failure, I know it didn't sit well with him. Sav, what about the other Ba'al, Apollyon's commanders?"

"If you will it, we will eliminate them by the score."

Jacob laughed and slapped his hand on the table. "I will it. Give the order, Sav. The Grigori shall march to join The Destroyer and slay his officers. However, I have an important aspect of your task you must follow."

"Yes, master?"

"Do not shed any blood until the Legion first reach the walls. If he is given the chance to regroup, your work will not be as effective. Wait until the walls are nearly breached, and the Ba'al make ready to join the Legion. Can you communicate effectively in such a matter to coordinate your attacks?"

Sav smiled at Jacob before standing. "The will of the Shay'tan is absolute."

"General Piotyr, there is a matter of import I must speak to you about." Piotyr looked up from his maps and saw the Seneschal standing there, wringing his hands.

"Go ahead, what is it?" The man bowed his head and moved close to him before lowering his voice and speaking in soft tones.

"I have... *very* recently been informed that you may have encountered certain individuals on your journey. Certain individuals who live in a rather cold place."

Piotyr frowned, he had told no one. He grabbed the Seneschal and directed him away from the tent and into a quiet alcove in the Plaza. "I find that troubling, how did you come by this information?"

Whispering now, the Seneschal looked at Piotyr with wide eyes before softly answering. "I know this because *they are here,* General. Your presence is most humbly requested at the river landing."

Piotyr smiled, and clapped the man on the arm. "Tell no one, who else knows?"

"Just two guards and a page. The guards are stationed at the entrance from the landing to the catacombs, and the page was sent to summon me. I had him return to the river landing."

"We need to isolate those three. You don't have to kill them unless you think you have to, but keep this information from reaching any other ears. Under penalty of death. Come with me."

The Seneschal cocked his head and looked at Piotyr quizically. "As you wish, General."

They made haste back through the bowels of the Palace, and nearly ran all the way to the stairs leading down into the depths. Piotyr could barely restrain himself from sprinting, but the last thing he needed was to fall and break something. Then he would have to send the Seneschal for Joshua... no, better just to slow down and be careful.

He had no real idea why he was here or what his purpose was beyond leading the army in the siege, but he had taken to it with a zeal which felt completely natural. He loved it, and felt a passion for it that he couldn't understand.

The Seneschal struggled to keep pace, but Piotyr was not worried, the man wouldn't suffer from a brisk walk. Finally arriving under the dungeons, Piotyr was relieved to see two guards and a page there at the stairs leading down into the darkness. The air was damp here and he could faintly hear the river. Strange that he had only just arrived back from this place yet it already felt like a different world to him.

"Ah, excellent, they are still here."

"Yes, I took the liberty of having them stay here until you arrived."

Piotyr looked again at the man, quietly catching his breath. "Well done, Seneschal. You are good at your work. Find them some suitable refreshments and make them comfortable when we are done."

"Men."

"General!" The Legionnaire stood at attention and waited for him to speak.

"Men, what did you see down here?" Piotyr spoke loudly and firmly, and waited for a response.

"General, a man, a Ba'al from the look of him, though a bit plain looking, but a Ba'al came up those steps and asked us..."

"Wrong!" Piotyr bellowed to interrupt the man, who blinked and dropped his head.

"What you saw here was not a damned thing. You haven't seen a damned thing since I arrived, and you won't see a damned thing after I leave. Nothing strange, no visitors, and nothing whatsoever to tell a damned soul. Isn't that right Legionniare?!"

The man looked at him with wide eyes. "Ah... yes General. We didn't see anything."

"Good!" He bellowed loud enough that he was sure anyone listening in would have heard him. "Good guards should be rewarded for doing their job, and not seeing a damned thing! Right?"

"Ah... yes General. We didn't see anything."

Lowering his voice somewhat, but still speaking loudly, he continued. "Seneschal, send them extra rations of meat and ale. They are not to leave their posts unless relieved by you personally, or me. The page is excused from duty as well, the three of them will remain here unless informed otherwise."

"Yes, Piotyr. What about..."

"I'll handle it. Wait here, all of you."

The guards, page, and Seneschal waited at the landing, not really sure what was going on, he gathered. That was unimportant, the Seneschal had nothing to do with Piotyr's plans, and he would make do with what he was told.

Descending into the darkness and damp, he felt strangely comforted. This was the only memory he had that was his own, that he had made without any outside influence. When he met up with the undead man on the river, he got the sense that he knew him well, and that there was much the corpse wanted to tell him. Corpse? Hell the thing looked healthier than any living being he had seen since arriving in Sheol. He wondered why people called him that.

He shook his head. There was a lot he didn't understand, but here in the darkness of the cavern river landing of Styx, he felt that he was possessed of all he needed to know. He walked along the path to the water proper and wasn't surprised to see a camp, complete with tents, banners, and torches. Unable to contain his smile, he called out to a patrolling sentry, who waved to him and brought him before Sammael. Piotyr was thrilled to see picket lines and Frost wyrms tethered beyond the camp next to the river.

"Hail! What brings you here, my friend?" Piotyr felt as warm and affectionate as he could remember when he greeted him.

"As I said, Son of Adam. I have a debt to pay."

Kasim awoke to an empty room. Han and Joshua were gone, and so was Dhermina. There was a large platter of food on the table and a note addressed to him. The smell of food made his mouth water and stomach growl. By all that was graceful he was hungry.

He grabbed a slab of beef and shoved it in his mouth as he read the letter.

My love, eat well and regain your strength. It has all been tasted, so you are safe from Grigori poison. Ba'al Apollyon is two days away and marching with speed. I am with Joshua assisting with final preparations. He said he performed an Invocation of Metabolism on you to speed up your appetite, which should last for this meal. Come find us when you have eaten and feel stronger.

Han also fortified the food, which was prepared by Ve'kal's Master of Kitchens. You will feel better soon. -Dhermina

He smiled as he shoved more meat into his mouth. He counted fowl, beef, venison, and fish in the greatest quantity. Some thin flatbread, but mostly meat. The cook was a wonder, with the meats spiced perfectly and with plenty of olives, onions, and other pungent condiments to make it one of the best meals he had ever had. His eyes closed as he sighed in pleasure while eating. The platter would have fed three men normally he would wager, but he was starving and it was delicious.

He was actually sad when he finished it. He felt like he could keep eating but at the least he did feel stronger. He stretched for a couple of minutes and did a simple calisthenics routine to warm up. Feeling limber, he performed a few short forms just to get the feel back. He felt good.

He grabbed a metal carafe from next to the platter noticing it was chilled and covered in condensation, and sniffed. Mint and honey. He drained the tea in two large gulps and sighed. He was ready to continue so grabbed his tray and carafe and left the infirmary. The door was immense and heavy, but he managed to open it. Passing through the doorway he felt a chill on his skin. *Warded. Han.*

He appreciated the added security. He was more or less helpless over the last several weeks and would have been easy prey for the Grigori. *Not any longer.*

He walked along the hall, passing a lab filled with beakers, flasks, and other alchemical apparatus he wasn't really familiar with. He passed a library packed with books and his nose picked up the scent of Han's favorite incense. He smiled. His friends had kept a close watch on him.

He passed several more wards as he progressed through the bowels of the palace and finally found daylight leading up past a stairwell into the plaza. It was a kicked anthill of furious activity with servants, Legionnaire, Fallen, and even some Ba'al hurrying about. The command tent was frenetic and Kasim saw Piotyr and the Seneschal heading inside. Kasim thought about going to say hello, but he had been told that Piotyr had lost his memory on his quest to obtain the water which now had healed Kasim's veins.

It would probably be a distraction, he thought. He would thank him properly once he remembered who he was. Additionally, Piotyr looked focused and very busy. Kasim at the moment was not crucial to the battle preparation.

He asked a Legionnaire guard where he could find Joshua and Dhermina and was directed to the ramparts above. Thanking the man, Kasim was almost shocked when the man nodded and said "You are welcome." The Templar must be having quite a positive influence on the city.

Kasim found them after a short search. He noticed the walls had been completely repaired, but it was still strange revisiting them after his last time, when he and the other monks had battled hard to clear them of siege engineers and archers to clear the skies for Piotyr and his brood. It seemed a lifetime ago, yet was not even two months.

"Well look who is up and around?" Kasim smiled as Joshua called out a greeting. Dhermina ran to him and hugged him, which he enjoyed immensely before giving her an impassioned kiss. He was feeling far, far better.

"Aye, my friend. Your healing has done wonders. I can never repay you, Joshua."

Joshua smiled and then coughed before he began speaking, though to Kasim's ears he sounded a little better than he remembered. "Not just my healing. Han's arcane efforts were as important, and without Piotyr and the First retrieving the water, it would have been impossible."

"Nevertheless, I thank you for your part. Are you feeling better? You sound like it."

"A little. I have a remedy that may cure me completely, though I doubt it. Han is confident, but I am not. Either way, I won't take it until the battle is over. Han and I discussed it and we are afraid that if I cure myself, the plague may weaken or even fail. We need the undead. I'll wait until this is over, one way or another. I did a small experiment with the water though, and I am quite functional. I feel like I am merely sick, instead of constantly dying."

"Well, I'm glad for that at least. So I hate to ask, but I feel your Metabolic Invocation is fading, and I am already hungry again. Could I impose?"

Joshua laughed again, and though it was raspy, he was able to get through it and start a sentence without hacking. Progress indeed. "Hah, it is no imposition. I expected as much, and I'm glad you have your appetite. Here."

Joshua intoned the Invocation in the common tongue and Kasim immediately felt his stomach grumble. Dhermina looped his arm in hers and smiled at him. "Come, I'll get something to eat with you. Then we need to attend to some combat training. It will help your strength return."

He smiled at her, and kissed her again. "Will that be alright, Joshua? I don't want to be useless in two days."

Joshua's smile dipped. "Oh, you won't be, but I have to be honest in that our odds aren't very good. Do what you can to get as strong as you can, then go see Han. He will be finalizing preparations either with Piotyr and Ve'kal or by himself in the command tent. Be well, Kasim."

"You as well, Joshua. May peace be ever upon you."

Joshua's eyebrows climbed, and Kasim knew why. Kasim had never spoken a warrior's greeting to Joshua before, though the man had certainly earned it. "And on you, Kasim."

Having heard the response, he and Dhermina left to find more food. By God he was hungry.

You are crazy, corpse. You think this will work? You will fall and shatter upon the earth long before this makes any difference.

Having made the adjustmets to Eirygaile, he had copied the method on another fifty dragon spears gathering dust in the armory. He sat now admiring his work there and was pleased.

"There are nearly twenty of us that are powerful enough and intelligent enough to make this work, Lokryg. Though I am the First among us in both skill and knowledge, I am not the only one who is worth far more than any ten Legionnaire or Fallen. You must trust my judgement."

I trust your judgement about as far as you respect gravity, it seems. What makes you think that Aruc or Ulis will go along with this?

"You are their brother, and I trust you to make my case. It *will* work."

They are already here, you know. They arrived less than an hour ago and are currently roosting above the southern parapets.

"I know, and I would like to go ask them. Will you assist me?"

I will ask, but I still think you are insane. It won't work.

The First was more than pleased with that response. If nothing else, that Lokyrg was willing to advocate for him to his siblings would suffice. He didn't need his approval, just his willingness.

They noticed quickly that the walls were cleared significantly in advance of the southern parapets. Small wonder, he thought, once he saw the two massive red wyrms coiled about them. "You certainly grow quickly, that is true."

They do, not "you" do. I am no longer one of them.

"Forgive me, I did not mean to slight you."

I know, just know that they may not treat me the same as they once did.

The First was aware of that possibility, but he had to try. He could easily guard the walls with the other Plague Lords, or lead sorties against the ground troops of The Destroyer, but of far more concern were the Ba'al which would darken the sky. That was where the battle would be won or lost, and that was where he wanted to put the considerable talents of the Plague Lords.

He stopped short of the parapets by a good fifty paces, and politely knelt with his head bowed. Wyrms were known for their pride, and he had relatively little. It hurt nothing to acknowledge their greatness.

It was Ulis, he thought, who first raised her head lazily and acknowledged him. He only thought so because she was smaller than the other, and unless things had changed significantly in the last couple of months Aruc was larger by a good margin.

He did not expect her to speak to him, his understanding was that human speech was a trait that Hellfire wyrms did not develop until much older. Piotyr had told him as much. "Aruc and Ulis, son and daughter of Piotyr and Asya. I have come to ask a boon for the coming battle. Will you speak with your brother on the matter?"

We will speak with him. The words came to his mind with a serpentine affect. Her words were not as clear as Lokyrg's.

"I trust you, my friend. This will work, please do your best."

Shut up and let me do this, then.

The First nodded his assent and stood patiently while the siblings spoke. He wished he could have heard it, but he also respected their privacy. He hoped it would work out in his favor.

Has he treated you well, brother? Ulis began the exchange.

Yes, he has. We had some disagreements in the beginning, but it has become a good partnership. He is most skilled, and my thirst has been sated often. How is mother?

Aruc followed. *Heavy with our new siblings. She laments not being here, though she laments father being gone more. Is it true, is his mind shattered? We felt it close off not long ago, and feared the worst.*

Not shattered, just damaged. We met a woman, a mortal of all things, who was powerful beyond reason. Though I was not there for it, we gathered that she tricked father into drinking from an enchanted, or cursed spring. He has visions of the future now, but can't remember anything from before his journey. He doesn't remember any of us.

Ulis broke in next. Do you think he will live through the battle? It does not look like his side has a chance of winning. We flew out to see the forces coming, and they number untold.

I believe he will live, though they may lose the battle. My hope is that if it goes poorly, he can be convinced to come away with us back to mother.

That would be good, brother. Ulis again. This was going better than Lokyrg had expected.

My undead companion here has an odd request, but one that he feels will greatly affect Father's chances in the battle. I know that no one has ridden either of you in combat except Father... well and Han... sort of, but he has a plan involving harpoons and the other Plague Lords that is completely crazy, but it could actually work if you are willing.

Is that what has been deemed best by father? Aruc asked pointedly, and Lokyrg would not lie to his brood. The First *had* gotten Piotyr's permission, but mostly it was a simple dismissive comment that they were using to even have this conversation. Piotyr had said yes, that if the dragons arrived, and yes, if they allowed anyone to ride them as cavalry, then The First could do whatever the hell he wanted with them. that two dragons would make little difference.

No, but he didn't say either way. If he has another use or idea, he will tell you I'm sure.

Aruc and Ulis looked at each other before turning back to The First. In unison, they answered him. *We will do as you ask, brother. Fight well.*

It was past dusk and Han was tired again, but he had gotten a decent nap earlier in the infirmary and he could sleep for a few hours as soon as he was done. He would check again tomorrow, but he couldn't rest until all of his plans, troops, and support logistics were ready.

Kasim had found him a couple hours ago. Han had to admit that the man looked well. His cheeks had filled out, his color had returned, and his skin no longer sagged. His recuperation was going very well and quickly. He would not be at full strength when the siege hit, but he would be very, very close. Another full day of food, exercise, and hopefully some time alone with Dhermina and Kasim would be nearly ready.

The catacombs were no longer a place of dark terrors for Han, and as his thoughts wandered his mind, his feet meandered the dark stone corridors. Once a place of despair and horror, Han liked to think of them now as a place of learning and purpose. The wraith-walkers and leech-walkers were all ready, their tunnels having been completed. They could be within the enemy ranks within minutes of leaving their prison.

The insects had been breeding like, well, flies, and the flash crystals and wind shunts would get them out onto the field in seconds. Combined with the already secured plague-walkers and diseased waterways that Abaddon would have to contend with, Han was confident that with Piotyr commanding the defenses, the city could hold against the Legion on the ground for weeks, if not months. Supplies would run out before they need fear the forces of the Destroyer breaching their walls from the ground outside Sheol.

That left the Ba'al and the Fallen who could fly. His spies and scouts couldn't count accurately, but by even rough estimates well over one hundred thousand would blacken the sky above the city walls less than two days hence. It could be ten times that many. He had no realistic answer for them, other than his own destructive energies.

He mused on that a moment as he made his rounds, checking on his abominations and machinations. He was tired, so rest would definitely be a priority tomorrow, but he would be able to wield a considerable amount of power once the battle truly began. Would it be enough to last the day? Two? When the Patriarch of Haven Invoked Holy Fire... immense storms of Divine Wrath that burned the Legion to ash... it took a terrible toll on him. Han remembered how weak and frail the old man looked after the day's battle, and how every day he returned to the walls to fend off the Destroyer one more time. Did Han have it in him? Did he have the old man's strength?

He slowly made his way back to the warded lab and library that he and Joshua called home. He was thankful that so many useful rooms had been below ground when the Cataclysm happened. The palace had been blasted into nothing, but a dozen floors underground survived relatively intact. Libraries, armories, barracks, servants quarters, storage, dungeons, and all manner of variations striated through the earth like a honeycomb. Ve'kal had told him that the Shay'tan had been a vain sort, and most of the palace aboveground was dedicated to decadence and debauchery. Good riddance to such frivolity.

Joshua was not in for the night yet, which didn't surprise him. Joshua had his own last minute preparations to make, with his elixirs and healing restoratives and innoculations to oversee. Han wished Joshua had been able to delegate more, but he understood the man's desire to look after important things personally.

Han sat in his chair and sighed, lighting an incense stick and closing his eyes. Joshua's ingenuity had given the defenders on the walls a much bigger chance than Han had initially calculated. While every Ba'al or Fallen that cleared the wall on Abaddon's side would die once felled, the same would not be true for Sheol's guardians. Wounds would knit, flesh would heal, and limbs would reattach. In the chaos of war, it might be some time before it was even noticed, but by the time Abaddon's forces learned that every one of their victims had to be slain ten times over to be counted out it may well have turned the tide enough for Han to make a difference.

The pieces were in place and there was little else Han could do to prepare. He relaxed as best he could, and finally slept. Tomorrow would be the last gasp before the plunge.

chapter twenty-seven

All the days of the afflicted are evil: but he that is of a merry
heart hath a continual feast.
- Proverbs 15:15

The village was nearly a ghost town. He and Markov had stayed the night after the Grigori assassins and the other, non-fighting Watchers had left. After eating, they would make their way to Sheol. Home, he supposed. It felt strange to think of that way, but he was beyond questioning what he had been told. It made sense. He had killed the Shay'tan, but somehow it had been in such a way that the title passed to him.

He had theorized a number of explanations. Perhaps it was because he had killed him right by the Throne itself. It could be that it was due to Jacob being within the Apotheosis at the time. Maybe it was as simple as the Shay'tan being killed by a mortal somehow broke the rules of succession. It really didn't matter. All that mattered is that it happened. Jacob was the Shay'tan.

In his heart, he knew that was why his Soul Fire didn't diminish when he used it now, whereas it did for Markov.

He looked at Markov and smiled. The man smiled back, but it wasn't the easy, relaxed smile he had when they escaped the valley. It was guarded, suspicious. How could it not be? Jacob was what they had both vowed to fight until their last breath. Granted he was still Jacob, a man and a Templar, but he was also the Devil, and Jacob was not surprised Markov's demeanor had changed towards him. He was thankful Markov wasn't outright hostile.

"Are you ready?"

"Yeah, I'm ready. Let's see this to the end, Merethius."

"Markov. You are a good man, and I call you a friend and brother. Know that no matter what, even though things have changed, I am grateful we met."

The man snorted, but did crack a slight sideways smile. "Well if we hadn't, I'd still be stuck in that fucking valley, so I guess I'm thankful as well." With that, he extended his hand. "Godspeed, Shay'tan Merethius. I'm ready."

Jacob smiled and shook hands. He Invoked the Sword, and the transformation hardly changed his appearance at all. His form was already perfect. Lucifer was but a pale shadow. He was the pinnacle of Adam's Seed, and the Shay'tan as well. None would stand before him. "To Sheol, then, and an end to it."

Ve'kal awoke with a start and looked at the sunlight in the room. Dawn had come. She hurried to her feet and dressed, splashing mint water in her face and throwing open the window to her room in the Shay'tan's quarters. The horizon was choked with dust. *Abaddon will crest those hills today. Tonight we will be under siege.*

She opened the next room and was startled to see Nezmyr's bed empty. She opened the door to their suite of rooms and stopped to ask the house guard where her son was.

"Downstairs eating breakfast, mistress."

She thanked him and hurried downstairs, and was relieved to see her son sitting at a table eating some bread and drinking what she hoped was milk. She hadn't been able to supervise him much of late, and he was growing up far too quickly. He liked soldiers entirely too much, and to her dismay they liked him just as much.

"Good morning, Nezmyr. How did you sleep?" She stole a quick glance in his cup. Inwardly she sighed. Milk.

"Fair enough, mother. Though it will be a long, anxious day for everyone I fear."

"Yes it will. May I join you? I would like to have..." she stopped herself from saying one last meal.

"It's ok, I understand. Please." He gestured to an empty chair at the table. "It won't be our last, but the fact that it could be means we ought to enjoy it, right mother?"

She smiled at him. She tousled his hair and nodded, blinking back tears. He was too old for her to show such weakness. "Right, my son. Come; let us raise our glass in a toast to the future."

He smiled and clinked his mug to hers before taking a big drink. "The future, and to Jacob. For fallen friends and family."

Her smile faded, but she clinked again. The boy didn't know his own father, or his brothers. They were dead shortly after he was born, and he had been in Thrall his whole life since then, until Jacob freed him. Jacob was the only father he had ever known, and that was all too brief.

"To Jacob." She had never savored a meal more.

"You have time for a meal with us, Ba'al Joshua. It has been too long, and it may be a long time again before we have the chance." K'had was speaking, though Ulraen was nodding emphatically. They were in a smaller plaza, some distance from the Throne. Joshua had been dispensing more elixirs, restoratives, and vaccines when his disciples had ambushed him.

"I have much to do to oversee the final preparations, my friends. There isn't time."

"Oh give it a rest, would you? The food is ready; we ordered it especially for today. It was made by Priolt and his staff, and we had to give him a great deal of our treasure from Sheol Am to get him to take the time. Please. Sit with us." That from Ryrig... who by merely bringing up Sheol Am made Joshua feel obligated. That was probably by design. Jaz'rih looked at Ryrig approvingly. It was clear they were all in on it.

He sighed, but seeing the pages with the platters of food and his disciples already setting the table for their whole group? He *was* hungry, and he could spare an hour. Preparations would never be completely finished anyway.

"Very well, do you have wine?"

Ulraen grinned like a child up to mischief, and clapped K'had on the arm. "Told you he'd listen. Wine!" He clapped his hands and a flat door on the ground door was opened, leading down, Joshua assumed, into a wine cellar. Joshua's eyes climbed as dozens of people he knew from Ithera and M'zal, as well as from Sheol Am came out of the wine cellar and also from outside the plaza. The small gathering grew tenfold in minutes.

There was Garysh and M'lor setting up tables with Sajhal and Arein, the four of them looking, as far as he could tell, quite happy. He wished he had had more time with everyone, they were among the first to follow him.

The tables and chairs were set up in haste. He was surprised to see more and more food brought in, as well as cases and cases of wine. He frowned as he worried that his disciples planned to drink to excess, but the small plaza was soon filled with dozens, no, hundreds of people. He grew quiet as he recognized more and more were from the cities and villages he had liberated... and wiped out.

He saw Qirin and Yuari playing with Pal, with his father Priam looking on in approval. He had felt so sorry for the boy and his father, but seeing them now he was sure they were happier than the misery they lived in before he brought the plague to their home.

Amazing scents greeted his nose, even through his illness, and he was silently thankful he had taken a small amount of the curative he and Han and made from the Hell waters. He deserved to enjoy a meal.

Hazuk'tyr carved the roasts and Byral the swine, and all manner of breads, roasted vegetables, sweet and savory pies, fruit, and cheeses all were stacked high on tables with everyone he could think of. "Don't look so surprised, Ba'al Joshua. When you appointed me Master of Provisions, I took the job seriously."

M'lor was one of the most dour men Joshua had ever met, but in that moment Joshua saw an inkling of warmth from the man. "I don't think anyone would ever accuse you of not being serious, M'lor."

"Nor should they accuse him of taking too little credit, I think." Ryrig had joined them, and his smile gave away the lie that he was upset.

"Bah, I never said I did it alone, Ryrig. Of course the quartermaster helped."

Joshua smiled at both of them as Jaz'rih brought him a class of wine. "Don't tarry, make sure you get something to eat, Ba'al. Tomorrow dawns a difficult day, enjoy this while you can."

"Thank you. All of you. I wasn't aware how much I missed such things." They raised a glass to him, and he drank deeply, and sighed in pleasure as the wine settled in his chest and then stomach with no hacking or coughing.

He made his rounds of the food tables and spoke with everyone he could. An hour turned into two. He was glad the celebration had begun at midday. The food was incredible, by far the best he could remember eating, and though he was careful with his wine, he didn't ignore it either. They could all be dead tomorrow, or in a week, or who knew how long. It was worth it to have a momentary respite from planning for death and destruction.

He found K'had and Ulraen telling a group of survivors from M'zal about how they had met. He stopped for a moment to listen, and was pleased that *some* of the details were left out. People were eating, after all. He waited until they were done, and had a good laugh at his expense before he got their attention.

"I'm sure that story never gets old, you two?" He smiled as he said it. It surprised him how good he felt.

"Never. It's nice to let people know that even a mighty Ba'al once was not so grand." Ulraen winked as he spoke to him.

"I'm not really a Ba'al, though."

"Oh shut up, not this again." It really didn't matter which of them spoke, as they could have been twins in speech as well as appearance, but that was K'had.

"Fine, fine. No argument here. Just curious, but were any of the walkers asked to come?"

They looked at each other before Ulraen answered. "Ah, no. We did tell the First that we were doing this... and we asked that you be left alone for a time. Nothing personal... of course, but they make a lot of people uncomfortable."

He supposed they would. Hell, some of them *were* loved ones from Ithera or M'zal or Am. "No worries. I would have liked to share this with them, but only because they deserve thanks for their part as well. I understand, though."

"That's the spirit! We aren't unkind, but well they don't eat... and some of them are rather uncouth still."

"It's fine, thank you both for this. I needed it. We all needed it, I think."

"Agreed. When it's all over we'll find you a woman, too."

He blinked, then smiled. He was used to it by now. No reason to tell them, at that particular moment. "Yes... when it's all over. Thank you both."

They smiled and he made some last rounds saying hello to people he hadn't seen in weeks, and some he had never met. They were his people and he had changed their lives. He brought death to them and their loved ones, but he also liberated them from a terrible life. Like many things, there was balance in it.

It was as fine an afternoon as he had spent in years, even going back to before his damning by the Patriarch. When he finally made his departure, two hours had turned into three. He had no regrets, but he had work to do. Tomorrow dawned a difficult day indeed.

Forty Plague Lords and two hundred intelligent plaguewalkers stood with The First in the southern courtyard. The parapets overlooked them and Aruc and Ulis lazily watched them arm and armor themselves as they sat coiled around the towers in the sun.

The forty Plague Lords were equipped with the finest weaponry and armor in Sheol, repurposed from the private collection of Lucifer's Heir himself. Staring at them would probably hurt the eyes of a mortal, but the First merely saw purpose and potential. Acid dripped from halberds, Heart of Cocytus glimmered off of warhammers, and licks of Hellfire danced across bastard swords. The armor was enchanted as well and The First knew well that these weapons had been bound to the souls of countless mortals to achieve these effects.

Hefting Eirygaile in his hands, he couldn't judge... even if he cared about such things. Ba'al Moloch had one of the finest greatspears in all of Hell. Now it was his, and Lokyrg's soul was tethered to it. He was no hypocrite, and beyond that, the souls had already been torn from their owners in the forging. They were weapons, meant to be used... what better than to slay Ba'al with them?

He looked in approval as Secundus practiced throwing a harpoon at a target across the plaza, one hundred paces away. He skewered it, dead center. The other Plague Lord was not as proficient as he, The First was, but he had been given a name befitting his aptitude. His language was also quite advanced, and his body was completely healed, if not the near flawless specimen of himself.

The two of them would ride Ulis and Aruc in battle as cavalry, and would each carry a couple dozen harpoons secured to their mounts along with the rest of the simple barding and weaponry. There wasn't a lot of suitable barding for the wyrms, but there had been enough that was hellfire resistant to cover their softer vital areas, and enough to affix a saddle on both of them. He and Secundus riding the wyrms would be a primary defense against Abaddon's Ba'al once they attacked the walls.

That had rankled the dragons at first. They wanted to be out razing the infantry, but The First had been adamant that such tactics, while certainly effective, would ultimately do little to keep Sheol defended. The walls had to be protected, and the two cavalry units would be far more useful staying back from the outside chaos.

The wyrms had agreed, though reluctantly, deferring to him after getting confirmation that Piotyr approved of it. The Templar had made no time to speak individually to him but had sent messengers relaying details of the siege he thought important. He had confirmed that reserving the dragons for siege defense was the best use of them and had then told him how best to utilize the Plague Lords as well. It amazed The First that Piotyr's plans were identical to his own.

In tests, both he and Secundus were able to fire a harpoon in close to a second, and retrieve it via the attached rope in another. They simulated the motion of flying Ba'al by launching bags of clay out of catapults. Neither of them missed. As long as the spears didn't break, and the ropes held, the two of them would slaughter Fallen and Ba'al alike.

The other Plague Lords and lesser walkers in the plaza were there as shock troops to engage airborn foes in support of Aruc and Ulis. The equipment was there to hasten their killing, and in turn accelerate their development into greater walkers. The Fallen and Ba'al would produce a feast of souls for the small force The First had sequestered here, and by the time it came to open combat within the city, it would be a force far more powerful than the one waiting in the plaza now.

The undead, now equipped as they were, would be stationed evenly along the walls with the sole purpose of sweeping any Ba'al who got close enough to land on the parapets. Unlike the dragons, they followed orders implicitly, without any reservations. Many Ba'al would want to be among the first attackers to reach the Walls and the Plague Lords would answer them swiftly and decisively. The lesser two hundred undead would support them, getting kills when they could, though the First secretly hoped that they would be close enough to the kills of the Plague Lords to leech some of the souls. He had grown quite powerful after the death of Ba'al Am and he hoped that could be repeated here for his other intelligent undead. It was a good plan, not enough to guarantee success, but nonetheless a good allocation of important resources.

He was overseeing the final preparations of his soldiers without pride, though he did feel that they were prepared and well-suited to this task. He had sent a messenger to Joshua explaining his absence, as he didn't feel it would have been wise to attend the Templar's feast in the plaza. None of them needed to eat and their presence would only make some of the mortals uncomfortable. That was fine, this preparedness and martial atmosphere was all the well wishing he needed. A thought did occur to him then. It was fine for him, but mortals were different and he perhaps thought Joshua could use a message of support from him.

Summoning a messenger page, he had the boy write down a very simple note to be delivered to the man whom the First could honestly say was as close to a friend as he had. "Good luck, and we'll see you on the other side."

The command tent was quiet for the moment. Piotyr had ordered everyone out except for a few messengers and servants, himself, Han, and Ba'al Geir, who had been given the command of the Sheol Legion. He had done so to give them a chance for a quiet meal and drink before chaos came to their gates. From the dust on the horizon, this was the assuredly the last day. As he ate and drank, he went over preparations in his mind.

The First had his own unit that Piotyr had given him autonomy over as the undead would know best how to use his own. He felt conflicted over the dragons, as he knew they were his children, but with no memory of them and death marching on them all, he opted to use them as he saw best. Held in reserve with the undead... to kill any flying Fallen or Ba'al who cleared the walls was the best use of them, as their hellfire could strafe their air with impunity without fear of damaging soldiers on the wall. With the dragons protecting the skies above the parapets and the most lethal of the plague-walkers defending the walls, Piotyr felt that the First was in command of a very important aspect of the siege defense.

That left the garrison itself to command, and Ba'al Geir had apparently distinguished himself, according to Ba'alat Ve'kal. He didn't trust such things on any one person's word, but after investigating, Piotyr had confirmed that the man was an apt and motivated commander. He was careful with his men, and for a wonder actually valued their lives. Han had called him the first of a new breed of Ba'al and explained briefly that it had something to do with Kasim but he hadn't cared about the details right then. If the man was capable, so be it. Ba'al Geir had his orders and would be trusted to carry them out. The orders were simple enough. The Sheol Legion would run sorties when the need arose. The invading infantry would get close enough to use siege ladders or towers, but only if the wall defenders failed to dislodge them would Piotyr direct Geir to send out a sortie. Primarily they would fire artillery from the walls and form defensive units with tower shields and archers to take out Ba'al and Fallen on the wing as they cleared the ramparts. Simple enough commands, and upon the words of the others, he trusted Ba'al Geir to do what was required.

Ve'kal, blessedly, had agreed to guard the Throne itself and stay away from the command tent when the Ba'al attacked. Piotyr did not question her intelligence or determination, but the last thing he needed was another commander questioning him or getting in the way. Besides, while the Throne technically was safe from direct assault from the onset, it *was* the ultimate goal of the Destroyer. If it came to it, Ve'kal would have to defend it with fire and steel. It did, however, free him from having to answer anyone or communicate once the siege began. His visions had grown more still, more focused, but they still flickered in his mind with any adjustments he made to the battle plan.

Once blood was drawn, he would have to adjust quickly and without interruption. He had twenty runners ready to relay orders at a moment's notice, and twenty more in reserve in case he ran out. The Destroyer was no fool, and once he saw that his force would not have an easy time of it, the tactics would change and Piotyr needed to be ready. It was good that Ve'kal was going to be elsewhere.

The Seneschal had a far simpler, though critical, task. If things went poorly, which was certainly a strong possibility, his task was to take the non-combatants from their secure location underneath the palace ruins through the bowels and to the rivercraft Piotyr had made ready for them. He wouldn't leave them to be butchered or worse if they couldn't protect the city. The Seneschal was to oversee the evacuation and, hopefully, relocation to other parts of the empire if Piotyr failed. The exodus would hopefully never occur, but Piotyr had to plan for every possible outcome, and their death and defeat by Abaddon was certainly one potential outcome.

He smiled to think of Sammael's forces helping the Seneschal prepare the riverboats. There were hundreds of boats along the supply docks below gathering dust. The Shay'tan had not utilized Styx as a transportation artery, but at one point someone had commissioned them to be made. Sammael was being kept a secret for now, one that he didn't intend to reveal until Ba'al had already flown over his defenders, but as the Seneschal already knew of him, it made the most sense to have him oversee the process. Provisions had been moved under the guise of clearing out storage for the secondary defense of the keep should the battle go badly and now were staged by the river down below. In the case of the battle being lost, the Seneschal could quickly move the non combatants from the palace bowels to the river landing and get them out of the city to safer territory very quickly. Hopefully it would not come to pass, but if it did, it was good to have it handled beforehand.

Sammael was patient and said he understood Piotyr's decision to keep him in reserve for the time being. Nearly a thousand winged angels stood ready to fly at his command and it would have been folly to reveal them now. Let Abaddon react to them once he saw them butchering his Ba'al. Piotyr had hand-written special messages to Ve'kal, The First, Joshua, Han, and Ba'al Geir about Sammael, and he would send runners with them just before The Destroyer's infantry reached the walls. The element of surprise was a factor, but his commanders *did* need to be made aware of them at some point before they appeared. The messages were cryptic, lest they be intercepted by spies, but they did explain that Piotyr had another contingent of forces, their colors, and their use.

Joshua was also left to his own command, though really there wasn't much for him to do that wasn't reactive. Once his insects were released among the invaders, he would give them limited redirection as needed, but his main task would be to oversee the healing, reprovisioning, and repositioning of the mortal defenders of Sheol should the need arise. Piotyr knew the new troops, though dedicated and fiercely loyal to Joshua, would not stand long in battle. They were kept within the walls, armed to utilize arrow slits, murder holes, and otherwise attack without reprisal. Joshua had some elite troops with him, but their task was to keep him safe, not engage Abaddon's forces. His restoratives and elixirs had already done much to improve their chances, but they were to engage *after* the Sheol Legion, not before.

That left Han, and Piotyr had left him alone to do what he had to. Han would command nothing, and instead would be responsible for keeping Abaddon contained and at bay should he manifest as The Destroyer. All their preparations were for naught unless Han could do just that. If he had the chance, certainly he could use his power to kill troops, but Piotyr was not getting involved in that, the choice for how to use his abilities fell to Han and Han alone.

Sitting quietly with Ba'al Geir and Han, he smiled at them and raised a glass. He could hear the war drums coming from outside the gates. "To tomorrow, and war."

Han raised his own glass and returned the gesture. "To tomorrow, and war." He took a deep drink and sighed. He was already tired, and this was only the beginning. Joshua was right, he hadn't rested enough. He would do his best that night to sleep as long as he could. The marching would last all night, he calculated, but it was unlikely that Abaddon would be in position to attack before morning, and mid-morning at that. He just had too many troops to move.

"I'm going to turn in, Piotyr. I have one more stop to make, first, but then I need to rest. Is there anything else for me, tonight?" He didn't expect that there was, but it was polite to ask. Piotyr might not remember anything from before, but he was still his friend.

"No, Han. Get your rest. Have Ba'al Geir accompany you. These walls aren't safe."

Han agreed, though they had been safe since Kasim was attacked, he was sure the deaths in the city were not random. The attacks had slowed appreciably over the last week, though. A Legion captain there, two guards here, always delving, always at a place where he and Joshua *could* be but never were. Too bad there hadn't been a way to just end them. He assumed the Watchers were still trying, but Hell was not finished with the Templar. Han listened to the voice of Hell, and it kept him safe.

Ve'kal had occassionally questioned why his meetings were sudden, unexpected, and in random places, but she didn't need to know his reasons. He wasn't mad, not any longer, but telling anyone the evil of the place was communicating directly with his mind was not a way to instill confidence in his sanity.

He nodded to Piotyr. "Indeed. Good luck on the morrow. Call for me if he marches on us tonight."

"Of course. Rest well."

Han waved Ba'al Geir to him and the two men walked out of the plaza and down into the bowels of Sheol. He needed to deliver a letter to Kasim before he turned in, but he expected the man was still recovering in the sanitarium. Han marveled at how quickly Kasim's damaged body had repaired itself, but far more important was how fast his rehabilitation was getting him back to full strength. Han had a small part in that, but mostly it was Joshua. The man could heal anything, sure, but it looks like he could also make anyone whole in but a few short days.

"Don't go that way, Ba'al Geir, assassins await. Send word at the next checkpoint that I'm headed to the southern parapet to investigate the undead." *Strange, he did not sense that it was Grigori. Perhaps Apollyon has his own assassins.*

Ba'al Geir nodded and, to his credit, didn't even question him. Han had wondered at the wisdom of promoting the boy after Kasim killed his father, but Obistal had proved to be unique among all the Ba'al that Han had encountered in Hell. He had a good soul. It was difficult to think in those terms, but evil hadn't taken root in the boy... well young man at least. He was not a child.

Han had seen elements of goodness in Ve'kal and had even seen some aspect of care and nurturing from her when it came to her son. However, there was still a tremendous darkness within her and a hunger for power that dwarfed any kindness she may have. He theorized that Jacob had done something to spark that positive element but, now that he was dead, the growth had stopped. Obistal was different, and the boy Nezmyr as well. If they survived this, he wanted to study more of the Ba'al children recently freed from Thrall. He hoped that it was the case in all of them, and that their imprisonment and torment at the hands of the parasites who possessed their bodies had shielded them from becoming like their parents.

Small chance of surviving, but if they did, perhaps there was a seed of good which could be sown. Stranger things had happened, he was sure. Perhaps not many.

Ba'al Geir relayed the message at the next checkpoint, and Han then led them both on an indirect, safer path to his library and Joshua's lab. He had told Joshua what he needed to do many times over the week. Though tempted to have a drink and talk with his friend, he really needed sleep and couldn't spare the time. Joshua couldn't either, they were both worn down.

It was without incident that he and the Ba'al made their way to his warded wing of the cellars. He bade his Fallen companion good night and was surprised when the man smiled at him. "Good night, master Han. Rest well."

A seed of good indeed.

"Good night, get some sleep yourself. Tomorrow the tide shall rise."

He closed the door behind him as he walked through the first set of wards. He had attuned the wards to let himself, Joshua, Kasim, and Dhermina pass. Anyone else whom he did not specifically align with the ward prior to entering would be unable to pass. The city was ancient, however, and he feared secret passages or entrances, so within he had placed different traps and alarms.

If someone were to somehow pass the warded entrance without his attunement, they would not pass undetected. If the alarm raised didn't scare them off immediately, then the pain waves would follow and incapacitate anyone. He had left far deadlier ones in Kasim's room, but he and Joshua were certainly not unprotected here.

He yawned as he thought wryly that he could just kill anyone with a thought who managed to get here anyway, but one could never be too careful. Kasim had nearly died for thinking himself safe, and his friends had not been so lucky. He grabbed his letter from his robe and smiled to see that Kasim's door was closed. Hopefully he and Dhermina were both resting peacefully, and that he had eaten yet another large meal. Kasim would be needed before the end, though he didn't know it yet, and Han didn't know exactly *how*, either. His letter explained everything that he knew, though. He left it on a small table outside their door and placed an unlit candelabra over the corner. He yawned again as he made his way into his library and the bed he had there. God he was tired. Tomorrow. He could worry about things tomorrow.

He crawled into bed and pulled his blanket over his chest. His last thoughts as he drifted off were of the Patriarch. He hoped he was up to the same task.

A half-finished tray of meat and cheese sat on his table as he lay in bed while Dhermina dressed. He finally ran out of appetite, and he had no interest in finishing the food... and his love had even helped him with it. He felt well, and his convalescence felt complete. His muscles had filled back in, though he had to admit he was leaner than he had been before the attack. Sustenance, Prayer and Invocations both Arcane and Divine from Han and Joshua had brought him back to if not complete wellness, then very, very close. He was still tired, but even that was fading. On the morrow, he would be able to fight.

He watched Dhermina dress, but smiled as she stopped once her small clothes and tunic were on. She had said she heard someone, but once that was investigated, she would return. He didn't want to be without her on this last night.

"Anyone there?" Kasim asked as she opened the door.

"No, but there is a letter here. It looks to be from Han. Shall I bring it to you?"

Kasim thought briefly that the letter could be poisoned if the Watchers still wanted him dead. He shook his head though, no one other than the Templar could get in to deliver it without raising the alarm. The Seneschal and Ve'kal couldn't be here either unless Han allowed them specifically to accompany him through the wards. It was safe.

"Please. I wonder that he didn't just deliver it himself."

"You aren't the only one who is tired, my love. He probably wanted to sleep." He nodded as she handed him the letter and closed the door.

He stood to get a glass of chilled spiced tea, not bothering to dress as he did. Dhermina took off her clothes as well and hopped back under the blankets. There had been one more piece of his recovery that now, blessedly, had been addressed. Being intimate with her had been just as important for his body and soul as had everything else.

He had his tea as he sat by the lamp, turning it up slightly to see the letter. He read it slowly as he drank.

Dear Kasim,

I know you are feeling stronger every hour, and by the time Abaddon marches on Sheol you will feel well enough to join the battle. That is why this will be hard for you. You will feel ready, but I must ask you to stay behind for the time being. One more pair of hands, no matter how proficient at violence, will not turn the tide, and I know that we will have need of you before the end. It will not be far from the end, though. Do not think this insulting, or condescending, but I ask you to stay out of the battle for now. Rest, eat, do whatever you need to prepare, but do not join us yet. You are an assassin, not a soldier, and right now having you with us as one more sword-arm would be meaningless. Stay your hand for now, my friend. This battle will not be won or lost tomorrow. I will send for you.

Your friend and brother,
Han Fei-tze

"Hmm. Not what I expected, take a look." Standing, he handed her the letter and the lamp, and finished his tea as he waited.

"He means for you to sit out the battle?"

"Not all of it, by the sound of it, but yes, he doesn't want me to fight."

"Why not? You are worth many Legion."

"I think he is right, in that numbers on the ground won't mean much. Abaddon's Legion will be decimated just in reaching our walls, and we have enough defenders to repel them for months. This is a well designed city, and our defenses are strong. Not as strong as Haven, but enough to keep them at bay. I won't be of much use out there."

"What of the walls then? Surely Han fears for the Ba'al and Fallen to attack in mass?"

"He does. In that too, I would be of use, but it sounds like he doesn't want to risk me dying or being injured before something else he has planned."

"What do you think that is?"

"I'm not sure, but he mentions specifically that I am an assassin, so I imagine he has a target, or targets in mind."

"That seems rather overprotective."

"Yes, and though he isn't wrong in analyzing my skill set, I won't cower in here while the rest of the city bleeds. I will be careful, but tomorrow I will join them on the wall. The letter doesn't tell me to stay hidden, it just says to stay out of the battle. I believe I can do that, for now. Piotyr won't be in the battle either, unless things go poorly."

"So tomorrow, join them at the command tent?"

"No, I don't think so. They don't need any distractions. I will probably just observe the battle from the walls, and stay out of sight."

"No."

Kasim's eyebrows climbed high as she spoke. "No? Why not?"

"You don't see? The walls will be chaos tomorrow. There will be no better chance for the Grigori to strike you down."

He frowned. So that was what Han was doing. Keeping him away from any attempt to assassinate him. "I hadn't thought of that."

"Nor had I, but that is what this letter is. He is saying you are too important to die a meaningless death on the battlements."

He sighed. "I have a mind to disagree. Is that foolish pride?"

She smiled at him as she put the letter down and grabbed his hand. "Yes, Kasim. Listen to him. I don't want you to die, either, but beyond that, you *are* more important than the regular forces. If he has something in paticular for you, allow him to plan for it. Stay here. I'll let you know what transpires."

"I want to be very clear, right now, that if you are on the walls, I will be as well."

Dhermina frowned and Kasim knew an argument was coming. "The letter says nothing about me."

"I don't care. I will not leave your side once this starts. There will be no argument. If you go, I go."

"That isn't fair. You are keeping me here against my will, when I could help save lives."

He hated seeing her look at him that way but he wouldn't budge. "You are less of a soldier than I am, Dhermina. I may be specialized, but I lived and breathed warfare my entire life. I am no stranger to defending a city. You are. If Han thinks he can spare one soldier manning the parapets, he can spare two. I will not leave your side."

"You are being selfish. You would put yourself in harm's way for no reason, and suggest that I can't take care of myself."

"Dhermina, *thousands* of Ba'al could storm the walls tomorrow. If that happens your life will be measured in seconds. Do you not remember Astaroth? He nearly killed us both, and that was merely one of them, and one that wasn't fit to join the actual war at Abaddon's side. Death is coming to Sheol tomorrow, and if Han wants me to stay safe for something later in the siege? Then he damned well will do without you as well. I am being selfish? If you die I will be worthless, and I promise you my death will follow yours within heartbeats."

"So now you speak of suicide? You are better than this."

Kasim sighed and rubbed his eyes. He did not want to spend the night arguing. "You speak of what I am better than, yet you rush to join the battle for what reason?"

She was quiet, and Kasim didn't need his inner sight to know that he was exactly right. He could read her without trying. "That isn't it."

"So you rushing to draw infernal blood has nothing to do with the others from Sagarmatha being murdered?"

He had no other way to say it, but he still felt ashamed as her eyes watered. No, he would not feel guilty for speaking the truth. She was stubborn, but in this case, wrong.

"They were my brothers and sisters..."

"I know, my love. It also broke me when they died, in more ways than you know. I shall tell you more of what transpired between life and death some day , but suffice it to say that their deaths are as much a part of me as your love."

"I did not mean to imply that you didn't care."

He smiled and sat down next to her on the bed, holding her hand. "I know. I also know that vengeance is a powerful tool. In this case, trust and faith is more powerful. Stay with me for now. We will have our chance."

She was quiet for a moment. "I do not know if I can sit idly by as the siege begins. I might wish to remain by your side, but I don't think I can once the sounds of our men dying begin."

Kasim nodded, as another idea came to him. "There is a way we can both be satisfied. Do you remember the child I freed from Thrall in Tolmryk?"

"Of course, I had feared that night you would slay the demon children as well as their parents."

He moved behind her on the bed and wrapped his arms around her. He sighed as she relaxed in his embrace. No more fighting, then. "When I saw the girl, I was able to use my inner vision to see the parasite feeding on her soul. I was then able to leave my body completely, my spirit engaging in a psychic battle with the thing."

"You told me a little of this. Why do you bring it up now?"

"I can do it again, and see the battle in person even as our bodies remain safe here. If it goes badly, I can return and tell you, then I promise you we will join. Is that fair?"

She was quiet for a moment, then nodded her head. "That is fair. If it even looks like we have a chance of being overrun, we will help?"

"With all my heart, yes. I am no coward, Dhermina, but I will do what Han asks if he feels it gives us a greater chance for victory. Agreed?"

"Agreed."

He wasn't sure why he was so tired all of a sudden, but he felt it might have to do with fighting with her. He wasn't used to it, and did not care for it. She must have been tired too, as it was not long before she dozed off, her head resting peacefully on his chest. He took a bit longer for sleep to overtake him, but it came as well. His last thoughts before slipping into dream was that it was going to be very hard staying away.

Ba'al Mirish grinned as The High Sheol crept slowly into view. Ranks upon ranks of Legion marched down the hills surrounding the city, and blood would flow soon. He laughed out loud at the sight, bringing a few odd looks from nearby officers and a few Fallen. He scowled at them. How could they not feel the joy he was right now?

"Do you not see, Ba'al Keryx? We march on Sheol with The Destroyer, and he will be Shay'tan!" Mirish was able to elicit a wry grin from the giant black-winged man, which given his reputation for ill humor, was probably as good as he would get.

He didn't let it dampen his spirits though. Ba'al Apollyon was the greatest military mind Mirish had ever seen, save Michael himself, and was a far greater general than Lucifer or his heirs ever were. Lucifer was a terror in combat, as his sons had been, but none of them had the shrewd, keen mind of Apollyon. There was a bigger prize than Sheol tonight. That bitch Ve'kal was but a small bump to be easily crushed and smoothed out on the way to the real goal.

Haven *would* fall, he knew it. He felt it in his bones, that after the siege was over... if their pitiful resistance could even be called that... but after the siege was over, a small time to regroup and restore the city, then march back to the portal and finish this damned thing. Six centuries had come and gone, and it would finally be over.

He flew up a few dozen paces and laughed again at the endless array of troops. Legion mostly, but broken into units led by Fallen officers and Ba'al Overseers. The Destroyer would not arrive until midday tomorrow, but by that time the first ranks of the Legion would be in position to charge the walls. Hundreds of thousands would die, perhaps even millions, but Mirish secretly believed they could take Sheol without the waves of Ba'al that Apollyon held in reserve to breach the walls. Yes, the Templar would be adept at defending against a siege, but there were simply too many Legion to repel. Enough would get through to allow the siege engines to close, and once the ladders were out it was over. House Ve'kal would break, and her feeble claim to the Throne would be a joke told to amuse soldiers for millenia.

He smiled again. Or perhaps she would be forgotten completely. Once this was over, why not just write her out of history entirely? A better fate, to be sure, and a better one than she deserved. Pity she would likely be dead before she could be brought to justice. If she didn't die during the battle, she would be wise to kill herself and her son. If she didn't, she was a fool, and deserved the torment she would receive.

He broke himself out of his reverie and flew the several miles to the supply officers. He found Ba'al Hakkur and landed, nodding to the man in greeting. "It is time. Distribute the innoculations. Remember, no one is to drink until the order to charge is given." The special orders he had been given by Apollyon were very specific about when to distribute the plague vaccines.

"Very well, Mirish. It will be as ash-Shay'tan wills."

Mirish winced inside. That was an ill omen, and foolish. "He doesn't have the Throne yet, Hakkur. Don't curse our fortunes."

The smaller man snorted. "Choke on your superstitions. This battle is ours. I'll give the order, fear not."

Mirish ground his teeth. *Fear* not? Perhaps Hakkur would have an accident during the siege. "Just don't fail him. If they charge the city without the innoculations, you won't like what happens." He stopped and cocked his head to the side before smiling and laughing. "Neither will the Legion."

Hakkur laughed as well. At least the image of a million dying Legion falling over and becoming undead amused them both. "I won't. Is there anything else?"

Mirish shook his head and left. He flew to a high vantage point overlooking the valley. It was all here, within their grasp. He stood and patiently watched the inevitable march of doom. Not just Ve'kal's doom, but also that of Adam's Seed. Smiling as he envisioned salting Haven's earth... he sighed and allowed himself the pleasure of visualizing what the actual prize was. What it always had been, what they had fought for so long for.

Ve'kal, Haven... and Elysium.

chapter twenty-eight

And it came to pass, when Joshua was by Jericho, that he lifted up his eyes and looked, and, behold, there stood a man over against him with his sword drawn in his hand: and Joshua went unto him, and said unto him, Art thou for us, or for our adversaries?
- Joshua 5:13

Jacob landed, barely winded even after flying for hundreds of miles, in sight of a terrifying vision. "By God, there is no end to them."

Markov brushed himself off. Being carried by Jacob was not exactly a graceful or comfortable method of travel. "No, no there isn't. What are you going to do? Even in the Apotheosis, it will take forever to kill this many of them. They will crush the city while we are out here trying to drain the ocean with a teacup."

Jacob was dumbfounded. There were simply too many of them. He had no idea how to approach this.

"We need a plan, Jacob. Something is better than nothing."

"Unless that something gets you killed, Markov. I can summon the Soul Fire with impunity, you can't. You may be willing to sacrifice yourself again for humanity, but this army will outlast your Apotheosis, of that I am sure."

"Well, with two of us, we'll make a big dent. Yeah, I'll die, but you won't. Maybe we can slow them down enough for the defenders to hold them off?"

Jacob thought about it, but another thought entered his mind. If he manifested, so would Abaddon. He knew it in his heart. He and Markov wouldn't be able to engage the Legion. The Destroyer would come and the battle would be fought between the three of them.

"I think we should wait and see how the siege goes for at least a short while."

"Are you mad? Look at that army! It will be a massacre!"

"Hear me out. I think Abaddon is a cautious commander, and he will throw troops that he can afford to lose against Sheol, just to see the defenses and what he is up against. His vanguard will be his worst soldiers, and he expects them to die."

Markov frowned, then looked out across the valley. "That seems a bold gamble, are you sure?"

"I am sure, it is how he thinks. I know from my life as a mortal, and I feel it now as Shay'tan. He will be content to throw tens of thousands of lives away, though only the Legion, if it gives him a better sense of the real strength of this defense. If we attack now, we will carve through them like wheat, but we will be revealed, and he will attack us directly. I think more of his army stands to fall if we wait and see what my brothers can do."

Markov looked at him, then back at the army before throwing his hands up. "Well, fuck it then, what do we do, just sit and wait and eat some goddamn popcorn?"

Jacob blinked for a moment, then looked at his mortal companion. "What is popcorn?"

Piotyr stood on the walls, patiently waiting while the Legion marched ever closer. He was in full battle armor, though armed only with his greatsword. He didn't remember forging either, but Han and The First had both agreed that they were made by his hand. They fit perfectly and didn't smolder on his flesh as other untreated clothing and armor did. That greatspear that the undead wielded was also his, he was told, but he gladly lent it to the man. What was a Cavalier without a lance, after all?

He stood, hands clasped behind his back as he watched. The march played out in his mind exactly as he had foreseen. He smiled. No deviations yet, so no reason to change his plans. He had everything in place to utilize in due time, and it would all happen as it should. He watched as the first ranks of the Legion fanned out and crossed the first waterway. No talking, no posturing, just unyielding inevitability. The plague-walkers would erupt as soon as the first Legionnaire fell to Joshua's disease.

He waited, smiling, then his smile faded as they kept marching and no undead burst from the ground. A blinding flash burst across his eyes for a split second and he felt the course of the battle deviate. This was not what was supposed to happen. He cursed and bellowed at the top of his lungs. "Ready archers and artillery!"

Secretly Han had hoped for a slower start, had hoped that the Legion would stall and that Abaddon would close to discuss terms. For what, Han didn't really know, but he still hoped. He had hoped that the Legion would slowly cross the valley and, when suing for Sheol's surrender, the plague and Joshua's undead would begin their work in earnest.

It was not so. Han's throat seized and he felt a brief surge of panic rise as a collective roar powerful enough to rattle his teeth burst from the Legion. They didn't run, at least. He fought back his fear as they methodically crossed the valley floor in rank upon rank. He saw winged Ba'al in the skies, hundreds of them already in flight, though he knew tens of thousands more awaited in reserve. This was just a delving to see if Sheol would break under the first assault.

He clenched his jaw and waited. They crossed the first waterway. He couldn't help but hold his breath. Long seconds went by and his heart sank. It wasn't working. Sighing, he turned to the herald next to him. "Tell Joshua what has happened, and

Ba'al Geir to give this order. If one siege ladder touches Sheol, make ready. If two hold position on our walls, call up all reinforcements. If five pierce our defenses and their Legion manages to stand and hold on our ramparts? Have their men drink the restoratives."

Inwardly, he had a firm grasp on his terror. He had come this far, and as waves of arrows fell from the sky on the Legion below, he forced his breathing, raspy and jagged, to be as even as possible. There was no chance that this first push would reach the walls, but looking out at the sea of Abaddon's forces, Joshua had little reason to think the attack would stop for any reason.

He wondered at that. The first soldiers attacking the city in a siege had to know they had no chance of surviving. What could motivate them to march headlong into a meat grinder? Joshua looked down the walls to both sides, and it was an unbroken line of archers, siege equipment and engineers, and Legion infantry waiting for the combat to reach the parapets.

His undead were there as well, though not the masses that were sitting unused in the fields. The damned Legion must have developed an innoculation of some kind. That was a miscalculation, and one he hoped didn't cost them everything. His walkers along the wall would help, but they hadn't been bound with the other parasitic undead like the ones down below had.

The first rows fell to the hail of arrows, but he frowned as the numbers game played out. More of them survived than would be acceptable from each volley. Explosions rocked the advancing waves as the trebuchet and catapult shots fell on Abaddon's Legion. Some standard siege missiles landed as well, but Sheol's surplus souls had largely been put to use bound to siege ammunition. Acid, hellfire, and concussive force fell in equal measure to the iron and steel.

Thousands died, and thousands marched behind them. No Ba'al were in the initial assault. Just infantry, and swarms of them. Joshua counted ranks before the first siege ladder could be seen. It was close to twenty. Each line had to have ten thousand men, at least. They stretched the entire length of the city. Could Abaddon really just march two hundred thousand men to their deaths just to bring the first breaching equipment to the walls?

He sighed as he realized he could probably lose twice that many and it wouldn't matter in the slightest. In the distance, almost back to the hills over the miles of valley floor, he saw giant brown pieces of something being assembled. Siege towers he assumed. If those didn't take long to assemble, and the infantry could close all the way to Sheol on this first push?

Though he had faith in the strength of his mortal followers, and the Sheol Legion would let blood flow like rivers... things would go badly if the fight went to the walls within the first day. Their elixirs would last for hours, so at least The Destroyer would find the walls would not yield simply because his army crested their ramparts.

That was a losing venture, though. The defense of the city required the virulence of the plague as well as the infected walkers in the tunnels beneath the valley. If that cascade didn't start, they were doomed. The archers at least had been trained very well, he noticed. The fourth rank of Legion finally died, but it was only a handful of archers that he could see that had fired at the same rank more than twice.

Piotyr must know what he was about in this sort of thing. Maybe each archer had a certain number of shots he was supposed to fire at the advancing rank before moving on to the next? That would probably cut down on arrows being wasted by two defenders shooting the same target.

The fifth rank he noticed, unfortunately, actually reached firing range for their own archers. Only five ranks in, and Abaddon was in striking range. Only a handful from that rank got close enough, and Joshua blinked as they fell instantly to crossbow bolts. Every fifth Legion infantry had stepped forward and wielded a heavy crossbow.

This was an expected part of the defense then. The sixth rank closed, and also died to a man. The pace of slaughter slowed, though. Ranks seven and eight closed, and men still stood from both as the numbers swelled below the walls. The archers maintained their rotation, and the crossbowmen thinned as fast as they could, but ladders were inching forward. The walls would see combat before the end of the day.

Kasim sat cross-legged on the floor as Dhermina nervously paced around the small room. He thought of asking her to be still, that the distraction made it harder for him, but he didn't want to invite another argument. It could be harder for him to let go, it was alright.

There were pages outside of the library that they could ask for news, but the battle was so new he didn't want to increase his anxiety at all. He let it be, for now, and sat while he evened his breathing and let his consciousness drift.

It was a process that was graceful and easy. When he did it at Tolmryk, he had done so really without thinking... instinctually. Here, he was anxious and distracted, but he still was able to ease himself out of his physical shell without strain. He slipped away out of the room, noticing that Dhermina was also anxious and nervous on his way out.

The wards were visible while he was moving as his spirit. Giant webs of blue and purple energy guarded each threshold to the doors as he passed through them effortlessly. Physical or spiritual did not appear to matter, as he was still Kasim.

He made haste up through the tunnels and out into the plaza, finding his way easily to the closest tower leading up to the ramparts. He spared a quick glance here and there to gauge morale, and for the most part, it was holding. There were a lot of green troops that had swelled the Sheol Legion's ranks, and some were too old or too young. A nervousness ran in many of them which would be of worry should the battle go too poorly too soon, but they were not in danger of breaking, at least not yet.

He saw Piotyr's offspring coiled on the southern parapets, with two very powerful spirit forms mounted on their backs. One glowed a brilliant gold so bright it hurt to look at, and the other, while certainly not blinding, was also a very bright bronze hue. He couldn't see any flesh underneath the aura, but he assumed it was The First and the other Plague Lord Joshua had called Secundus. They must have been held in reserve for another portion of the siege defense, as for now they watched in what he could see was stoic patience.

As he crested the ramparts, the morale and focus of the Legion went up tenfold at least. These were men and women who knew what was at stake and were prepared to fight for it. Archers, engineers, undead, Fallen overseers, and an occassional Ba'al were in orderly units, raining fire and death upon the massive sea of invaders below.

He tried not to focus on the sheer size of the invasion force but he was taken aback at the endless ocean of spirit forms moving unwaveringly towards the city. There were so many he couldn't really get a sense of distinct forms, but he did see distinct, darker and larger souls towering above the flood. Ba'al, he assumed, though from this distance he couldn't see much distinction.

Something had gone poorly already, he saw. There should have been the sick and decaying spirits of the undead already tearing through the enemy ranks, easily discernible, yet he saw nothing of the sort. Why not? A critical portion of their battle plan involved those undead, and more importantly, the ones infused with Han's parasites, and the plague.

Scowling, he hopped down into the fields to investigate. Something had gone terribly wrong.

Mirish was getting annoyed arguing with Ba'al Ezliel about the battle. The idiot kept complaining about how many troops they were losing. Was he blind?

"For the last time, and then I'm finished with this, the battle is going *better* than anticipated. We have already reached the castle, and our ladders will be up by nightfall. Abaddon had anticipated that a full three days might have gone by breaking their archery range, and by then the innoculations would have begun wearing off."

"I understand that, Mirish, but how are we supposed to finish Haven without the Legion? They will all be dead first, at this rate."

Sighing, he rubbed his eyes and the bridge of his nose. "No, they won't, but many of them will, and that's fine. We might lose a few months rebuilding enough of an infantry to crush them, but what is a couple of months? Once this is handled, there is no more opposition, anywhere. We'll be there soon enough, Ezliel. Just shut up and enjoy the moment."

Jacob watched with dismay as the rate of stopping the invading ranks slowed. The sun dipped lower and lower towards the horizon, and before dusk there would be siege ladders in place and towers close enough to fire upon the defenders. He looked at Markov and he saw it etched on the younger man's face. The battle went poorly.

"When do you want to get involved?"

Technically, he was the older man he supposed. It was hard to remember that. "Not until Abaddon's forces take and hold a section of the wall. I know that sounds harsh, but I want to maximize our chances at making a difference."

"It's your show, Merethius. Shay'tan."

The title made him feel awkward. Shame was there in a small way, shame that he was now that which the Templar had fought against for centuries. Shame even more for the pride he felt. He *was* the Shay'tan, and he could do powerful and incredible things. "Then we wait, for now."

It was quiet between the two of them for long minutes as they watched. The battle wasn't going well, but it wasn't over for Sheol. They fought well, and effectively... just slowly losing ground.

"It's corn, dried out and separated from the cobb. You then pop it in a pot and eat it. It's fucking incredible. I'll show you someday."

Jacob turned to look at Markov and had to laugh. Popcorn. Someday indeed.

It was almost dark the first time a siege ladder made contact with the upper ramparts. Giant barbed hooks attached it to the stone and Abaddon's Legionnaire did their best to scamper over the top to make an insertion point to break the siege. More ladders crept closer, but the first one could have been a tipping point. Piotyr need not have worried, as the Legion on the top of the ladder lasted less than a heartbeat before falling to a hail of crossbow bolts. More scampered up but never managed to take a step past a ring of steel which butchered them instantly. His visions had not changed much since the initial chaotic torrent when the undead failed to rise out of the valley, but they were still dismal. He supposed no critical variables had altered, though every time Han blasted a ladder or tower he felt a blurring of future memory for a split second. Otherwise, the plan was mostly unchanged over the past several hours.

It was good to make the undead the first line of melee defense. The more they killed, the stronger they would become. Foolish to think that the mortal defenders would not be needed as well before it was over, but for now, it was to their advantage to preserve all of their resources. He didn't want to utilize one ounce of strength that he didn't have to. The Ba'al and Fallen coming to wing over their walls was still a far greater threat.

He saw a group of undead hack away at the barbs hooked to the walls and sever them. With a push, the first siege ladder tumbled back to the ground, taking dozens of Legion with it. The second was already touching the wall further down the ramparts. The first one *was* the tipping point. The battle was truly joined.

Han spared a small amount of strength and blasted apart the first siege tower that was completed. His lance of psychic energy ripped the structure apart like leaves. He was more concerned with how the well of suffering felt afterwards and was relieved to not feel any appreciable difference. Still, looking at the next fifty towers, he checked his optimism. He would have need of every drop of it before the end, and blowing apart one of them did nothing to slow the rest of Abaddon's advancement.

He was also worried, as even though the well itself did not feel to have dimished, he could also feel that it was not infinite. It was the changes he had implemented. Sheol had once been a place of eternal damnation and torment, which in turn endlessly supplied the pool of suffering he could draw on.

He had put a stop to all of that, had treated its people justly, and freed the innocent from the dungeons. Hope bloomed in Sheol for the first time, and though he felt very good about what he had done, he was now paying the price. Kindness has lessened their war resources. Was it better than the alternative?

He shook his head as a fifth siege tower made it to the wall. Technically it was over the twentieth, but this was now the fifth that was still upright and attached. They had destroyed more than a couple of dozen, but the rate was increasing, not slowing. Three more were already near, and Legion poured up the five in place. The defenders held, but couldn't sever the hooks fast enough to keep the Legion from advancing.

Han blasted the closest one into oblivion, and feeling that their morale was critical, he blasted another one as well. The surging defenders closed to the remaining three and in a frenzy of blood and steel pushed Abaddon's forces off the wall and sent the ladders crashing back into the swarm below. Archers still rained death on the ranks advancing, and artillery still crushed and impaled Legion by the thousands.

The three new ladders touched the walls at nearly the same time, and another four were not far behind. Han sighed and ground his teeth. He didn't feel much of a loss in power, but he *did* feel it. He had to be careful. More ladders were in reach of the walls, hundreds it seemed, and dozens of siege towers could be within reach while the night was still young. Midnight, perhaps.

He clenched his fists and watched as the defenders did what they had to and he kept his power in check. He had to be patient.

Joshua knew that it was foolish to hope for a respite at night, but he had to admit a small part of him stupidly hoped that darkness would slow the assault. If anything, it made it worse. Torches were lit, but Legion and Fallen alike could see almost perfectly in the dark. He had to Invoke Night Sight, but between that and the torches it was just like midday for him, if of slightly higher contrast and less colorful hue.

The ladders were no longer an issue, they simply were in place and would not be repelled. They kept coming as well, but the larger issue was that the siege defenders were now pressed into melee across most of the wall. He knew his men at some of the insertion points would have already taken their elixirs, but he had given the order to hold out until the last possible moment. Some areas were not yet under assault directly and any seconds ticking away on the duration of the restorative would be seconds later needed and not available.

Still, minutes were in question, not hours. Han had detonated another of the siege towers, but they crept forward like a creaking, inevitable doom. Each one had to have hundreds of Legion ready to pour out over the walls, and the undead, though becoming more powerful with every sword stroke landing true, could not hope to hold out alone against the tide rising against them. The mortals would be fighting for their lives before dawn. Some of them already were.

He cursed as he once again lamented their battle plan. They had feared an innoculation within Abaddon's forces, had even expected it was a possibility, but the battle was nearly half a day old, and Joshua couldn't believe that the disease had failed so completely. Abaddon must have had very skilled or powerful apothecaries or physicians in his service. If the plague didn't work, the cascade wouldn't start, and the most powerful of the undead wouldn't have their criteria for their orders met. There wasn't anything else they could do right now, as their other defenses would hinder their own defenders as much as the invading Legion. Han could still help, but if he exhausted his strength and power now, they were doomed anyway. The Ba'al, or The Destroyer, would sweep them aside like dust.

He stood far away from the combat. He was well aware of his own martial skills, and he would do no one any favors by wielding a sword in combat. He knew which end went where, but he had no natural talent for it. He would do better in the plaza at the medical center he had set up. He had waited as long as he could watching the siege play out. Soon there would be the first large influx of wounded arriving. Defenders who were either too late to consume their elixirs, or too soon and got hurt after they wore off. The towers inched closer, they would start cresting the walls within the hour. Han could stop them, but he wouldn't, nor should he. If they couldn't repel Abaddon's infantry for even a day, the battle was lost. It might be tomorrow rather than tonight, but it was still lost. Wish a wistful shake of his head, he left the wall and went to the triage area. Everything was crumbling.

Kasim didn't know what was supposed to have happened, but it was certainly not this. He looked over the endless sea of Abaddon's forces, and knew that this was wrong. The first two siege towers had been engulfed in flames from Sheol's siege defenses, and a third had been detonated by Han he assumed. Two more now sat open, their bridges spanning the gap to the ramparts and their housing empty. Both the towers were on fire, but it hadn't been enough and hundreds of Legion had poured out onto the walls. Kasim couldn't see how that fight went, but he hoped and trusted that it was being contained. Frowning, there were another half dozen towers that would engage Sheol within a quarter hour. Another thirty within the hour.

It was happening, the city was being slowly overrun. They hadn't been able to stop them without the undead and the plague beginning to decimate the forces behind the siege line. The plague must have failed to take root, which meant there was an innoculation of some kind. Kasim had to believe that they couldn't count on it then, which left the undead laying in wait under the earth. They had been instructed to wait until the plague began to work before emerging... but these were mindless undead, not the intelligent ones that waited at Sheol with Piotyr's drakes. They wouldn't change their plans, and even if they had been given a contingency plan to begin their attack, who knew if they were capable of understanding?

A worse thought occurred to him as he feared that maybe they didn't have orders at all. If they were truly mindless, it would have had to be external stimuli which caused them to act. It wouldn't have been the plague itself, he didn't think. They already had the disease and wouldn't know the difference between it being active around them or not. No, it had to be something else, something simpler. Dhermina and Joshua had set this up as a trap. What did traps need? Some sort of triggering mechanism or bait.

He ran swiftly through the ranks, dodging infernal forms that were far too arrogant and confident in their emotions. It was easy to read the morale of Abaddon's Legion, it was soaring... full to bursting. They were winning and they knew it. He could have probably killed a few of them, but it would have taken time and energy and made no difference in the long run. No, there was something else he wasn't seeing, something else he needed to do.

He slipped slightly as he ran, not on actual terrain, as his spirit form was weightless and didn't need traction... but rather the height of the earth dropped and he realized he was now standing in a water channel. He didn't get wet, as his incorporeal body had no mass to attract any other substance, but he did notice that he was lower and that the brackish, foul substance he was knee deep in was water. Scowling, he moved across the channel and took one step up the other side when a lancing pain shot up through his foot and he yelled in agony.

He looked down and some... *thing* had grabbed onto his foot and was now chewing on it. He kicked out with his other foot and gasped in relief as the black, shapeless mass that was attacking him released his foot allowing him to scramble, hobbling, up the embankment and stare in horror at a seeping wound in his spirit. How was that possible? He had no blood in this form, yet it was leaking out of him the same.

He shuddered in terror. It wasn't blood... it was his soul. That thing had ripped open his essence and it was now trailing behind him as he stumbled away. He hadn't gone five steps when he was relieved to see the seeping stop, but then his heart froze as a hideous black shapeless entity rose up out of the soft earth under the water and moved towards him.

It wasn't entirely shapeless, Kasim saw, but it was shifting, changing forms. It definitely had eyes and a mouth though, and Kasim knew without a doubt he was now being hunted by the thing. He hobbled away through the pain and was relieved that as he moved the pain diminished and his form healed itself somewhat. Looking back, he was also surprised to see that the creature hadn't moved. It strained against some invisible tether as if...

He understood. *That* was one of the things Han had bound to the undead, it just couldn't escape its host and its host was still underground. It couldn't leave unless the undead beneath it did. He laughed then. Traps needed bait. Kasim could run, now, if a little pained. He got close to the creature and smiled as the thing snarled and lashed at him.

He didn't have a mouth here, but he projected his thoughts out of his mind as loudly, clearly, and mockingly as he could. *Come and get me, little wraith. Tell your friends, too. There is food out here for all of you, you just have to reach for it.*

The thing strained and stretched, and Kasim saw other black shapes emerge from the earth as well. He watched very carefully. The first crack of earth was displaced as something underneath it struggled to emerge. He had done it.

🛡️ ☪️ 🏳️ ⚕️ 🔺

Ve'kal was seeing her life collapse in front of her. She had been a fool to trust the Templar. Even now, she could see Han's observation area and Piotyr's command pavillion on the walls and couldn't feel anything other than disgust for them.

Han had blown up a few pieces of siege equipment, but the walls were slowly being overrun. She had been worried about the

Ba'al? She snorted bitterly. She would be dead long before a single Fallen flew over the walls of Sheol. What was the point of any of it? Why had Jacob even come to her if the result was worse than where she was at her estate?

Nezmyr was freed from Thrall, which had been wonderful, and the Shay'tan was dead... but she had hours left to live at best unless she took her child and fled into the wilderness. She would be hunted until the end of her days, and so would her child... all because these damned mortals couldn't finish what they started.

She sighed and fought off tears as she watched another tower crest the rampart and drop another hundred legion on the laps of her defenders. When should she seek out Nezmyr and end his life? She wouldn't let the Ba'al have him, any more than she would let them have her. Torture and torment were the only possible outcomes from her capture... for her and anyone in her house. They would probably even kill her cook. Haj'ur, too.

It would be soon, then. She would watch another hour, less if Abaddon's Legion pressed further and faster, but then she would find her child and give them both a philter of the poppy. Oblivion and death would be preferable to what else awaited them. It was over.

She watched stoically as the battle continued to go against her. She wanted to draw steel and join the fight. A clean death in combat would be more honorable than suicide, but she couldn't take the risk that Nezmyr would be captured. Her job now was to keep him from being brutalized, not kill a handful of Legion from a force of millions.

Time went faster than she expected, and with a heavy heart she made ready to leave. It was time to end it. She turned to leave the ramparts and was surprised to see a human mortal standing before her. He had two swords strapped to his body, one a shorter blade on his side and another long blade on his back. She thought he was there by mistake, but when she moved towards him he didn't yield.

"Too soon, my lady, far too soon."

That voice... he knew her, and she knew him. It was one of the two madmen who were at the Throne after Jacob killed the Shay'tan. What was he doing here?

"Get out of my way, whoever you are."

"Look past the walls and tell me you still want to kill yourself and your child, or Nezmyr."

Idiot, Nezmyr *was* her child. What was he babbling about. She thought about drawing on him, but he had humbled her before, and she was in no mood for it to happen again. She glared at the impudent dog and walked back to her vantage point. She looked past the melee on the rampart and instead looked to the fields below.

She saw nothing at first, just the endless advance of the Legion of The Destroyer. Wave upon wave of lethal steel crushing her forces one rank of soldiers at a time. She seethed, and then her breath caught. She sprinted to an area with no ladder close to it and grabbed the stone in a death grip as she looked out into the sea of approaching doom.

There was chaos spreading back in the ranks, and although she couldn't tell at first what was going on just by looking at it, it was spreading along the waterways. The undead had begun their attack. She wept in relief, and began sobbing softly as she felt a faint ray of hope blossom in her mind.

"Thank God." She didn't even realize the irony as she spoke, trembling with relief.

chapter twenty-nine

Regard your soldiers as your children, and they will follow you into the deepest valleys; look upon them as your own beloved sons, and they will stand by you even unto death.
- Sun Tzu

"Holy Shit! Look at those motherfuckers die!" Markov was nearly bounding with enthusiasm as he said it and Jacob was also feeling an incredible sense of relief. So much that Markov's bizarre words didn't even phase him.

"I don't know what happened, but that just saved the city." He wasn't exaggerating. An hour ago, it was over. Jacob had been just about ready to attack when something started reaping through the invasion force like a scythe. It had a very slow beginning, but sped up like a boulder falling down a mountain.

It was still hard to see exactly what was occuring, though with far-sight Invoked he could see Joshua's walkers wreaking havoc on the enemy ranks. "This looks planned. I'm not sure at all why they would wait this long to launch an offensive like this, but I don't imagine this was incidental."

"Yeah, I don't know. About time, though. The walls were going to be overrun. Still might, if those things push away from the walls and not towards them."

Jacob frowned, and looked intently at the developing attack patterns... or lack thereof. Markov was right, it could go either way. It looked as if the walkers were spiraling out of several central lines, but did not appear to be making any concerted push back towards the walls. The damage was devastating, but the defenders on the wall were hard pressed.

"You are right. If those lines don't fall back towards the city, they will still lose the walls. We'll need to intervene if they don't do something quickly."

Markov nodded at him and clapped his shoulder. "Well you didn't want to miss the entire battle, did you?"

Piotyr's mind swam as entire branches of the outcome of the battle ripped through his thoughts and vanished, superceded by a host of new ones as the walkers shredded the enemy ranks. He looked out from the ramparts and smiled, blood dripping off his blade. The fighting hadn't been the fiercest at his section of the wall, but it hadn't avoided it, either.

The entire tide had shifted in a few short minutes, and now the Legion would be hard-pressed to keep up the pace of the assault with the undead carving them up along ten different lines. The waterways had finally yielded half of what they were supposed to. He didn't know why the plague hadn't worked, but now at least they had their shock troops breaking the siege momentum.

Unfortunately, that didn't do anything for the troops already on the walls or the tens of thousands closer to Sheol than the undead reavers behind them. He briefly contemplated signalling for Sammael, and as he did more possibilities of the outcome flowed through his mind in blindingly fast flashes of blood and fire. It was too soon, and he would need to hold them in reserve for now.

The defenders *had* to hold, and they had to do it without reinforcements for now. Yes, this helped, but without the plague to accelerate things it was still a losing numbers game. The Ba'al were still coming, and he needed his reserves for them.

More torrents of outcomes passed through his head, this time far more favorable. He smiled again. There was something he could do now, though.

Bellowing as loud as he could to be heard above the melee, his shout caused several nearby Sheol defenders, mortals of course, to flinch and stare at him in surprise. "Cavalry! Sweep the base of the city!"

Han's hands shook in relief as the defenders finally pushed the invasion force back to the edge of the ramparts in his section of the wall. God, but it had been close. He had helped sparingly, only attacking when he saw an imminent risk of a break into the city proper... but there had been several instances. He could feel a pronounced difference in the remaining pool of destructive power left in the city. Even worse, as hope blossomed in the men, every time they pushed back an advance or Piotyr's wyrms incinerated another fifty men... as that hope surged he felt Sheol's power ebb.

He was acutely concerned that even now, with the Legion of Abaddon stymied, the battle loomed impossible to win. Even assuming they could stop the Ba'al, it was up to *him* to hold The Destroyer at bay. He hated to admit it, but it might only be possible if the defenders begin to be routed and despair takes over. It was a very difficult balancing act. On the one hand, there had to be enough physical resistance to the Legion and then also to the Ba'al when they came to not simply be swept aside like ants. Balanced to that was that the defenders could not feel so much hope that Han's power source dwindled too quickly to hold off Abaddon.

He couldn't worry about it yet, but he feared he would soon. The battle soon changed focus, as Sheol had held. With fire and steel, the last of the siege ladders currently on the wall were dislodged, and the advance was not strong or fast enough to crest the walls again. Han allowed himself a nervous smile, but anxiety spiked in his heart with every cheer the men and women on the walls gave out. He could feel the sea of pain recede. Not much, but it was noticeable.

Siege towers dotted the plains still, but they stood impotently unmoving without enough Legionnaire to push them. The force below was by no means broken. Millions of Legion still stood, and the vast majority would still be living hours, if not days from now, but the additional lines of combat had been opened and it was fiece and bloody. Han's wraith and leech undead were tearing through Legion fast enough that the onslaught against the walls had slowed to a trickle. They would hold. Now the only question was what would Abaddon do about it?

● ☾ ♜ ⚕ ▲

Having returned to the walls briefly, when he heard the ladders had been dislodged, Joshua felt a perverse pride as he watched the walkers etch out curved lines of death from their points of origin along the waterways. He and Dhermina and the engineers had placed them effectively to create maximum disruption and carnage to the passing siege force. The lines of the rapidly evolving and improving undead were like snakes crossing desert sands, ess shaped waves in the ranks rippling with screams and agony.

He was their father, and though he was not a violent man, he felt immense satisfaction watching them work so effectively on the plains. One last wave of hot air ripped the sweat from his face and dried his moist lungs, and he saw Ulis and Aruc finish their strafing run before banking back over Sheol to land on the southern parapets. He felt a brief pang of sadness that Piotyr did not remember them. He imagined the pride the Hellfire Knight would feel as something akin to what Joshua did watching his walkers.

Partially anyway... Han had infused them with the other creatures... and it wasn't as if they were actually his progeny, but he still felt proud. More so of The First and now Secundus. He wondered if there would be more like them after the battle below?

He shuddered to think about The First with a wraith bound to him, or a blood-drinker. The man was already lethal in war. He coughed for a moment, but it was subdued and controlled, not the hacking, debilitating cough he usually suffered. His restoratives had helped him immensely.

His smile faded as he watched the plains because it was clear there had been an order for the Legion to stop advancing. Abaddon's forces to a man turned away from the walls of Sheol and either fell back to their lines on the far side of the valley if they were close or converged on the undead if they weren't. Abaddon was no fool, and once it was clear he couldn't take the city with his initial push of infantry, he had changed his tactics. Joshua swallowed past a lump in his throat the size of a walnut. He didn't fear for his undead, they would live or die as needed, and they could hold their own against a far superior force... even surrounded, for some time.

No, he feared for what was to come next. If the Legion slowed their advancement, that meant The Destroyer would be moving onto his next course of action to take the city. One of two things was coming, and soon. Either terrified him.

He had finished his run and now loped with ease back towards Sheol. Kasim had lured the last of the entrenched plague-walkers out of their warrens successfully and now returned to tell Dhermina of the progress of the siege. He looked behind him often. He was faster than those things bound to the flesh of the walking corpses, but he didn't want to be caught unaware, lest his soul be rent again. He had no idea where Han had found those things, but it was somewhere dark and terrible indeed.

He smiled, though, as he glanced behind him and saw three of the things shred Legion like a cook chopping cabbage. He was halfway back to Sheol when the battle changed. He could feel it in the air before his eyes made sense of it, but the Legion of Abaddon had shifted tactics. They no longer pressed the city, instead falling back to either surround the undead or moving quickly away from those battle-lines back to their staging area.

Worse, he saw most of the Legion fall behind tower shields and form shield rings around whatever undead could be surrounded. It was containment then. They couldn't match them in violence, so they would stymy their offense. Abaddon was shrewd, Kasim had to grant him that. He glanced to make sure he was clear from any wraiths at the moment, and worriedly watched the far side of the valley from the small hill he was on. He stared, and then glowered. Dhermina would have to wait, Fallen and Ba'al were taking to the skies by the thousand.

Ezliel was laughing at him, which made Mirish' blood boil. "Are we done enjoying the moment, yet?"

The order had come much sooner than he had expected, but with the stalling of the assault, it wasn't surprising. Every Ba'al there knew that they would likely be the ones breaking the city. The Legion was fine for what it was, but these Templar knew their way around a siege. The chances of their land infantry winning the battle on their own were low. The fact that they almost had was far more surprising than Abaddon now signaling the Ba'al to get ready.

"I'll enjoy this more than watching half bloods, mongrels, and uppity mortals take the credit for our victory. The Legion is meant to be thrown into the grinder. *We* shall liberate the Throne from that bitch usurper, Ve'kal."

A low, dissonant horn called out and quieted much of the din. Once to ready arms.

"Oh I agree, but I did say that this would not be so easy. We *did* lose too many troops to finish it quickly. It was always going to be our blades that ended this, Mirish."

The horn called again, Mirish and Ezliel joined a chorus of bared steel and tightened leather. Hundreds of thousands of Fallen and Ba'al awaited the final horn call, which would cause them to take flight and storm the city. It would fall within hours.

"You are right, you should tell Apollyon that, once this is over." *Damned fool. I hope he dies early on, officer or not.*

Ezliel snorted, but didn't respond. He apparently *did* know when to shut up.

The horn called again and Ba'al Mirish was about to ask Ezliel if he fancied a wager when the other man cursed and slapped his neck. Mirish's eyes rose as Ezliel's rolled back in his head and he fell over, dead.

"What..." was all he could get out of his mouth as he saw Ba'al fall left and right. Hundreds... *thousands* fell over without a single blade being drawn against them. Mirish spun around and saw nothing but Legion support around them. No Sheol forces, no Templar magic that he could see. Simply Legion, yet while many Ba'al took wing, many also fell over dead.

He took flight himself, and with no idea what was happening, he flew high up and looked for commanders and officers up in the sky to see what was wrong. He looked for a long moment before finding another of his rank, Talthael. Not the most powerful among them, and like him not an officer, but she was known for her cunning and speed.

"Talthael, what is happening?"

"I don't know, but I'm headed to Sheol anyway. This is nothing, a drop in an enormous bucket. Come Mirish, don't let your reputation precede you. For once in your life, be bold and not cautious."

The comment rankled him, but it really was a minor reduction in their numbers. Not even one in ten had fallen, though it bothered him that it was right after the third horn call and appeared very coordinated. He frowned, and looked at Talthael flying rapidly towards the city. He made to follow, but not as quickly. Something was wrong, he just didn't know what.

chapter thirty

*I am come as Time, the waster of the peoples, ready for that
hour that ripens to their ruin. All these hosts must die; strike, stay
your hand - no matter.*
- The Vision of God: Bhagavad-Gita

"That was flawlessly executed. Do you think they realize what
has happened?" Jacob watched with a keen eye for any signs of a
change in the attack or for any reluctance from the Ba'al and
Fallen. He could see none, the winged monsters blacked out the
sky with no pattern or discernible order to it.

"No, it doesn't look like it. God, those assassins are good."

Jacob could only agree. The timing had been perfect, and as
soon as the signal to attack had come, the Grigori had decapitated a
significant portion of the command structure. He could see it here,
from a distance, though he doubted in that dense madness of the
attacking force if anyone noticed the chaos. A few pockets were in
their proper ranks, which was to be expected. The Watchers would
have been unable to kill all of the leadership, but they had done an
incredible job of thinning the officers.

The force now was still incredibly overwhelming, but
disorganized. That was critical and an advantage the defenders
could exploit. He had seen it far too many times at Haven and
other Sanctuaries in his life. The enemy was overconfident when it
had superior numbers and was not cautious. They would expect

their sheer size to overwhelm the city, and if Piotyr was leading the defense, the man would not break. This was about to get very bloody for Abaddon, unless something was terribly wrong with his brothers.

"Yes. Yes they are. Now look. Disorganized, overconfident. Abaddon probably didn't put too much care into a redundant command structure. He will regret that, shortly."

"Do you want to move in?" Jacob could hear the excitement in Markov's voice. It *was* hard to remain on the side, merely watching it play out, but it was still not time.

"Soon, I imagine. When this push also fails to break the city, Abaddon will be forced to adapt his strategy. When that happens, the door will open for us to settle this. It may be awhile, though. There are many Fallen."

Markov scowled, but nodded. Jacob understood. He wanted to be there as well.

Piotyr felt the tide change in his mind like a bolt of lightning. Something had just happened to tilt the odds more towards Sheol, though it was still an uphill struggle. The sea of Ba'al approaching them made it clear that bodies were about to litter the ramparts, but it was not as desperate as it was even one minute before. He had allies nearby, of that he was certain.

It was time to open the floodgates. If they couldn't stop this tidal wave, it was all over. He grabbed the signal horn from off the table and gave it two short, low blasts.

That was all he needed to communicate. Both Han and Joshua knew exactly what he meant, and that he needed it immediately. He did not have long to wait. Han did his part, and from what he could see, Joshua did his as well.

The noise hit like a storm. A buzzing and vibrating tornado of vermin burst from tunnels prepared in the hills outside the city. It spread like the darkening of night itself through the incoming onslaught of Fallen. He smiled as more tangents of positive outcomes danced through his mind, his artillery and defense orders changing accordingly in his mind as the scenes became certain in his thoughts.

These were not beings new to warfare, but no creature alive that he knew of could easily ignore billions of swarming insects swirling around their face. There were so many, flight itself became challenging and the rush of incoming Ba'al slowed, not stopping, but slowing. It was impossible to tell what exactly was happening in that cloud, but he imagined it involved a lot of yelling, cursing, blindness, and confusion. Certainly not enough, but it gave him precious time.

He again raised the horn to his lips and sounded one long high note. Ba'al Geir looked at him in confusion, as did the pages, aides, and servants in the command area. Only a handful of men knew what that signal meant, by design.

The swirling maelstrom of chaos above Sheol lingered, still, for what Piotyr felt to be the longest handful of heartbeats in his life. Time slowed for him as he felt for the tremors below that would signal what he hoped was their salvation.

It was a sight that was so awesome and terrible that it left him momentarily speechless. He knew it was coming, and it still took his words right out of his mouth. The first to be consumed by the Frost wyrms were spared from the horror of their impending death by the thick veil of the insects, but Piotyr could still hear faint screams as some of the Ba'al must have seen them.

Sammael's forces erupted from the ground in an explosion of earth, frost, and screeching roars. Piotyr felt his heart surge with adrenaline as he saw the forces, *his forces*, emerge from the ground beneath the plains of Sheol to devour his enemies whole. Thousands of Ba'al died in the initial push, but Piotyr was not foolish enough to think a few score wyrms would tip the balance. Yes, each one of them ate Ba'al by the handful, but that would not matter. The Host of angels that burst forth with them, however, made a far larger difference.

Sammael's Host was perhaps no more than a thousand, but with the wyrms, the carrion swarm, the erupting earth still raining down on their enemies? It was a slaughter, at least for the moment. Piotyr had prepared for this well and knew that surprise as well as visibility would play a crucial role in this part of his defense.

The angels all wore veils or masks that would keep the vermin at bay and Piotyr had also provided a repellant in the form of a resinous musk that every single Fallen Angel under Sammael's command had rubbed their armor down with, as well as that of the wyrms. Joshua's creation, though he had no idea why Piotyr had needed so much of it. Plans solidified in his mind as he directed his archers and artillery to concentrate on various parts of Abaddon's bewildered and frantic flight of Ba'al.

Some of the Ba'al broke free and fled the swarming morass to rush Sheol, easily picked off by reserve archers who held off firing at the main host for just such a purpose. Even so, some few made it to the walls, but were in such a state that they were easy prey for the wall's defenders.

Not a few others managed to escape and flee above the stinging black cloud, but Aruc and Ulis were there to consume and incinerate them. Those few they couldn't kill fell to Secundus or The First and their harpoons, fired like blurred ballista bolts from impossibly strong undead arms.

The siege had gone from hopeless to managed in the span of an hour. Ironic, he thought, that chaos now favored his forces instead of The Destroyer's Legion.

Another horn signal came from Abaddon's camp and Piotyr nodded to himself. It was expected. The Legion had been given the order to advance again, which either meant the blood-drinker and wraith imbued undead were handled, or that Abaddon no longer cared about sparing his troops.

Piotyr suspected the former, but regardless, the battle was about to be fully engaged on all sides. There would be no more tricks, no more surprises. It now fell to executing his orders, adjusting to Abaddon's decisions, and placing his troops where they needed to be. The course of the battle played out constantly in his mind. They had a chance.

Han took the chance to rest and preserve his strength. His talents were not needed at the moment. He felt the hatred in Sheol dip again at the hope of the defenders, but that appeared to be tempered by the despair of the Ba'al being consumed or shredded in mass in that black death cloud of vermin and blade wielding angels.

It was now a waiting game for him. Abaddon's forces would be brutalized for a time, but numbers were still vastly on his side, and in time their confusion would dissolve. Han was impressed at the job Piotyr was doing, and even more impressed with how everything was coming together after the near disaster of the beginning of the battle.

It was impossible to count, or measure the casualties, but from all appearances the vast majority of the dying was being done by Abaddon's side. The Legion losses were incalculable, though the force still stretched across the entire valley. Ba'al fell out of that cloud with pleasing frequency, though Han still was cautious in his optimism. It was not over, not even close, and if the battle even looked to be close to being won by Sheol? He had no delusions what would come next. It was for that, he saved his strength. *It was worth it, my Patriarch. I have no regrets, as long as I have the strength I need this day. God grant it to me.*

Joshua was relieved that his triage area wasn't the nightmare he feared it would become before it was over. His job had been simple enough once Piotyr signaled for his vermin and he had directed them as he was asked. That was hours ago. After that? He waited in reserve for wounded to come in and supervised their care or comfort. It was, so far, an easy task. He knew Abaddon's forces had to be dying on a massive scale, but he had expected that to be matched by their own forces.

As of yet, that had not happened. He patiently waited for the hammer to drop, however. His restoratives by now had surely all run out, but they had allowed the mortal defenders of Sheol to survive the initial push, and that was what mattered. The moon was rising high and the screams of the wounded and dying resounded in the night air. He had plenty to do, and many wounded came in, but not in the numbers he had feared. He and his support staff were able to keep up, assisted mainly by Ryrig who had developed a taste for helping those wounded in battle. Men and women came in, missing a hand here, an eye there.

If they had the damaged or missing part, he had little trouble mending and restoring them, and if they didn't, he helped them purge infection and mend the damage as best as possible. He was in his element, and unless someone was brought in already dead, he had little fear he could help them. He also felt energized and powerful. He hadn't had this much energy since arriving in Hell, and as the battle went on and the moon climbed high and then low again, he had saved or had helped save hundreds, if not thousands of defenders.

He did begin to grow tired towards dawn, but lack of sleep and constant action had far more to do with that than did his Invocations of Healing and Regeneration. He yawned, and asked an assistant to bring him some black tea. Sleep would have to wait, the siege would keep bringing in wounded all day.

He sat, rubbing his eyes during a brief respite, when suddenly he felt an incredible voracity start in his stomach and spread throughout his veins. A hunger built within him, and energy poured into him like a lightning bolt. He staggered to his feet and hissed at Ryrig, who was standing over a patient who had lost his arm at the shoulder.

"Something has happened... please find out what."

His friend looked at him wide-eyed, and then nodded and ran off towards the rampart steps. Joshua sat again and drank more of his tea, with hands shaking and fighting off the urge to vomit. God he was hungry, and hadn't felt this charged in months... years. His sickness was still mostly kept at bay from his elixirs, but he felt that his current ailment was related. His breathing evened and smoothed out, and his chest hurt a little less as he waited for Ryrig to return.

Joshua feared the worst, which was why he sat dumbfounded when his disciple returned with a smile.

"No worries, Ba'al Joshua. We are winning. The plague has finally triggered. The Legion of The Destroyer turns to dust and we are holding against the Ba'al. Sheol has held."

Joshua coughed, then laughed. So that was it. His plague was no longer held at bay. Why did he feel so hungry?

Kasim had done what he could to seek out the information he could, but the Ba'al could fly and he could not. The battle had turned to chaos so quickly that he didn't know what good he could do. He had scouted as best he could, avoiding the wraiths and memorizing all that he could about The Destroyer's forces before running back to Sheol and his warded room. He smiled in relief as he realized that Dhermina was still there, though pacing. Clearly from her aura she was angry... and he was the reason why.

Steeling himself, he returned to his body with a gasp and spoke before she had a chance to lay into him. "I was attacked while observing, but it was that attack which led me to releasing the undead. I know it wasn't what we agreed on, but I did not do it willfully."

"What do you mean you did not do it willfully? Did someone *make* you break your word?"

He couldn't help but smile, and he trusted that their bond would allow her to see the meaning why. There was no mockery in him, especially not to her.

"The waiths never arose until I crossed the threshold of the waterways. I was scouting, in truth I really was, but I lured them out by accident and they attacked me. I had no intention of staying out, but once they gave chase I was committed. Far better to lure them into the enemy lines than uselessly back to Sheol's walls."

She sighed as he spoke and he knew that she could feel the truth in his words. There would be no lies between them. Not now, and not ever.

"I am glad you are well, my love. So was it effective? Are the wraiths now tearing through Abaddon's forces?"

"They feast on their souls. The day is not won, but I have faith that Piotyr will see us through to face The Destroyer himself. His minions shall not take our walls."

"Then rest, Kasim. You may need your strength if that comes to pass."

Ve'kal knew that their advantage would not last forever, and in fact she was grateful it had gone so well for as long as it had. She parried another flurry of blade strokes from a winged form fully armored in black and green. This Fallen *was* skilled but she did not think she faced the Ba'al of House Utha'ryyk. She spun inside his reach and slit him from armpit to hip between his cuirass plates. No, definitely not Ba'al Utha'ryyk himself.

House colors were everywhere, but in the chaos of the fighting on the wall it was near impossible to tell Ba'al from Fallen, other than how many men were falling to them before they were brought down. Hyksin, Garag, Jalthus. The Houses were myriad, and the colors flashed in the blood of the wounded and slain as well as the black of the vermin. By Lucifer's Oath it was a boon that the swarm was able to discern Sheol defenders from attackers. If the chaos was not one-sided it would have been over already.

She whirled to face another foe and blinked in surprise as the expected downstroke of the winged form in the blue and bronze of House Posgh never descended, instead hanging in mid-swing before the form fell over. She smiled to thank his slayer, then scowled and cursed as again the mortal man who had spoken to her of her child stood behind the dead form.

"Ba'al Posgh, my lady."

She opened her mouth to demand the man get off her battlement when she felt a push from behind her force her to the ground. She rolled to her feet to see the mortal standing above her, swords raised in defense as another mortal hacked two Fallen apart in a blinding series of axe-slices. She recognized the blond man as well.

"Ba'als Yag and Aszil, my lady."

She got to her feet angrily and spun away from the men to re-engage the defense when her breath caught. *No... please no...*

There was a break in the swarm and a full squadron of Fallen descended directly upon her location at full speed. "Legion, to me!"

The words were meaningless, there was no time for enough...

The two mortals sped into motion in front of her and engaged the Fallen... no, some Fallen but she recognized at least half of them as Ba'al. She blinked in confusion as the men...*blurred* was all she could think to describe it as they winked into and out of individual melee engagements. Sorcery?

She tried to follow what was happening but it was over in heartbeats. The attacking Ba'al and Fallen all lay dead within seconds, and the two men were untouched. *What are these men?*

She breathed hard, waiting for them to say or acknowledge her in any way. It was a long moment before the blond man spoke to the other.

"I told you, what good is a Herald with nothing to announce?"

The dark haired man with two blades nodded to him, and then to her. "It isn't over yet, my lady."

She could only nod, dumbfounded. Why were they protecting her?

The moment came less than a minute after Jacob knew it would. He saw... he *knew* that the battle to take Sheol quickly and simply was over. The defenses were astounding. He knew in his heart that it was Piotyr defending the city. No one else alive could have woven so many threads of resistance so deftly and effectively. Maybe Jacob could have. Maybe the Patriarch. Barring that? Piotyr had defeated Abaddon at Sheol's walls. It had to come to this, and now it had. He saw it. A silence that went beyond the siege, beyond the screams of the dying.

Silence that drifted along the wind to his perfect hearing and flawless vision. The Frost worms, the Hellfire dragons, assassins decapitating the Fallen leadership, vermin blinding and deafening and tearing at the flesh of the Ba'al. Undead infantry holding back the Legion of the Destroyer, terrible and ravenous other undead ripping through the heaviest ranks of Abaddon's best siege lines...

Piotyr had done it, and now it must be. Jacob felt the terrible emanation coming across the field even before he saw the cause. A sight he had seen before rose to greet him, but not before his soul screamed in challenge to The Destroyer manifesting across the plains.

Dawn was breaking and the sunlight brilliantly illuminated the bloody warfare occurring across the valley around Sheol. The lull in the combat lasted for but an instant before the shrieking call rose above the din and the massive shape of The Dragon arose above Abaddon's forces.

"It is time, Markov. Will you join me?"

Jacob allowed himself to be opened fully to the divine connection in his mortal soul, though this time it was not a torrent that flooded him, merely what felt like a simple completion to his already immense power. He sighed as his wings opened fully and dripped a golden nimbus of light, then smiled as he saw Markov follow suit. He hoped the man would not die from this, but there was no greater cause.

The two men took flight, and sped towards the greatest Demon Lord of them all.

"Merethius, how will we fight him? He is immense!"

Jacob had given thought to that as well. He trusted that he was faster than The Destroyer, a trust solidified by having seen him assault Haven more than once. The Patriarch had always forced him back, in part because The Destroyer was slow. Lumbering.

"With Holy Fire and Sword, Markov. Always stay moving, never hold still. If you can't harry his flank or strike him safely, keep moving!"

He flew across the plains as a golden plume of holy wrath, his wake causing fire to blossom in the flesh of Abaddon's Legion and Fallen alike. He smiled briefly at seeing one of the Watchers, hidden in plain sight as a member of the invaders, stand impervious to his divine flames.

The undead were also spared, which was curious to him as he streaked across the plains, though he saw the wraith spirits ignite and burn as he neared them. Their power came from conflicting sources, it seemed.

He drew Duskfall and laughed at how weightless the now easily twice the span of a man tall weapon was. He casually swung it downwards into a pack of screaming Legion and sent those who weren't smashed apart flying at least a dozen paces. *So this was how it was for Lucifer's Heir to fight my forces. Like brushing aside gnats.* "FLEE BEFORE THE SHAY'TAN! FLEE BEFORE JACOB MERETHIUS! YOUR LORD AND MASTER COMMANDS IT!"

He saw the effect on the morale of the nearby Legion, but it was too small an influence when compared to the size of the force Abaddon brought. Meaningless. He stopped caring about anything other than The Destroyer and honed in on his attack vector.

A roar split the sky as he neared and he felt a brief pang of apprehension. God, he was even bigger than he remembered from Haven. *Stop it, you are the most powerful being to have ever drawn breath. He is no match for you.*

He believed the words as he looked back to make sure Markov was close to him, and with a final nod to the other Templar, he broke upwards and ducked under a slow wing buffet. Well, slow to him, but he saw it knock prone hundreds of Legionnaire.

He accelerated over the beasts spine and delivered a crushing blow along Abaddon's shoulder blade. He kept moving as he struck, a strafing series of impacts along the neck that resonated across the land with the sound of boulders cracking.

The Destroyer roared and spun around, but too slowly as Jacob continued to burst faster and faster around its neck, striking all the while. He heard more roars of pain than he was causing, and he knew that Markov was landing his hits as well.

"DIE, ABADDON THE FEEBLE! DIE BEHEMOTH! DIE, ZIZ THE WEAK!"

He and Markov were ripping Abaddon apart, and their battle was not slow nor closely contested. When he landed his most telling blow, smashing the Dragon in the eye and watching with satisfaction as the blood geysered out of the now-gaping socket he could not help but feel arrogant. What was this worm compared to the might of the Shay'tan?

He and Markov pulled up mid-flight to watch as the neck went slack and fell to the earth, shockwaves rippling outward as even more of his own forces fell to the collateral damage of his enormous bulk.

"Fuck, that really wasn't that hard, was it?"

Jacob was in agreement. It really wasn't.

Piotyr frowned as he saw the golden forms methodically tear town The Dragon. The course of the battle had shifted completely within his mind once Abaddon manifested. He adjusted some of the troop directions, though mostly what hc saw unfolding over and over were variations on The Dragon advancing to Sheol. Those Golden figures were fools to stay there. They hadn't won, not even close.

Shay'tan? Jacob? He was sure that should mean something, but at the moment all he was concerned with was that those idiots had killed the weakest form of The Dragon in his visions. He swore and shook his head as the two flying men appeared to be celebrating. He gave his orders to reinforce the sections of the wall about to be hard pressed and grit his teeth as Abaddon rose up with two sinuous necks and hissing mouths where once there was one... roaring in defiance.

"Damned fools. Ready Catapults for Abaddon!" He could ill afford to lose the artillery support for the massive army still trying to smash his gates down, but he saw it very clearly. Abaddon was going to reach the gates, and once he did, he would break them and it was over. Once the Legion entered the city in mass, his forces couldn't hold them back. He had to slow the Dragon enough to... to wear down the siege force by attrition he supposed.

He had no idea why these idiots had attacked him directly, but his chances had been better before they had. Abaddon was faster now, and his necks were not the only part of him that had grown more agile. They were attacking him again, but this time his maws were forcing them to be on the defensive far more. Good, maybe it would keep them from killing him again. Fools! His plans had been working, and now his timing was off. He no longer had the time for his defense to work and it was their fault. Watching them be hard-pressed by The Destroyer, he hoped it killed them. Damned idiots.

Han had seen the Patriarch do this repeatedly, but it still hadn't prepared him for the incredible drain he felt Invoking Holy Fire at such a distance and in such a large area. He had summoned the flame storm right over the beast's head, and smiled as it screeched in pain and receded... but his eyes immediately felt weighed down by exhaustion. God, he was tired after one Invocation. How had the Patriarch done this day in and day out for years?

He was in shock at seeing Jacob there... the Shay'tan no less! But it did explain why Ve'kal had been unable to assume the Throne. He had his suspicions, but to see it now confirmed, and in such stark clarity, was jarring. The other golden man fighting with him was a mystery. Another angel, perhaps? If Piotyr had found such an ally, perhaps Jacob had as well.

Han focused anew on his far more important task of keeping The Destroyer at bay. It advanced on Sheol... slowly still but always forward. Piotyr's defense plan required killing as many of the invaders as possible for as long as possible. If Abaddon reached the walls? It was over, and the flood of his Legion would drown the city.

Han knew he couldn't hold The Dragon back with Holy Fire alone, and he drew a tremendous amount of suffering from the pool that surrounded him. He coalesced it into a giant lance of destruction, and launched it with the force of a thunderbolt at Abaddon. He grinned in satisfaction as the thing struck his foe, and then the blood drained from his face as the lance harmlessly dissipated against the beasts' scales.

No! He is immune! Han felt bile rise in his throat. He couldn't use his most potent weapon against Ba'al Apollyon. They were doomed... unless Jacob... *unless the Shay'tan...* could stop him. In impotent despair Han watched The Dragon advance closer as Jacob and the other figure attacked it. Han could see their blows still rang true, but not at the speed they had struck with at first. They were wounding it, but it walked closer to Sheol by the minute. If only the terrain were not so flat...

Frowning, he wondered. He couldn't hurt Abaddon directly... but perhaps indirectly? He gathered more of the essence of pain and shaped a great blade above and in front of The Dragon, then plunged it directly into the ground in a fountain of earth and stone. Legion were shattered where the plow hit, but more importantly a trench had been dug in the path of the approaching Destroyer.

Yes... it would work, but it would take time, but he wasn't sure if it was the best use of the resource available. *Yes, if he reaches the walls it is finished. It won't matter how many Legion or Ba'al you have slain if that sea of infantry breaches Sheol.*

Decided, he worked quickly to create deep, staggered pits and trenches, alternated with grabbing giant clumps of terrain and throwing them at Abaddon to distract and enrage him. When he felt his wind restored, he would Invoke Holy Fire in giant storms over The Destroyer and smile as it caused a roar of pain while The Dragon would stop his progress, screeching in agony.

He worked with all his will, endurance, and focus. Sweat poured off of him. He grew exhausted and on his fourth storm he Invoked, he nearly fell to his knees, catching his hands on the ramparts for support. He watched, weary, and then blinked as Abaddon fell. He peered intently, seeing Jacob... seeing the Shay'tan and his companion wheel from what must have been the killing blow and hover in mid-air in victory.

Han allowed himself a weak smile and thought of Invoking his voice to call out a greeting, but decided he didn't have the strength to spare and that Jacob would come soon enough. He sighed in relief, and turned from the view to go find Joshua.

He stopped as the first roar sent a cold knife into his heart. Blinking slowly, he saw bodies of Legion, Fallen, and Ba'al alike littered the ramparts and blood flowed off the stone to trickle down below in a slow waterfall of gore.

His eyes opened wide in horror as a second roar followed the first, and the sounds of the battle near him faded away. He saw but did not hear the archers, siege engineers, Legion battling or Ba'al in flight. The insects went silent.

He turned as the third roar pierced his veil of quiet and the sound of the battle ripped back into life. The Dragon stood, and Han saw a second head rise from the carcass, both of them moving faster than before, with the body matching them in speed as it resumed the march of annihilation towards the city.

It would not be enough.

Be careful what you wish for, fool. Joshua admonished himself as he feverishly worked to save as many as he could, and felt no guilt for healing the Ba'al loyal to Ve'kal and sending them back to the battle. Their numbers were so inferior that attrition could hardly matter, but every single body he could mend was another sword-arm.

His tent was a madhouse of frenetic yelling for bandages, water, and medicinals. He and his dozens of assistants were working in constant motion doing what they could. Screaming Legion stumbled in missing eyes, ears, limbs... half their faces. Ba'al were more composed, but if they had to leave the ramparts, they were in dire shape, with gashes exposing internal organs or bone piercing their skin.

Far too many were carried, dead, by non-combatants. They were usually the old, young, or infirm carrying the deceased, as able-bodied women had been conscripted into the defenses from the beginning. Unfortunately... them being old, young, or infirm made them ill-suited to triage the wounded in the field, and much time was wasted looking at corpses. He couldn't fault them though, to most eyes there was no difference between one near-death and one already dead. Joshua could tell at a glance. These volunteers could not.

He had ordered no updates on the battle in the medical tents, but everyone knew what the roars from outside meant. The Destroyer had manifested, and every roar heard meant annihilation marched that much closer to everyone there.

His fear was present, but he controlled it with an iron hand. He could control what was in front of him, not what was out there. He healed, and his strength did not wane in the slightest. His illness also was barely noticeable. He worried at that in a small way in the back of his mind, but the reasons were unimportant. His hands knitting flesh or setting bone was important. That sliver in his mind knew that the undead plague was empowering him... God it might even be nourishing him, but that didn't matter.

Joshua Danner at the moment was a healer, and nothing more. With no shortage of dead and dying, he had plenty of opportunity to earn the title.

Kasim and Dhermina raced from their chamber when they heard the roar outside. It was chaos outside the tunnels in the medical area, but they fought their way through the throng and up to the ramparts with as much urgency and haste as they could. No words were spoken as they went, none were needed. His health was no longer at issue. The Destroyer came, and their lives were all forfeit if he reached Sheol.

The ramparts were a slick and caucophonous maelstrom of bloodshed, but he and Dhermina were masters at their craft. With his wind saif in hand, Kasim nimbly struck down any Legion foe in his way, and Fallen were no different for the two of them in unison. Ba'al were present as well, and though normally he would be more cautious around them, with the din of the melee all around them as well as the chaos of the vermin swarm? With he and Dhermina being in perfect harmony even Ba'al fell quickly to their blades.

The four roars in quick unison gave him pause. They arrived at the forward command center with Piotyr in time to see the giant beast attacking a pair of golden winged beings with the speed and ferocity of a desert viper.

"Kasim, who are those men?"

He frowned, and opened his inner sight to a blinding display. He had seen it before, and it was the same. Jacob glowed with the glorious radiance of The Apotheosis, and amazingly so did the other figure. Two of them?!

He felt a brief surge of hope in his chest... Jacob lived! He then had to avert his eyes as the blackness of Abaddon darkened the radiance of the two angelic figures. There was some sort of... sameness to their auras that was hard to explain, but he knew it to be true. Abaddon had the same magnitude and similar effect radiating from him... though it was dark and perverted. Could Abaddon Invoke his own Apotheosis?

"That is Jacob, though I know not how. The other man is another like him, and they both have Invoked The Soul's Last Fire. It will be decided among them."

He watched helplessly as The Destroyer snapped and lunged at the two figures. Sheol's defenders would be as ants in an anthill against such might. He was relieved to see Jacob and his companion engaging their enemy effectively, though he also noticed that only Jacob appeared to be fast and agile enough to avoid the snapping heads of Abaddon and still strike back with any real capability. His companion held his ground to a degree, but landed no strike on The Destroyer that he could see. It would be Jacob and Jacob alone then.

He looked around at the rest of the battle outside Sheol, but to his eyes, it was little more than a slow stalemate. Legion surrounded the city like a sea of hate, but undead infantry and Han's wraith and leech-walkers still cut huge swaths through them and ground them up like sausage. Frost worms still bored in and out of the ground, tearing up the enemy formations and feasting on Legion, Fallen, and Ba'al alike by the thousands.

In the sky, Aruc and Ulis ringed the huge cloud of vermin, fiery blasts of hellfire incinerating escaping Ba'al by the score, with their riders piercing just as many. Angelic forms flew in perfect formations, phalanx and wing formations breaking Fallen and Ba'al groups apart with ease. Gazing with his inner sight, Kasim was also surprised to see that they had allies among the Legion of Abaddon, as Fallen and Ba'al died under attack from assailants unseen to normal eyes.

Under any other circumstances, this would be a route, with Sheol completing a near perfect siege defense... but Kasim could see the inevitable march of doom coming towards them. He saw a burst of Holy Fire rain down on Abaddon. Han was doing his part as well. More, it seemed, as Kasim couldn't think of any other origin for the immense chasms and pits blocking The Destroyer's path. Under any other circumstances, victory would be at hand, but even with everything brought to bear against his forces... Ba'al Apollyon still advanced.

Kasim looked at Dhermina and smiled sadly. "If he gets close, I have to go."

"If he gets close, we are all dead, my love."

She was right, so what matter if he died a little sooner?

Apollyon took his steps forward in measured patience, which was hard with the hatred burning him from within. The two golden figures were mercilessly fast, but his four snapping heads were nearly as fast. He allowed them each to act independently of each other, as well as his own direction. It was better that way, more efficient. He had been surprised when they had been able to fell his last two so quickly. It was unlikely they would do so again.

He was patient by nature and had always had an intense dislike for opening himself up to Hell's Blood. When he did, and thus manifested as The Destroyer, he became less patient. A lumbering, rage fueled beast was not what he was as Ba'al Apollyon. He wanted to win without it, but as with Haven, he just couldn't break the defenses of Sheol.

He hissed in pain as this fool calling himself the Shay'tan landed another hard hit against one of his heads. No Son of Adam could ever equal Lucifer or his heirs. If by some fluke this mortal actually had managed to kill the last Shay'tan, it mattered not. He was a fly to be swatted, nothing more. With The Blood of Hell flowing through his body and soul, Apollyon was invincible. He cursed and roared with pain as one of his heads was smote to the earth. Damn that man! Dragging it behind him would slow him even more and make it easier for whoever was on the walls burning him with Holy Fire to impede him even further.

It was intolerable, even for one as patient as he was. He had waited millenia, served willingly and brilliantly under Lucifer as well as his heirs, and now even as the acting commander of the Infernal Legion, he *still* had to wait as he slowly progressed across the plains of Sheol. The city was tantalizingly close, yet still so far away.

He wanted to release the essence of Hell itself. He wanted to revert back to his true self and fly with haste to Sheol's walls, but that was foolish. He was near invulnerable as The Dragon, a true Dragon, not these pitiful lizards the mortals had somehow tamed. He longed to fly and lamented that his form as the Destroyer was far too cumbersome and heavy to achieve flight even if his wings could somehow lift his immense body.

Another titanic blow struck the side of a head and followed-up against his torso. The mortal wasn't a complete fool, though he was sorely mistaken if he thought Apollyon a mere hydra. His body would yield no more satisfaction for Adam's Seed than his heads would.

He screamed as another cloud burst of Holy Fire rained upon him. The agony of his flesh searing in the Divine Wrath clouded his vision and the ensuing hatred for whomever was on the walls nearly darkened his sight completely. It was exactly like Haven! Damn them all! He had faced the Patriarch countless times. To face his counterpart at Sheol was maddening. He grit his teeth. Patience would win out. He grunted as the fire ceased and he stumbled forward through the pain, stumbling on another of these damned pits.

He looked in dismay around him as more thousands of his troops appeared to be dead in the deluge. Apollyon was not wasteful, and lamented every single loss of a fighting Legionnaire. The skies were worse. He had not imagined in his worst, most catastrophic predictions of the siege that so many of his Fallen and Ba'al would die. He recognized House Sammael in the skies, which sickened more than shocked him.

Betrayer. Coward. Sammael had *agreed* with The Morning Star, yet had not taken up arms at his side. Now, thousands of years later, he took up arms against him. Sammael would pay with his life for this, his whole House would.

The Hellfire wyrms and the undead he had expected, though certainly not these voracious things that tore through his ranks like paper. Ve'kal had upgraded her forces to an unbelievable extent. Apollyon had expected to take Sheol with little resistance, and now found himself with Hell's Blood flowing through him just to reach the city. It was *exactly* like Haven and he refused to let this turn into a prolonged affair. He was patient, but he couldn't afford to let this fester. He had to secure the Throne, and he had to unify Hell again. A broken Empire with no true Shay'tan could not finish Haven... could not finish Adam's Seed. Taking Sheol was crucial, even if the resulting setbacks to his army made him wait even longer to take Haven.

A second head fell limp, and he screeched. It would be worse now. With only two heads, and his body dragging the extra dead weight, the Golden Warriors would tear him apart. Well, the one calling himself Jacob would. The other was slowing, significantly. Apollyon almost did not need to concern himself with him.

The one called Jacob, however... the pretender? He was vicious, brutal, and powerful. A fine Ba'al to have at his side, and an implacable enemy to have against him. He grunted as the attacks came faster and more telling. He thought about laying still and letting his metamorphosis take place, but every step he could manage was a step closer to his prize. He just needed to reach the Throne and it would all be over.

A third head toppled. It was almost pointless, but progress was progress. He mused as he lumbered forward that he didn't even want the damned title, but in order to unify things he had to become Shay'tan. It could have been Ve'kal if she was stronger, but the woman was not fit and he could think of no other who was. It would have to be Ba'al Apollyon who became Shay'tan. Briefly he wondered if this Jacob was someone the mortals would follow. Would he be a good leader for them?

His thoughts turned to healing as his last sinuous neck and head were crippled, and he fell limp to the ground. He felt the blows continue to strike his unmoving body, and for a moment, he applauded the mortals' tenacity. He felt the surge of Hell's Lifeforce enter his soul and his body split to accompany two more heads snaking out of his torso. Wryly, he wondered if the mortals would notice the third head sprouting low to the ground with a much shorter neck... or the face... *his face,* finally carved out of the flesh on his body itself. *Four heads beget three more, and his true face now upon him, the face of Ba'al Apollyon crowned with three horns.*

His seven flailing heads were now too much for the second golden figure, and he withdrew from combat. The pretender, Jacob, was now outmatched, and Apollyon laughed as he finally gashed the winged form's flesh with one of his horns. His heads lashed out with teeth and horn and sent Jacob into a flurry to avoid his gnashing. Ba'al Apollyon grinned in triumph as he raced onwards towards Sheol. Holy Fire burned his eyes and flesh again and again, mounds of earth were flung at him, great pits opened in the ground before him. He cared not, and the pain invigorated him as he accelerated.

He felt the strikes come as fast as lightning from Jacob, his torso and necks battered and bashed into pulp, but he cared not. His will kept him going, and he roared in triumph as he neared the walls. Seven mighty roars called out to the skies in triumph as he finally achieved in Hell what he never had on Earth. Ba'al Apollyon... Abaddon The Destroyer... broke through to the walls of the last city guarded by a Patriarch, and brought its walls down.

chapter thirty-one

I am Alpha and Omega, the beginning and the end, the first and the last.
- Revelation 22:13

Jacob watched in helpless rage as The Destroyer broke through the city. *His* city. Rock, stone, and dust filled the air as The Dragon smashed the outer wall at his point of impact, and his ensuing roars of triumph nettled Jacob to his very soul. The wing buffets and tail swipe finished carving a giant hole in the side of Sheol, and once the cries of pain and suffering ceased, Abaddon's Legion would pour into the city. He had maybe minutes before the slaughter began.

He flew with haste towards the ground, blinking in confusion as the form of The Dragon vanished. He wondered if something about the connection between Abaddon and the source of his manifestation as the Destroyer prevented him from entering the city proper in his form.

Either way, it mattered not. The city had been broken, and Apollyon would win within the hour. The defenders simply could not stop the flood of Legion which would burst through the ruined walls. The siege was over, and the slaughter would begin. His friends had done well, but he had failed them. He could not defeat The Destroyer, though perhaps he could kill Ba'al Apollyon now that he was no longer manifested.

He couldn't see anything through the debris, but he didn't have to. Abaddon could only have one prize in mind, and that is where Jacob went at the speed of a diving eagle. He flew over the ruins of what looked to be the command area, and though he couldn't see Piotyr, or Han, or Ve'kal for that matter, he felt their presence within the confusion and pain. They lived, for the moment.

He could not stop, he had to get to The Throne before Abaddon. Dropping down along the ramparts he dove at full speed into what was once the plaza where he slew The Shay'tan. It was a disaster area, and medical tents had been thrown up all over the place. He landed, and watched as thousands of wounded mortals, Legion, Fallen, and not a few Ba'al all flung themselves back in awe.

The ones who could move did so, the ones who could not lay still with mouths agape.

"Clear the plaza. Now. Ba'al Apollyon comes to challenge me."

His voice held the iron command of The Shay'tan, as well as the resilient confidence of the greatest Templar Earth had produced in its centuries of warfare. The functional wounded cleared those which were too maimed to leave. He saw Joshua among those there, and he smiled and shook his head as his old friend moved to approach him. *Not now, Joshua.* He thought the words and the healer understood. It was not the time.

Jacob looked at The Throne, and briefly glanced upon his epitaph next to it. He smiled and closed his eyes for a moment, bathing in the power he felt emanate from The Throne. *His* power. He was Shay'tan, and Apollyon was the usurper. He opened his eyes as he felt the presence of his challenger.

"Greetings, Destroyer."

The three-pace tall figure was nothing like Lucifer's Heir had been. Apollyon was fully dressed in black plate armor, his entire body covered in metal. It was adorned simply with Angelic Script and scrollwork, glowing brightly from the etching. He wielded a longsword in one hand, clearly a fine blade, but lacking the obvious malevolence he expected. No souls screamed silently on its surface, and no ichor dripped off the man. If Lucifer's Heir was ostentatious in his evil, Ba'al Apollyon was understated in his.

"We are beyond pleasantries, Son of Adam."

"I am so much more, now."

"You are nothing more, not now and not ever."

Jacob smiled as he raised Duskfall, its Golden Light glowing brightly and falling in soft waves off of his morningstar and body. "End it."

Ba'al Apollyon raised his blade and the two men charged each other. Black blade met golden haft, and the power from both of the weapons knocked any standing observers in the plaza prone. Blow after blow from both men clashed against each other's weapon and the ringing from the parrying shattered glass in windows.

Jacob was as good a warrior as drew breath in all of existence, but even with all of his skill and channeled power from The Throne, there was an equal force flowing into Apollyon. It felt like it did when he fought the Shay'tan the last time. He knew it was true even as the two men perfectly matched blows. This duel would last forever without one of them winning, and though the balance favored him personally just as much as it did Apollyon, it did not favor the city, or his friends. Apollyon could wait... Jacob could not. The invading Legion would breach the walls within moments.

He saw the answer even as he parried with ease every stroke from his foe, not even becoming frustrated that his own were just as easily met by Apollyon's blade. The Throne was powering both of them. He didn't know how or why The Destroyer was sharing The Shay'tan's power, but it didn't matter. He could feel it as clear as day. They couldn't destroy each other with The Throne in play. The solution was clear.

He stepped back out of combat and noticed wryly that Apollyon was in no hurry to press the attack. The man was shrewd. He also knew that time favored him, and whether or not he knew the reasons behind their stalemate, he knew the situation. He could be patient and was in no hurry.

"Well fought, Destroyer. I'm almost sorry I have to end it now."

The greatest of the Ba'al snorted. "Always so arrogant, is the seed of Adam. I'm not even The Destroyer right now, and yet you think to taunt me to gain some advantage? Raise your weapon, human. You will end..."

Jacob didn't care what the man had to say, he only wanted to distract him. No sooner had Apollyon started to speak that last word than Jacob turned and sped in a blur to The Throne and brought Duskfall down in a full arc on the seat itself with all of his channeled and Invoked Strength.

It cracked right down the middle. Jacob spun to stand at Apollyon, who was just standing there. With his face behind his visor Jacob couldn't read his expression, though he guessed it was shock. Jacob laughed quietly as the power drained out of him. The Apotheosis still flowed within him, so he released it before the power of The Throne was gone. He felt like a river within him was drying up and he instinctively knew it was within Apollyon as well.

"Well, Destroyer. So ends the power of The Shay'tan." He sprung forward and landed a glancing blow off Abaddon's breastplate. The Ba'al was able to raise his blade to turn Duskfall, but not fully. The scales were no longer in complete balance. There could be a victor. It would be him.

Jacob whirled and swung his morningstar with fury and righteous vigor, Invoking Strength, Focus, Endurance, Agility, everything he could think of while attacking Ba'al Apollyon. The man was now significantly stronger than Jacob was and his mass made for an advantage, but Jacob was a seasoned warrior in his own right and had faced Ba'al before. The battle was evenly matched, and both men came close to landing killing blows.

The sounds of battle outside the plaza drew close and Jacob knew it was almost over, one way or another. He did not want to Invoke the Soul's Last Fire without the power he had from The Throne. He instinctively knew it would kill him now without the buffer. He had lived last time because he slew The Shay'tan, but this time there would be no second chance. To Invoke it was to consume his own soul.

He would if it came to it, but he felt he could beat this man without it. Jacob fought with all of his skill and might, and thought he had a slight edge but the man was covered in armor and was a monster in combat. A slight edge could still mean the duel could last an hour, which Sheol didn't have.

He was surprised, though relieved when Markov flew down into the plaza from above. The golden light from his friend had dimmed into a barely flickering bronze glow, and his wings could barely support his weight. The Apotheosis had nearly consumed him, and it was a testament to the bravery of the other Templar that he still held onto it.

The element of surprise was gone before it meant anything, though Jacob could imagine Apollyon was not pleased to face the two of them again. Markov wasn't a lot of help, but he was some, and Jacob felt the battle was going his way. He landed hits on Apollyon often, though they were not enough to kill him, not even close. Duskfall was the perfect weapon against the heavy plate, but it was still very good armor, and the Ba'al was a terribly powerful opponent.

It wore on, with Markov flanking as best he could while staying clear of Apollyon's reach. That blade was not the equal of Lucifer's Heir, but it was still lethal. Jacob still had the upper hand, but it was not going to be over any time soon. He feared he would beat on Apollyon for an hour without killing him, even with his Invoked Strength. They were out of time.

He had to create an opening, and the only way he could think to do so was to open his own guard up and let Apollyon strike him. It would be a mortal blow, but he could retaliate quickly enough to kill him in return, especially with Markov there. Joshua could heal him afterwards. It wasn't a perfect plan, but he had no other options. If he didn't end it within another minute, it didn't matter.

He spun just outside of his opponents reach and inched closer as he lowered Duskfall just enough to give the Ba'al the chance to finish him. Markov made ready to strike as well, though he was feeble and exhausted. He would die within minutes, too.

Jacob waited, breath coming with difficulty, but Ba'al Apollyon just stood there, waiting. The seconds stretched, and the armored figure showed no signs of engaging.

"Coward."

Steam hissed from the armored visor as he answered. "No, just patient. While you try to kill me, my Legion is butchering your forces. I am in no hurry."

Jacob didn't know what to do other than attack again, but time favored Apollyon, and he simply could *not* kill the man quickly. God, he might not be able to kill him at all at this rate. Even striking him as frequently as he was...

He blinked as a sight appeared perhaps fifty feet in the air behind and above Apollyon gave him pause. One of the Sheol defenders, too small to be a Legionnaire, had hopped one of the ramparts and dashed up an archers tower. He wasn't sure why he thought it was odd, but it distracted him for a moment.

"I am the Shay'tan. Your forces won't accept you as my replacement unless you kill me."

"Won't they? You sundered The Throne. Perhaps it no longer matters."

The figure appeared again on the top of the tower, and Jacob stopped looking at him, it wasn't important. He sighed, and lowered his weapon while stepping back. It was over.

"Markov, release it before you die from it."

"Sorry, Merethius, I tried." Markov let go of his aura, and in exhaustion stepped back out of the combat. A gentle wind blew through the plaza, though enough to nearly knock Markov to the ground.

Ba'al Apollyon laughed. "Yet again, Adam's Seed fails. So the both of you were in the midst of your Soul Fire and still could not best me? How did you pathetic fools ever manage to..."

Jacob blinked as the figure he saw from the tower dropped out of the sky a good twenty paces above Ba'al Apollyon and landed directly on his back, plunging two blurred blades down deep into his torso from in between the gorget and the breastplate. Kasim twisted his blades neatly and hopped off the armored behemoth, lightly landing on his feet before his weapons simply vanished into nothing but a gust of wind. Apollyon wheezed and fell to his knees before slowly collapsing to the ground, blood pooling out of his armor.

Jacob stood, panting with breath, and was about to speak when Kasim raised a hand to stop him. "It is good to see you, brother, and I smile to see you alive. However, the city is being overrun, and you must stop it. Absorb Abaddon's soul, quickly while his life force still lingers in his flesh."

Jacob frowned. "I don't know how."

"Yes you do. Just finish him, Shay'tan."

He trusted Kasim, but didn't know what the man was talking about. Regardless, he raised Duskfall high overheard and brought it down in a crushing arc directly on Ba'al Apollyon's armored skull. He brought it down again and again, making sure he was dead, when a red veil passed over his eyes and he felt a cool, electric mesh settle over his skin and absorb into it.

"As it must be. Jacob, call off *your* troops, they will listen to you."

He flew into the sky, feeling almost as powerful as he had before he broke the Throne. Was that what that red mist was when he killed denizens of Hell? Was that what Haj'ur Ve'kal had spoken to him of so long ago? He admitted that it must be so, if Kasim said it as well. He knew better than to question the man. Jacob knew very little about the workings of Hell and Kasim clearly had been here the entire time Jacob was either dead or gone.

He gained enough altitude to see a good vantage of the breach The Destroyer caused, and he Invoked Voice and shouted at the top of his lungs. "YOUR SHAY'TAN COMMANDS YOU! I HAVE SLAIN ABADDON THE DESTROYER AND TAKEN HIS SOUL! SHEOL IS MINE, LAY DOWN YOUR ARMS AND JOIN ME, OR SUFFER MY WRATH!"

He watched as the battle almost immediately came to a stop. The breach was the last part to stop moving, but even that was only a few seconds after everyone else halted. From his point of view, it was clear that Apollyon's Legion had been only moments away from complete control of the walls. The ramparts had been nearly overrun, and only a handful of defenders remained alive in the breach itself. He hoped Piotyr and Ve'kal, and any others had fallen back.

The city grew eerily quiet as he hovered in mid-air. He waited to see if his commands would be obeyed. He sighed in relief as across the city, and then beyond in the plains, millions of Legion threw their weapons into the dirt and knelt. It was over.

Kasim had sprinted to the plaza as fast as he could once The Destroyer had neared the walls, and he had told Dhermina to go there as well and watch for him in case he failed. The impact from the breach had knocked him off his feet, but he already knew what was happening there, and there was nothing he could do about it. He had hopped back up and gone as fast as he could to a tower overlooking the plaza, avoiding throngs of survivors and wounded defenders headed to the medical area. He was slowed by the crush of people clogging the city, but still made it there in a few minutes. He had no delusions about succeeding where Jacob had failed, but he had to try... and he had not believed the opportunity he was given when Jacob had broken the Throne.

It was as he had hoped when he arrived, with Jacob and Abaddon having beaten him there and fighting in the plaza. He opened his inner sight to watch them, and was surprised to see a giant black cord connecting both of them to the Throne, which burned with a black light so brutally intense he had to look away. It was a dark mirror to the Throne Kasim had seen in his travels through death.

He had watched the combatants trade blows for a time and knew instinctively that the black cord was directly serving as a conduit for both of them. Neither would be able to die with that tethering them to the Throne. Kasim stealthily made his way to a ladder partially concealed from the plaza by a crenellation and dashed up to a stone parapet above the tower, dropping prone to watch the fight from the shadows. It only lasted a few minutes before Jacob did what Kasim knew he must, and sundered it. The cords shot away from both of them and the black energy dimmed immediately and gurgled slowly out of the Throne like a weak geyser.

It was time. He had a chance to make amends. He moved slowly, taking great care not to be seen by either man. He had faith that Jacob would be able to hold his ground in combat long enough for him to get in position. He had worried that Jacob might see him and react to his presence, but had trusted for Apollyon not to be concerned with one mortal nearly one hundred paces away even *if* he turned to look.

It was an assassination well within his means, with his current gifts. Long ago, it would have been much too far, but with the wind as his ally the jump was easy. He called his saif into existence and Invoked Speed and Grace before leaping at full sprint off the tower and directing the wind to push him and then slow his descent.

He drifted out over the plaza, and when the angle and position were right, dropped out of the sky like an arrow and sunk his blades deep into the flesh of the first being he had ever failed to kill. It was made right that day, though he by necessity allowed Jacob the killing blow. A minor, if important detail. *His* blades had severed the man's spine and pierced his lung and heart. The Destroyer had fallen at his hands.

The rest was up to Jacob, and Kasim's inner sight was correct in revealing what had to be done. He watched Jacob absorb the soul, then take flight and end the battle. Dhermina came to join him as he stood in the plaza over Ba'al Apollyon's corpse and they shared an embrace and kissed. It was over.

Joshua unabashedly wept as Jacob took flight and the battle was over. His undead responded to his will in ceasing their attacks, and gazing far up into the sky, he could see The First and Secundus waving down to him, signaling that they had also stopped.

The wraiths were beyond his control, so were the blood drinkers, but Han could handle those. For the rest of it, he would leave sorting everything out to Jacob, Ve'kal, or whomever wanted the responsibility. He had wounded to care for, and that crash when Abaddon brought the wall down would have caused thousands more deaths.

He called his undead back to help clear debris and find survivors. He dispersed the vermin. Though they would return on their own to feast... he was sure. The battle was over, but his task was only beginning. He smiled at Ryrig and was rewarded with a return grin. There were people to save.

Han was still amazed that Jacob was there, and in that capacity no less... but mostly he was tired. He had run away from the walls like everyone else when Abaddon closed and now he barely had the energy left to climb the steps up to the ramparts to look out at the plains. He sighed in exhaustion and could scarce believe the devastation outside Sheol.

How many millions lay dead? Ten? Fifty? It was impossible to tell, though the bodies covered the plains like pollen on the ground after spring's blossoming. He couldn't directly command his improved undead to stop fighting, but he was able to effectively corral them at this distance and force them into the pits he made to slow Abaddon. God he was tired. Even this minimal effort made him want to sleep for a year.

Had the pits even worked? Abaddon had broken the city walls despite Han's efforts, and nearly all of Sheol's defenders lay dead. Mostly Legion, and almost all of the non-fighters within the city had been spared, but it was still daunting.

In spite of the casualties, he had to be secretly pleased with the end result. He was alive, his friends were alive, and Abaddon was dead. Jacob had done it, or more accurately, with help had done it. Han smiled tiredly as he surveyed the aftermath. Sheol's well of suffering wasn't completely depleted, but it was nearly so. He had enough left to draw upon to help repair the city walls and clear rubble, which he would begin as soon as the survivors moved away from the debris. He closed his eyes briefly. Sleep would be wonderful, but there were people trapped under the rock. Some would still be alive.

He turned away from the fields to look down at the collapsed and broken section from The Destroyer's rampage. Abaddon's

Legion had already begun to help clear the stone and so had some of his Ba'al. The other Fallen and Ba'al who hadn't fled had also begun to descend, looking to Han confused and without purpose.

They had won, but it would be some time before anyone knew what was going on. Jacob had his work cut out for him. Sighing and stretching, Han wearily climbed down to help find survivors. He had his work cut out for him, too.

🛡 ☪ 🏛 ⚕ 📕

Piotyr had seen in his mind that Abaddon would breach the walls a solid five minutes before he did. The possibilities had stopped being vague about that particular result and he had given the orders early for his officers to clear out. Ve'kal had survived, as had Ba'al Geir, the Seneschal, and nearly the entire command pavillion. He would have ordered the imminent breach area to be cleared as well, but those defenders couldn't leave without allowing Abaddon's Legion to penetrate too deeply into the city. They had to stay, which meant they were going to die. He could spare the chain of command, though.

The order to fall back was obeyed, but after that, there was little he could do to stem the tide. He had done what he could and now his mind showed him that his role in the battle was over. This Jacob would either win, or not. Piotyr was done with it.

He had quietly passed the word to his men to prepare for invasion, but he left it up to everyone individually whether they wanted to fight Abaddon's Legion once they breached the city or to give up and hope for mercy. Abaddon might not want to butcher the city, or he might, depending on what sort of leader he was. Piotyr didn't know, nor did he care. He had given his final orders, then consumed the flask prepared for him by the Oracle.

The flood of memories had returned to him in full, and sitting on a quiet stone bench while the rest of Sheol lived or died based on events beyond his control allowed Piotyr to absorb his fate. He was angry at first, grinding his teeth in rage at his treatment of that bitch in the cave. His anger transferred to Abaddon, then to his friends for not telling him more about who he was... but quickly dissipated as he felt relief that Jacob lived, at least for the moment, and that so did his wife and children.

The relief won out quickly. Only a few minutes after drinking the philter, he was of clear mind and moving to the back of the city. He called out in his mind for his drakes to meet him on the western edge of Sheol.

He passed all manner of people fleeing, crying, and cowering. He didn't stop to comfort anyone. The battle was over, he was sure of it, one way or another. His elixir had wiped the future threads from his mind, and he was glad for it. Jacob had either won or he hadn't, but there was no sense worrying about it. He was tired of fighting in this war.

He smiled as he entered the small western plaza and saw his drakes standing, perched upon the stone. God they were big! He called out in his mind and told them both how relieved he was to see them alive and well.

It is good to see you as well, father. Is your mind restored?

Yes, Ulis. It is my own again, and I am well. My heart is glad to see you both, and that you survived the battle unharmed.

Unharmed and sated, father. I feasted on many flying demons, today.

Piotyr laughed, and crossed to Aruc, rubbing his head gently. Ulis joined in, and Piotyr sighed deeply in relief. "Come, lets get this barding off of you and get out of here. I long to see your mother."

She longs to see you too, father, though only if you are finished here.

"I will tell you both, clearly, that I am. I want to go home."

A soft throat clearing to his side made him spin and draw his blade. He relaxed when he saw the two undead men standing in the shadows of an archway.

"My apologies, Piotyr. I did not want to intrude. Are you well?"

Piotyr sheathed his sword, and crossed over to The First. He laughed and embraced the man. He released him, and laughed again as he saw the hint of a smile on the corpse's face.

"I will never forget what you did for me, and I name you brother. Fare thee well, my friend."

"Fare thee well, Piotyr. I shall miss you, and your son, as well. As fine a warrior and weapon as I could have hoped for."

Taking his son from the zombie felt like coming home. I have missed you, Lokyrg.

In your stead, the corpse has slain uncounted foes. It was a good departure.

It was as it should be, and he turned to nod to his friend. "Be well, King of Corpses."

To his own shock, Piotyr felt genuine sadness at leaving him. He wasn't even alive, but Piotyr would miss him. Hardly fair to call him a corpse, though. God, his features were flawless, and he looked healthier than any of the other humans or Legion Piotyr had seen that day.

"You as well, Piotyr. I just wanted to say goodbye. Jacob and Kasim have killed Abaddon, if you are interested."

He clapped The First on the arm and smiled. "I am glad. Tell them both good luck, Han and Joshua as well. They will know where to find me, if they want to. Also, find Sammael and tell him goodbye as well. Jacob can deal with everything afterwards."

"I will tell them, my friend. Secundus, are you ready?"

"I am. Shall we find Joshua?"

Piotyr looked at the other Plague Lord and shook his head in wonder. Secundus was also nearly flawless. Strange sorcery in these undead.

Piotyr removed the armor from his drakes, and nodded a final time to the undead men. It had never felt so good to leave a place in his life.

I am coming home, my love.

Ve'kal had been torn once the walls came down. She longed to run to Nezmyr, but that would ultimately mean nothing if Jacob lost, so she instead followed the throng of wounded to the plaza of the Throne.

Her heart had leapt when she saw Jacob on the plains. He lived! Once it became clear that he couldn't stop Ba'al Apollyon, though, her heart had turned to ash. What good was his survival and return to Sheol if he couldn't defeat The Destroyer?

She had stilled herself though, and stopped that line of thought. No one could kill The Dragon while manifested, but he couldn't enter the city, either. Destroy its walls? Certainly, but he could not approach the Throne. That, at least, was a precedent that could not be ignored. Jacob would get his chance.

Getting away from the ramparts had been easy, especially once Piotyr gave the order for everyone except one section of the wall to fall back. There were some opponents to dispatch, but not once did any of The Destroyer's Legion or Fallen come near her. The mortals at her side, the blond man with the axes and the dark-haired one with the swords continued to guard her, to her irritation as well as relief. They said nothing, and neither did she. They did seem intent on insuring she continued to draw breath, so she let it go. It made the chaotic trek to the Throne plaza faster, at least.

She had missed much of the duel it seemed, and her breath caught and her mouth dropped when she saw the Throne laying cracked in two. *What could have done that, and what will that mean?*

She watched as it dragged on. The nearness of the invading Legion pressing into the city and starting the slaughter of everyone nearly unhinged her, but she calmed herself and made herself watch the three men fight. It was clear that the other golden mortal was a non-factor, but Jacob more than held his own. She thought he would win, but there would not be enough time. She had nearly accepted that the battle was lost and they would all die when Kasim had appeared out of nowhere and ended it.

The shock of the moment lasted a long time for her. It was over. *They had won.* She wanted to run to Nezmyr and shout in joy at the victory, but she was transfixed by Jacob. He hadn't died... that was why the Throne was not hers.

"Remember what I told you, my lady. The King is dead. Long live the King."

She remembered. She looked at the two mortals, and the familiarity of the situation was intense. It was different, yet the same. She looked at Jacob Merethius, this mortal man who had come to Hell and unhinged it, and shook her head.

She was not the Shay'tan, because he was. Her lover, Nezmyr's surrogate father. What did that make her? *Not the Shay'tan, but more than Ba'alat Ve'kal.* She waited for Jacob to see her, and when their eyes met, she smiled at him. He smiled back.

More than Ba'alat Ve'kal, indeed.

epilogue

I summon all
Rather to be in readiness with hand
Or counsel to assist; lest I, who erst
Thought none my equal, now be over-match'd.
- John Milton: Paradise Regain'd Book Two

Markov had never been so glad in his life to see signs of civilization. He had walked for what seemed like years, but he knew in truth it had only been a few short weeks. By now, he was sure that Sheol was no longer the shit storm it was when he left, but he really didn't care. He didn't belong there, he belonged here.

Well, not here exactly, but it will do for now. The signs of years of Legion occupation were already beginning to wear down. He smiled as he knelt on and felt the soft grass, just beginning to come back after being trampled by Legionnaire, Ba'al, and God only knew what other monstrosities.

He rounded the bend and there it was. Haven. It wasn't San Luis, but there *were* some strong similarities. The portal was far behind him, and he hoped he had seen the last of Hell. He was home, or as near as could be for now. His Sanctuary had been razed to the ground by The Legion over a year ago. He felt pride that it held almost to the last. This, though... *had* held to the last.

It was an impressive city, not as large as The High Sheol, but even more defensible. It was built on a hill, and the entire thing was ringed with three tiers of what must have been thirty pace high stone walls. A great moat encircled the entire city, and Markov could barely imagine the staggering death toll trying to take the city would force. He had seen what Piotyr did with the defense of Sheol, but if an entire army of Templar Priests were defending Haven? No wonder The Destroyer had never taken it.

He sighed as he watched. San Luis had been nearly as impregnable. From what he gathered from the now loyal Ba'al and Legion at Sheol, it had simply been a matter of throwing bodies at it until it gave. It had been salted, but at least the population had been mercy killed. No brutalizing of the population had occurred. He was thankful for that.

"I hope your descendants, if your sorry ass had any kids... I hope they died without pain and without fear, Lou-ees. Sorry I couldn't have done enough the first time. Rest well, my friend."

He could feel his soul, flickering weakly, still there. He hadn't burned it all, though nearly so. That guy, Han, had told him it didn't burn out because he was in Hell, but that if he tried to use the Soul Fire on Earth, it *would* kill him. He didn't really care any more. He had given everything he had to Jacob and that battle, and he was done with war. He had done enough, perhaps too much in some ways. He looked forward to meeting the Patriarch of Haven and telling him of what had transpired. The Templar had all given him personal messages to deliver. Once he did, he hoped he could get a small contingent of volunteers to accompany him south to the Divide. He knew it would be destroyed, but it was his home, and he wanted to see it.

He patted his satchel with the scrolls written by the other Templar and started down the path. A few more miles and he would be back with his own kind, though never really his people, not after how much time separated them. He was centuries removed. Still, better here than Hell.

Markov whistled an old tune as he walked and smiled. His fate had not been kind, but it could have been worse. Hell, it can always be worse.

The End of Earth's Sowing, Book Two of The Apotheosis Trilogy.

And Solomon said: Hear, O my son, and receive my sayings, and learn the
wonders of God. For, on a certain night, when I laid me down to sleep, I called upon that
most holy Name of God, IAH, and prayed for the Ineffable Wisdom, and when I was
beginning to close mine eyes, the Angel of the Lord, even Homadiel, appeared unto
me, spake many things courteously unto me, and said: Listen O Solomon! thy prayer
before the Most High is not in vain, and since thou hast asked neither for long life,
nor for much riches, nor for the souls of thine enemies, but hast asked for thyself wisdom to perform justice. Thus saith the Lord: According to thy word have I given unto
thee a wise and understanding heart, so that before thee was none like unto thee, nor
ever shall arise.

Grimorium Verum

James Bishop (born September 24, 1979) is an American author of science fiction and fantasy fiction.

His first book, Hell's Reaping, was published in 2012, which is also the first book in The Apotheosis Trilogy.

www.ingramcontent.com/pod-product-compliance
Lightning Source LLC
Chambersburg PA
CBHW070351260626

47161CB00001B/104